PUFFIN BOOKS

Praise for the Bodyguard series:

Brilliant Book Award 2014 – Winner

Hampshire Book Award 2014 – Winner

'Bone-crunching action adventure'
Financial Times

'Breathtaking action . . . as real as it gets'
Eoin Colfer, author of the bestselling Artemis Fowl series

'Bradford has combined Jack Bauer, James Bond,
and Alex Rider to bring us the action-packed thriller'
Goodreads

'Wholly authentic . . . the action and pace are spot on. Anyone
working in the protection industry at a top level will recognize
that the author knows what he's writing about'
Simon, ex-SO14 Royalty Close Protection

'A gripping page-turner that children won't be able to put down'
Red House

'Will wrestle you to the ground and leave you breathless. 5 Stars'
Flipside magazine

'A gripping, heart-pounding novel'
Bookaholic

Chris Bradford is a true believer in *'practising what you preach'*. For his award-winning Young Samurai series, he trained in samurai swordsmanship, karate, ninjutsu and earned his black belt in Zen Kyu Shin Taijutsu. For his new Bodyguard series, Chris embarked on an intensive close-protection course to become a qualified professional bodyguard.

His bestselling books are published in over twenty languages and have garnered more than thirty children's book awards and nominations.

Before becoming a full-time author, he was a professional musician (who once performed for HRH Queen Elizabeth II), songwriter and music teacher.

Discover more about Chris at *www.chrisbradford.co.uk*

Books by Chris Bradford

The Bodyguard series (in reading order)

HOSTAGE

RANSOM

AMBUSH

TARGET

ASSASSIN

FUGITIVE

The Young Samurai series (in reading order)

THE WAY OF THE WARRIOR

THE WAY OF THE SWORD

THE WAY OF THE DRAGON

THE RING OF EARTH

THE RING OF WATER

THE RING OF FIRE

THE RING OF WIND

THE RING OF SKY

Available as ebook

THE WAY OF FIRE

BODYGUARD
FUGITIVE

CHRIS
BRADFORD

PUFFIN

Warning: Do not attempt any of the techniques described within the book
without the supervision of a qualified martial arts instructor. These can be highly
dangerous moves and result in fatal injuries. The author and publisher take no
responsibility for any injuries resulting from attempting these techniques.

PUFFIN BOOKS

UK | USA | Canada | Ireland | Australia
India New Zealand | South Africa

Puffin Books is part of the Penguin Random House group of companies
whose addresses can be found at global.penguinrandomhouse.com.

www.penguin.co.uk
www.puffin.co.uk
www.ladybird.co.uk

First published 2018
001

Text copyright © Chris Bradford, 2018

All rights reserved

The moral right of the author has been asserted

Set in 10.5/15.5 pt Sabon LT Std
Typeset by Jouve (UK), Milton Keynes
Printed in Great Britain by Clays Ltd, St Ives plc

A CIP catalogue record for this book is available from the British Library

ISBN: 978–0–141–35951–9

For all my Bodyguard fans –
stay safe!

'The best bodyguard is the one nobody notices.'

With the rise of teen stars, the intense media focus on celebrity families and a new wave of millionaires and billionaires, adults are no longer the only target for hostage-taking, blackmail and assassination – kids are too.

That's why they need specialized protection . . .

BUDDYGUARD

BUDDYGUARD is a secret close-protection organization that differs from all other security outfits by training and supplying only young bodyguards.

Known as 'buddyguards', these highly skilled teenagers are more effective than the typical adult bodyguard, who can easily draw unwanted attention. Operating invisibly as a child's constant companion, a buddyguard provides the greatest possible protection for any high-profile or vulnerable young person.

In a life-threatening situation, a buddyguard is the **final** ring of defence.

Gripping the stick tightly, Connor Reeves smashed the silver-masked wrestler in the belly as hard as he could. The wrestler spun round, reeling from the blow.

'*Dale! Dale! Dale!*' screamed the crowd in Spanish, urging him to hit again.

As the wrestler swung back at him, Connor wound up for a second strike. His devastating blow split the wrestler's stomach open, causing his guts to spill out across the tiled floor. The crowd cheered and Connor was almost knocked over in the rush as everyone surged forward. Peeling off his blindfold, Connor was astonished at the excitement a piñata could generate, even at a fourteenth birthday party. Then again he'd only ever imagined fruit and sweets to be stuffed inside the papier-mâché figure, not fistfuls of dollar bills, gold bracelets, glittering necklaces and sparkling rings! But this was Mexico and the party was being held by a super-rich business tycoon.

'That's a powerful swing you have there, Connor,' said Carlos Silva, the birthday girl's father, his English smoothed out by his Latin American accent.

Connor shrugged and, by way of an excuse for his surprising strength, replied, 'I've played a lot of cricket, Señor Silva.'

'Well, you certainly hit El Santo for six!' Carlos gave a rolling laugh and nodded at the effigy of the famous silver-masked Mexican wrestler, now hanging forlorn and battered from the ceiling. 'Tradition says the piñata symbolizes the devil. You have to hit him hard to make him let go of all the good things he's stolen. The devil has clearly stolen a lot from you!'

Connor responded with a bittersweet smile. There was more truth to the tycoon's words than the man would ever realize. He wished that hitting the piñata could bring back his father, who'd been taken from him when he was just eight years old, killed in an ambush while protecting the US ambassador in war-torn Iraq. And now the devil seemed intent on taking his mother too. She was battling the advanced stages of multiple sclerosis. Only his gran seemed to defy the devil, soldiering on despite her ageing years and a failing hip.

Connor offered the piñata-buster back to his host.

'No,' insisted Carlos. 'Keep it as a reminder of defeating one of the greatest legends in Mexican sport.'

'Thanks,' said Connor, slipping the rainbow-striped stick into the back pocket of his jeans.

The tycoon patted him firmly on the shoulder. 'Enjoy the party, my friend.'

As Carlos wandered off, joining his wife on the veranda to watch dusk settle over the haze of Mexico City, a boy with slick black hair, bronzed skin and a swagger straight out of a hip-hop music video approached Connor. He wrapped an arm round Connor's shoulders. Eduardo was the son of a high-ranking Mexican politician and the Principal whom Connor had been assigned to protect. The boy already had two muscle-bound security guards accompanying him wherever he went, but Connor was his 'invisible shield' – the teenage bodyguard no one suspected. Despite Connor officially protecting Eduardo, the two of them had hit it off the first day they'd met and over the past few weeks had become firm friends.

'Hey, didn't you get anything from the piñata?' asked Eduardo, a clutch of cash and candy in his own hand.

Connor shook his head. 'Too busy hitting the devil.'

Eduardo unwrapped a bright orange lolly and popped it into his mouth. 'Well, you sure missed out.'

'No, he didn't!' In a glittering white dress and her long honey-brown hair braided with miniature red roses, Maria left no doubt about the identity of the birthday girl. 'Connor, I saved *this* for you . . .' With a coy smile, she fastened a gold-chain bracelet around his wrist.

'Err . . . thanks!' said Connor, unsure how to respond. 'That's really something.'

'It should be,' said Eduardo, rolling the lollipop from one cheek to the other. 'It's solid twenty-two carat gold!'

Not your standard party gift then, thought Connor. But he knew such extravagance shouldn't have really shocked him. Now on his fifth assignment, he'd witnessed many flamboyant excesses of wealth. When protecting the sons and daughters of the elite and super-rich, it simply came with the territory. Yet he felt uncomfortable accepting a gift worth thousands of dollars. He unclipped the bracelet. 'I'm sorry, I can't take this. It's too much.'

'Sure you can,' Maria protested. 'It's *my* party and I can give gifts to whoever I want.' She fixed him with her bewitching brown eyes. 'You don't want to upset the birthday girl now, *do you*?'

Shifting uneasily on his feet, Connor put the bracelet back on. 'Of course not –'

Suddenly a thumping Latino beat blasted from the terrace's sound system and the disco lights flashed and spun overhead.

'Come on, let's dance,' said Maria, grabbing Connor's hand and dragging him on to the terrace with the other guests.

Connor glanced helplessly back at Eduardo. He was keenly aware that he should stay at his Principal's side. But Eduardo just laughed as Maria's girlfriends surrounded Connor in a circle, preventing his escape. Each girl began to dance with him in turn and Connor found himself flattered by all the attention. Checking on Eduardo again, he reassured himself with the fact that the house and grounds were secured by high walls and razor wire as well as CCTV and numerous security guards. His Principal was as safe as he could be, as long as he stayed within Connor's line of sight.

With one eye on Eduardo, Connor danced with Maria and her friends late into the evening. With each song, the birthday girl drew a little closer and Connor found himself getting into an awkward predicament. When the DJ put on a slower track, Maria appeared to be plucking up the courage to make her move, wrapping an arm round his waist and . . .

The delicate moment was thankfully interrupted by a call on Connor's mobile. He glanced at the screen. It was Charley.

Excusing himself, Connor headed over to the veranda, leaving the birthday girl with a wounded frown. He answered the video call and Charley's warm wide smile appeared on the screen. Her head rested against a pillow, her corn-blonde hair poking through a tight wrapping of bandages.

'Hi, Connor,' she said, her voice soft and weary. She caught the thumping sound of the disco and the flashing of strobe lights in the background. 'I'm not interrupting you, am I?'

'Of course not,' Connor replied, overjoyed to see his girl-friend. Between his assignment and her spinal treatments, they hadn't spoken for nearly a week. Charley was in China undergoing pioneering surgery and intensive physiotherapy for the spinal injuries she'd sustained on a mission that had gone terribly wrong. For the past two years she'd relied on her wheelchair for mobility after being paralysed from the waist down. Not that she let it stop her from doing any-thing: she was operations leader for Alpha team and one of the most experienced recruits in the whole Buddyguard organization. 'How did the surgery go?' he asked.

'I still feel a little groggy and I'm having a few odd dreams, but the doctor says the implantation was a success. I'm starting physio now that I've recovered. There's a long road ahead but the doctor's very hopeful.'

'That's great news –'

'Connor, come back and dance!' implored Maria, appearing at his shoulder.

Charley's brow furrowed. 'Sounds like you're having fun.'

Connor responded with an awkward smile. 'Birthday party,' he explained. 'My Principal was invited by Maria, one of his school friends.'

'Well, I think the school friend wants a dance with you,' said Charley, her voice tight.

'Charley . . . you're the only one for me,' Connor reassured her. And that was the truth – he'd never met a girl like Charley. She was everything to him. 'I'd *never* betray you. Besides, you'd kick my arse if I did!'

Charley let out a laugh. They both knew that was true. Charley was a force to be reckoned with when it came to unarmed combat sessions – many a recruit had learnt the hard way not to underestimate her abilities just because she was in a wheelchair.

'And after your therapy,' Connor went on, 'I'm sure it won't be long before I'm dancing with *you* –'

He flinched as a deafening explosion ripped through the air.

Connor looked around for Eduardo as the sky lit up overhead. Screaming, Maria and her friends rushed towards the veranda.

'Problem?' asked Charley, her expression now tense and alert.

'No, just fireworks!' Connor laughed with relief, locating his Principal by the balustrade. 'It's the end of the party. I need to get my Principal home.'

Charley relaxed back against the pillow. 'Well, stay safe. I miss you.'

'I miss you too,' said Connor, touching her face on the screen before signing off.

Fireworks coloured the sky in showers of sparkling red, blue and gold. The guests *oohed* and *aahed* as rockets whizzed high, and firecrackers burst in glorious rainbows of shimmering light. Then, with a final ear-splitting boom, a galaxy of falling stars marked the end of the celebrations. The guests collected their belongings and headed to their respective drivers.

Connor, putting on his jacket and resuming full

bodyguard mode, kept close to Eduardo. While the mansion compound was a safe zone, the streets of Mexico City were a potential battlefield, the city known as the kidnap capital of the world. Drug cartels and criminal gangs regularly targeted the families of the rich and powerful, ransoming hostages for ever-increasing amounts of money. Such high-level risks made this assignment particularly hazardous. Yet, three weeks in, the worst Connor had experienced so far had been sunburn and a few mosquito bites.

'You looked like you enjoyed the party,' said Eduardo, grinning as the two of them ambled down the flood-lit drive, escorted by his two wide-necked, gun-toting bodyguards.

'Absolutely,' Connor replied, his new bracelet jangling on his wrist. 'You've got some very generous friends.'

Waving goodbye to the birthday girl, Eduardo nudged Connor. 'Well, Maria definitely likes you.'

Connor glanced back. Maria waved at him, her dark eyes smouldering. He raised a tentative hand in farewell and she blew him a kiss.

'She'll be wanting your phone number next,' said Eduardo with a wink.

Connor's thoughts turned to Charley. 'I'm already spoken for.'

Eduardo shot him an astonished look. 'Surely she can't be as gorgeous as Maria?'

Connor simply smiled.

Eduardo laughed. 'Well, if that's the case, I'll have to

become a buddyguard myself. Your kind attracts all the best girls!'

Exiting the main gate, they headed over to the awaiting SUV. The number of guests had meant their vehicle was forced to park on the other side of the street. This was by no means ideal. From a security point of view, it left them exposed to potential danger for longer than was necessary. Connor instinctively heightened his awareness and scanned their surroundings. Blacked-out SUVs lined the road on either side. The traffic itself was light and posed no obvious threat. Besides the departing guests and their bodyguards, there were few other people on the street and none that raised any immediate suspicions. Yet Connor wouldn't relax until they were back safe and sound at his Principal's villa.

Flanked by their own heavyweight security, Eduardo and Connor waited at the kerbside while a blue-and-white telecom van passed by. The driver inside caught Connor's eye and Connor noted that he was wearing a white pollution mask. *Understandable in a smog-filled city*, thought Connor, *although surely the driver's got to have air-conditioning . . .*

'I'm starving after all that dancing,' said Eduardo. 'Let's stop off on the way home and grab some tacos –'

Suddenly the van screeched to a halt in the middle of the street, the back doors flew open and five masked men leapt out, wielding assault rifles.

Eduardo's two bodyguards drew their weapons, but were taken down in the first hail of bullets. Connor – his sixth sense triggered by the pollution mask – had already shoved Eduardo to the ground and was crouching in front of him as more rounds *zinged* overhead. The security personnel for the other guests returned fire. They killed one of the gunmen and wounded another. But their only priority was to save their own Principals. Eduardo wasn't their concern at all.

Retreating to their vehicles, the bodyguards were eager to make a quick getaway from the kill zone. And with Eduardo's security detail dead, that left the two of them to fend for themselves, Connor now his Principal's sole source of protection.

Connor glanced back and cursed. The gates to the compound had been automatically sealed shut against the attack. That meant they were cut off from their nearest escape route. This left them just one option of survival – their bulletproof SUV.

'Keep your head down,' Connor instructed as he thrust Eduardo behind the shelter of a parked car. Peering through the side window, Connor saw the masked gunmen closing in. He was stunned at the bold and brutal nature of their ambush. Targeting a secure compound with multiple armed bodyguards, the attackers were taking a serious gamble. But their audacious assault meant this was an all-or-nothing mission. They clearly had a specific target in mind . . . and, considering both Eduardo's bodyguards had been shot dead in the first few seconds, Connor could only assume that target was *Eduardo*.

In the street, now littered with bodies of the dead and

dying, a full-on firefight raged. Connor heard the screech of tyres as another guest's vehicle pulled away, then veered off the road and crashed into a lamp post. With the street turning into a war zone, Connor had to evacuate his Principal at all costs. He peeked over the bonnet of the car they were hiding behind and spotted Eduardo's driver cowering below the SUV's dashboard. The driver couldn't see them but at least he hadn't fled the scene . . . not yet, anyway.

As Connor calculated their chances of reaching the SUV alive, Eduardo cried out, '*Cuidado*, Connor!'

Connor spun round to see a masked man sneaking up behind them, a Glock 17 pistol aimed at them. Grabbing the piñata-buster in his back pocket, Connor struck out with lightning speed at the man's outstretched hand. There was a sharp *crack* as a wrist bone broke. The man grunted in pain and dropped the gun. Then Connor whipped the stick hard under the attacker's chin, snapping his head back. A final blow to his knee crippled the assailant and he collapsed to the pavement, barely conscious.

Eduardo stared wide-eyed and awestruck at Connor's lethal martial arts skills.

'Move!' Connor commanded, pulling Eduardo to his feet. 'To the SUV.'

Gunfire roared around them as they sprinted towards their vehicle. Connor did his best to shield Eduardo from the shots with his own body. He felt a round clip his shoulder, but the bulletproof fabric of his jacket absorbed the worst of the impact. The driver, spotting their approach in his rear-view mirror, unlocked the vehicle. Bullets pinged off the armoured panels. Eduardo cried out and stumbled but Connor kept him on his feet. Wrenching the tailgate open, he bundled Eduardo into the back, leapt on top of him and slammed the tailgate shut. The thud of multiple rounds hammered the metalwork like hail.

'*VAMOS!*' Connor screamed in Spanish.

The driver hit the gas and the SUV roared away. But another van appeared, blocking their escape. Executing a handbrake turn, the driver now drove straight at the two remaining gunmen. The attackers dived for cover as the SUV rammed the corner of the first van at speed, sending it spinning aside with a bone-shuddering crunch. Having forced its way out of the kill zone, the SUV weaved between the traffic, the reinforced rear window ringing with the impact of more high-velocity rounds. Then their vehicle turned a corner and they left the ambush behind.

Clear of danger, Connor lifted himself off Eduardo. 'Are you all right?' he asked.

But Eduardo didn't respond. His face was pale and his breathing rapid and rasping. At first Connor thought it was just shock, but then he noticed the spreading pool of blood on the boy's shirt.

'*Please, no!*' Connor gasped. Leaping over the back seat, he grabbed the medical kit from the footwell. Finding a sterile dressing and applying pressure to Eduardo's chest wound, he ordered the driver, '*Al hospital. Ahora!*'

CHAPTER 3

Connor stood at the kerb of the pick-up zone at London Heathrow Airport Terminal 5. But no car came to collect him. His suitcase dumped at his feet like a bodybag, he waited a full half-hour, hoping it was simply traffic holding up his ride. But as he watched the other passengers being whisked away in limos, picked up by family and friends, and numerous taxis come and go, he realized that the traffic wasn't the problem.

He tried calling Buddyguard HQ but got no response. He guessed Alpha team must be occupied sorting out the mess in Mexico – not surprising really. He'd failed in his assignment.

His Principal was dead.

Despite the driver having gone flat out, they'd reached the hospital too late. And, even though Connor had done his best to stem the bleeding, Eduardo had died from massive internal haemorrhaging. The post-mortem report concluded that a bullet had struck Eduardo in the upper chest, passing through his left lung before ripping through a main artery.

In the aftermath of the attack, Connor had sent Alpha team a short report, too devastated to do much more than provide the bare facts. Eduardo's father, beside himself with grief and rage, had dismissed Connor on the spot. Connor hadn't argued. Numb and shell-shocked, he'd simply gone back to the politician's residence, showered the boy's blood off himself, packed his bags, then taken the first available flight back to the UK.

The fact that HQ hadn't sent a car to collect him clearly meant that he was in disgrace.

Not sure what to do next, Connor took a taxi to Paddington Station. On the journey there he contemplated heading straight home to his mum and gran in East London. But how would he explain his unexpected return? Too many questions would be asked. And he didn't have the answers. His mum still had no idea that he worked as a covert young bodyguard, protecting the sons and daughters of the rich, famous and powerful. She thought he attended a private school on a sports scholarship programme – and that the bruises, knocks and scrapes he came home with at the end of each term were the result of energetic rugby games, mountain bike accidents and martial arts tournaments.

His gran knew the truth, though. Despite her age and frailty, her mind remained sharp as a tack and she'd seen straight through the 'scholarship' smokescreen. Connor had confided in her about the true nature of the so-called school in Wales that was headed by the formidable Colonel Black. And, although she disapproved, his gran begrudgingly understood the necessity of the job. The Buddyguard organization funded the medical support for his ailing mother, including the provision of a live-in carer – without which his mother would likely have to go into a nursing home, his gran into a care home and Connor into fostering. Those weren't desirable options for any of them. And, without his father around, Connor felt responsible for keeping the family together.

So he couldn't go home – not yet.

Boarding a fast train to Cardiff Central, Connor took a seat in a half-empty carriage and stowed his Go-bag in the luggage rack overhead. He'd picked up a sandwich for the journey but now found he had no appetite. Slumping in the threadbare seat, he stared blankly at the passing view instead, a blur of grey towns and industrial estates eventually giving way to green fields and rolling hills.

Entering a tunnel, his world was suddenly plunged into darkness and Connor briefly saw a red flash of gunfire. A distant cry of pain echoed in his ears . . . and Eduardo's face, pale and lifeless, swam before his eyes.

Connor shuddered at the ghostly vision in the window. A second later a train shot past and jolted him back to reality, daylight burning bright as they exited the tunnel. Connor pressed the palms of both hands to his eyes and took a long, slow breath. He knew he was burnt out. It had been one mission too many. And he'd made a mistake – a fatal error of judgement that had resulted in the loss of a boy's life.

Why didn't I warn the other two bodyguards of my

suspicions about the pollution mask? Should I have tried getting back to the compound instead of making a dash to the SUV? What if I'd picked up the dropped gun and shot back? Or just stayed behind the cover of the car and waited for reinforcements? Would Eduardo still be alive? Would he have even been shot? What if I'd . . . ?

Connor felt the hot sting of tears and the view outside the window became even more blurred. So many *what ifs*. Every time he thought of Eduardo a surge of anger, sadness and guilt overwhelmed him – anger at the gunmen who'd launched the attack, mixed with sadness at the boy's tragic death. And guilt at the fact he'd failed in his duty to protect his Principal.

Wiping away the tears with his sleeve, Connor knew in his heart that it was time to quit – to leave Buddyguard for good and put his days as a 'hidden shield' behind him. Somehow he'd have to find another way to pay for his mother's care . . .

But his father, a decorated SAS soldier, had *never* quit. Had he *ever* even failed a mission in his life? If so, how had he coped with the crushing guilt? But Connor could never imagine his father failing at anything. Even when he was shot and mortally wounded in Iraq, his father had still managed to get his Principal to safety. On that fateful mission the Principal had been none other than the US Ambassador Antonio Mendez, a man who ultimately became President of the United States. What would Eduardo have become if he'd survived the attack? Now no one would ever know . . .

Connor blinked away yet more shameful tears. How he wished he could be with Charley at this very moment, wrapped in her arms, and forget all about Mexico and Eduardo, and the bullet that had ripped through his Principal's chest. Thinking of his girlfriend put his own situation into perspective. Unlike Charley, who had lost the use of her legs, he was alive and – apart from a painful bruise on the shoulder – uninjured. So he was the lucky one.

But what would Charley think of him now? What would the others in Alpha team think of him? Ling, Jason, Richie, Marc and Amir – they all depended upon one another, trusted each other with their lives. Now they had good reason *never* to put their faith in his bodyguard skills again.

Connor rested his head against the carriage window and felt the thrum of the wheels on the track. Jet lag finally catching up with him, he closed his eyes . . .

When he next opened his eyes, the train was pulling into their final destination – Cardiff Central.

Retrieving his Go-bag and suitcase, Connor wearily made his way to the empty passenger collection point. He'd sent Alpha team a message informing them of his travel plans and arrival time at the station. But still no one had turned up to meet him. Colonel Black must be *really* furious. Connor may have decided to quit Buddyguard, but it appeared Buddyguard had already quit him!

Getting money from a cash machine, Connor hailed a taxi and gave the driver directions. The driver, a large man with grey stubble, hangdog eyes and a belly that threatened to consume the steering wheel, shot him an incredulous look. 'That's in the Brecon Beacons, in the middle of nowhere!'

'I know,' said Connor, putting his suitcase in the boot and clambering into the back seat with his Go-bag.

The driver whistled. 'It'll cost you an arm and a leg. Sure you don't want to take a bus?'

Connor shook his head. 'The school's a long walk from any bus stop.'

'All right, boyo,' said the driver with a shrug.

An hour later they were wending their way between stone-walled fields of green and hills dotted with sheep.

'Are you sure this is the right way?' asked the driver as the road narrowed and entered a hidden valley. 'Doesn't look like there's anything down here.'

Connor nodded. 'It's a private school.'

'Must be very private.'

As they were nearing the brow of a hill, a cattle truck came speeding over the rise and blasted its horn. Cursing, the driver swerved sharply into a thorn hedge, narrowly missing a head-on collision.

'Bloody farmers!' said the driver, as the cattle truck thundered on. 'Think they own the roads round here.'

His heart still in his mouth, Connor could only nod in agreement as a delivery van followed in the truck's wake.

'Bloomin' rush hour, by the looks of it!' snorted the driver before continuing down the lane, far more cautiously this time. A few minutes later a pair of wrought-iron gates came into view.

'You can drop me off just here,' said Connor.

The driver frowned. There was no building in sight. Just a long gravel drive with open fields on either side. 'Don't you want me to take you to the door?'

'No, thanks,' said Connor, handing over several crisp notes. It was still a fair walk to the old school, but he didn't want the driver to see the training facilities. 'Keep the change.'

Watching the taxi go, Connor stood before the gates. Perched atop the arch like a bird of prey, a winged shield glinted in the morning sunlight. It appeared to be an ancient coat of arms but was in fact the emblem for the Buddyguard organization. Connor remembered the first time he'd passed through these gates, driven by his close-protection instructor, Jody. He'd been nervous, excited and unsure what his future held. Now that he knew, he wished he'd *never* set foot inside the grounds.

Surprisingly, the gates were open. They were clearly expecting him. *But what sort of welcome will I get?*

With his suitcase weighing as heavily as his conscience, Connor set off down the driveway. He passed the hidden CCTV camera that would have observed his arrival and crossed one of the many concealed perimeter alarms encircling the estate. Then, as he crested a rise, the familiar old castle-like building of Buddyguard HQ came into sight. Familiar . . . except for the ominous spiral of smoke rising from its roof and the body lying in the centre of the gravel forecourt.

CHAPTER 4

Connor dropped his suitcase and ran towards the smoking building. *What the hell had happened? Who was the casualty?* He couldn't tell at this distance. Was it a client? One of the instructors? A recruit? Or . . . an intruder?

Connor stopped dead as sense took over from reflex, his initial shock hardening into professional instinct. Rushing into a situation without thinking was the equivalent of jumping out of a plane without a parachute. He could just as easily become a casualty himself before he had a chance to help anyone. First, he had to ACE the incident.

Assess the threat.

Counter the danger.

Then, in this instance, rather than *Escape the kill zone . . . Enter it!*

Taking a moment to sweep his eyes over the terrain, Connor searched for threats in the grounds and surrounding fields. At this stage he didn't know for certain what the actual danger might be. The casualty could simply have tripped down the entrance steps while escaping the building; or been overcome with smoke inhalation; or even suffered a heart attack. The smoke indicated there was a fire in one section of the school building. But Connor had to assume the worst-case scenario: an attack or a bomb had caused the fire.

His gaze scanned the small lake, football pitch, summer house and old well in the gardens, spotting no one at all. That was unusual in itself – unless everyone was gathered at the evacuation point on the tennis courts on the far side of the building. A dense patch of woodland to the north and low stone walls bordering the estate provided potential cover to any hostiles. Yet Connor couldn't see any apparent threats.

That wasn't entirely surprising. Apart from clients – whose self-interest ensured their confidentiality – and the select few in the know, Buddyguard was a well-kept secret. So the idea of an assault on its covert headquarters was highly unlikely.

Still, after Mexico, he wasn't taking any chances. Crouching low, Connor followed the line of the drystone walls to make himself less of a target and to avoid spooking the sheep in the nearby fields. As he scurried along, he was acutely aware that this wasn't the most direct route, but it paid to be paranoid in his line of work.

Darting diagonally across the football pitch, Connor approached the main building from the east. With the sunlight behind him, he had the advantage of clear sight, while any hostile would be looking straight into the sun. Reaching the corner of the building, he peered round it. The body still lay face down in the forecourt.

Up close, Connor could now see who the casualty was and felt his stomach lurch. He instantly recognized the shaved dark head of his combat instructor, Steve Nash. An ex-British Special Forces soldier with a physique that out-gunned the movie star Dwayne 'The Rock' Johnson, he was the toughest member on the staff. If someone had managed to take him down, then –

Connor started laughing to himself. How stupid could he be! This was simply a training exercise, like one of the dozen or more he'd participated in during his own close-protection course. Whenever possible, Colonel Black insisted on authenticity to ensure his recruits were ready for real-world encounters. His combat instructor was simply play-acting the role of a casualty.

'Steve!' called Connor, stepping out of hiding.

No response.

'*Steve!* It's me, Connor. Is this a training exercise?'

Still no response. Connor began to feel uneasy again. If his instructor was play-acting, then he was doing a convincing job. With a final check round, Connor hurried over to him. As soon as he laid a hand on his instructor's muscled forearm, he knew something was deeply wrong. Steve's skin was cold to the touch. Two fingers to his neck confirmed he had no pulse. With great effort, Connor managed to roll him on to his back. Connor gasped at the sight. Blood stained the gravel a dark inky red and there were several small yet distinct holes in his instructor's broad chest.

Shock numbing his grief, Connor stared a full minute at his dead mentor before snapping back to high alert. His eyes darted around for the shooter. He noticed the gravel in the forecourt was churned up all around him, indicating a number of large vehicles had arrived and left at high speed.

But that didn't mean the place was clear of hostiles.

Unable to do anything for Steve, Connor rushed over to the school entrance and took cover. No wonder he hadn't received any response to his calls and no one had come to pick him up. Buddyguard had been under attack.

Aware that the surviving instructors and recruits might still be fending off the intruders, Connor took out his XT tactical torch from his Go-bag and, with a flick of the wrist, extended the hidden baton. More effective than a piñata-buster, this self-defence weapon could knock an assailant out with one strike. Switching his Go-bag to the front and tightening the shoulder straps, Connor prayed he wouldn't need the protection of its bulletproof inner panel . . . or, for that matter, the trauma kit stored in its side pocket.

Taking a deep breath to steady his nerves, Connor stole up the steps and into the school's entrance hall. On first glance everything appeared normal. Still, a deathly quiet hung in the air. Then Connor noticed the oil painting above the fireplace was skewed at an odd angle. Bullet holes peppered the wood-panelled walls and blood was smeared across the polished parquet flooring. There'd been splatters on the steps too. Steve had evidently put up a fierce fight.

Turning towards the wide sweeping staircase, Connor listened for signs of a battle upstairs but heard nothing.

Deciding it was wise to clear the ground floor first, he crept down the main corridor towards Alpha team's briefing room. Passing various classrooms, he noticed desks overturned, chairs kicked over and computers missing. In the dining hall, breakfast was still out on the tables. As he crept inside, Connor caught the lingering whiff of tear gas and spotted the spent cartridges of several flash-bang grenades – clear evidence that this wasn't a straightforward robbery.

The silence was unsettling and Connor felt an icy finger of fear creep up his spine. *Where is everybody?*

Connor started coughing and his eyes began to sting. Despite the smoke escaping through an upper window, the dining hall was still hazy with gas. He retreated back into the corridor. Even more on edge now, he continued towards the briefing room. A window in the hallway was broken, glass scattered across the carpet. Careful not to step on any shards, Connor crept past. The briefing room was in the same state as the others: furniture in disarray and computers missing. Here the door seemed to have been barricaded shut. It may have held for a while, but scorch marks indicated an explosion and the door now hung off its hinges.

By the look of things, the attack had been brutal and unexpected. *But why wasn't the alarm raised? How did the intruders overcome the security systems?*

Connor went over to the main desk and tried the phone. The line was dead. He retraced his steps and headed to Colonel Black's office, passing more ransacked rooms and broken windows on the way. The office's heavy oak door had been kicked in, the lock broken and the state-of-the-art LED display on the wall smashed. But, to Connor's surprise, the intruders didn't appear to have discovered the colonel's personal computer. The heavy mahogany desk had been swept of its personal effects and its drawers rifled through. Yet Connor knew that an advanced multi-core computer was built into the desk's frame and a slim glass monitor concealed in a hidden recess. Perhaps he could use the colonel's computer to access the security systems and find out what had happened. Maybe even discover where everyone else was . . . dead or alive.

Setting aside his baton, Connor sat in the colonel's high-back red leather chair and pressed his thumb to the discreet fingerprint scanner on the inside of the armrest. A small digital display flashed: ACCESS DENIED. He knew it was pointless but Connor tried again anyway. As the display blinked stubbornly red again, Connor heard a crunch of glass in the corridor. Snatching up the XT torch, baton at the ready, he darted over to the open doorway.

There was another tinkle of glass. *The intruder was right outside the door!* Connor leapt out to take him down first . . . only to discover the corridor empty. Too late, he realized that the crunch of glass had been a distraction. Behind, he heard movement and something struck him in the back. A searing pain blazed through his body and his muscles went into spasm. Connor felt as if he was being beaten with a dozen baseball bats at once. The convulsions overcoming him, he collapsed to the floor.

Connor's eyes blinked open. He couldn't have been out for more than a few seconds. A warm sizzling sensation – the same feeling as if he'd put his tongue on a 5V battery but amplified a hundredfold – slowly faded from his pulsing nerves. Every muscle in his body was now sore as hell and he felt utterly drained, as if he'd run a triple marathon. Then a surge of anger, fuelled by survival instinct, rose in him. He sat bolt upright and stared into the dark eyes of his attacker.

'I'm really sorry!' said Amir, holding up his hands. He brandished a Taser X2 Defender stun gun, its conductor wires still trailing from the muzzle to the two electrode darts embedded in Connor's back.

'You *tasered* me!' cried Connor, glaring at his friend.

Amir offered a sheepish grin. 'I thought you were one of them.'

'Didn't you recognize me?'

Amir shrugged defensively. 'You're supposed to be in Mexico.'

Connor forced himself to calm down, the flood of

adrenalin that the stun gun had released only now beginning to pass. He sighed heavily. With all the chaos going
on and the phone line down, he realized that Amir wouldn't
have got his messages. Glad his best friend was alive and
well, Connor embraced him.

'Yeah, I missed you too,' said Amir, detaching the barbs
from his back and helping him up. Connor's legs still felt rub-
bery and Amir had to support him over to the colonel's chair.

Connor collapsed into the soft leather seat. 'What happened here? It's like a war zone.'

With a nervous glance towards the door, Amir pulled
up another chair. He looked in a complete state: his thick
black hair was matted, his eyes red and watery, his jeans
torn and soaking wet, and his top smeared in grime. Amir
wearily shook his head. 'I honestly don't know. We were
dealing with the fallout from the Mexico operation and –'

'Yeah, I messed up badly, didn't I?' interrupted Connor,
shifting in his seat, his gaze dropping to the floor.

Amir looked at him. 'It wasn't just your mission. Several other assignments went haywire at the same time.'

'*What?*' said Connor, stiffening.

'Never experienced anything like it. A bomb threat in
Thailand, a shoot-out in America, a carjacking in South
Africa. *All* our operations seemed to have been targeted at
once.'

Connor stared wide-eyed at Amir, unable to believe
what he was hearing. 'You mean Bravo, Charlie and Delta
teams were hit *too*?'

Amir nodded gravely. 'Elsa's in hospital, critical. Sean's

missing. We were waiting to hear back from David, but . . . while we were distracted managing those disasters . . . HQ was attacked.'

'When exactly?' asked Connor.

Amir swallowed hard, looking on the point of tears. 'Around breakfast this morning. Completely without warning –' His voice faltered. 'It just all happened so fast. We were totally unprepared. Crazy, if you think about it. We're bodyguards! We're trained to deal with exactly these sorts of situations!'

Connor rested a hand on his friend's trembling shoulder. 'I know, I know, but we don't expect to be targeted ourselves. Now tell me all you can about what happened here.'

With his head cradled in his hands, Amir went on. 'They seemed to come out of nowhere. They were literally *inside* the building before we even knew it. I was having my cornflakes, had just poured the milk, when flash-bang grenades went off in the dining hall. That was the *first* sign we were being attacked! Our instructors reacted fast, though. Tried to evacuate us. But –' he glanced up at Connor – 'the enemy seemed to know all our action drills *in advance*. They had the exits covered and the safe room locked down. Some teams managed to barricade themselves in. I made it with Ling and the others to Alpha team's briefing room. But they blew the flippin' door off!' Amir snorted in stunned disbelief. 'We were overrun. Steve and Jody put up a fight, allowing us to make it out into the fields. But . . . then we heard gunfire and screams.'

'Yeah, I saw Steve, outside,' said Connor.

Amir looked up hopefully. Connor replied with a shake of his head. Amir gazed out of the window, his eyes glassy and brimming. 'Steve sacrificed himself for us. And for what? We were all captured anyway. There were gunmen waiting at the boundary walls. We never had a chance.'

Connor gave Amir a questioning look. 'So how did *you* escape?'

Amir responded with a hollow laugh. 'As I was running away, half-blinded by tear gas, I fell into the old well. Almost broke my leg! It took me ages to climb back out. But that well saved my life. None of the attackers thought to look down there.'

'So, where's everyone else now?'

'I think I'm the only one left, apart from you.'

Connor felt as if all the air had been knocked from his lungs. 'You mean they're all *dead*? Ling, Marc, Rich–'

'No! They were rounded up and loaded on to a cattle truck. They took all our computers too. Spent a good time stripping the entire place. Very odd.'

'*A cattle truck?*' questioned Connor. 'I almost had a head-on crash with one as I arrived. There was a delivery van too.'

'Yeah, that would be the computers and the gunmen,' said Amir bitterly.

Standing up, Connor shook the feeling back into his legs. 'Well, at least we know our friends are still alive.'

'Yeah, but for how long?' Amir asked. 'We don't know where they've been taken . . . or why.'

'Well, do you have any idea *who* attacked us?'

Amir shook his head. 'They were all wearing masks and balaclavas. Never saw a face.'

Connor frowned. 'Can you access the CCTV footage from the colonel's computer? That might give us a clue.'

'I think so,' said Amir, settling himself into the colonel's chair. He pressed his thumb to the fingerprint scanner. The display blinked red: ACCESS DENIED. 'Administrator override 43XGT97,' he said and the display turned green, a laser keyboard lit up on the desktop and the slim glass monitor rose from its recess.

'What I don't understand is why you didn't get any warnings?' said Connor, pacing the room. 'What about the perimeter alarms? Security cameras? Pressure detectors? The school is a virtual fortress. The attackers shouldn't have been able to get anywhere near HQ.'

'That's what I've been asking myself too,' replied Amir, his fingers flying across the laser keyboard as he called up the surveillance network. He studied the screen for a moment, then frowned deeply. 'Nothing was triggered. Not the perimeter alarms. Not the pressure detectors. Not the window sensors. They've *all* been deactivated. The CCTV cameras too. Footage for the past twenty-four hours has been entirely erased!' He typed some more, pulling up different screens that meant nothing to Connor. 'Our communications were disrupted too. All incoming and outgoing messages blocked!'

Connor stared at Amir. 'How's that even possible? I thought you told me it was a closed system.'

'It is,' Amir replied, his eyes locked on the streams of code. 'To have overcome our security firewall and remotely accessed the system, these weren't some fly-by-night hackers. They had to be high-level professionals –'

'Or someone on the inside deactivated the alarms,' suggested Connor.

Amir's mouth dropped open. 'Are you serious?'

'It's a possibility we have to consider.'

'But who?'

'Your guess is as good as mine. To be able to locate this secret facility and cripple our security systems *must* require insider knowledge, though.'

Amir leant back in the colonel's chair. 'Or else unlimited resources, like a government intelligence agency. The fact that multiple missions were disrupted at the same time, in different locations around the world, points to an extremely powerful organization.'

Connor thought over his assignments before Mexico. 'The Russian mafia perhaps? Possibly the Russian government? Or maybe both!'

'Well, they were definitely foreign,' agreed Amir. 'But they weren't Russian. When I was in the well, I overheard a couple of the gunmen talking. It sounded like Japanese or Chinese. I couldn't understand what they were saying but there was *one* word I did recognize –' Amir hesitated, a pained expression clouding his face – 'repeated a number of times, a name actually.'

Connor stopped pacing and turned to his friend. 'Whose name?'

'Your name.'

CHAPTER 6

Connor felt as if he'd been punched in the gut. 'Are you saying *I* was the target?'

'It looks that way,' replied Amir. 'I mean, your operation was the first to be attacked. But, judging by the way they stripped HQ, I'm guessing they were after something else too.'

Connor thought back to Mexico. The assault had been well-planned and executed with the same brutal efficiency, the attackers timing their drive-by to the exact second. As the van had passed, Connor remembered the driver had glanced at *him*, not Eduardo. And, when the gunman had raised his Glock 17, the pistol had been pointing at *his* face. It dawned on Connor that the attackers hadn't been trying to kidnap Eduardo at all – they'd been trying to kill *him*! Connor's legs lost their strength once more and he slumped down in the spare chair. Was he *really* the reason for the attack in Mexico and on HQ? The thought sent a chill through him. He stared aghast at Amir. 'What do they want with me? What were they looking for?'

Amir shrugged. 'I've no idea. As I said, I didn't understand a word. But I'm hoping Colonel Black might know.'

Connor sat up straight. 'He *wasn't* captured?'

'No,' said Amir with a shake of his head. 'He was off-site at the time.'

A wave of relief rippled through him. The colonel wasn't only the head and founder of Buddyguard; he was the closest Connor now had to a father. 'Where is he then?'

'Well, I don't know exactly,' replied Amir. 'The colonel got a call from Bugsy last week and left as a matter of urgency.'

'So Bugsy's OK too!'

Amir nodded. 'He's been away on some pre-mission appraisal – a high-level assignment, judging by the secrecy surrounding it. Bugsy wouldn't even tell me where he was going and I'm his logistics deputy!'

Knowing that both the colonel and their surveillance tutor hadn't been captured in the assault, Connor started to feel more hopeful about their situation. 'Have you tried to contact them?'

'Of course!' said Amir. 'But I've had no response . . . although I think I now know why.' He pointed at the computer monitor where a line of code flashed red. '*That* is a back door to our entire system, planted without our knowledge. The enemy have had access to our entire security network, communications and all mission databases. They've basically been in control!'

Connor gasped. 'For how long?'

'Who knows? They've hidden their tracks well.' Amir's fingers raced over the laser keyboard, his brow a knot of concentration. 'Multi-rootkits . . . time-based evasion . . .

internal data obfuscation . . . stego-malware! The combination of evasion techniques is truly exceptional. I'd be impressed, if only it weren't directed at us –'

'I've no idea what you're talking about, Amir, but is there any way we can track the colonel down?'

'Give me a minute, then I'll access his private agenda. Don't want our friends snooping on us any more.'

Lines of code reeled across the screen. To Connor it was gibberish, but to his friend the hieroglyphic-like fusion of letters, numbers and symbols were as accessible as a picture book.

After several minutes of furious typing, Amir hit *enter*. 'There, that should kill it,' he said, leaning back in the chair with a satisfied smile.

The screen flashed white, then went blank.

'Is it supposed to do that?' asked Connor.

Amir's smile faded. 'No.'

He tried to reboot the computer. Nothing happened. Amir slapped his palm to his forehead. *'How could I be so stupid?* Of course the malware had a self-destruct command. It's crashed the entire system. Permanently.'

As Amir tried in vain to get the computer back online, Connor pulled out his mobile. 'What about my phone? Can we use this to contact the colonel? Or is it compromised too?'

'Most likely,' said Amir with a grimace. He waved for Connor to hand it over, then, with a flurry of input commands, accessed the phone's operating system. 'Well, there doesn't appear to be anything obviously suspect. After the Cell-Finity bug issue during Operation Hidden

Shield, we upgraded the security on all mobile devices. They're near impossible to hack, though you can still be tracked via your signal –'

All of a sudden the phone vibrated with a message. Amir did a double-take, then passed it back to Connor. 'It's an encrypted text from the colonel.'

With Amir peering over his shoulder, Connor pressed the fingerprint authorization to decrypt the message:

> End mission immediately. HQ compromised.
> DON'T involve authorities. DON'T communicate.
> Lives at stake.
> Meet at <u>31.224484, 121.487966.</u>
> 1030hrs local time 16/5.

'He knows about the attack at least,' said Amir flatly.

'Let's check the coordinates –'

'No!' cried Amir. But Connor's thumb had already instinctively hit the hyperlink.

'Sorry,' said Connor with a feeble smile. 'I thought you said there was nothing suspect.'

'It's not your phone that's the problem,' said Amir. 'It's the wireless router it's automatically connected to. That's still potentially compromised.'

'Well, it's too late to worry about that now,' said Connor sheepishly as a global map appeared on the phone's screen, then zoomed in on a sprawling city. He exchanged an astonished look with Amir at the destination. 'Shanghai, China. They're on the other side of the world!'

Amir checked his watch. 'That gives us barely twenty-four hours to reach the rendezvous point.'

Connor rose from his seat. 'We'd best pack our gear then.'

'First I need your phone,' said Amir. After noting down the colonel's coordinates on a scrap of paper, he took out the SIM card and snapped it in half. Then he dropped the phone on the floor and stamped on it repeatedly, until it was little more than a pile of broken circuitry.

Connor forced a laugh. 'I was due an upgrade anyway! But how's the colonel supposed to contact us now?'

'He can't. But neither can the enemy track us,' Amir explained. 'We have to go dark. New phones. New kit. New everything.'

As they headed out of the office and down the corridor towards the logistics supply room, Connor gazed round at the destruction. It was sad to see their training headquarters in such a sorry state. This had been his home for almost two years. Here he'd learnt the life-saving skills of a bodyguard, made lifelong friends, met Charley. So many good memories were attached to the place. And now it was a wreck, a broken shield that no longer protected anyone.

'Are you sure we shouldn't call the police?' said Amir, noticing the downcast look on his face.

Connor shook his head. 'You saw the colonel's orders. We can't involve the authorities.'

'But what about Steve? And the others?'

'I guess . . . we bury Steve,' said Connor glumly, 'and pray for the others.'

Connor stood amid the devastation that was his bedroom. The place had been ransacked, just like the rest of the facility. His clothes lay scattered, his bed upended, his desk emptied and his personal effects tossed on the floor or missing. The attackers, whoever they were, had done a thorough job. Connor couldn't work out if they were looking for something in particular or simply carrying out wanton destruction.

He got down on his hands and knees and began to hunt around. Eventually he found what he was looking for: a scratched plastic key fob. But this wasn't any old key fob. It contained the faded photo of a tall tanned soldier with dark brown hair and piercing green-blue eyes the same as Connor's: his father. Previously the fob had held a photo of himself, aged eight years old. His father had died with it clasped in his hand. Now the fob was Connor's talisman. He gripped it tightly in his palm for comfort and strength, then slipped it into his pocket.

During his hunt Connor had also come across the dog-eared copy of the *SAS Survival Handbook* that Colonel

Black had given him prior to his African assignment. While the colonel wasn't by nature a warm or emotionally open man, he often showed his affection and care towards Connor by more practical means, the manual being just one example, and it had proved essential to his survival during that unexpectedly hazardous operation in Burundi. While Connor didn't foresee any use for it in China, the handbook did contain one essential item. Flicking through its pages, Connor was relieved to discover, still tucked inside, a dark blue American passport. Presented to him on his first-ever assignment in recognition for services protecting President Mendez's daughter, it granted him US citizenship. He'd been using it as a bookmark, but now Connor thought a second passport could come in very handy.

Unzipping his Go-bag, Connor added the passport to his other travel documents. Their plan was to travel light, so all he needed was a fresh set of clothes. As he sorted through the pile on the floor, he unearthed a framed picture of Charley. Blonde, beautiful and with eyes as cobalt blue as a cloudless sky, she'd had the photo taken the day before leaving for her spinal therapy. It had been a bright spring morning, full of hope and new life – just like Charley. Connor recalled her excitement and trepidation at the prospect of being more independently mobile – possibly walking or even surfing again. As a former junior surf champion, that was her ultimate dream. *No promises*, she'd said. And he'd reminded her of her own words to him: *if you think you can, or think you can't, you're probably right*. The frame's glass had been cracked, but she smiled defiantly through it – as she did through most of life's challenges.

Connor prayed that Charley was all right, that she hadn't been targeted in an attack like everyone else. But why would she be? Charley wasn't on a mission. She hadn't actively been part of Buddyguard for nearly two months since beginning her therapy. Why would the attackers pursue her? Or even deem her a threat?

Nonetheless Connor couldn't help but worry. If he knew anything about their mystery enemy it was that they were methodical and ruthless. He needed to get in contact with Charley, confirm that she was safe and warn her of the danger. She might even be worrying about him now that his phone was out of action. But lacking a guaranteed secure line, there was no way he could call her without alerting the enemy to her location ... that's if they didn't know it already.

Shanghai, China ... That's where Charley's medical facility was situated. Surely Colonel Black's coordinates couldn't be mere coincidence. Maybe the colonel had already reached her, hence the choice of rendezvous point. At once Connor felt reassured by the thought and was even more impatient to leave.

He glanced out of the window. From his room, he could see the old school chapel with its small tree-bound cemetery at the rear. A pile of freshly dug earth and a makeshift cross marked the shallow grave of Steve Nash. Connor wondered if they'd done the right thing, burying their instructor. They might have destroyed crucial clues as to who his killers were. Should they have left him where he was or put his body in the kitchen's freezer instead? But he and Amir didn't know how long they'd be gone, or whether they'd even return. Out of respect and necessity, the burial had seemed the best decision.

'I've salvaged what I could,' said Amir, entering the room with his own Go-bag brimming. 'Since we're travelling with only hand luggage, I've selected items we can carry through airport security without drawing attention.' He passed Connor items from his bag. 'Spare stab-proof T-shirt . . . new bulletproof jacket, given your old one had taken a hit . . . night-vision sunglasses . . . contact lens camera . . . fresh batteries for your XT tactical torch . . .' He glanced up with a tight uncertain smile. 'I didn't think we could get away with red-gel pepper spray, even disguised as a deodorant can . . . so, besides the extendable baton, our only other self-defence weapon is an iStun.'

Amir handed Connor a standard-looking smartphone, the key difference being the two metal studs at the top of the device, which delivered a three-million-volt shock. After Connor's recent experience of being tasered, he was wary of taking the phone off Amir.

'Don't worry,' said Amir, misreading his reluctance. 'We should be able to get them past security – their internals are essentially the same as a normal working phone, just a larger battery. Of course we can't use them to communicate with since they could be compromised. But I struck lucky with these babies.' Amir presented Connor with a slim black wristband watch. 'Only arrived yesterday and they were overlooked during the search.'

The time appeared on the display as soon as the watch was strapped to Connor's arm. 'At least we won't be late for our rendezvous,' he said.

'It's a new-generation thermic smartband,' Amir explained. 'Powered by your body's own heat, the watch supplies full biometric read-outs, has an encrypted end-to-end text messenger and a locator beacon that will allow us to communicate with one another securely, track each other's movements and share key data on our medical status. Could be useful if we get separated.'

Connor held up the iStun. 'But what about a smartphone that won't fry our ears off?'

'I'll buy us new disposable ones at the airport,' said Amir. He glanced at the read-out on his own smartband. 'Our flight's in a little under five hours. We'd best get moving.'

Downstairs, they passed through reception and Connor entered the transport office. Much of the contents had been rifled through, but he found the keys they needed. Hurrying outside to the car park, Connor unlocked Jody's Range Rover.

Amir snatched the keys off him. 'You haven't got a licence!'

Connor shot his friend a look. 'Nor have you!'

They'd both been trained in defensive driving but due to their age weren't legally allowed on UK roads.

Grinning, Amir jumped into the driver's seat. 'I know, but I drive faster.'

CHAPTER 8

Ling's eyes flickered open but she saw nothing. Her world was swallowed in darkness. She could hear the rasping breaths of people pressed close against her, their heavy limbs pinning her down. Her head was thick and woozy and she felt like she might throw up at any moment. She reached out a hand, slowly feeling her way across a prone body. Her muscles were aching and unresponsive as if drained of every ounce of energy. After an immense effort her fingertips touched cold rough metal. *A wall?* No . . . the side of a container. A bright flash of memory flickered in her sluggish mind:

She, Jason and the other recruits being herded from the back of a cattle truck into a large shipping container . . . Their captors wielding electric cattle prods to ensure their compliance . . . Then the metal doors slamming shut, plunging them into tomb-like darkness . . . Gunner, Jody and the other instructors had kicked and shoulder-barged at the doors, shouting out for help, until Richie had noticed an unnerving hiss and an acrid stench tainting the air . . . Then, one by one, they had each passed out and flopped to the floor in a pile of bodies . . .

As her eyes adjusted to the darkness, Ling could make out the vague shapes of her friends. Next to her lay Jason, his muscular bulk and jutting jaw familiar and reassuring to her.

'J-*Jason*,' she croaked, her voice no more than a cracked whisper. Whatever gas had been pumped into the container had seared her throat too.

Jason didn't respond, but she could feel his chest moving up and down. He was breathing at least.

'What's your cargo?' said a gruff official-sounding voice.

Ling jerked her head round, seeking out the person who'd spoken.

'Livestock,' replied another man, his tone low and frosty.

The voices were coming from outside the shipping container.

'What sort of livestock?'

'Sheep.'

Ling tried to cry out for help, but her throat was dry as dust. She crawled over the comatose body of Jason and banged weakly on the side of the container with her fist.

'Are you sure they're all right?' asked the gruff voice.

'They'll settle down on the journey. They've been sedated.'

Fighting her feebleness, she struck the metal container again – a dull *thung* sounding out. Silence followed and Ling panicked that their one hope of rescue had gone. She tried to call for help, this time managing a bleating croak.

'Sounds like one of them's in pain,' said the gruff voice.

'It'll live,' came the reply.

Hearing the sound of footsteps fading, Ling became desperate. She pounded on the container's side with all her remaining strength before collapsing with exhaustion. The sedative gas was still in the air. She could taste its bitterness and her exertions had made her breathe in more of it. She felt herself slipping away again . . . seconds passed . . . each one feeling like an eternity. The men *must* have heard her. They *couldn't* ignore the noise.

Then the gruff voice ordered, 'Open up the container.'

Ling fought against passing out. She had to ensure they were rescued.

'Is that really necessary?' The other man sighed. 'Clearance should've already been granted.'

'*Don't* make me ask you again.'

In her delirious state, Ling listened as the two men tramped to the far end of the container. There was a heavy rattle of a padlock and she smiled weakly to herself. They were going to be saved!

'Arthur! What are you doing?' called out a new voice, breathless and panting.

'Inspecting the cargo, sir.'

'No need for that,' came the sharp reply. 'All the documents are in order. I attended to them myself.'

'But –'

'No buts. Just sign the customs clearance and I'll handle it from here.'

Ling slumped in despair as she heard the padlock snap shut and the man she presumed was Arthur walk away, grumbling to himself. *No! This can't be happening*, she thought.

'I trust the *duty fee*'s been paid?' said the new voice, oily and conniving.

'In full.'

'Excellent! Then everything's in order. Thank you for your business, sir. I do hope your cargo reaches its destination without any further hitches.'

'So do I,' replied the other man. 'For their sake.'

Heavy footsteps plodded away and with them any last hope of rescue. Ling lay across Jason, clinging as desperately to him as she clung to consciousness. She heard the faint ring of a mobile phone. One of the men still remained outside. Ling struggled to follow what he was saying, her mind growing ever more fuzzy and only hearing one side of the conversation.

'Buddyguard headquarters have been destroyed, along with any evidence . . . No . . . Colonel Black was not on-site. We must assume he's still in China . . . No sign of the flash drive either . . . I've rounded up hostages. They'll make good bargaining chips . . . What about Connor?' Ling's ears pricked up at the mention of Connor's name. The man now sounded annoyed. 'He survived the ambush?' The man swore an oath. 'You should have left it to me. Where is he now . . . ? *Shanghai!* You wish me to intercept . . . ? I understand.'

The man ended the call and his footsteps faded away, leaving Ling to the darkness.

CHAPTER 9

'Excuse me, young man, is this your bag?'

Connor glanced round at the airport security officer and nodded. He'd been momentarily distracted by a Chinese man in the queue who'd appeared to be staring at him. But the person had moved to a different line and was no longer looking his way.

'Can you open it for me?' said the security officer. Her black hair was pulled so tightly into a bun that her expression seemed to be one of perpetual severity: her eyes slightly too wide, her cheekbones sharp and her lips stretched so taut that her words came out clipped and stiff.

Connor unzipped his Go-bag. As the officer began to rifle through the contents, Connor felt his heart rate rise. Usually, he'd have put his self-defence gear and weapons in hold luggage to avoid any unnecessary questioning. But they were under pressure of time and couldn't risk being delayed at the other end waiting for baggage.

The officer pulled out one of his T-shirts. Interwoven with a graphene fibre that made it both stab-proof and capable of withstanding a round from a standard handgun,

Connor knew that it was indistinguishable from a normal thick cotton top. Still, in his eyes, the T-shirt was screaming *suspect*! Setting it to one side without further inspection, the officer took out the XT tactical torch, tested that it worked, then dug deeper into his bag.

Connor began to sweat. What was she looking for? Had the X-ray scanner picked something up? He was certain he'd taken out his father's old survival knife and the red-gel pepper spray. Was the liquid body-armour panel an issue? Connor shot an anxious glance in Amir's direction, his friend having just passed through the body scanner behind him.

'Found it!' said the officer in a triumphant tone. Then she added sternly, 'This item exceeds the hundred-mil limit.'

She produced a can of Coke that Connor had bought at Paddington Station earlier that morning and forgotten all about. She tossed it in the bin. Breathing a sigh of relief, Connor began to gather his things.

'Not so fast,' said the security officer, her eyes alighting upon the iStun. She picked up the smartphone and frowned. 'I haven't seen this model before.'

Connor's eyes widened as she put her fingers on the two metal studs. All she needed to do now was flick up the volume switch and she'd get quite a shock. 'Ermm . . . those are –'

'Dual aerials for improved signal,' Amir interrupted with an eager smile. He waved his matching iStun in the air. 'I've got one too. Downloads twice as fast. Forget 4G – this is 8G!'

'Hmm,' said the security officer, examining the smartphone in her hand. Her expression softened. 'I'll have to get one myself.' She passed the phone back to Connor. 'You have a good flight, young man.'

'Thanks,' Connor mumbled, hurriedly repacking his Go-bag.

'Well, I think that went pretty smoothly!' Amir said, walking up to look at the departures board.

'For you maybe,' replied Connor, his heart still thumping.

'Right, I'm off to buy us new phones,' said Amir. 'I'll meet you back here in twenty minutes.'

As his friend hurried to the electronics store, Connor headed for the newsagent. He bought them some snacks for the flight and a can of Coke to replace the one that had been confiscated. Then he spotted a payphone in a quiet corner of the departure lounge. *That line won't be compromised*, he reasoned. Dropping in some change, he dialled home. His mum and gran would become worried if he didn't check in regularly and he didn't want them attempting to contact his 'school'. The phone rang once . . . twice . . . three times . . .

By the fifth time, Connor had started to grow anxious. Had the enemy got to his family too? The thought filled him with dread. Then the call was picked up on the eighth ring.

'Hello?' croaked a familiar voice.

'Hi, Gran – it's Connor.'

Her voice brightened instantly. 'Connor! Are you back?'

'Yes, sort of . . . but I'm off again.'

'*Already?*' His gran's tone instantly turned reproachful. After his assignment in Burundi, Connor had promised his gran that would be his last mission for Buddyguard, and that he'd put in a request to be stationed at HQ for future operations. But then Russia had come up, followed by Mexico. Like his father, Connor craved action and felt the irresistible urge for always *one more mission*. But this time was different . . .

'It *isn't* an assignment,' Connor reassured her, although he questioned whether the trip might be even more dangerous than a typical operation.

'I'm glad to hear it,' said his gran. 'Am I to assume that you've spoken with Colonel Black?'

'I . . . haven't had a chance,' he replied honestly. 'Besides, I don't think there'll be any more missions for a while.' With Buddyguard HQ out of action and the instructors and recruits abducted, Connor wondered if there would *ever* be any more assignments. In the back of his mind, he also worried what would happen to the care package that provided for his mum and gran. Would that end too?

'Oh, why's that?' asked his gran.

'I'll explain another time. More importantly, how are you doing?'

'Oh, I'm as fit as a fiddle and as right as rain. Sally's doing a great job of taking care of us.'

'And Mum?'

There was a pause on the line.

'Why not speak to her yourself?' suggested his gran. Connor heard the phone being passed across.

'Hello, darling. How's school?' His mum's voice was weak and fragile. That told Connor all he needed to know about her state of health. Her MS was taking its toll.

'Fine,' Connor replied as cheerily as he could. 'I'm just calling to let you know . . . the school's phone line is down. So don't try and contact them. Should be fixed in a couple of weeks or so.'

'OK. How are your studies getting along? Have you managed to improve your maths grade yet?'

The last concern in Connor's head was maths! Nonetheless he had obtained a C grade in the most recent test, a vast improvement on his previous E grades. As his mum chatted with him, he became aware of the Chinese man from the security queue. Thin, narrow-jawed and with a bowl haircut, he perched at the end of a bench in the waiting area. He wore a plain dark blue suit and was reading the *Financial Times*, both signs that he was a businessman or banker. But Connor didn't like the regularity with which the man glanced over in his direction.

'So how's Charley?' asked his mum. 'Have you spoken to her recently?'

'Ermm . . . fine. We haven't had much chance to talk. The time difference doesn't help and she's undergone surgery and been in and out of physiotherapy sessions like a yo-yo. They're pushing her pretty hard by the sounds of it.'

'Any progress?' Confined to a wheelchair herself, his mum was eager to hear of any improvement in Charley's condition.

'Too early at this stage, she says. But Charley's hopeful. So am I.'

Connor glanced over his shoulder. The man with the bowl haircut had gone. Then, out of the corner of his eye, he caught a glimpse of someone he thought he did recognize. Someone he *never* wanted to see again. Someone who made his blood run cold. 'Sorry, Mum – I've got to go.'

'I understand, darling. They do work you hard at that school! You take care.'

'Give my love to Gran.' Connor put down the receiver and darted over to the cover of a pillar. Peering out from behind it, his eyes rapidly scanned the crowd. He spotted the man's charcoal-grey suit first, then clocked his pallid complexion. Yet Connor couldn't see his face fully so couldn't make a positive ID. But the way the man walked – no, the way he *stalked* like a panther – through the crowd was chillingly familiar.

Could it really be . . . *Mr Grey?*

On his last assignment in Russia, Connor had shot the assassin in the chest. But the man had survived somehow, most likely due to a bulletproof vest. Ever since, Connor had been expecting the assassin to exact his revenge. But days . . . weeks . . . then months had passed, and Connor had forgotten all about him.

The suspect peeled away from the main crowd and ducked down a side corridor. Connor dashed out from his hiding place in pursuit. For his own safety and security, he *had* to confirm whether it was Mr Grey or not. As he reached the corner, his suspect headed up a flight of stairs. *Where was he going?*

Following the man up to the next floor, Connor watched

as he entered a code into a digital keypad on the wall and disappeared through a set of double doors. Before they could lock shut, Connor ran down the hallway and slipped through the gap. He found himself in a marble-floored room with an artificial waterfall and misted-glass privacy screens.

'Excuse me, young man! You're not allowed in here.'

An elegant woman in a flight attendant's uniform hurried out from behind a reception desk. She pointed to a sign that read: MEMBERS' LOUNGE – FIRST-CLASS PASSENGERS ONLY.

'Sorry,' said Connor, trying to look past her into the lounge.

'I'm afraid I'll have to ask you to leave.'

She ushered him out of the door, but not before he snatched one last glimpse of the man. His back to Connor, he was drinking an iced water at the bar, a warped reflection of his lean face tantalizingly visible in the rows of glass bottles. Then the doors closed on him.

As Connor retraced his steps back to the departure lounge, he pondered the reflection. Had that been Mr Grey? It was hard to tell. Whatever, he was sure the man had been looking at him . . . and he'd been smiling, a thin sadistic smile. Or had that been merely a distortion of the bottles?

Connor began to wonder if he was becoming paranoid. After the multiple attacks on Buddyguard, who could blame him? But, if it was Mr Grey, did that mean the assassin was involved in the assault on HQ? Surely revenge didn't extend *that* far . . . yet if it did, Connor would have to be even more on his guard. The assassin was as ruthless as he was relentless.

'There you are!' cried Amir, laden down with shopping bags. 'They've already called our flight. Here's your new phone, and you'll never believe what I managed to get my hands on. The latest ultra-thin hybrid tablet with –' He noticed Connor's intense expression. 'Are you all right?'

Connor nodded absently as an announcement sounded over the tannoy: 'Final call for Flight VS250 to Shanghai Pudong. Please go to gate twelve for immediate boarding.'

CHAPTER 10

Eleven hours and five thousand, seven hundred and fifty miles later, their plane touched down at Pudong International Airport on the east coast of China. After negotiating passport control on a pair of hastily obtained student visas, Connor and Amir made their way to the connecting Maglev station.

'Do you know this train hits a top speed of *two hundred and sixty-eight miles an hour*?' said Amir, looking out of the window as they rocketed towards the centre of Shanghai. 'It's the world's fastest magnetic levitation train in commercial operation and covers the nineteen-mile journey to central Shanghai in under eight minutes –'

Connor was only half listening. For most of the overnight flight he'd been preoccupied with thoughts of Mr Grey; even his brief sleep had been troubled by nightmares of the ruthless assassin. But now his attention was distracted yet again by the presence of the man with the bowl haircut. As Amir read from the downloaded travel guide on his new fancy hybrid tablet, Connor kept a careful watch on the man, who sat in the next carriage, facing their direction yet steadfastly avoiding any eye contact. This, as Connor knew from his training, was unnatural behaviour. Most people would at least glance in the direction of someone looking at them.

'This train is amazing,' Amir declared as building upon building whizzed by at warp speed. 'The guide says it arrives at the station with on-time reliability – to the second – of greater than 99.97 per cent. In England we'd be lucky to get *one* train arriving on time in a day!'

'Uh-huh,' Connor murmured as Amir went on. His suspicions had been aroused when Bowlcut, as he was now beginning to think of him, had boarded their plane at Heathrow. Repeated sightings were a strong indicator of surveillance and Connor had seen Bowlcut in the security queue, in the departure lounge, on the plane, and now he was on the Maglev. During bodyguard training, Bugsy had taught them that *once is happenstance, twice is circumstance and three times means enemy action.*

Although this was the fourth sighting, Connor still wasn't absolutely certain that it meant enemy action. Bowlcut could well be a Chinese businessman simply returning home on the same flight as them. There weren't many variations of route someone could take in an airport. So none of the sightings were conclusive proof that Bowlcut was following them. However, when the train arrived at the Longyang Road terminus, Connor planned to hang back with Amir to allow the suspect to go ahead of them, to rule out the possibility, once and for all, that Bowlcut was tailing them.

'We just hit maximum velocity!' exclaimed Amir, pointing to the digital display above the carriage door.

Connor glanced up at the read-out: *09:32 . . . 431 km/h . . .* The train didn't feel to be going that speed; the ride was so smooth and quiet. In the next carriage Bowlcut was talking on his mobile. After a minute or so he ended the call. At the exact same time Connor heard a flip-phone snap shut a few seats behind.

Coincidence? Connor thought not. A phone call was a classic handover technique between surveillance operatives. If Bowlcut thought he'd been clocked, he'd swap with another accomplice.

Connor rose from his seat. 'Going to the toilet.'

'Really?' said Amir with a puzzled frown. 'We'll be at the station in less than two minutes.'

'Can't wait,' Connor explained. But he could. In fact, he had no desire to visit the toilet at all. He simply wanted an excuse to leave his seat and get a good look at whoever had made the call behind them. As he headed to the toilet, his gaze swept over the passengers. A couple of excited tourists. Several travel-weary businessmen. And two seats behind, next to a Chinese woman with steel-framed glasses, was a heavyset man in a black shirt and a black tie. He had a square jaw, shaved head and appeared to be local. The man didn't look up from his magazine as Connor passed. Nor did he pay any attention when Connor returned to his seat.

'Told you,' said Amir, retrieving his Go-bag as the Maglev pulled into the terminus.

'Hold on,' said Connor, making a show of searching in his own bag.

Amir shot him a questioning look. 'You lost something?'

'No,' he said under his breath, 'but I think we're being followed.'

Amir's eyes widened in alarm. But he kept his cool and didn't automatically glance round – an instinctive reaction that would have alerted any operatives to the fact that they were aware of their surveillance.

After waiting for the carriage to empty, the two of them disembarked.

On the platform Bowlcut had gone; so too had Black Shirt.

'Looks like I was wrong,' Connor admitted. 'But stay sharp.'

Amir nodded. Entering the colonel's coordinates into his phone, Amir studied the digital map, then headed towards the escalator. Catching the metro, Connor and Amir got their first taste of Shanghai: TV adverts floated in the air outside the windows as the train hurtled down the tunnel.

'I think . . .' Amir said, staring in fascination at the futuristic illusion, 'the tunnels are lined with LCD screens that display the ads at the same speed as the train. Ingenious!'

Then the adverts disappeared and they arrived at their stop. Emerging from the metro station into the heart of Shanghai, Connor and Amir were immediately confronted by a jaw-dropping cityscape of glittering skyscrapers and impossibly tall office blocks. The streets criss-crossing this immense urban forest were a flood of cars, taxis, motor-bikes, scooters and bicycles. The noise from the traffic and the surrounding building sites was almost overwhelming. Hordes of people, many wearing white elasticated pollu-tion masks, surged along the pavements – a situation made more hazardous by the constant stream of scooters and bikes that appeared to use the pavements as much as they did the roads.

Connor had always thought that London was noisy and crowded. But Shanghai was on a totally different level. A mega-city. As he and Amir headed for their rendezvous, they needed three-hundred-and-sixty-degree vision just to cross the roads and negotiate their route through the chaos. Then, all of a sudden, the city landscape opened out on to a wide spacious promenade alongside the Huangpu River.

'This is the Bund,' said Amir, checking the map on his phone. He pointed across the water at a megalithic series of skyscrapers that stretched high into the haze of smog. 'That's Pudong, the city's finance and trade zone. The sky-scraper that looks like a massive bottle-top opener is the Shanghai World Financial Center. At the top is a sky walk with a *glass* floor. Then next to it is the Shanghai Tower, one of the tallest buildings in China. It also has the world's fastest lifts. And the rocket-shaped domed structure is the Oriental Pearl TV Tower. At night it supposedly lights up like a Christmas bauble –'

Connor realized his friend was gabbling to hide his tension and nerves. So, while Amir led the way, Connor scanned the area for Bowlcut and Black Shirt, just in case. But it was a task easier said than done. Thousands of people strolled up and down the promenade. For Connor to spot two Chinese men among so many of their fellow citizens would be nigh-on impossible. To make matters worse, he and Amir were virtually the only foreigners in sight and stood out like sore thumbs. If someone wanted to follow them, then it wouldn't be hard.

He glanced at his smartband: 10:09 a.m. They were running out of time. 'So where's the rendezvous point?'

Amir was still studying the map. 'We got off at the closest metro stop. But I didn't appreciate how *vast* Shanghai is. According to the map, we've got at least a twenty-minute walk!'

'You need a tour guide?'

Connor and Amir spun round to face a hip-looking Chinese teenager in tight jeans, a loose-fitting T-shirt and red baseball cap, tufts of black hair poking out from underneath.

'No, it's all right. I think I've already got one,' replied Connor, smiling and thumbing in the direction of Amir.

The teenager eyed Amir dubiously. 'But he doesn't know Shanghai like I do. I can show you the real Shanghai.'

The guide pointed in the direction of a gleaming motorcycle with a leather-seated sidecar, the logo *Shanghai Insiders* emblazoned on the body.

'Nice motorbike,' remarked Connor.

'No, not that one!' said the guide irritably. 'The one next to it.'

Connor shifted his gaze to a clapped-out-looking rickshaw powered by a rusty bicycle. A handpainted sign on the side announced: *SHANGHAI SURPRISE! Tours to open your eyes!*

'Errr . . . thanks, but I think we'll take a taxi.'

'No taxi!' protested the guide with an indignant look. 'This is the only way to travel. My electric rickshaw is fast through traffic, friendly to the environment and fun for you!'

'Sounds wonderful,' said Amir with a gracious smile, 'but we aren't here to sightsee.'

'I give you a good deal,' the guide insisted. 'Special offer for not-sightseeing tourist.'

While Amir did his best to discourage their persistent guide, Connor hunted around for an available taxi. That's when he spotted the woman with the steel-framed glasses. The *same* woman from the Maglev. Although she'd now donned a pollution mask, Connor recognized the glasses. She was on her phone and looking in their direction. This *couldn't* be a coincidence. Connor rebuked himself for overlooking the obvious. Women often made far more effective covert surveillance operatives than men due to their ability to blend into different environments with ease. Black Shirt hadn't been the handover – *she* had!

On instinct Connor glanced behind him. Three heavily built men were converging on them.

Connor grabbed Amir's phone. 'You know this

location?' he asked the guide urgently, pointing to the red dot on the digital map.

The guide nodded. 'Fifty yuan, I take you there.'

'Done,' said Connor, striding purposefully in the direction of the rickshaw.

'We've been had!' Amir hissed, hurrying along behind Connor. 'According to my guidebook, a taxi there should only cost twenty yuan!'

'*Get in*,' Connor ordered, leaping into the back seat of the rickshaw, 'before it's too late!'

CHAPTER 11

'My name is Zhen,' said their guide with a flash of a smile. The teenager had a slender build and Connor questioned if the boy would be strong enough to cycle with them both in the rickshaw – let alone fast enough to get them out of their imminent danger. Then he noticed the electric motor rigged under their seat.

'Can we go?' urged Connor, glancing back anxiously at the woman and three men advancing towards them. 'We're short on time.'

'Sure!' said Zhen.

First adjusting the baseball cap, their guide slipped on a grimy mask and mounted the bike. Without looking, he pulled out into the traffic. A car honked furiously. Zhen ignored it and zipped between a bus and a taxi. The three men hurried to the kerb and for one horrifying moment Connor thought they might try to follow them into the road. But the traffic soon swallowed up the rickshaw and their pursuers were left behind.

'Welcome to Shanghai,' said Zhen proudly as both Connor and Amir let out a sigh of relief. 'Its name means *upon-the-sea* and is home to the world's busiest container port. But you won't see the port or ocean from here. The city stretches over one hundred and twenty kilometres north to south, and nearly one hundred east to west. One of the most populated mega-cities in the world, Shanghai has –'

'Watch out!' cried Amir as a taxi ahead of them stopped without warning.

Zhen niftily swerved round the vehicle, barely avoiding a collision, and continued the tour commentary as if nothing out of the ordinary had happened: '– over twenty-five million people living here. Across the river, you can see the Jin Mao Tower. It looks like bamboo pieces stuck together to make a super-tall glass pagoda –'

His heart in his mouth as a scooter shot across the rickshaw's path, Connor held on tightly to his seat, his knuckles going white. Having narrowly escaped capture, he began to question whether they'd now escape with their lives from the rickshaw ride.

Amir's dark brown eyes registered mute panic as their guide cut across four lanes of traffic and turned off the Bund. He whispered to Connor, 'Do you think we lost them?'

'No sane person would follow this suicidal rickshaw rider!' replied Connor through gritted teeth. Nonetheless he looked over his shoulder to check if anyone was on their tail. He'd last glimpsed the woman with the steel-framed glasses frantically hailing down a blacked-out silver Mercedes. It was hard to tell among the maelstrom of traffic, but he couldn't spot the car. They appeared to be in the clear.

'This area of Shanghai is called Old Town,' announced their guide, turning down a narrow road and through a stone gateway carved with dragons. On either side of the street squatted ageing two-storey buildings, somewhat dilapidated yet quaint when compared to the modern glazed towers of Pudong district. Telephone and electricity lines criss-crossed above their heads in a confused cat's-cradle, and people's laundry festooned windows, eaves and wires like a festival of tattered prayer flags. 'It's the original heart of the city, the only part remaining from the 1850s –'

The rickshaw slowed to a crawl, wending its way through the crowded lanes and backstreets. Wafts of steaming noodles and frying meat billowed out from tiny Formica-tabled restaurants, and locals stared in lazy curiosity as Connor and Amir glided by, the only foreign faces in the whole area. As Zhen negotiated a turn, Connor leant close to Amir and said under his breath, 'I'm guessing the people who followed us belong to the same organization that attacked HQ. You were right about the compromised Wi-Fi router – they must have intercepted my phone signal when I called up the colonel's coordinates.'

'Do you think it's safe to go to the rendezvous point then?' questioned Amir.

Connor gave a reluctant shrug. 'What other choice do we have? Besides, if the enemy knows where we're headed, why bother following us? Why try to grab us off the street?'

'Well, since your original message was encrypted, they don't know *who* or *when* we're meeting, only where,' said Amir.

Connor ducked as a shirt hung out to dry almost hit him in the face. 'That's a good point.'

Their guide took another sharp turn and Amir checked the map on his phone. Leaning forward, he tapped their guide on the shoulder. 'Are you sure we're going the right way?'

'Shortcut! Now on Fangbang Middle Road,' Zhen announced as the street opened up and the rickshaw rejoined the stream of traffic. He waved his hand at the passing buildings. 'All this used to be old houses and old offices. Now New Shanghai!'

Connor and Amir gazed in awe at the gleaming shopping malls, shining skyscrapers and towering apartment blocks that sprouted from the countless building sites. The modern urban sprawl was barely a few metres away from Old Town yet a whole world away from its crowded backstreets, cramped houses and overhanging laundry. But every so often a cluster of little homes and shops defied the city's advance. One small area looked like it had been bombed out – only a few houses were left standing in the middle of a barren wasteland.

'We call those "nail houses",' Zhen explained, pedalling hard to keep up with the traffic. 'Homeowners refuse to move. So developers can't build until the tenants are bought out, pushed out or – since many are old – carried out.'

'That sounds harsh,' said Connor, amazed that the ramshackle nail houses were still standing.

'That's progress!' replied Zhen, pulling off the main road and into a car park. 'Here we are.'

The rickshaw squealed to a halt in front of a concrete office block. Not as new as the surrounding glazed towers, the block stood alone and defiant amid its bigger, flashier brothers. A building site on its doorstep was forested with tall yellow cranes, industrial-sized diggers and heavy dumper trucks. From one nearby crane a large wrecking ball hung like a pendulum over the gutted remains of a demolished building.

'Are you sure this is it?' asked Connor, dubiously surveying the scene. The car park was mostly empty and the office building itself looked to be vacant.

Zhen nodded. Amir checked the map on his phone and nodded too. Stepping from the rickshaw, Connor took out a fifty-yuan note and handed it to their guide, who pocketed it eagerly.

'I wait for you here,' said Zhen, tugging off his mask and shooting them an expectant smile.

'Thanks, but we might be a while,' replied Amir.

'No problem.' Zhen settled into the rickshaw's back seat to wait, apparently not getting the hint.

Leaving their tenacious guide behind, Connor and Amir headed to the office entrance. They kept an eye out for anyone suspicious, but there was nobody around. *Perhaps our mystery enemy doesn't have the coordinates after all*, thought Connor. A sign by the door listed a number of companies in Chinese, but none bore the Buddyguard logo – although that didn't surprise Connor, considering the organization's covert nature. On the wall next to the sign someone had spray-painted what looked like a J and K in a red circle.

'The place seems a bit run-down,' Amir observed.

'I expect the colonel chose a place that wouldn't draw too much attention.'

Amir frowned at the piles of rubbish, cardboard boxes and discarded mattresses that littered the forecourt. 'But do you *really* think this is the rendezvous point?'

'Only one way to find out,' replied Connor, pushing through the glass doors and entering the lobby.

A lone security guard sat behind a desk, looking bored. Connor approached the man. 'We're here to see Colonel Black,' he said.

The security guard pointed to the lift.

Connor glanced at Amir. 'Well, it seems we're in the right place.' He turned back to the guard. '*Xièxie*,' he said, using what little Mandarin Chinese he knew to thank the man.

Amir went over and pressed the button to call the lift. The doors pinged open and they stepped inside.

'Which floor?' Connor asked.

The security guard pointed up, gesturing several times irritably.

'I suppose that means top floor,' mumbled Amir, thumbing the uppermost button.

The doors slid shut and the lift began to rise.

'I'll be glad to regroup with Colonel Black and the others,' said Amir, his foot tapping impatiently as the floor numbers blinked by.

'Me too,' agreed Connor. He was most looking forward to seeing Charley again. They'd been apart for over two months and every day he'd missed her like crazy. After all that had happened, their reunion would be even more emotional.

The lift doors pinged open on the sixth floor and they stepped out into a sparse reception area. Standing behind a wooden counter, a receptionist greeted them with a tight smile.

'Colonel Black?' enquired Connor.

The receptionist nodded and led them down a hallway into a meeting room. 'Wait here, please,' she said in accented English. Apart from a conference table and eight office chairs, the room was empty.

'Where's Colonel Black?' asked Connor.

'In a meeting. He won't be long.' The secretary gave him another tight smile, then left, the door clicking shut behind her.

Connor gave Amir a troubled look. 'Where's everyone else?'

'Perhaps we're the first,' Amir replied, taking a seat at the table.

Connor glanced at his watch: 10:26 a.m. Maybe his friend was right. But, too agitated to sit down, he paced the room instead. A door at the far end led to an adjoining office. Through its small glass window, Connor spied a figure sitting in a tall leather chair at a desk, back turned to the meeting room. He went to knock on the door –

'Hey, look!' said Amir, pointing at the main window. 'A drone.'

Connor turned to see a small remote-controlled drone hovering in the air, then it darted away. 'Did it have a camera?' he asked, his tone urgent.

'Probably,' said Amir. They exchanged a look, both knowing what that meant.

The enemy had found them.

Connor strode over to the door through which they'd entered and spotted the receptionist hurrying into the lift. He also noticed that the reception counter was bare – no computer, no stationery, not even a phone.

'Something's wrong,' said Connor. He tried the door, only to discover it was locked. He yanked on the handle, but it still wouldn't budge. He rushed over to the other exit, Amir joining him. This was locked too. Throwing their shoulders against the door, they burst into the office. The occupant still had his back to them, but Connor immediately recognized the distinctive silver-grey hair.

'Colonel, we've got to leave. Now!'

When he didn't respond, Connor spun the chair round and was confronted not by Colonel Black ... but by a mannequin in a wig.

CHAPTER 12

'Is this some kind of joke?' said Amir.

They both stared at the shop dummy in bewilderment. 'What the hell's the colonel up to?' said Connor.

'Perhaps this is a ghost rendezvous,' Amir suggested. 'A way to check if we were being followed or not. Bugsy must have spotted the drone and they pulled out.'

'But why the elaborate set-up?' Connor's smartband vibrated, alerting him it was 10:30 a.m.

The office strip lights flickered out and the room darkened to an ominous gloom.

Amir looked round and started backing away to the door. 'I don't like this,' he said. 'We should get out of here.'

As he spoke, a huge *boom* sounded outside and the building shook to its foundations. Dust and plaster rained down on them from cracks in the ceiling.

'Was that a *bomb*?' gasped Amir, trying to keep his feet as the floor beneath them shuddered.

'Sounded like one!' Rushing to the window, Connor looked down into the car park. The security guard and receptionist were running for their lives. Their guide Zhen was waving his arms madly up at them, gesturing to one side of the building. Connor peered through the glass and saw what the boy was pointing at. A huge grey wrecking ball was swinging towards the building on a direct collision course with their office.

'RUN!' Connor shouted at Amir, shoving his friend towards the door.

Feet skidding across the carpet, they dived into the meeting room just as the wrecking ball smashed into the office window, shattering the glass panes in a shower of lethal shards. The huge ball ploughed on through the office, taking with it the desk, the chair and the mannequin in one heavy swoop. The floor was eaten away and the ceiling caved in. The noise was like an avalanche of rock and rubble, the air turning thick with dust, as the whole building trembled from the impact.

Then the steel wrecking ball slowed its savage path of destruction, pausing for a brief moment before retreating. With a screeching groan, it fell away, leaving a jagged hole in the outside wall. The wind whistled and papers fluttered out into the empty sky like birds with broken wings.

Amir coughed and spluttered as Connor blinked away the dust and debris hanging in the air.

'That was close,' wheezed Connor, shaking the plaster from his hair. Then he saw Amir's eyes widen in alarm.

The wrecking ball was coming back.

Scrambling to their feet, they raced for the door. But in their panic they'd forgotten it was locked. As Amir frantically yanked on the handle, the wrecking ball hurtled closer and closer.

'It won't open!' cried Amir, throwing his full weight against the door.

Connor delved into his Go-bag and pulled out the XT tactical torch. Gripping it like an ice pick, he smashed the hexagonal strike-ring into the door's narrow window. The pane shattered. Amir reached through, undid the lock and they kicked the door open just as the demolition ball punched another hole in the office block.

Racing down the hallway, Connor could hear the wrecking ball pursuing them like an out-of-control steamroller. The five-thousand-kilogram comet of steel demolished all in its path. Partition walls crumbled. Floorboards split. Ceiling panels fell.

'The stairs!' shouted Connor, his heart screaming in his chest as the grey juggernaut thundered after them.

Amir was almost at the stairwell when another demolition ball powered through the side wall. It rocketed past Amir, missing him by a whisker, though it took out the floor at his feet. Connor grabbed for Amir's Go-bag as his friend tumbled into the abyss. Catching hold of the strap, he was jerked forward by Amir's weight and pulled to the floor. All the breath was knocked from him, but he stopped his friend from breaking a limb in the fall. It also saved Connor's life. The wrecking ball behind had reached the end of its arc and the steel whisked over Connor's head on its way back out of the building.

Amir dangled over the floor below. '*Don't* let me go!' he pleaded.

But Connor had no choice. The other demolition ball was also on its return swing. Forced to release his grip on the strap, he dropped his friend and rolled away as the ball carved out another slice of concrete.

Then all was quiet again, the only sound the light pitter-patter of dust settling.

Connor called through the haze to the floor below. 'You all right?'

'Yeah!' groaned Amir, rubbing his backside tenderly.

Before the wrecking balls made a repeat visit, Connor lowered himself over the hole and dropped down to the fifth floor. The whole level was stripped of furniture, light fittings and partition walls. Connor now realized the building was just a shell – a vacant office block.

Amir nodded towards the main stairwell, which was blocked with concrete lintels, bricks and debris. 'How do we get out of here now?'

'Fire escape,' said Connor, pointing to a green sign with an arrow. But they'd barely taken a step towards the fire door when the first wrecking ball smashed in the corner of the building. Connor and Amir were knocked off their feet and a section of the sixth floor caved in, cutting off that escape route.

The building shuddered yet again as the second demolition ball hammered into its side. Bricks and concrete support pillars exploded from the catastrophic impact, and morbid creaks and groans began sounding from the entire office block.

'Another few hits and this building's going to collapse like a house of cards!' cried Amir, crawling over to Connor.

As the wrecking balls tore their way through the building once more, Connor looked desperately around for another fire escape. But there didn't appear to be one. Then he spotted the bright yellow plastic of a builder's rubbish chute poking through an open window. 'There! That's our way out.'

He dragged Amir to standing and they dashed over to the plastic tube.

'You've got to be kidding,' said Amir, peering down the dark hole to nothing. 'We're five floors up!'

'It's either this or being flattened like a pancake!' Connor replied as the building let out another pained groan. 'You go first.'

Amir stared at him. 'Why me?'

'I want something soft to land on!' He took off his Go-bag and threw it down first. 'There, that should take the sting out of things.'

But Amir was still reluctant and Connor didn't blame him – they were likely to crash-land on to rubble, bricks and glass. And that's if they were lucky! Then a wrecking ball blasted its way through the fifth floor, forcing his friend to make up his mind. Amir tossed his own Go-bag into the tube and leapt in after it.

Connor decided to give his friend a count of five to

allow him time to move out of the way. However, before he finished the countdown, the second demolition ball smashed through the wall beside him. It sent masonry flying like shrapnel from a bomb, and a brick struck Connor on the back of the head. He was knocked to the floor, stars bursting before his eyes and his head ringing like a bell. For a moment he thought the room was spinning. Then with utter horror he realized it *was* – it was collapsing.

Fighting his sickening disorientation, Connor staggered back over to the chute and jumped in. He flew down at breakneck speed, a straight run to the ground. A second later he was spat out into a skip, landing hard on a pile of wood, cardboard and junk. The skin was taken off his elbows and his back jarred against the edge of a filing cabinet.

'What kept you?' asked Amir, pulling him to his feet.

Connor grimaced with pain and rubbed the back of his head where a large bruise was forming. 'Thought I'd admire the view.'

Grabbing their Go-bags, they tumbled out of the skip. The wrecking balls continued pulverizing the office block and the entire building started to reel like a concussed boxer. Bricks rained down as Connor and Amir ran for the safety of the street. Then the structure gave way entirely and the building collapsed in on itself. A monstrous roar preceded the tidal wave of bricks and masonry. A huge dust cloud billowed out, enveloping them and plunging their world into a murky darkness. Unable to see or breathe, they staggered blindly across the car park. Then the air cleared a little, the building exhaled its last wheeze and they found themselves beside the rickshaw, bruised, bloodied yet alive.

'We could've been *killed*!' gasped Amir, bent over double, his hands on his knees.

Connor stared at the demolished building, now little more than a dark corpse in the haze. 'I think that was the whole point.'

CHAPTER 13

'You two are *lihai*!' exclaimed Zhen, their guide applauding them, his pollution mask back on against the dust.

Connor coughed. 'What?'

'Hardcore! Entering a building marked for demolition, then sliding down that tube.'

Connor glared at Zhen. 'What do you mean, *marked for demolition*?'

Zhen frowned. 'Didn't you see the red painted circle? It said *chāi* – demolition.'

'You could've warned us!' cried Amir.

'I thought you could read Chinese,' said Zhen with a shrug.

'Whatever makes you think that?'

Zhen pointed to Connor. 'He said you're a guide.'

Connor gave a wheezing laugh. 'That was a joke.'

Their guide blinked. 'Oh. Sorry. I don't understand English humour. I learnt your language from books and Hollywood movies.'

As the dust cloud began to disperse, Connor spotted a ghostly figure sprinting through the haze towards them.

The man was large and powerfully built and wore a black pollution mask with mirrored shades. Whoever he was, he certainly wasn't a demolition worker.

Connor turned to Zhen. 'Get us out of here.'

'Sure. Where do you want to go?'

'Anywhere! Just do it,' ordered Connor, handing over more money and jumping into the rickshaw's back seat. Amir had spotted the menacing figure too and, tossing in his Go-bag, leapt in beside Connor.

Zhen, unaware of the approaching threat, raised a slim eyebrow in surprise at the handful of yuan notes. 'OK, I give you extra-special Shanghai Surprise tour,' he said, mounting his bike and pulling out of the car park. 'We start at People's Square, before heading into French Concession, then we will make our way back to Old Town for the Yùyuán Gardens and Confucian Temple. After that I will show you the *real* Shanghai, explore the backstreets and visit some local homes –'

'Sounds great. Let's go!' said Connor, barely taking any notice of their guide's tour plan. His eyes were fixed on the figure emerging from the dust cloud. The masked man was waving angrily at them as their rickshaw merged with the traffic and slipped away. Then a white telecom van pulled up at the kerb, their pursuer leapt in and the van gave chase.

Amir looked at Connor with a horrified expression, the dust on his face making him appear pale with fright. 'I think they intend to finish the job!'

Connor shouted to their guide. 'Can't you go any faster?'

'You two always in a hurry!' remarked Zhen with a laugh. 'Lucky for you the battery is fully charged!'

Zhen flicked a switch on the handlebars and the electric motor kicked in. The rickshaw took on a burst of speed and they zipped along the road. Behind, the van forced its way between the lanes of cars, scooters and taxis, determined not to let them out of its sight. But the rickshaw's smaller size and nimbleness allowed them to weave through gaps in the traffic and they steadily pulled ahead.

'We're losing them,' said Amir with relief.

But then the rickshaw came to a halt.

'What's the problem?' asked Connor.

'No problem,' Zhen replied breezily. 'Traffic lights.'

As the lights stubbornly stayed on red, the traffic began to clog up. A dozen or so cars back, the telecom van had stopped too and the masked man got out. He started to wend his way towards them.

'Know any more shortcuts?' Connor asked.

'Of course!' replied Zhen, pulling off the road and on to the pavement. Manically ringing the bike's bell, Zhen forged a path through the crowds of pedestrians, then turned off down a side alley and cut through to an adjacent road. As they swung left to join the traffic again, Connor glanced back and spotted the masked figure standing at the far end of the alley. Their pursuer had apparently given up the chase.

'See the red building ahead? The old one with the curved roof?' Zhen called out as he continued with the tour, oblivious to everything that had gone on behind.

'That's the Dàjìng Gé Pavilion. It sits on top of the last remaining section of the old city walls. Originally built in the sixteenth century to protect Shanghai against pirates, now most of it has gone . . .'

As their guide pedalled them in the direction of People's Square, every so often pointing out landmarks and rattling off guidebook facts, Connor and Amir engaged in a frantic whispered discussion.

'Mannequins! Wrecking balls! What the heck happened back there?' asked Amir.

'We were set up,' said Connor.

Amir wiped the dust and grime from his face. 'By the *colonel*?'

'If he's the traitor, then yes.' Connor frowned deeply. 'But that doesn't make any sense. Why would he want to destroy his own organization? Why would he want to kill *us*?'

Amir shrugged. 'The enemy could've intercepted the message, or else the text was never sent by the colonel in the first place.'

Connor's concern for the colonel spiked and he swallowed hard as a stark realization hit him. 'If they've got his encrypted phone, then they must have him too.'

Amir slumped back into the rickshaw's plastic seat. 'So what do we do now?'

'Stay alive,' said Connor grimly. 'Whoever attacked HQ clearly wants us dead. Their aim must be to wipe out the entire organization. We're going to need all our bodyguard skills just to protect one another. Then our next priority is to contact –'

'Hold on. Do you hear that?' interrupted Amir.

'What?'

'That high-pitched buzzing.' Amir looked up and searched the sky. 'There!' He pointed to a small drone hovering high over their rickshaw. It appeared to be the same one that had spied in through the office window. 'We've got to get off the street and into hiding, otherwise we'll never evade their surveillance.'

Connor tapped their guide on the shoulder, interrupting his commentary. 'Is there somewhere we can stay?'

Zhen nodded. 'I know a good hostel. Cheap! Well, cheap for Shanghai.'

'Take us there then, but can you –'

Suddenly the rickshaw gave a jolt as a vehicle shunted them from behind.

'*Báichī sīj ī!*' yelled Zhen at the driver, waving his fist in fury.

The driver evidently took offence at this and rammed into the rickshaw again, the impact lifting the front wheel off the ground. Almost bucked from his bike, Zhen screamed abuse at the man as they were forced at increasing speed down the road. Clinging to the rickshaw for dear life, Connor turned round to see a silver Mercedes on their bumper. In the front passenger seat sat the woman with the steel-framed glasses.

'STOP! STOP!' cried Amir, pointing ahead in panic. The rickshaw was on a collision course with the back of a parked truck.

Zhen battled to regain control of his steering as the

Mercedes' engine revved and growled, accelerating them towards the truck. Bracing himself for the impact, Connor had a sickening vision of his own mangled and bloody body sandwiched between the wreckage of the rickshaw and the silver bonnet of the Mercedes. But at the last moment the rickshaw's front wheel touched back down and Zhen swerved violently to the right. There was a screech of tyres as the Mercedes narrowly missed the truck itself. But the sudden turn had been too sharp for the rickshaw and it began to keel over like a ship in a storm. Almost thrown from their seats, Connor and Amir clung to the frame.

With the rickshaw at tipping point, Zhen yelled, '*Lean!*'

Connor and Amir both threw their weight into the turn and the rickshaw righted itself. As soon as all three wheels were back on the ground, Zhen twisted the electric engine's throttle to the max and shot away down the pavement.

Wheels spinning and rubber burning, the silver Mercedes followed, mounting the kerb and driving with homicidal speed. People leapt aside in panic, cyclists collided with each other, and those on scooters went hurtling into shop fronts.

'Faster!' Connor shouted as the Mercedes gained on them.

'I'm going . . . as fast . . . as I can!' gasped Zhen, his legs pumping and the electric motor whining. Sweat poured from his brow and his breathing became ragged and strained.

The Mercedes was almost on top of them when, in a

skilful and unexpected manoeuvre, Zhen veered off the pavement and down a side lane. Connor heard the Mercedes brake hard, tyres squealing on tarmac.

He looked back. The lane was too narrow for the car.

'Good work, Zhen. We got away!' Amir yelled.

But Connor wasn't so jubilant. The insect-like buzz of the drone continued to hound them from above.

CHAPTER 14

Exiting the lane on to a backstreet, their guide braked and the rickshaw came to a shuddering halt. 'You two OK?' asked Zhen.

Connor and Amir nodded. Back up the lane, the woman in the steel-framed glasses was stepping out of the car and talking rapidly into her phone.

'Sorry about that,' Zhen continued, his jet-black almond eyes expressing deep regret. 'Shanghai drivers can be a *little* impatient.'

'It isn't your fault,' said Connor, glancing up into the grey sky. The drone's high-pitched hum was setting his nerves on edge. They needed to get moving and into hiding. Fast.

Noticing Connor's troubled frown, their guide asked hesitantly, 'You . . . want to end the tour?'

'No, no, let's keep going,' Connor insisted with an encouraging smile.

'And lose that drone,' added Amir.

Zhen looked up at the tiny craft hovering above the rooftops. 'Is that thing *following* you?'

Amir offered their guide a sheepish look. 'Er . . . maybe.'

Zhen narrowed his eyes. 'Why? Are you in trouble with the police?'

'No,' Connor replied truthfully.

'Then what?' demanded their guide, stubbornly refusing to set off.

A guttural roar of engines alerted them to two motorbikes thundering down the lane, their riders nodding briefly to the woman in the steel-framed glasses as they zoomed past the Mercedes. A second pair of motorcycles raced into the backstreet, closing in on either side of the rickshaw to block them in a pincer movement.

'No time to explain,' said Connor. '*Please* just go!'

Zhen stared open-mouthed at the approaching bikers. 'Wh-who are they?'

'GO!' urged Amir as the lead motorcyclist drew a handgun.

Still their guide didn't move and Connor realized he'd gone into shock. The instinctive reaction to an unexpected threat was fight, flight or freeze. And, just their luck, their guide had opted to freeze!

Before Connor could bring Zhen to his senses, the motorcyclist took aim and fired. The bullet hit Amir square in the back, his friend having dived to shield their guide. Amir cried out and flopped forward in his seat. Ducking down, Connor threw himself protectively over his friend as a second bullet pinged off the brickwork.

'GO! GO! GO!' he yelled, kicking out at their guide.

The boot to the back of his seat snapped Zhen out of his

frozen state. Twisting the throttle and pumping the pedals, he bolted down a nearby alleyway. The motorbikes followed in hot pursuit.

'Amir! Speak to me!' pleaded Connor. He feared a nightmare repeat of Eduardo's tragic death, blood staining the rickshaw's plastic seat, a bullet having ripped through his friend's heart.

Amir rolled in his arms and groaned. '*Oww*, that really hurt!'

Connor exhaled with relief. The bulletproof jacket had done its job. Amir was alive. But Connor knew from bitter personal experience the extreme pain his friend was going through. The bullet might not have penetrated his jacket but the blunt trauma from the gunshot was the equivalent of being kicked by an angry mule. Amir would be winded at best, and could even be suffering a broken rib or two. Either way, his friend would be out of action for the next few minutes at least.

Another bullet whizzed overhead, shredding through the overhanging laundry.

Zhen let out a yelp. 'Why are they trying to kill us?'

'No idea,' Connor shouted, doing his best to shield Amir with their Go-bags. 'Just lose them!'

'I can lose the drone . . . in the backstreets of . . . Old Town,' their guide panted, cutting a sharp left down a market street and weaving manically between irate shoppers. 'But you'll have to deal . . . with the motorbikes!'

Connor looked behind. The four bikers were hard on their tail, darting and buzzing like angry wasps. People scattered and shouted abuse as the convoy ploughed through the throng. One of the bikes edged closer on their left-hand side, trying to overtake them.

'Swerve left!' Connor ordered their guide.

Zhen veered hard and sealed the gap, forcing the rider into a stall selling mobile-phone accessories. As glittering plastic covers and selfie-sticks went flying, a second biker tried to slip past on the rickshaw's other side. He was almost through . . . until the sudden appearance of a moped from an alley blocked his attempt, forcing him to brake sharply and fall back. But, with engines faster and more powerful than the rickshaw, Connor realized it was only a matter of time before their pursuers managed to overtake them. Thankfully, the busy streets prevented the lead biker from attempting another potshot at them with his handgun.

'I can't . . . keep this up . . . much longer,' gasped Zhen, his voice high and panicky.

With the electric engine whining in protest, the rickshaw zigzagged madly through Old Town's backstreets. Quickly lost amid the laundry and overhanging rooftops, they appeared to have shaken off the drone. But the bikers continued to hound them like a pack of wild dogs. Connor knew he'd have to go on the attack himself if they were to stand any chance of escaping their pursuers. As the rickshaw skirted past a hawker selling plastic buckets, pans and brushes, Connor snatched a wooden broom from the man's cart.

'*Zéi!*' shouted the man angrily before his cart was

knocked over by the racing motorbikes, his buckets and pans getting crushed beneath their wheels.

Armed with the broom, Connor fended off the nearest biker. He stabbed at the man's chest in an effort to dislodge him from his seat. This kept the rider at bay but had no effect in stopping their pursuit. So Connor changed tactics and thrust the broom up into the air, where it caught an overhanging telephone wire. He yanked down hard and pulled the line loose from its fastenings. Almost jerked from his seat in the process, Connor lost the head of the broom but left the wire strung out across the road like a garrotte. The nearest biker was going too fast to avoid it. The wire wrapped itself round his throat and wrenched him off his speeding motorbike. While the rider was left dangling like a puppet from the line, his bike carried on and careered into a shop that sold copper piping, the metalwork cascading in a clattering tidal wave into the street.

'One down!' Connor shouted, but his triumph was short-lived as the other three bikers ducked beneath the wire, swerved round the copper piping and powered on after them.

Left with just the broom shaft, Connor jabbed fiercely at the approaching bikers as if trying to spear a frenzy of tiger sharks. As one fell back, another moved in. Then two of the motorbikes split off down different streets. Meanwhile the lead biker stayed on their tail. Zhen switched right along an alley, then cut across a road, dodging the traffic. Car horns honked and a screech of tyres resulted in a crunch of bumpers. The biker darted round the accident and shot after them into the next lane. Blessed with a clear run, he drew his gun.

'Go for the wheels!' gasped Amir, peering over the back seat.

Risking all, Connor threw the broom like a javelin at the motorbike. The shaft hit its target, spearing the spokes and locking out the front wheel. The bike flipped and the rider was tossed into the air. He flew head first into a restaurant, crash-landing on a table and sending bowls of noodle soup into the faces of the customers.

Connor punched a fist into the air. 'Two down!'

Amir sat up with a grimace of pain. 'And looks like we lost the others too.'

'No, we haven't!' Zhen yelled, brakes squealing. 'They've cut us off!'

Ahead, the two motorbikes had blocked the road and the lane itself was too narrow for the rickshaw to make a quick U-turn.

'Down there,' Connor instructed, pointing to an open gateway between two buildings.

At the last second Zhen diverted left along a pinched alleyway, the path barely wide enough for the rickshaw. Sparks flew as its metal frame scraped the walls on either side. Electric engine whining, they burst from the alley into a small gloomy courtyard. Laundry dangled like cobwebs from eaves and windows, and bedsheets hung like sails from numerous washing lines. Connor caught a glimpse of a steaming kitchen and an old woman's startled face before he was enveloped in a blue polyester sheet and heard their guide yell, 'HOLD ON TIGHT!'

The rickshaw came to a sudden and ignoble stop as it hit a wall. Connor and Amir were flung forward in their seats. Zhen, flipping over the handlebars, struck the brickwork and slid dazed and bloody to the concrete floor.

Shaken but unhurt, Connor fought to disentangle himself from the bedsheet as the growl of two motorbikes reverberated down the alley and echoed through the courtyard. Flinging the sheet aside, he leapt from the rickshaw. Amir clambered out after him, clutching their Go-bags.

The two Chinese bikers, one with a goatee and the other wearing a pair of aviator-style shades, dismounted and advanced on them. Goatee pulled a knife on Connor, while Aviator went for Amir with a length of steel pipe. Connor leapt away and ducked beneath a clothes-line as Goatee slashed at his face. Driven back with a flurry of thrusts, Connor retreated across the courtyard using the laundry for cover. Amir, holding up his Go-bag as a shield, blocked the first brutal swing of the pipe from Aviator. But he was still too weak from the gunshot to fight back. A second hit drove him to the ground.

Unable to help his friend, Connor dived behind a hanging bedsheet. A moment later the tip of Goatee's knife plunged through the thin polyester material. In a matter of seconds the sheet was ripped to shreds by a series of wild slashes, then Goatee's grinning face leered through the gaps. Behind Connor the old woman let out a cry and fled the little kitchen in which she was boiling a large pan of water.

There's no such thing as knife defence, just knife survival. The words of his late instructor Steve resounding in his head, Connor knew he had to disarm the man at all costs. He grabbed a towel from a nearby clothes-line and flicked the end into his attacker's eyes. There was a stinging *thwack* and Goatee cried out in pain. His attacker temporarily blinded, Connor wrapped the towel around the man's forearm. Then, with a disabling kick to the knee, Connor yanked Goatee forward and thrust the man's hand holding the knife into the boiling water. Goatee screamed in agony. As the man's hand turned red as a lobster, Connor struck him in the side of the neck, targeting his carotid artery and momentarily cutting off the blood supply to his brain. Goatee dropped like a sack of rice. Out cold, he lay sprawled on the ground, his hand still steaming.

'I suppose that's what you call Chinese cooking,' Connor muttered to himself.

Then he heard a rasping cry for help from Amir. Rushing across the courtyard, he found his friend pinned to the ground, Aviator on his back, the steel pipe wedged against his throat. As Aviator choked him, Amir's eyes bulged and his face turned a deep purple. His fingers were stretching out desperately towards his Go-bag. Connor saw what he was reaching for and grabbed the iStun from inside. Flicking up the volume switch, he thrust the two metal prongs into Aviator's tattooed neck. The man convulsed and slumped to the floor, the pipe clanging across the concrete.

'*You . . . took your . . . time*,' Amir gasped as Connor helped his friend to his feet.

'You should have called!' Connor joked, handing back the iStun.

Amir managed a weak smile in response, retrieved his Go-bag and stowed the lethal smartphone inside.

By now Zhen had recovered from the crash and was staring at them in wide-eyed astonishment.

'We can explain,' said Connor, holding up his hands in a calming gesture. 'I know you're probably in shock, but first we need to get out of here –' he indicated the two comatose bodies – 'before these two come round.'

Zhen blinked. 'Shock? Of course I'm in shock. Just look!' He pointed to his rickshaw. The front wheel was bent and misshapen. 'This tour going to cost you plenty extra!'

CHAPTER 15

'Are we in a movie?' asked Zhen, eyeing them both hard.

While the rickshaw was being repaired in a bicycle shop across the street, their guide had taken them into the cover of a nearby bird, fish and insect market and found a tiny restaurant to hunker down in. With little more than a few rickety benches and an open wok, the restaurant's sweaty chef nonetheless served up a mouth-watering concoction of noodles, spices and crispy veg. Having only eaten an insubstantial breakfast on the plane in the early hours of the morning, Connor and Amir were now ravenous and heartily tucked into their meal.

'What makes you say that?' said Amir through a mouthful of noodles.

'Collapsing buildings, car crashes, motorbike chases, martial arts fights – it's like *Fast and Furious*!' Zhen looked over his shoulder. 'Or is this some reality TV show? Am I on camera?'

'Not any more,' said Connor, glad to have lost the drone at last. 'This is no movie or TV show. But this *is* reality. And we're all in real danger, including you.'

Zhen blinked. 'Me?'

Connor nodded. 'As long as you're with us, you're a target too.'

Their guide leant forward across the Formica table, apparently more intrigued than scared. 'So, are you *spies*?'

Connor shook his head. 'Bodyguards.'

Zhen laughed, clearly unconvinced. 'Who for?'

Connor offered a strained smile. 'Well . . . at the moment, for ourselves! But usually we're protecting the sons and daughters of the rich and famous, those who might be a target for kidnapping, blackmail or assassination.'

'Kid bodyguards!' smirked Zhen, slurping on a can of soda. 'This has *got* to be a movie!'

'Perhaps this'll convince you,' said Amir, lifting his jacket and shirt to reveal the dark red bruise spreading across his back where the round from the handgun had struck. 'In a movie, bullets don't hurt the actor.'

Zhen's jaw fell open. For a moment their guide was stunned into silence, then he asked, 'How did you survive that?'

'Bulletproof jacket,' Connor explained, shovelling in another mouthful of food with his chopsticks while he had the chance. One of the first things he'd learnt as a bodyguard was to eat, drink and relieve himself at every opportunity, since on an assignment one never knew when the next meal or toilet break might be. And on this mission he realized each and every meal could well be his last.

'So why were those people chasing you? Why do they want you dead?' asked Zhen.

'That's what we came to Shanghai to find out,' Connor replied, crunching on a particularly crispy piece of veg. 'Our base was attacked and our friends and fellow recruits abducted. The office you took us to was supposed to be the rendezvous point with our commander, Colonel Black.'

'Not the best place to meet!' snorted Zhen, arching a slim eyebrow. 'Considering it was about to be demolished.'

'That was a trap,' explained Amir as he teased out a crumb of cement still lodged in his tangle of black hair. 'We can only assume the colonel's been captured too.'

Zhen bit at his lower lip and gave them both a sympathetic look. 'So what are you going to do now?'

Connor put down his chopsticks. 'Without any official back-up of our own, we need to contact the British Embassy here in Shanghai and tell them what's happened. See if they can help in any way.'

'I'll take you there,' offered Zhen.

Connor shook his head. 'No, you've risked enough for us already. We'll catch a taxi.'

'And put *that* driver in danger?' said Zhen. 'At least *I* know what's going on.'

Amir glanced at Connor. 'He has a point.'

'Then we'll walk,' said Connor.

Zhen laughed. 'You have no idea how big Shanghai is! It'll take you hours – if you don't get lost first. I know Shanghai better than any taxi driver and I can avoid the drones.'

Connor rubbed a hand across his chin. 'OK,' he agreed reluctantly. 'As soon as the rickshaw's ready, you drop us off at the embassy. But that's as far as you go. I don't want you putting your life on the line for us any more.'

'Deal,' said Zhen, sticking out his hand. 'The fare's three hundred yuan.'

'Three hundred!' exclaimed Amir, pulling a face. 'Exactly how far is this embassy?'

Zhen gave a cocksure smile. 'Oh, not far. Ninety per cent of the fare is danger money.'

Stung by their guide, Connor admired the boy's negotiating skill and handed over six fifty-yuan notes. The three of them resumed eating, Zhen slurping noisily on his noodles as Amir scooped up another mouthful of crispy veg.

'You like the food?' asked Zhen, peering up from his bowl.

Munching hungrily, Amir nodded. 'The noodles are tasty, but what are the crunchy bits?'

'Centipede.'

Amir choked. Then retched. He spat out the half-eaten mush into his bowl. 'Are you *serious*?'

'This is an insect market,' explained Zhen matter-of-factly. With his chopsticks, he selected a crispy brown wedge that looked like a beetle and popped it into his mouth with a grin. He pointed in the direction of the greasy-faced chef, who was about to lower a wriggling red centipede into the wok. A loud hiss and sizzle filled the air as the multi-legged creature was stir-fried with other insects and freshly chopped vegetables.

'I think I'm going to be sick,' said Amir, his dark complexion somehow turning green. 'Where are the toilets?'

'At the back,' Zhen replied with a smirk.

Amir rushed through the beaded doorway, clutching his stomach. Connor was too hungry to care what he was eating. He'd consumed snake and fried rhino-beetle larvae on a previous mission to Africa. A stir-fried centipede wasn't anywhere near gross enough to put him off his food.

Zhen wiped his lips with a napkin and finished off his soda. 'I'll go and check if the rickshaw is ready.'

Connor nodded. 'OK, I'll pay up and we'll meet you there.'

Zhen hurried off through the market. Connor wasn't unduly bothered if their guide decided to bolt with the three hundred yuan in his pocket. In fact, he hoped the boy would. Zhen didn't seem to appreciate the true scale of the threat. The enemy had followed them all the way from England, attempted to kill them in a demolition, tried to crash them into the back of a lorry, and finally shot at them, chased them across Shanghai on motorbikes, then attempted to murder them in a backstreet courtyard in clear view of a witness. The enemies' actions proved they were bold, ruthless and relentless. And, most worrying of all, it appeared they had no concerns about the police or security services.

Their power and influence clearly went above and beyond the law.

Having paid the chef for their centipede stir-fry, Connor passed on the man's offer of a deep-fried tarantula and stepped out of the little restaurant into the crowded market to wait for Amir. His ears were instantly assaulted by a cacophony of animal cries – cats mewing, birds chirping, dogs barking and monkeys howling. The stench of stale urine and musty animal feed hung in the cloying air. Multicoloured fish flitted about in large water tanks, while caged chinchillas peered through their bars with shell-shocked stares. Fat snakes writhed in neon-lit glass caskets. Mice scuttled over one another in crowded plastic rat runs. And shell-less turtles tried to crawl from their glass prisons like swarms of little aliens.

The strange market completely overwhelmed Connor's senses. Then above the noise he heard an intense buzzing. *Is the drone back?* Connor ducked behind a glass enclosure containing a green-striped lizard that eyed him with cold disinterest. Searching around, Connor quickly realized that the high-pitched tone was actually emanating from the legions of tiny wicker baskets on sale at the various insect stalls. Peering closer, he saw the baskets housed thousands upon thousands of crickets, all calling out in a roar of chirps and buzzes.

'No use hiding,' said a voice as chilling as a winter wind.

A shiver sharp as a razor blade ran down Connor's spine. It was a voice he knew only too well. And one he'd hoped never to hear again.

CHAPTER 16

With dread, Connor slowly turned to confront the assassin 'I could've guessed an insect like you would be crawling around here,' he said, trying hard to suppress the tremble in his own voice.

Mr Grey stared at him, his expression absent of all emotion. 'That's no way to greet an old friend.'

'I didn't think you had any friends.'

Connor was struggling to maintain his composure. Being in such close proximity to the ruthless assassin made his skin crawl, as if a dozen centipedes now scurried across his body. Cold-blooded as the lizard in the cage, Mr Grey struck a baleful figure as he emerged from the shadows of the market stall. While of average height and build with a plain lean face, the assassin's pallid complexion and dead-eyed look gave the impression of a walking corpse – the Grim Reaper in human form. And by all accounts he *should* be dead.

'I shot you,' said Connor defiantly.

'I haven't forgotten,' Mr Grey replied, drawing uncomfortably close, to the point where Connor could smell the assassin's nicotine breath. He fixed Connor with his slate-grey eyes.

Despite the mesmerizing horror of it, Connor held the man's gaze. 'You were at the airport, weren't you?'

A twitch of a smile passed across the assassin's thin bloodless lips. 'They don't allow minors in the first-class lounge. More's the pity – we could have had our chat there and then.'

'What do you want?' said Connor, though he knew there could be only one thing the assassin wanted – *revenge*.

Extending a pale hand towards him, making Connor flinch, Mr Grey reached beyond him and picked up one of the wicker cages from the stall.

'According to Chinese folklore, crickets bring good luck,' he said, tipping the chirping insect into the palm of his hand. 'They can also be highly valuable. Some prized crickets sell for over a thousand dollars.' He prodded the bug's antennae, goading it to attack with its mandibles and forelegs. 'You see, cricket fighting is a lucrative pastime in China. Fortunes are bet on the outcome of matches. Are you a gambling man, Connor?'

Connor shook his head.

Mr Grey raised an eyebrow. 'You surprise me, considering you gamble with your life every day.'

Connor shifted on his feet, preparing to fight or flee the assassin.

But Mr Grey continued to inspect and torment the specimen. 'The best crickets, I hear, are bred in the Shangdong province. Fierce, tough and unyielding, they're born with an indomitable spirit to survive.' He glanced up to ensure he had Connor's full attention. 'Much like you. You refuse to die easily or without a fight. But I'm afraid your luck is fast running out.'

With brutal indifference, Mr Grey crushed the cricket in his hand, the insect's hardened body crunching into little shards. The assassin dusted his hands of the dead creature. Connor tensed, every muscle in his body ready to battle for his life. But the assassin didn't make any move to kill him. Instead he asked, 'Where's Colonel Black?'

Connor was thrown by the unexpected question. 'I . . . don't know.'

Mr Grey sighed irritably. 'That's a shame. For you, at least. Because, unless you know where the colonel is, you and your friend, throwing up in the toilet, are expendable. So I'll ask you again: where's Colonel Black?'

'What do you want with the colonel?' demanded Connor, baffled as well as playing for time – if Amir joined him, they might have a chance to overcome the assassin. Then a horrifying realization hit him. 'It was *you* who attacked HQ, wasn't it? Did you abduct my friends too? Were you –'

Mr Grey tutted and wagged a finger. 'Remember what I once said to you? Curiosity killed the cat.'

'Just answer me!' Connor snapped. 'Is this your idea of revenge? *All* because I shot you in Russia!'

Mr Grey snorted. 'Don't flatter yourself! This goes way beyond our little disagreement. Although it's true to say you *are* the catalyst for Buddyguard's destruction. Your intervention in Russia ruffled a few feathers and the people I represent have decided to shut your organization down. Permanently.'

Connor frowned. Viktor Malkov was dead. So it couldn't be his organization. Then a missing piece of the puzzle clicked into place. 'Are you talking about ... *Equilibrium*?'

'Your knowledge of its existence is the very reason Buddyguard has been targeted. You really *shouldn't* have told Colonel Black. Now, where is he?'

A spark of hope ignited in Connor's heart. If Equilibrium didn't have the colonel, then their situation wasn't as desperate as it appeared. They still had an advantage to play. 'No,' said Connor, squaring up to the assassin. '*You* tell me where my friends are first.'

Mr Grey tapped a bony finger on the side of a glass tank housing a long brown snake, trying to rouse the creature, as if bored by Connor's defiance. 'Contained,' he eventually replied.

'What do you mean *contained*?'

The assassin shrugged. 'They're still alive, if that's what you're worried about. For the time being. And, unless you want that time to dramatically shorten, tell me where Colonel Black is.'

Connor's jaw tightened. Through clenched teeth, he said, 'You'll never find him.'

Mr Grey narrowed his eyes. 'Well, if you don't know where he is, I'll just have to ask Charley.'

The mere mention of Charley's name from the assassin's lips sent a surge of rage through Connor. He felt his stomach knot into an iron ball, his fists clench and his neck muscles stiffen. *'You leave her alone!'*

Mr Grey smiled, or what at least passed for a smile formed on his lips. 'Touched a nerve, have I?'

Struggling to control his fury, Connor was determined to keep the assassin away from Charley at all costs. 'I'll find the colonel,' he vowed. 'Just leave her out of this.'

'That's the spirit I was talking about. Call this number when you do.' He handed Connor a business card with a single line of digits. 'By the way, don't even *think* about going to the British Embassy or the Chinese authorities. Report this to anyone and I'll be paying Charley a personal visit.'

Connor couldn't contain himself any longer. He went for the assassin. But a lightning-fast spear-hand to the base of his throat choked off his air supply and he was stopped dead in his tracks. Spluttering for breath, he collapsed to his knees, all the fight taken out of him in one single strike.

'Don't test my patience, Connor,' said the assassin, walking over to a plastic cage full of mice. Opening the lid, he pulled one out by its tail. 'Rest assured, when this Equilibrium business is concluded, we'll settle our score, once and for all. Until then –' he dangled the squirming mouse over the glass tank containing the brown snake – 'you have a stay of execution.'

The assassin dropped the mouse into the tank where it

scampered over to the corner and frantically tried to claw its way out. The snake stirred and uncoiled itself.

'But remember, in the end, the snake *always* gets the mouse.'

Connor watched as the snake slowly and deliberately glided towards its prey. The mouse fled for the opposite corner. But the snake struck. Its fangs clamped into the little animal before winding its scaly body round the mouse and constricting it to death. Connor, still struggling for breath himself, felt sickened as the snake started to swallow the mouse whole.

When he managed to tear his eyes away from the gruesome scene, Mr Grey had gone.

CHAPTER 17

Amir stepped out of the restaurant and saw Connor kneeling on the floor, his hand to his throat. 'You've been sick too?'

Connor shook his head and, supporting himself against the glass tank, rose unsteadily to his feet.

'Then why so pale?' Amir asked, grimacing as he noticed the half-consumed mouse lodged in the snake's jaws. For a moment it appeared he might throw up again.

'I've just seen a ghost,' Connor rasped.

Amir frowned. 'You must be jet-lagged. What are you talking about?'

'Remember that suspect you identified for me in Russia with my contact-lens camera?'

'You mean the nobody man?' Amir had been unable to trace any background information on Mr Grey. Facial recognition had drawn a blank, his identity and records having been apparently globally erased from every database: criminal, civilian and governmental. It was as if the assassin didn't exist.

Connor nodded. 'Well, he was here.'

Amir's jaw dropped. 'In *Shanghai*! What did he want with you?'

'I'll explain on the way.' Connor hurried out of the covered market and headed across the street to the bicycle repair shop.

Zhen waved cheerily to them. 'Rickshaw's fixed. We can go to the embassy.'

'Change of plan,' said Connor as their guide rolled the rickety vehicle on to the road, its front wheel hammered back into shape. 'We no longer require your services.'

Their guide looked up, stunned and clearly offended. '*What?* But you already paid!'

'The threat level has escalated. No amount of danger money is worth the risk for you,' Connor explained. He knew the presence of Mr Grey meant that anyone associated with them became a target, and the assassin would have no qualms in killing Zhen to achieve his ends.

Zhen shrugged it off. 'As my grandmother says, once your toe is wet, you may as well dive in up to your neck!' Mounting the rickshaw and donning his pollution mask, he beckoned the two of them to climb aboard. 'A deal's a deal. I'll take the risk.'

'Come on, Connor,' urged Amir, jumping into the back seat. 'If things are truly as bad as you say, we don't have time to waste. Let's get to the embassy while we can.'

'We're not going to the embassy,' said Connor.

Amir blinked in surprise. 'Then where are we going?'

Connor glanced up and down the crowded street, pedestrians spilling off the pavements and scooters zipping past in every direction. But there wasn't a taxi in sight and, beyond a name, he had no idea where he was headed. The address for Charley's clinic had been on his old smartphone. Even if they were lucky enough to hail a cab, it was doubtful the driver would speak English as fluently as their guide, if at all. He turned to Zhen. 'Do you know where the 1933 Building is?'

Zhen nodded. 'Lao Changfang? Sure! It's in Hongkou district, north Shanghai.'

Reluctantly Connor clambered aboard and sat next to Amir, praying his decision to use Zhen wasn't sentencing their guide to death. As the rickshaw pulled away, Connor felt hostile eyes upon him and shot an anxious glance over his shoulder. Mr Grey stood in the shade of a market stall awning, a roasted black scorpion on a stick held between the fingers of his bone-grey hand. With his glacial stare locked on to Connor, he bit clean through the scorpion's tail and chomped on its bulbous toxic stinger. Connor shuddered. He realized if he was to have any hope of beating Mr Grey, he would need every ounce of wit and martial arts skill just to survive. But would that be enough to vanquish such a cold-blooded killer?

'What's at the 1933 Building?' Amir asked as the rickshaw turned a corner and the assassin disappeared from view.

'Charley, I hope,' replied Connor, settling uneasily back into his seat. 'Mr Grey has threatened to pay her a visit if we don't find Colonel Black.'

Amir stared at him in horrified bewilderment. 'But we don't know where the colonel is!'

'Nor does Equilibrium, apparently.'

The rickshaw bumped over a pothole in the road as Zhen took a left turn and headed north past the old city wall.

'*Equilibrium?*' questioned Amir.

'That's who's behind the attack on Buddyguard.' Connor clenched his fists in fury as he thought of their friends being 'contained' somewhere by the secretive and sinister organization.

Amir's brow creased. 'I remember. You mentioned Equilibrium in your Russian operation report.'

'Yes, but I've no idea who or what the organization is, except that Mr Grey works for them. As far as I could gather at the time, they were funding and protecting Viktor Malkov in an attempt to gain political influence in Russia.' Connor clicked his fingers as he was struck by a thought. 'Come to think of it, that might be how Equilibrium infiltrated Buddyguard HQ – through Malkov and his communications with the colonel! There might *not* be a traitor.'

'We still can't rule that possibility out,' said Amir.

'After reading my report, Colonel Black assigned Bugsy to investigate Equilibrium further.'

Amir nodded thoughtfully as if several pieces of the puzzle had just fallen into place. 'That must be why Bugsy was so secretive about his trip. He must've uncovered something significant or damaging about Equilibrium, which explains why the colonel left HQ in such a hurry.' He looked at Connor. 'So what's the plan now?'

'We get to Charley first, ensure she's safe, then somehow locate the colonel. She may even know where he is –'

A familiar hum whirred above their heads.

Connor glared at the tiny hovering craft. 'Well, there's a surprise!' he said, his tone sarcastic. 'Mr Grey wasn't going to let us out of his sight for long. Zhen, ditch the drone!'

'No problem,' said their guide, cutting down a back lane. The laundry hanging from the criss-cross of washing lines provided cover as the rickshaw changed direction up a side street, then shot along a narrow alleyway. After a couple more switchbacks, they popped out on to a main road and merged with the traffic.

Zhen grinned. 'Easy!' But the smile fell from his slender lips when the incessant buzzing returned with a vengeance. Their guide cursed in frustration and pedalled on. The road led straight on to the Bund and they soon found themselves beside the Huangpu River again, the drone hovering over them like a malevolent wasp.

'We'll never lose it out in the open,' said Amir.

'Don't worry,' replied Zhen. 'I have a plan.'

Bearing right off the Bund, their guide ignored the red no-entry sign for bicycles and entered a tunnel beneath the river. The air was thick with exhaust fumes and Connor and Amir were forced to cover their mouths. But Zhen hadn't gone far when he stopped the rickshaw and turned against the flow of traffic. Cars and taxis honked angrily and a white van swerved to avoid them as they exited the tunnel the wrong way. But the risky manoeuvre had done the trick. The drone operator had fallen for Zhen's ploy and sent the craft to the tunnel's exit, on the opposite side of the river.

'Good work, Zhen,' congratulated Connor, looking up into a drone-free sky. He hadn't wanted the assassin following their every move. Then an unnerving thought dawned on him. If Mr Grey knew where to find Charley, then so did Equilibrium. They could be watching the place. And who was to say they didn't have her already? Of course, there was a slim chance the assassin had been lying, but –

Connor pulled out his new phone and dialled a number from memory.

'Who are you calling?' asked Amir.

'Charley. This phone's secure, isn't it?'

Amir nodded uneasily. 'For the time being at least. But hers might not be.'

Connor decided he had to take the risk. The line rang twice before connecting. He heard a series of escalating beeps, then the phone cut off. Connor tried again, hoping he'd just lost signal. The same beeps greeted him, except this time an automated message followed: *We're sorry, but you've reached a number that is unavailable or no longer in service . . .*

'No answer?' said Amir.

Connor shook his head. 'Disconnected.' His concern for Charley exploded into panic. Had Equilibrium got to her already? Or had Charley received warning from Colonel Black and ditched her phone?

'Can't you go any faster?' he urged Zhen.

'Always faster!' gasped Zhen, maxing the throttle and pedalling harder as they crossed over a bridge into north Shanghai. 'Be there in five minutes.'

Those five minutes were the longest in Connor's life, the

traffic seeming to grind their journey to a snail's pace as the rickshaw squeezed its way between cars, taxis and lorries, fighting off mopeds and delivery bikes for gaps. Amir kept a watchful eye on the skies, while Connor grew more and more agitated in his seat.

'That's it up ahead,' said Zhen eventually, turning off the main road and pointing to an immense four-storey concrete building at the end of the street.

'Stop here,' ordered Connor. As desperate as he was to find Charley, he couldn't take unnecessary risks. He had to surveil the area before making his approach.

Zhen pulled over to the kerb.

'Doesn't look like a medical clinic to me,' remarked Amir, his gaze sweeping over the grey and oppressive concrete block that stood beside a wide canal. An ominous lattice of round and square windows faced west on to the street and gave the building the appearance of a rectangular multi-eyed spider. The whole construction was both formidable and menacing.

'The 1933 Lao Changfang used to be a slaughterhouse,' explained Zhen, automatically going into tour-guide mode. 'Its architecture is unique.'

'You can say that again,' remarked Amir.

'Over the years, the building has been a medicine factory, a cold-storage facility and a boutique shopping centre. Recently it was bought by a Chinese billionaire and closed to the public. There is a rumour that it is now an advanced medical research facility.'

Connor scanned the area for threats. Almost at once

he spotted a number of CCTV cameras dotted along the drab concrete walls and two security guards at the entrance. Opposite, more CCTV cameras lined a modern glass-and-steel office block, although interestingly they were pointed *towards* the 1933 Building. The road leading up to the entrance was light of both traffic and people and there was no obvious sign of enemy surveillance, but that didn't mean agents weren't watching.

'Zhen, can I borrow your mask?' asked Connor. Their guide handed over the grimy pollution filter and Connor used it to conceal his face before stepping out of the rickshaw. 'Stay here,' he instructed Amir. 'If you notice anything unusual, buzz my smartband.'

Nodding, Amir watched the street and skies as Connor headed towards the building. He kept to the far side and followed casually behind a couple of office workers. Up close, it was even more intimidating. He looked up at the gridwork of windows, the building's black eyes giving up nothing of what was inside. Then Connor caught a glimpse of sun-blonde hair in the top right corner. Squinting, he spied Charley on the rooftop balcony, gazing out across the city skyline. His heart soared and, as he raised a hand to attract her attention, his smartband buzzed urgently –

A white telecom van screeched to a halt in front of him. The side door flew open. Strong hands reached out and Connor was dragged inside before Charley had a chance to look his way.

The Director gazed out of the window of the Chairman Suite on the eighty-seventh floor of the Grand Hyatt Hotel, atop the Jin Mao Tower in the affluent Pudong district. Few knew the true identity of the head of Equilibrium, but the reflection in the glass revealed her to be a short woman with a bob of black hair as smooth and dark as the velvet jacket that cloaked her compact frame. Her watchful eyes were the colour of unrefined oil. And from her slim alabaster neck hung a vibrant jade-green pendant of a fire-breathing dragon, the curled creature nestling in the small hollow above her slender collarbone.

By now the bright midday sun had burnt away much of the polluted haze and the view from the Chairman Suite stretched across the cityscape as far as the eye could see. But not as far as the Director's domain extended – which was why she was so vexed that a pair of teenage boys had somehow slipped her net.

Savouring a sip of Dragon Well green tea from an antique porcelain cup, she turned to the two Equilibrium agents responsible for the screw-up: a middle-aged man by the name of Heng with a narrow jaw and bowl haircut; and a younger woman called Yuan, whose steel-framed glasses hardened her otherwise pretty looks into a permanent stony stare.

'Explain yourselves,' said the Director, taking another slow and unhurried draught of tea.

'It isn't my fault,' Heng cut in first. 'I tailed the targets all the way from London before I handed over to –'

'You needn't have handed over to me if your surveillance hadn't been so careless!' retorted Yuan, shooting her associate a sideways glare.

'I wasn't the one to lose them on the Bund,' snapped Heng, a flush rising in his cheeks. 'That was *your* fault. I'd done my job –'

'If you'd done your job properly,' Yuan continued, her tone harsh yet even, 'then all *four* targets should've been crushed to death in the demolition.'

Heng's mouth flapped open like a goldfish's as he struggled for a response. 'Th-th-the other two didn't show! I can't be held responsible for that. And no one could've anticipated the boys' insane escape route – sliding down the builders' rubbish chute like sewer rats! Anyway, *you* had multiple opportunities to kill them after that and *failed.*'

'They hospitalized four of my men,' said Yuan fiercely, rounding on her associate. 'Thanks to your lack of intel, we seriously underestimated the targets' capabilities. The failure is as much yours as it is mine, if not more so –'

The Director held up a hand for silence. 'Enough of this

blame-gaming. What I want to know is *where* our targets are now, and what you're going to do about it.'

Yuan straightened. 'I've agents hunting them down as we speak. They can't have got far. Their faces don't exactly blend in. In fact, I expect confirmation of their capture any moment. As for the other two targets –'

A knock at the door interrupted her and a hefty security guard escorted a charcoal-suited man into the luxurious hotel suite.

'Ah! Mr Grey,' said the Director, raising the teacup in greeting. 'I trust you bring me better news?'

The assassin nodded. 'I tracked down the rickshaw to a bicycle repair shop in Old Town. The targets were "enjoying" an early lunch in the insect market.'

She looked past the assassin. 'So where are they then? Or did you execute them on the spot?'

'I let them go.'

The Director almost dropped the teacup. 'You did *what*?'

'We only have two targets in our sights,' Mr Grey explained. 'We need bait for the bigger fish. Why not let Connor reel them in?'

The Director drained the teacup. 'Excellent work, Mr Grey.' She shot Yuan and Heng a withering look. 'At least someone round here shows initiative. Shame on you both that a *lǎowài* has shown you up!'

The two agents bowed their heads and stared resolutely at the carpet.

Setting aside the fine porcelain teacup, the Director

ushered Yuan and Heng out of the Chairman Suite with a wave of her hand. Being on the top floor of the five-star hotel, the exclusive suite led directly out on to the uppermost balcony of Jin Mao Tower's world-famous atrium – a vertigo-inducing barrel-vaulted space of circular golden corridors and staircases that wound in a spiral all the way down to the hotel lobby, thirty-one floors below.

Before allowing the security guard to close the door on the two agents, the Director addressed Yuan. 'As lead agent, the success or failure of any operation is your sole responsibility. Don't *ever* fail me again.'

Red-faced, the agent replied, 'I promise I won't.'

As she bowed her head, the Director glanced at the muscle-bound guard manning the door. 'Show Heng out first.'

Nodding, the guard seized Heng by the collar of his jacket and belt of his trousers. Then, picking him up like a piece of garbage, he tossed the bowlcut-haired agent over the balcony rail. Heng flailed and tumbled, screaming all one hundred and fifteen metres of the way down, until he smashed into a bloody and broken heap on the crimson carpet of the hotel lobby below.

The Director smiled in satisfaction at his departure, then turned to Yuan, whose eyes had widened into saucers behind her glasses. 'No, Yuan, you will not fail me *unless* you wish to check out early too.'

CHAPTER 19

Connor fought for his life as the van accelerated away and careered round a corner.

'Get off me!' he snarled, struggling in the man's iron grip. His abductor was broad and solid as a brick wall, his square-jawed face hidden behind a pollution mask and his eyes obscured by a pair of mirrored shades. Managing to wrench an arm free, Connor caught his assailant with a crunching roundhouse punch to the jaw. Then he wound up for a second strike.

'Whoa! Hold up, Connor! It's me!'

Connor froze mid-punch. Having dislodged the mirrored glasses with his first blow, he now got a good look at his abductor's flinty eyes and sharp crew cut of silver-grey hair. Rather than wanting to punch him, Connor could almost hug the man. In fact he did. Overwhelmed by the unexpected reunion, he wrapped his arms round the soldier's broad chest. 'Colonel! Sorry, I didn't realize –'

In a rare moment of tenderness, the colonel returned his hug. Then, stiffening back into his usual stony demeanour, he extracted himself from Connor's arms. Lowering the black mask, he wiped away a thin stream of blood from his lower lip with the back of his hand. 'Solid punch, Connor. Someone's trained you well.'

Connor laughed with relief. 'Yeah, Steve's a good instru–' he stopped and corrected himself – '*was* a good instructor . . .' He trailed off, his initial rush of joy dissolving with the memory of his murdered combat teacher.

The colonel stared at him, unflinching, but he didn't need to ask any further to understand. 'I feared as much. The others?'

'Taken,' replied Connor. 'But we've no idea where or why.'

Colonel Black slumped against the side of the van and hammered his fist into its metal panelling, leaving a knuckle-sized dent.

'Everything all right?' asked a familiar voice from the driver's seat.

'Bugsy!' exclaimed Connor, his joy returning at the sight of his surveillance tutor. Twisting his bald head round, Bugsy shot him a wink and grinned. 'That'll be the first and only time you get away with hitting a commanding officer!'

To Connor's ever-increasing amazement, Amir now peered round the edge of the passenger seat. An elated smile was plastered across his face too, clearly glad to be reunited with his logistics mentor. 'Wait till I tell the others you floored the colonel! They'll never believe me.'

'Don't worry, Amir. I'll be your witness,' Bugsy told him, laughing.

'Steve's dead,' said Colonel Black flatly.

The tragic news cut Bugsy's laughter short and his grin

sagged into a fierce glower. 'Murdering scum!' The engine roared as he drove the van even harder. 'What about Jody? Gunner? The recruits?'

Amir answered with a sorrowful expression. 'Captured. But we've reason to think they're still alive.'

'Equilibrium won't kill them,' said the colonel, rising to his feet. 'Not yet at least. Not while we possess this.' He pulled a discreet flash-drive stick out of his pocket. 'They'll use them as leverage to get this back.'

'What does that contain?' asked Connor.

'Everything Equilibrium doesn't want the world to know.'

Colonel Black braced himself against the van's roof as Bugsy weaved through the traffic and joined the city's middle ring road. Slipping the flash drive back into his pocket, the colonel nodded behind him and demanded, 'Now who's that? And why's he with you?'

In the darkened back corner of the van a small trembling figure lay huddled, eyes round and fearful.

'That's Zhen, our guide!' said Connor, noting with alarm that the boy's slim wrists and ankles had been bound with zip-ties. 'He's been helping us. You can let him go.'

Zhen offered the colonel a timorous smile and held up his hands. But Colonel Black shook his head. 'Sorry, but I don't trust anyone at the moment. First, explain what you two are doing here in Shanghai?'

'We got a text message to meet you,' Connor replied.

The colonel narrowed his eyes. 'At that office on Fangbang Middle Road?'

Subjected to his penetrating glare, Connor got the

distinct feeling he was being interrogated. He nodded. 'It turned out to be a trap.'

'Yes, we suspected as much. Bugsy scoped out the site first. That's why we didn't show. But we did see you and tried to make contact.'

Connor now recalled the masked figure emerging from the demolition dust cloud. 'That was *you*! We had no idea. Why wear the mask?'

'The same reason you're wearing one,' replied the colonel, nodding at the grubby pollution mask still covering Connor's mouth. 'As Westerners in China, our faces stand out like balls on a cow. Even if we did blend in, Equilibrium's reach is so extensive they'd soon track us down. So, if we're to stay alive, we must keep a low profile at all costs.'

Peeling off Zhen's mask, Connor asked, 'But how did *you* find us? Shanghai's not exactly a small place.'

'We received a message too – from you,' revealed Colonel Black. 'I believe you were the bait for us. Since then Bugsy's been keeping track of your movements.'

'That was *your* drone!' exclaimed Amir, clapping his hands at making the connection. 'Oh, man, it's super-cool. What's the resolution of the camera?'

The corner of Bugsy's mouth curled into a smile. 'Sixteen-megapixel with 8K video capability at twenty-four frames per second.'

Amir's face lit up. 'Wow! Speed?'

'Top velocity of seventy miles per hour,' boasted Bugsy, 'with a new-generation LiPo battery guaranteeing over sixty minutes of flight time. When folded, it's not much bigger than a regular water bottle. The camera's mounted on a three-axis gimbals stabilizer ensuring –'

'Enough of the tech talk,' snapped Colonel Black. 'What I really want to know is what you two were doing outside the 1933 Building?'

Connor was once again subjected to a stare as cold and piercing as ice. 'I was going to find Charley,' he replied, wondering why the colonel was being so hostile. 'Mr Grey is in Shanghai too. He's threatened to *visit* her if I didn't locate you. I'd just spotted her when you grabbed me off the street.' He turned to Bugsy. 'We need to go back and get Charley.'

'No!' said Colonel Black sharply.

Connor shot him an incredulous look. 'Why not?'

The colonel studied Connor for several seconds as if judging whether he was trustworthy or not. Then, evidently satisfied, he replied, 'Because you almost stepped into the wasps' nest. The 1933 Building is Equilibrium's Shanghai headquarters.'

Connor shook his head. 'That can't be right. It's Charley's spinal clinic.'

'That may well be the case,' said Colonel Black, 'but it's also the heart of Equilibrium's operations, otherwise known as the Hive.'

Connor felt his stomach plummet. 'We have to go back. Charley's in danger!'

'No, *she's* the danger to us,' corrected the colonel. 'She's the traitor.'

CHAPTER 20

Connor was stunned into silence, the revelation hitting him as hard as the wrecking ball that had destroyed the Shanghai office block. It was as if he couldn't breathe, all the air sucked from his lungs. It couldn't be true. Charley *couldn't* be the traitor. She was Alpha team's operations leader. The first female Buddyguard recruit. She was his girlfriend! This *had* to be a mistake. But why would the colonel say such a thing if he didn't believe it to be the truth? Connor's mind reeled as the van sped along the ring road, his thoughts as chaotic and fleeting as the passing traffic.

'Turn off here,' the colonel directed Bugsy.

Taking the exit ramp from the ring road, the van headed into a run-down industrial zone – a potholed grid of crumbling concrete office blocks and vast decaying warehouses. Workers in dirt-stained overalls shifted wooden crates on and off delivery trucks that looked more like rust-buckets on wheels. Jagged mountains of scrap metal and broken household appliances littered the forecourts, while car parks were dump zones for wrecks of vehicles being stripped of their spare parts. Turning left down an empty side road, the van disturbed a feral dog scavenging through a pile of rotting rubbish. It limped off along a darkened alleyway strewn with broken bottles and plastic bags.

'Nice neighbourhood,' said Amir, eyeing a burnt-out vehicle and what looked like a flattened piece of roadkill in the gutter.

'This is prime real estate,' smirked Bugsy. 'No CCTV, no police and no security means no surveillance.'

Passing beneath a flyover, the van approached a dilapidated warehouse. Half the corrugated roof had collapsed in and its upper tier of windows had been either shattered or boarded up. The brickwork was pockmarked and flaking; even the faded graffiti looked worse for wear. The van came to a halt in front of a large rusting metal shutter and Bugsy handed Amir a key. 'Do the honours.'

Clambering out of his seat, Amir hurried over to the entrance. He unlocked a heavy-duty padlock at the base and rolled up the shutter. The van eased cautiously inside, then Amir brought the shutter down with a clattering *bang* that reverberated round the warehouse's dank cavernous space.

Sliding open the van's side door, Colonel Black jumped out. Connor followed, but the colonel insisted that the bound Zhen should remain in the back of the van.

'Welcome to our top-secret base!' said Bugsy with a wry smile. He swept his hand round the crumbling shell of a building – a vast, cold and gloomy void of dirt and discarded rubbish.

Amir laughed. 'I can see why you keep it secret.'

Then, like a magician, Bugsy tugged away a dust sheet and revealed a workbench kitted out with computers, high-res monitors, surveillance equipment, drones, weapons and other essential gear.

Amir's eyes widened, trying to take it all in. 'Whoa! James Bond would be jealous of this set-up.'

Bugsy patted his student amiably on the shoulder. 'There's a cyber-market on Qiujiang Road, right under the elevated train tracks in north Shanghai, where you can buy almost anything – electronic processors, circuit boards, laptops, cameras, you name it. Legal or illegal, they'll have it . . . for a price.'

As Bugsy gave Amir a rundown of the equipment, Connor stood in the centre of the warehouse, lost in a daze. He still couldn't believe what the colonel had said. It didn't make any sense. Not *his* Charley.

'She's no traitor!' he shouted, his voice echoing off the warehouse walls and sounding more hollow and desperate than he liked.

Colonel Black rounded on him. 'Believe me, she is. We didn't discover the link between the clinic and the Hive until Bugsy hacked into their mainframe.'

'So what if the clinic's in the same place as Equilibrium's headquarters? That doesn't mean Charley's one of them. They must be holding her against her will.'

Colonel Black folded his arms across his chest. 'Did she look like a prisoner to you?'

Connor thought back to Charley on the building's rooftop, to all appearances unguarded and untroubled. 'I wasn't close enough to tell. But Charley's one of us – Alpha team's ops leader and one of *your* first recruits!'

'Which makes her all the more valuable to Equilibrium,' the colonel replied coldly. 'Haven't you wondered how Equilibrium knows so much about Buddyguard? Not only did they find the classified location of our headquarters, but they were able to hack into our systems, compromising our security and taking control of our communications. They gained access to *every* active operation! All evidence points to an inside job – and the backstabbing traitor is *your* Charley.'

Connor didn't know how to respond. Of course he'd suspected an inside job and had even voiced his concern to Amir. But never in a thousand years would he have imagined it to be Charley.

'You *must* be wrong,' he argued, his upset turning to anger. 'Charley came to China to try out a pioneering therapy for her spinal injury. A once-in-a-lifetime opportunity. That was her only reason – her *only* motivation. The fact that the clinic's in Shanghai, or that she left prior to the attack, is mere coincidence.' He glared fiercely at the colonel. 'After everything she's sacrificed for Buddyguard, how can you even *think* of accusing her of betrayal?'

Colonel Black sighed. 'If I can't convince you, then perhaps this will.' He beckoned Connor over to the workbench and flipped open a laptop. 'Bugsy discovered this during his hack into Equilibrium's mainframe.'

He ran a video file and Charley's slim perfect face flickered on to the screen. Connor instantly felt a surge of protective love towards her. Laid back against a pillow, she looked relaxed, calm, almost dreamy. Her head was in bandages, so Connor guessed that the video had been recorded around the time she'd called him in Mexico.

'How do you feel now?' asked a voice off-camera, male, doctor-like and heavily accented.

'Better,' she replied with a smile.

'The neuro-chip implantation went according to plan. Your physiotherapy begins tomorrow. Now, you must fulfil your part of the bargain.'

A slight frown creased Charley's brow as the voice asked, 'What is the location of the Buddyguard Headquarters?'

The frown faded and her eyes, wide and blue as a summer sky, looked unblinking into the camera. 'Wales, Brecon Beacons . . . five miles north of Craig-y-nos.'

'What's the access code to your security login?'

'Kerry4837#RIP.'

'What security measures are there at Headquarters?'

Charley chewed her lower lip thoughtfully. 'Perimeter alarms along the borders, hidden CCTV cameras at the gate, pressure detectors at ten-metre intervals beneath the ground, window sensors . . .'

Connor felt his heart sink as Charley reeled off each and every security feature.

Then the disembodied voice asked, 'Where's Connor now?'

A smile slid across Charley's lips at the mention of his name. 'On a mission in Mexico –'

Connor snapped the laptop shut. Swallowing back a bitter lump in his throat, he stared off into the far distance, tears welling up. Even though he'd seen the video with his own eyes, he still couldn't believe it.

I don't know what to believe at the moment ... Charley's own words in reference to Colonel Black came back to haunt him. He recalled her recent questioning of the Buddyguard organization, her growing distrust of the colonel, her frustration at no longer being the star recruit, and her vague and guarded responses whenever he asked about the spinal research group and how they'd contacted and selected her. In light of the fact that Charley had lost the use of her legs in a mission, it was understandable that she resented Buddyguard – but to the point of *betrayal*?

'I realize how hard this must hit you, Connor,' said Colonel Black. 'I've only just accepted it myself. But we have an important mission ahead. Perhaps the most critical we've ever embarked upon. Dare I say, the future state of the world rests upon our shoulders. So I need your full focus and capabilities if we're to succeed.'

Connor nodded numbly. Slumped in a rickety old office chair, Amir appeared to be equally shocked. His head was in his hands and his dark brown eyes glassy with tears.

'You too, Amir!' snapped the colonel.

Amir blinked, straightened and refocused on the colonel. 'Yes, sir.'

Colonel Black patted the flash drive in his pocket. 'The contents of this drive can expose and bring Equilibrium down. But, due to the extent of their power and influence, there's only one person in the world I'd trust enough to act on information this sensitive – Stella Sinclair, Deputy Director of MI6. So we have to get the drive out of China and into her hands.'

'Why not just email it to her?' suggested Amir.

'The files will never get past the Great Firewall of China,' explained Bugsy. 'A two-*million*-strong force of security officers monitor online activity, 24/7. With Equilibrium's invisible grip on the government, the net will be shut down the instant the files are uploaded and a kill switch activated to destroy them. We'll be left with nothing but an empty flash drive.'

'What about using an encrypted VPN?' asked Amir.

Bugsy shook his head. 'Even Virtual Private Networks are controlled by the state, and through them by Equilibrium. We've no option but to physically take the files out of the country.'

'How about approaching the British Embassy? Use a diplomatic bag?' said Connor.

Colonel Black replied with a thin mirthless smile. 'Equilibrium has even infiltrated the British Foreign Office. With agents in the Shanghai division, there's no guarantee the flash drive will reach Ms Sinclair. The only sure-fire route is to hand it to her personally. As all the airports are being closely monitored, the plan is to take the bullet train from Shanghai to Hong Kong, then catch a boat to Singapore, before flying back to the UK.'

'But what about the rest of the team?' asked Connor.

Colonel Black's expression hardened. 'The flash drive is our only priority.'

Amir looked aghast. 'But they're in trouble! We need to save them – to do *something* at least.'

'We are. We're taking this –' he pulled out the drive – 'to MI6.'

Connor stared at the colonel. 'But Mr Grey threatened to end their lives if I didn't find you for him.'

'You have.'

'But he's expecting me to call. What do you think he's going to do when he discovers we've left the country?'

The colonel's eyes turned stony. 'As much as I hate to say it, sacrifices may have to be made.'

Connor was taken aback at the colonel's hard-heartedness. 'We *can't* abandon them to that psycho assassin. Think about Jody, Gunner, Ling, Jason, Marc, Richie –'

'We're dealing with a ruthless organization,' cut in Colonel Black. 'This flash drive is the only leverage we've got. And it's the best chance for their survival. Until it's out of the country, *all* our lives are in jeopardy.'

'And remember, Connor, they're all bodyguards,' said Bugsy. 'Just like you and Amir, they've had hostage survival training. Coping mechanisms will be in place. They'll be looking for any opportunity to escape. And if they're all together they'll be even stronger. Our job is to ensure their efforts aren't wasted and to be there when they get out.'

With a heavy heart, Connor accepted the logic in Colonel Black and Bugsy's argument, even though it didn't feel right turning their backs on their friends like this. 'OK,' he relented with a sigh. 'Let's do it then.'

Bugsy cleared his throat. 'There's one small glitch in our plan. We need ID to purchase the train tickets. However, as soon as our names are entered into the system, Equilibrium will be on to us.'

From the back of the van, a voice piped up. 'I can get tickets.'

'What's that?' said Colonel Black.

Zhen poked his head out of the van's side door, wrists and ankles still bound. 'I said, I can get the tickets for you. My uncle works for the railway. No need for ID or passports. Even put them in Chinese names.'

Colonel Black looked at Connor. 'Can we trust him?'

Zhen offered the colonel a mercenary smile. 'Can you afford not to?'

Connor perched on the end row of a set of red padded seats, one among hundreds that lined the vast concourse of Shanghai Railway Station like a regiment of plastic soldiers on parade. A newly purchased pollution mask covered his face, and a baseball cap hid his spikes of brown hair. He kept his head bowed but his eyes up, constantly scanning the torrent of passengers flowing to and from the dozen or so platforms.

The bullet train to Hong Kong was due to depart in a little under ten minutes and there was no sign of Zhen. Connor exchanged an anxious look with Amir, who sat three rows over, facing the opposite way. He wore a pollution mask too, and a hoodie, to conceal his identity. He clasped his Go-bag to his chest, and his knee jittered nervously. Bugsy was stationed a little way over to Connor's right, browsing in a small newsagent's while eyeing the crowd through his sunglasses. Ensuring their group was dispersed enough to avoid obvious detection, Colonel Black stood next to a drinks vending machine, mirrored shades and mask on. Between them they maintained a three-hundred-and-sixty-degree arc of surveillance in a bid to prevent anyone sneaking up on them unnoticed. Still, Connor felt horribly exposed and vulnerable. CCTV cameras covered every angle in the station and security guards roamed the concourse.

'Anyone see Zhen?' asked Colonel Black, his voice tense and impatient through the discreet comms units that Bugsy had kitted them out with.

'Negative,' replied Bugsy.

Amir shook his head.

'He'll be here,' said Connor under his breath, placing all his faith in their Chinese guide.

'You'd better be right,' the colonel replied, glancing up at the departure screen. 'We're running out of time.'

Another minute ticked by.

'I reckon the weasel's bolted with our money,' said Bugsy, angrily stuffing a magazine back into its rack. They'd handed over ten thousand yuan to cover the ticket price and the uncle's 'service charge'. It amounted to a small fortune for a teenage tour guide.

'Or else he's turned us in,' said the colonel bitterly. He nodded in the direction of the terminal exit where a group of guards clustered. More were gathering near the opposite entrance.

Connor didn't want to believe either scenario. During their rickshaw escape from Equilibrium's agents, Zhen had proven loyal, brave and resourceful. He'd had the opportunity to walk away with three hundred yuan in his pocket at that time and hadn't. Yet, after seeing the video of Charley divulging all Buddyguard's secrets, Connor questioned whether he could trust anyone again. And ten thousand yuan was a lot of money.

'Heads up, Connor,' warned Bugsy.

A station security guard was wandering his way, randomly asking passengers for their tickets and proof of ID. Connor began to sweat as the guard drew closer and closer. Having neither ticket nor an ID he wished to declare for fear of alerting Equilibrium, Connor rose from his seat and turned to go, but bumped straight into another passenger –

'Sorry,' said Zhen, his face a little flushed from running. 'A few *technical* issues.'

'Did you get the tickets?' asked Connor.

Zhen nodded and surreptitiously passed him four printed slips. A quick glance confirmed the date, time and destination in both Chinese and English: *Kowloon*. 'Tickets look good,' whispered Connor into his concealed mic.

'Let's move then,' Colonel Black ordered. Sweeping past them both, he palmed one of the tickets out of Connor's hand. Bugsy, following the colonel's lead, covertly collected his too, then headed in the direction of platform eight. Shouldering his Go-bag, Amir scampered over, took his ticket and muttered a hurried thanks to Zhen.

'Yeah, you really came through for us,' said Connor.

'It was fun,' their guide replied with a wistful smile. His eyes lingered on Connor. 'Tour turned out to be more *Shanghai Surprise* for me than you!'

Connor laughed. 'I'd best go. Got a train to catch. But I promise to leave you a good review on TripAdvisor!'

'What about your change?' Zhen asked, pulling out a thousand yuan in crumpled notes from his pocket.

Connor blinked, surprised to see any money at all. 'Keep it as a tip. You deserve it.'

Leaving behind one stunned and happy guide, he rushed across the busy concourse after Amir and the others. They had less than five minutes to make the train. Fortunately, just one security guard oversaw the ticket barriers to the platform; otherwise the process was automated. All going well, the four of them should pass through unchallenged. Then it was a straight nineteen-hour journey to Hong Kong.

But, as Colonel Black neared the barrier, Connor spotted a familiar face in the crowd – a stern-looking woman in steel-framed glasses. Like a hawk, her gaze swept across the tide of passengers, though she hadn't yet seen him. But her eyes soon locked on to Colonel Black, who was a head taller than any other commuter.

'Our cover's blown!' hissed Connor into his mic. 'Colonel, steel-framed glasses to your three o'clock.'

Colonel Black glanced to his right. Three security guards, acting on the command of Equilibrium's agent, pushed through the crowd towards him. The colonel had nowhere to hide among the throng of shorter Chinese. Then a flood of newly arrived passengers surged out of platform nine on to the concourse, swallowing up the advancing guards.

Taking advantage of the confusion, Colonel Black ducked down and doubled back towards Connor.

'Take this!' he said, shoving the flash drive into Connor's hand.

'B-but what about you?' asked Connor as they were buffeted by the crowd.

'I'll create a diversion while you board the train. You've the best chance of smuggling this out –'.

'Colonel!' Bugsy barked into their earpieces. 'More hostiles approaching.'

Colonel Black peered over Connor's shoulder. In the reflection of the colonel's mirrored shades, Connor caught sight of two mean-looking security guards headed their way. The colonel squeezed Connor's shoulder, his grip firm and somehow final. 'Swear to me you'll deliver the drive to Stella Sinclair.'

Connor nodded. 'But how will I –'

'Bugsy, to your left!' warned Amir into their comms. Connor noticed that his friend had halted by the ticket barrier and was observing a thin man with a bulging jacket as he made a beeline for his mentor.

'Use the codeword *Gabriel* to gain access to her,' Colonel Black explained hurriedly to Connor. 'She'll know I've sent you and trust the information. *Now go!*'

He pushed Connor in the direction of platform eight as the two guards closed in on him. Standing up to his full height, the colonel charged at the two men, knocking them down like bowling pins. Then he shouted to the Equilibrium agent in Chinese, '*Wǒ zài zhè!*' before running in the opposite direction to Connor.

With the woman distracted by the colonel's escape,

Connor made a dash towards the ticket barrier. But a security guard spotted him and moved to intercept him. Retreat no longer an option, Connor tried to slip past, only for the guard to lunge at him with a baton. As the heavy stick swung towards his head, Connor ducked but knew he had little chance of evading it. Then out of nowhere a wheeled suitcase smashed into the guard's feet and sent him flying face first into the floor, his baton clattering across the polished tiles.

For a moment Connor couldn't believe his luck. Then he saw who'd launched the suitcase at the guard: a young slender boy in a loose T-shirt and red baseball cap.

'Come on!' Zhen cried, grasping Connor's arm and pushing through the crush of commuters.

As they joined Amir at the barrier and scanned their tickets, Bugsy's voice blurted over their earpieces. 'Hostiles are armed –'

His voice was cut off as a gunshot rang out. For a split second the whole train station came to a halt, commuters appearing to be frozen in time as they registered the ear-splitting report. Then Bugsy collapsed to his knees, blood splattering across the shoes of nearby passengers.

Amir's eyes widened in horror. '*BUGSY!*'

A second shot finished off his mentor and sent a shockwave of terror through the crowd. People began screaming, running in all directions, tripping over each other in their mad rush to escape. The shooter – the thin man with the bulging jacket – had pulled out a semi-automatic weapon and now fired randomly into the crowd, killing and maiming commuters left, right and centre.

As this slaughter was occurring, Colonel Black found himself trapped and surrounded by station guards. He held his hands up in the air. But one of the guards, completely disregarding his surrender, drew a handgun and shot the colonel point-blank.

'NO!' yelled Connor as Colonel Black crumpled to the ground. The image of the colonel lying in a pool of his own blood was almost too much to comprehend. The former SAS soldier and commander of Buddyguard had somehow seemed indestructible to him.

Amir appeared just as shaken by Bugsy's cold-blooded murder. In a daze he turned back to help his fallen mentor. But Connor knew it was futile. Their surveillance instructor was beyond all help. Grabbing his friend, Connor dragged him through the barrier as a shout of 'ZHÀDÀN!' triggered even greater panic among the passengers.

'BOMB!' Zhen translated for Connor and Amir, vaulting over the barrier, his act of fare-dodging going unnoticed amid the chaos. As they fled towards the platform escalator, Connor glanced back one last time to see the thin man place a small cylindrical tube in Bugsy's dead hand.

CHAPTER 22

Connor, Amir and Zhen hurtled down the escalator on to the platform. The bullet train was preparing for departure, the doors still open prior to the guard's final safety checks. The chaos from above had yet to filter down. But the muffled sound of screams and the sudden surge of people on to the platform caused commuters to turn and stare.

'I haven't heard an explosion,' gasped Zhen.

'Maybe they disarmed the bomb,' said Amir.

Connor shoved a passenger aside. 'Or it hasn't gone off yet!'

Ignoring the protests and irate looks, he fought his way through the throng. If they could just make it on board, they could leave all the mayhem and murder behind.

'Come on!' urged Connor, sprinting for the nearest carriage.

But the doors closed a second before they reached them. Connor hammered a fist in frustration on the window. A row of startled faces scowled at him, then disappeared as the train pulled away.

'What are we going to do now?' panted Amir, watching in despair as their planned escape route accelerated down the track.

Connor looked around in desperation. The platform guard was running towards them, blowing his whistle, while several armed guards descended the escalator from the concourse above. No train waited on the adjacent platform as an alternative getaway and he couldn't spot any emergency exits nearby. Their options weren't just limited – they were zero! Alarms started blaring as the station was put into lockdown.

'It appears you missed your train,' said a dry pitiless voice from behind.

Connor spun to confront the last person on earth he wanted to see – Mr Grey. Amir took an instinctive step away from the ashen-faced assassin. Zhen merely stared, frozen like the petrified prey of a cobra.

'We had a deal, Connor, and you broke it.' Mr Grey's glacial eyes seemed to express both disappointment and pleasure at the outcome. 'Charley will suffer for your failure.'

'You can't threaten me with Charley. Not any more,' said Connor, standing his ground as the armed guards spread out across the platform and advanced towards them. 'I know she's on your side.'

Mr Grey raised an eyebrow. 'No one's on *my* side. True, Charley has proven useful to Equilibrium. But that doesn't guarantee her safety. Nor does it mean you no longer have feelings for her.'

Like a knife in his heart, the assassin's confirmation of Charley's involvement with Equilibrium grieved Connor even more than witnessing Colonel Black's death. Moreover, Connor realized Mr Grey was right. He still cared deeply for Charley, whatever she'd done.

'This is between you and me,' insisted Connor. 'There's no need to involve her.'

Mr Grey sneered. 'I'm afraid you're in no position to negotiate. Now hand over the flash drive Colonel Black just gave you –'

The platform guard came striding up and seized Mr Grey by the arm. 'You are under arrest!' he declared officiously.

Mr Grey glared at the little man. '*Bùshì wǒ. Nánhái!*' he snapped in Chinese, pointing to where Connor had been standing.

However, in the assassin's moment of distraction, Connor had made a split-second decision and jumped off the platform on to the railway tracks. Amir and Zhen followed his reckless leap like lemmings off a cliff. As they bounded across the first set of rails, a train thundered past, missing them by a hair's breadth. The clattering roar of carriages and the rush of wind almost knocked them off their feet. Zhen stumbled over a rail, Amir and Connor just catching him before he was dragged under the wheels. At the same time the express train blocked Mr Grey and the armed security guards from pursuing them.

Crossing over the second set of tracks, Connor clambered on to the opposite platform. He hauled Amir after him, then reached out his hand to Zhen.

'Another train's coming!' yelled Amir.

This time it was on their side of the platform. Tearing along at over a hundred and fifty kilometres an hour, the high-speed train had no way of stopping. A horn blasted in warning as Zhen scrabbled like a rat to escape the tracks. Connor grabbed Zhen's wrist and yanked with all his strength. The train entered the station on a direct collision course, only the boy's light frame saving him as Connor heaved him out with unexpected ease. He landed beside Amir barely a second before the train shot by, a *whooshing* blur of windows and steel.

'That's one train I didn't want to catch!' gasped Zhen.

They lay panting and breathless on the platform, while dumbstruck commuters gaped at the three children with apparent death wishes. Then the train's last carriage passed and they were exposed once more. Connor scrambled to his feet, pulling Amir and Zhen with him. From the opposite platform Mr Grey – still and deadly as the eye of a storm – glared in silent rage at Connor.

'*TÍNG!*' shouted one of the security guards, taking aim with his gun.

Ignoring the order to stop, Connor shielded Zhen with his body and ran. He heard a crack of gunfire and felt a heavy bruising impact, but the Go-bag's liquid body-armour panel took the brunt of the blow. More rounds whizzed overhead, one clipping Amir's Go-bag and reeling him round. They jumped down to the next set of tracks, scurried across and climbed back up to platform level. The growing mass of passengers fleeing the concourse now obstructed the guards' line of fire.

'Follow me,' said Zhen, heading down the platform and away from the most obvious exit. Their movements lost amid the crowd, the armed guards struggled to locate the fugitives as a train pulled into the station, further blocking their view. At the end of the platform, Zhen dropped down to the gravel-strewn ground. Connor and Amir followed, sprinting along the tracks before cutting across to a hole in the security fence. They ducked through just before the train set off again.

Recovering their breath in a deserted side street, Zhen turned to Connor. 'That was some escape! I can't believe you jumped in front of that train.'

'To be honest, I had no idea a train was coming,' admitted Connor.

'*What?*' Amir exclaimed, his jaw dropping open. 'I thought that was part of your escape plan. That's why we followed you!'

With a sheepish grin, Connor replied, 'No escape plan. Just pure luck.'

'Who else shares this room with you?' asked Connor, looking round the shabby flat and noting a pink T-shirt and leggings among the various items of clothing strewn across the floor. Their guide had taken them back to his lodgings, a cramped one-room affair in an old block of flats in the Putuo district of West Shanghai. The white plasterboard walls were grey with dirt and pockmarked with dents and gouges. The vinyl flooring was worn, its marbled pattern having faded to an off-brown colour. A bare light bulb hung from the ceiling and a single-glazed window looked directly across at an identical block of flats. A thin mattress and duvet took up one corner and a battered microwave oven and tiny buzzing fridge another. That was the sum total of the furnishings, apart from an old TV propped up on a wooden crate. It was a sorry-looking room and one that reflected the fortunes of their young guide.

'Err . . . my cousin,' Zhen replied with an embarrassed smile, gathering up the clothes and stuffing them into a plastic carrier bag.

'When will she be back?'

Zhen shrugged as he continued to tidy up. 'She's visiting her family in her home town. A few days at least.'

'And your parents?' asked Amir. 'Where are they?'

Zhen put down the bag as if it had suddenly become too heavy. 'Dead. My mother from lung cancer. My father from heart disease.'

'I'm so sorry,' said Amir, shifting awkwardly on his feet and not knowing where to look.

'Don't be. Nothing you can do. It was many years ago.' Zhen found another carrier bag and began stuffing it with discarded noodle cartons and plastic soda bottles, the debris of many TV dinners. Having collected the most obvious bits of rubbish, he dropped the brimming bag in the only empty corner of the room. Then he walked over to the fridge, took out a couple of bottles filled with bright orange soda and offered them a drink.

Connor gratefully accepted. 'Thanks for taking us in,' he said.

Zhen smiled. 'It's the least I can do.'

With no chairs, they all sat down on the floor. Connor took a long swig of the fizzy drink. The taste was sharp and tangy but refreshing and he immediately felt better. Their fraught escape had left them dehydrated and drained of energy. They needed the fluid. But Amir barely touched his.

'You should drink,' advised Connor.

'They shot Bugsy . . .' Amir replied in a murmur, as if he hadn't heard him. His friend gazed distractedly at the bottle in his hands. 'And the colonel.'

Connor nodded. The shock of their deaths was only just beginning to sink in. Until this moment there had been no space to think. Their murders had left a gaping hole not only in the pair's escape plan but in their hearts too. Bugsy's demise took its greatest toll on Amir for he'd been his mentor and friend, bonding over their shared love of IT and technology. For Connor, the cruel killing of Colonel Black hit hardest. Tough, strict and unyielding as he was, the colonel had been a father figure to him: showing interest in his developing skills as a buddyguard, always pushing him to improve himself and expressing pride in his achievements – all the support and approval he'd wished his own father could have been around to offer. In fact, Colonel Black had been his last link to his father's past as a soldier. And, in losing the colonel, Connor felt he'd somehow lost his father again too. The pain cut so deep it numbed him.

'How did Equilibrium track us down so quickly?' asked Amir, glancing up with watery eyes.

Connor shrugged wearily. 'They must've been monitoring all the train stations as well as the airports.'

'No. I am to blame,' said Zhen.

Amir and Connor looked at their guide. 'What do you mean?' demanded Connor.

Their guide lowered his gaze to the floor. 'Remember I said there were *technical* issues in getting the tickets? Well, my uncle couldn't use Chinese names. He said an inspector would notice straight away you weren't Chinese. So he overrode the system and issued the tickets in English names of recent tourists. The problem was, their visas were out of date and this must have triggered a security alert.'

Connor laid a hand on their guide's shoulder. 'That isn't your fault. We always knew there'd be a risk.'

A television began blaring from the flat next door, the plasterboard walls barely damping the noise.

'So what do we do now?' asked Amir in a plaintive voice. 'We can't get to Hong Kong. Bugsy and the colonel are dead. Our friends are being held captive somewhere and Charley's turned traitor. It's just us two left!'

Connor pulled the flash drive from his pocket and held it up. 'I promised Colonel Black we'd deliver this to Stella Sinclair and that's what we're going to do.'

'But how?'

Connor rubbed his face and held his head in his hands. Exhausted and emotionally burnt-out, he could hardly think straight. Their situation was dire. They had no local contacts, few resources and were up against a powerful international organization they knew little about. Yet he wasn't willing to give up. They *couldn't* give up. Not with so much sacrificed and still so much at stake.

As he pondered their limited options, Zhen's attention was caught by the programme blasting from his neighbour's flat. All of a sudden he jumped to his feet and switched on his own battered TV set. A female news presenter flickered on to the screen. Zhen turned up the volume, drowning out the noise from next door. The report was all in Chinese, but Connor and Amir instantly recognized the image behind the presenter's head: the concourse at Shanghai Railway Station.

Connor sat up straight. 'What's she saying?'

'That state security forces stopped a terrorist attack . . .' replied Zhen, his eyes locked on the TV, 'by a gunman and a suicide bomber.'

Mugshots of Colonel Black and Bugsy flashed up on the screen.

Zhen continued to translate. 'There were several deaths and multiple injuries, but she says it could've been a lot worse if security forces hadn't responded so quickly and shot the terrorists.'

'They're not terrorists!' Amir exclaimed indignantly.

The programme switched to CCTV footage showing Colonel Black running through the crowd and wielding a gun. Bugsy was highlighted holding a cylindrical tube in his hand as people scattered in panic, some falling to the ground as if shot. Then a thin man, his face pixelated to conceal his identity, entered the picture and gunned Bugsy down. Security guards moved in to surround the colonel. He was seen to take aim with his handgun before a security guard took him out in what was clearly an act of self-defence.

'That *isn't* what happened!' cried Amir in outrage. 'They've doctored the video footage.'

Connor was too stunned to say anything. He just stared at the TV as his own face now appeared alongside Amir's.

Zhen let out a soft cry of astonishment. 'Police are hunting two suspects, believed to be connected to the terrorists,' he explained, rapidly translating the presenter's words. 'The two fugitives are suspected foreign spies, trying to smuggle top-secret documents out of the country. Although children, they should be considered armed and dangerous. Do not approach. Report any sightings to the police immediately. A reward of a million yuan is being offered for information leading to their capture . . .'

Connor turned slowly to Amir, whose expression mirrored his own deep shock. 'I can't believe how far Equilibrium has taken this. They set up a terrorist attack. Killed innocent civilians. Framed the colonel and Bugsy. And now they've turned us into enemies of the state!'

Amir swallowed hard. 'You know, if we're caught, that means life imprisonment, maybe even the death penalty!'

Connor's mind became sharp in its panic. 'We have to lie low, otherwise we'll never get out of this country –'

'I know the very place,' Zhen said.

Connor shook his head. 'No, you can't risk your life being linked with us any longer.'

'Too late,' said Zhen, nodding grimly at the TV.

On the screen was a grainy CCTV photograph of a young boy in a loose T-shirt and red baseball cap.

'I'm a fugitive too.'

The glaring neon-white strip light in the ceiling buzzed – not because it was broken but because its incessant drone gradually wore the cell's occupant down. Similarly, the hard bench along the wall was made too narrow and too short to lie comfortably upon, in order to induce sleep deprivation in the detainee. An acute sense of claustrophobia, as well as dislocation from both time and place, was soon felt by anyone unfortunate enough to be locked inside the tiny windowless cell. The temperature in the room could also be altered from bone-chillingly cold to stiflingly hot, depending upon what caused the most suffering. And a large one-way mirror ensured the inmate had no privacy whatsoever, remaining constantly under the impression they were being observed.

Strapped to a chair and unconscious, the cell's current captive had no awareness of these 'conditioning techniques' – at least not yet. A bandage wrapped around the shoulder seeped blood, but the chest still rose and fell with each laboured breath.

'Bring the prisoner round.'

Obeying his boss's order with a sharp nod, a gaunt weasel-faced man in a white medical lab coat injected a syringe into the left forearm. The prisoner stirred, groaning feebly and spluttering up bile. The head lolled forward and eyes, swimming with pain and drugs, flickered open. They took a moment to focus on the woman standing over them.

Ignoring the weasel-faced doctor at his side, Colonel Black slurred, 'Wh-who . . . are you?'

'The Director.'

'Where's . . . my lawyer?'

The Director laughed, high and humourless. 'I'm not the director of the police. You have no right of attorney here.'

Colonel Black weakly turned his head, surveying the four featureless walls of the grim little cell. 'And where's *here*?'

The Director waved away his question. 'Don't concern yourself with such troubling details. You're in Equilibrium's care. That's all you need to know.'

Colonel Black nodded, as if accepting his fate.

The Director drew closer, her dragon pendant glinting dully in the harsh neon light. 'You can make your stay with us as comfortable . . .' Her manicured fingers gently stroked his cheek. 'Or as painful –' she slapped him sharply across the face – 'as you choose. Now where's the flash drive?'

Colonel Black blinked away stars, his ears ringing and his cheek smarting, then he stared defiantly back at his interrogator.

The Director waited a full minute. 'Don't play this tiresome game, Colonel. To the outside world you're already dead. And you'll wish you were if you don't answer me.'

The colonel remained stubbornly silent. The Director nodded at the doctor and he inserted another syringe into their prisoner's arm. Colonel Black felt reality slide from him, the strip light overhead leaving psychedelic tracers across his vision and the Director's voice now sounding as if she was underwater.

'*Where's the flash drive, Colonel?*'

He bit down hard, fighting the urge to reply, knowing whatever drugs had been injected into him would make his tongue loose.

With a roll of the eyes, the Director turned to the weasel-faced doctor. 'The drugs aren't working. Show him the video.'

The doctor extracted a tablet computer from his waist pocket and held up the screen for the colonel to see. Colonel Black tried to focus on the jerky images, watching as a handheld video camera approached a rusty old shipping container. A gloved hand reached out, undid the padlock and swung open the creaking door. Light spilt into the container to reveal a huddle of frightened teenagers. They were crammed like cattle into the metal box, their faces gaunt, their eyes haunted, their clothes grimy. Colonel Black barely recognized Ling, Jason or any of the other recruits. They looked like prisoners of war. Then Jason, Richie and a number of other Buddyguards made a dash forward at their captors . . . only to be beaten back with electric cattle prods and steel batons. A heavy blow to Richie's skull dropped him where he stood, his blood splattering across the camera lens –

The footage ended and the doctor put away the tablet.

Colonel Black clenched his fists in futile rage and a vein began to pulse in his neck. 'They're just children!' he rasped, struggling against his bonds.

'Exactly,' said the Director, 'yet you use them as human shields for spoilt little rich kids. Now unless you want them to suffer a slow and excruciating death – starving or perhaps suffocating inside that container – tell me what you did with that flash drive.'

Colonel Black glared at the Director. 'If you hurt them, I'll rip your head from your body.'

The Director tutted at the impotent threat. 'Perhaps I need to rephrase the question. Where's Connor Reeves?'

Still glowering at his captor, the colonel remained tight-lipped.

'We *know* you passed the flash drive to him. We *know* you were headed to Hong Kong. We *know* they didn't catch the train –'

Colonel Black flinched at this.

The Director raised a slender eyebrow. 'That's news to you, I see. Who's the local contact?'

Thrown by the unexpected change in questioning, Colonel Black tried to hide his puzzled frown, but the drugs had made him woozy and unguarded.

'The Chinese boy with the red baseball cap,' clarified the Director.

'No one,' said the colonel.

'For a *no one*, he's going to great lengths to help Connor and Amir. Where's the safe house in Shanghai?' She waited impatiently for an answer. 'Tell me or I'll start killing your precious recruits one by one . . . while you watch!'

'As you said yourself, I use them as human shields,' Colonel Black replied coldly. 'They're expendable. So what do I care what you do to them?'

The Director let out a long sigh as if suddenly bored with the interrogation. 'Well, if you won't talk willingly, we'll have to do this the old-fashioned way.'

The door to the cell opened and Mr Grey strode in, a small black roll bag clasped in his hand.

'Extract the information we require, Mr Grey,' ordered the Director.

'My pleasure.'

'I know it is,' she said as the assassin placed the bag on the bench, undid the clasp and unrolled it to reveal a row of shiny metal dentistry tools. 'Enjoy your stay with us, Colonel Black. Though I don't anticipate you being here long.'

The Director left the cell and closed the door behind her, sealing in the colonel and his tortured screams.

CHAPTER 25

'*Xièxiè*,' said Zhen, climbing out of the truck's cab on to the darkened highway. As their guide was thanking the driver, Connor and Amir slipped quietly out from beneath the tarpaulin of the open flatbed and crept into the bushes at the side of the road. With a rumble and cough of diesel fumes, the old truck pulled away and disappeared into the night.

Zhen waited until the road was clear, then, peering into the gloom, hissed, '*Connor? Amir?*'

The two of them emerged from the bushes like skittish round-eyed gophers. Amir had his arms clasped around himself, chilled to the bone by the long drive out of Shanghai. Connor rolled his shoulders and stretched out his back, his muscles stiff and sore from his cramped position hiding among the bags of cement and other building supplies the truck had been transporting.

'Did the driver suspect anything?' asked Connor, dusting down his clothes and Go-bag.

Zhen shook his head. 'I don't think so. He talked about the terrorist attack the whole way, but didn't link me with it.'

A pair of headlights appeared in the distance, their super-bright halogen beams growing fast.

'We need to get off the road,' said Amir fretfully.

Following their guide, they clambered down the embankment into a farmer's paddy field. The car shot past without slowing, plunging them back into darkness. More feeling than seeing their way, they headed across the field. The ground underfoot was waterlogged, the rice crop yet to be harvested, so Zhen kept to a narrow dirt ridge that ran between the tall stems of grasses. Connor crouched low and, being careful not to slip, trod softly in his guide's footsteps. Although the paddy field looked to be deserted, a huddle of low buildings nestled in the near distance and Connor was wary of any guard dogs that might alert their owners.

All of a sudden there was a splash and a sharply muttered curse from Amir. This was followed by loud squawking and a furious flapping of wings. Connor instinctively ducked, shielding his face as a pair of startled birds flew overhead.

'Bloody ducks!' complained Amir, shaking the mud off his sodden shoe.

'Stay low,' Connor hissed, his eyes watching the nearby buildings for movement. The birds' racket must surely have caught somebody's attention.

Zhen hunkered down beside him. 'Eco-friendly farming,' he whispered to Amir. 'Instead of pesticides, farmers use ducks to eat the insects and weeds.'

'Well, I wish they'd build their nests somewhere else!' grumbled Amir.

'*Shh!*' warned Connor, peering into the darkness. Now the ducks had settled, the night was still and hushed once again. He waited a full minute just to be sure. Then he waved to Zhen to move on.

Moonlight glinted on the muddy waters as their silhouettes swiftly and silently flitted across the field. Reaching the far side, they came to a single-track road that led to the outskirts of an old town. The buildings here were a mishmash of squat single- and two-storey whitewashed blocks, their peaked roofs a ripple of clay tiles, each merging into the next like a sea of grey dappled waves. The streets were narrow and cobbled, illuminated by red oval-shaped lanterns hanging from doorways, their warm soft light welcoming and just enough to see by. There were few if any people around, a stark contrast to the hectic bustle of the city. In fact, the flash modernity of Shanghai seemed to have bypassed this quiet corner of China completely. As the three of them wended their way through the back alleys, concealing themselves in the shadows, they crossed over a number of ancient stone bridges, each spanning a network of canals. There were no roads to speak of, in fact no cars at all – only narrow paddle boats. It was as if they'd stepped back in time.

'Where are we?' Connor whispered as they scurried over yet another bridge.

'Zhouzhuang,' Zhen replied quietly. 'It's a water town, a hundred kilometres west of Shanghai.'

Heading down the lane opposite, their guide stopped beside a small unassuming house backing on to a canal. Its windows were shuttered and no lanterns lit. Above its modest entrance a dragon had been etched into the brickwork. Zhen rapped on the door.

Getting no answer, he knocked again, more urgently.

After what seemed an age, the door opened a crack and an old woman's wrinkled face peeked through.

'*Lǎolao*,' said Zhen, smiling warmly.

The old woman frowned, her wrinkles deepening into grooves across her weathered face. Then a spark of recognition twinkled in her eyes. 'Zhen?'

Their guide nodded and the old woman, short and shrivelled as a dried fruit, opened the door. But she stopped as soon as she spotted his two companions in the shadows. Her sharp eyes were quick to judge Connor's cement-encrusted hair, Western looks and surprisingly tall stature. She glanced in undisguised distaste at Amir too, noting with a downward curl of her lips his muddy waterlogged shoes.

Zhen spoke rapidly in Chinese. The old woman didn't take her eyes off the two of them as she listened, her expression inscrutable. She gave no response to Zhen's pleas and appeared to be as unyielding as a rock.

Connor began to feel uneasy standing so exposed in the street. Someone could come along at any moment. The woman was evidently not going to let them in. And at worst she might raise the alarm, even inform the authorities. A million-yuan reward was not to be taken lightly.

Then the old woman held up a gnarled hand, silencing Zhen, and begrudgingly beckoned them all inside. They stepped into a small courtyard, cluttered with pots that brimmed with herbs and flowers. From the weak glow of a light bulb hung above the door, Connor could see the central area had been kept clear and recently swept. The house itself was a humble single-storey affair, its plaster walls flaking paint and its windows crooked yet spotlessly clean. A simple kitchen unit with a concrete sink was housed outside beneath a plastic corrugated roof. Laundry hung from a washing line and a wooden chair was propped against a wall beside a small foldaway table. In one corner stood a tall wooden stand with long pegs sticking out at different angles – to Connor it looked like a *muk yan jong*, a wooden training dummy used in martial arts, but here its sole purpose seemed to be as a coat rack.

Once the door closed behind them, the old woman turned her scathing, critical glare upon Zhen. In a brusque and sharp tongue, she rebuked the boy, wagging her bony finger angrily. Connor didn't need to understand Chinese to know that Zhen was in deep trouble and being subjected to a severe dressing-down. The old woman was as fierce as the dragon engraved above her door.

After a three-minute tirade, she dismissed Zhen into the house with a flick of her wrist. Red-faced and scolded into silence, their guide scurried through an open door and disappeared. The old woman shot a sideways glance at Connor and Amir, narrowing her eyes, daring them to move. But Connor doubted they could, even if they wanted to, in the face of such a ferocious adversary.

The old woman stalked past to the little kitchen. Lighting a single-ring gas stove, she picked up a large cooking pot that looked far too heavy for her slight frame and rested it on top. Removing the lid, she gave whatever was inside a stir, then adjusted the stove's heat. As the food was cooking, she stood with her arms crossed, watching Connor and Amir like a cantankerous vulture.

'We should go,' said Amir out of the corner of his mouth. 'The woman's obviously angry. And raving mad!'

'I agree,' said Connor. 'Zhen's in enough hot water without us adding to it.'

'She's not angry with you. She's angry with *me*.'

Connor and Amir turned to Zhen –

But it wasn't their guide who emerged back into the courtyard. Instead a slender young girl with a cascade of black hair appeared.

'*Zhen?*' asked Connor, questioning his eyesight. Gone were the shapeless T-shirt and baseball cap that had hidden her long hair; now their guide wore a traditional qipao dress, the close-fitting robe – with its high neck, split skirt and short sleeves – patterned with pink lotus flowers.

The girl nodded, spread her arms and offered them a tentative smile. 'Shanghai Surprise!'

CHAPTER 26

'Meet Lǎolao, my grandmother,' said Zhen as the old woman dumped three bowls of steaming soup on the little table that had been set up in the centre of the courtyard. Having scavenged three rickety wooden stools from around the house, they all sat down to eat a late-night supper – apart from the grandmother, who stood over them like a stern and dour-faced headmistress.

'*Xièxiè*, Lǎolao,' said Connor, bowing his head in appreciation. But his attempts at courtesy were met with stony-walled silence. He glanced across at Zhen. 'Your grandmother doesn't appear too delighted at having us around,' he said through a clenched smile. 'Perhaps we should stay somewhere else?'

'Oh, don't worry, she's always like this. Especially with new faces,' replied Zhen, spooning in a mouthful of broth. 'Besides, where else can you go?'

Connor felt the old woman's fierce gaze upon him. He supposed turning up after dark with two foreign boys wasn't exactly cause for celebration. But their guide had a valid point. It was the middle of the night. They were fugitives on the run. Nowhere was safe and no one could be trusted. This austere backwater bolthole was their only option, for the short term at least. Picking up his spoon, he took a careful sip of the thick saffron-coloured soup before him. Tasting of pumpkin, ginger, coriander and a whole host of other flavours he couldn't identify, the home-made broth was instantly warming and satisfying. Having not eaten for hours, it took all Connor's willpower not to down the entire lot in one gulp.

'What is this soup?' he asked, savouring another spoon-ful. 'It's delicious.'

Zhen turned to her grandmother, who snapped, '*Qigōng tāng!*' before irritably muttering something else.

'*Qigōng* soup,' Zhen translated for them. 'It's her own special recipe. She says the soup nourishes your spirit and *qi*.'

'*Qi?*' Amir said, his gaze fixed upon Zhen.

'Your life force,' Connor explained, recognizing the term from his jujitsu training. 'The flow of energy through and around your body. *Qi* is a core principle of traditional Eastern medicine and martial arts. Basically, Amir, the soup's good for you.'

Amir gave a vague nod in response. Despite the mouth-watering aroma and the recipe's supposed restorative powers, he continued to stare over his bowl at Zhen. He hadn't been able to take his eyes off her since their guide's miraculous transformation. Connor couldn't blame him. Zhen was undeniably pretty. He had no idea how he hadn't seen through her guise before. Her slight figure, soft features and high voice should've been a dead giveaway. But her brazen attitude, covered hair and neutral clothing had effectively concealed her true identity.

It seems some girls are experts at deception! thought Connor, feeling a sharp pang in his heart at Charley's shocking betrayal.

'Why pretend to be a boy?' Amir eventually asked their guide.

Zhen slowly stirred her soup. 'My grandmother questions that too. That's why she's so furious with me. She thinks a girl should be a girl and be proud of it. But she doesn't understand how the modern world works.' Zhen laid down her spoon. 'You see, after my parents died, Lǎolao took care of me. This used to be a guest house for tourists –'

'I bet it got rave reviews for the service!' remarked Amir, flashing a toothy grin at the immutable grandmother. Connor elbowed him in the ribs, urging him not to taunt the fiery dragon.

'I helped her out, cleaning and cooking,' Zhen continued, 'but when she grew too old to cater for guests I had to look elsewhere for work to support us. In the city, it was just easier *as a boy* to gain employment. And as a tour guide . . . far safer.'

'Unfortunately, not with us,' said Connor. 'I'm sorry we've dragged you into our troubles.'

Zhen laughed. 'Don't be. This has been my most exciting tour ever! Besides, the police are looking for a boy in a red baseball cap. Not a *girl*.'

Connor immediately felt a weight fall from his shoulders. Of course, their guide – as she appeared now – was no longer a suspect and consequently out of immediate danger.

'But *we're* still being hunted,' he reminded her. 'Not only by the police who think we're foreign spies but by Equilibrium who want us dead.' He glanced up at Lǎolao, who returned his look with hostile suspicion. 'It's understandable that your grandmother is so angry having us under her roof.'

Zhen resumed eating her soup. 'She hasn't heard about the attack. She doesn't have a TV or radio, or even a mobile phone! You're two students on one of my tours as far as Lǎolao is concerned.'

Amir blinked in shock. 'Shouldn't you tell her? I mean, she's *unknowingly* harbouring enemies of the state.'

Zhen tried not to look up at her grandmother, whose eyes listened as hard as her ears. 'Oh, she knows we're in trouble. Nothing gets past my grandmother. She just doesn't know how deep.'

'You should explain the situation to her,' insisted Connor. 'It's only fair.'

Zhen gave a nod. 'I will. In the morning. Tonight we all need rest.'

Connor couldn't argue with that. After everything that had happened – from the surprise attack at the station, and the shooting of Bugsy and Colonel Black, followed by their fraught escape from the guards and Mr Grey, to the long and risky journey fleeing Shanghai – the three of them were on their last legs. The food had satisfied their hunger, but now their bodies craved sleep.

Connor scooped out the last dregs of soup. As soon as he'd finished, Lǎolao whipped his bowl away. But Connor thought he caught the shadow of a satisfied smile on her wrinkled face.

Amir polished his off too. 'Can I have some more?' he asked tentatively, then clearly wished he hadn't as he withered under her unrelenting glare. She snatched the bowl from his grasp. 'I guess not.'

Leaving the bowls in the sink, the grandmother pulled out two paper-thin bamboo mats, a pair of blankets and a couple of cushions, and tossed them in the corner of the courtyard. '*Chuáng*,' she said, pointing at the floor and what would be their beds.

'Make yourselves at home,' said Zhen, although it was obvious the translation had been softened by their guide.

Lǎolao shuffled into her house without further ceremony or bidding them goodnight. Then she barked for Zhen to join her.

'Sleep well,' said Zhen with a timid smile, before obediently following her grandmother inside.

The door to the house slammed shut behind her and a bolt was heard rattling across.

'Well, I'm *loving* Chinese hospitality!' said Amir as he rolled out his bamboo mat on the hard concrete floor. 'Some guest house this is!'

Connor set up his bed next to Amir's. 'Just be thankful we've somewhere to stay.'

Amir sighed. 'I suppose you're right. We've got four walls, what more do we need?' He looked round at the spartan courtyard, then glanced up. 'Oh, a roof would be nice!' he added sardonically. 'But we can't ask for everything, can we?'

With a strained smile, he settled on his mat and tugged the threadbare blanket over himself. Connor paid no heed to his friend's irritable comments. They were both shattered and strung out. A good night's sleep would set them straight. Connor lay down, tucking the blanket around himself. The night was cool but not cold, and the sky clear, the stars twinkling overhead, visible for the first time since their arrival in China.

When it is dark enough, you can see the stars.

He'd read that somewhere in a book. He hoped it was true. Because their current situation was the darkest he'd ever experienced and he still couldn't see any stars to light their way.

CHAPTER 27

The soup and sleep had done wonders. As the dawn light filtered golden and shimmering into the little courtyard, Connor awoke feeling rested and re-energized. Through the slats of a small window in the courtyard wall, he could see a man paddling his boat amid the morning mist on the canal. Smoke from a dozen kitchen ovens rose lazily into the pale blue sky and the aroma of boiling rice and dumplings wafted through the air. Zhouzhuang was just beginning to wake up.

Turning away from the window, Connor wasn't surprised to see Amir still fast asleep, lightly snoring. But he was surprised to find Zhen's grandmother up and in the middle of the courtyard. She stood, poised like a noble white crane, arms spread like wings, balanced upon one foot, the other pointed with the elegance of a ballerina. Exhaling gently, Lǎolao placed her lead foot on the ground and shifted her weight forward, pivoting in a slow arc while her hands circled as if caressing an invisible ball. Pushing at the air, she advanced, then retreated, mimicking the ebb and flow of a wave. Her breathing married to her motion, she moved with a serene grace that defied her old age. Connor was captivated and astonished at the grandmother's suppleness and skill.

Amir sat up and sleepily rubbed his eyes. 'What's she doing?' he asked, yawning.

'Tai chi,' said Zhen, emerging from the house, dressed in a red blouse, slim-cut jeans and sequined flat-heeled pumps, her long hair looped into a high ponytail. 'It's a daily ritual for Lǎolao; in fact for most Chinese. We should join her.'

'But I haven't a clue what to do,' said Amir.

'Just follow Lǎolao's movements,' Zhen told him, mirroring her grandmother's posture and falling into her rhythm.

Wishing to respect their host, Connor nudged Amir and rose to his feet. They joined Zhen and her grandmother in the centre of the courtyard. Lǎolao made no comment, not even acknowledging their presence.

Connor took up the old woman's current pose and followed her gliding actions. But what Lǎolao made look easy and graceful proved far more difficult in practice. Her every action was measured and precise, requiring absolute control over mind and body. By comparison the two of them looked like bumbling clowns; Zhen suppressed a grin as Amir got his footing wrong and stepped on a plant pot. But even that mistake didn't disturb Lǎolao's focus.

After a while, her beady eyes flicked briefly towards Connor and she muttered a few words. Thinking he'd done something wrong, Connor looked to Zhen for a translation.

'Let your limbs flow like water,' said Zhen. 'No resistance.'

Following the old woman's instruction, Connor relaxed his muscles. The series of movements immediately became more fluid and manageable. Then gradually he began to recognize stances and techniques from his martial arts training: *cat pose . . . a circular forearm block . . . a palm strike . . . a wrist lock . . . a front flick-kick . . .* All in slow motion, but all with definite purpose.

'*Hūxī*,' said Lǎolao as Connor began to grasp the routine and find his flow.

'Breathe,' translated Zhen.

Consciously inhaling and exhaling, Connor timed his breath to match each movement. And, like a key in a lock, he gradually and effortlessly slid into the spirit of t'ai chi. His body relaxed . . . his mind calmed . . . his spirit lightened . . .

Losing himself in the meditative motion, he felt like a feather floating on the wind.

Then Lǎolao brought her practice to an end and turned to Connor and Amir. Greeting her with a smile, Connor awaited some comment or praise on their progress. But she just grabbed a couple of brooms and shoved them into their hands.

'Is this still part of tai chi?' asked Amir, dubiously examining his brush.

Connor shrugged. 'I guess we clean up.'

As they swept the courtyard, Lǎolao attended to breakfast and Zhen busied herself setting up the table and stools.

Connor swept his way over to Zhen. 'Did you speak with your grandmother?' he asked quietly.

Zhen nodded.

'And?'

'Nothing fazes her; she's been through the Cultural Revolution,' said Zhen. 'I explained what *really* happened at the station. She says you can stay as long as you need –'

'That's wonderful –'

'– but no more than a week.'

'Oh.' He stopped sweeping, his relief cut short. They'd be under pressure in that time to plan and execute a new escape route. Then again he hoped to be out of the country by then. 'That's more than generous, under the circumstances. Please express our gratitude.'

Zhen smiled and nodded at the table. 'You can do that by eating all her *zhōu*.'

Connor turned to discover that Lǎolao had served up four bowls of congee, a thick rice porridge, which was flavoured with pickled vegetables and fermented tofu. *Not your typical Western breakfast of cornflakes and milk!* But he and Amir had no trouble finishing off the food, despite the unfamiliar combination. The exertions of the past seventy hours had left them with a ravenous appetite.

After breakfast, Zhen and her grandmother headed towards the courtyard's front door.

'Where are you going?' asked Connor, out of concern as well as curiosity.

'Market,' replied Zhen. 'We need more food, since there are more mouths to feed.'

Reaching for his Go-bag, Connor took out several yuan notes from his wallet. He offered them to Lǎolao. She waved his money away.

'You've already given enough,' Zhen explained. 'Remember the thousand-yuan tip!'

'That was for you,' said Connor. 'We don't wish to take advantage of your grandmother's hospitality.'

The corner of Zhen's mouth curled into a smile. 'Don't worry. She wouldn't let you. She said you can do the dishes.'

Connor and Amir were left alone in the courtyard. Through the wooden side shutter, they watched Zhen and her grandmother cross the bridge and disappear down a lane.

'Can we trust that old dragon?' asked Amir.

'We don't have much choice,' replied Connor. 'But Zhen's convinced her to let us stay for a week. So that's something.'

Picking up a wire scourer, Amir began scrubbing away at the rice pot. 'What's our plan then?'

Connor slowly and thoughtfully dried a bowl before answering, 'We need to lie low for a few days, wait until the heat dies down. In the meantime, work out another way to get to Hong Kong.'

'Why don't we just turn ourselves over to the British Embassy? Explain our side of the story.'

Connor shook his head. 'Remember what the colonel said? Equilibrium has infiltrated the Foreign Office.' Setting aside the tea towel, he took the flash drive from his pocket and studied it. 'Whatever's on this drive is worth killing for. We need to know what's on it before we know who to trust.'

Amir put the rice pot down. 'I can open the files if you want. Bugsy gave me the passcode.'

Connor offered his friend the tiny flash drive. 'Go ahead. Knock yourself out.'

'With pleasure,' grinned Amir, happily exchanging the soggy scourer for the drive.

As Amir booted up his new hybrid tablet and unfolded the keyboard, Connor returned to the washing-up. At the same time he kept an eye on the courtyard window. When Zhen returned from the market, he intended to discuss alternative routes to Hong Kong. But, with both the police and Equilibrium on a nationwide hunt for them, he didn't hold out much hope. Connor almost despaired at the challenge ahead of them. He hadn't let on to Amir just how low his spirits were. That was why he'd given his friend the task of examining the drive: not only to find out what was on it but to keep his friend's mind occupied and off their dire predicament. Yet Connor still believed there was a slim chance of escape. All they needed was Zhen's local knowledge, some careful planning and a whole heap of luck –

'*Damn it!*' cried Amir, cursing out loud and pulling at his hair in frustration.

And apparently luck was a resource in very short supply.

'What is it?' asked Connor.

'I've accessed the drive, but the files have re-encrypted

themselves,' explained Amir, glaring at the screen. 'And Bugsy's passcode no longer works!'

Connor dropped the rice pot in the sink. 'So we can't read the files?'

Amir shook his head. 'Equilibrium have used a mutating encryption key to secure their data. That means the passcode is time-sensitive and changes regularly.'

A sinking sense of hopelessness gripped Connor's stomach. 'Can't you break the encryption, like Bugsy originally did?'

Amir grimaced. 'Maybe. I'll give it a try, but Bugsy was a far better hacker than me.'

'How long could that take?' asked Connor.

Amir shrugged despondently. 'Who knows? Depends on how complex the encryption is. A 128-bit key is the equivalent of trying to find one specific grain of sand in the whole of the Sahara Desert!'

Connor offered his friend an encouraging smile. 'Well, you'd best get started then.'

Connor was just finishing the last dish when he spotted Zhen and her grandmother returning over the bridge . . . with two heavyset black-jacketed men in tow.

'I don't want to disturb your concentration, Amir,' said Connor, 'but we've got a problem – two big ones in fact!'

Amir set aside his tablet and joined Connor at the slatted window. 'I knew we couldn't trust that old dragon!' he muttered as the two goons made their approach. 'Zhen must have told her about the million-yuan reward. Now her grandmother's gone and turned us in!'

After Charley's betrayal and now Zhen and her grandmother's, Connor wondered if he'd ever be able to put his faith in anyone again. Amir hurriedly packed away his tablet and grabbed his Go-bag. Snatching up his own Go-bag, Connor prepared to make a run for it with Amir – although he had no idea *where* they'd run to. The water town of Zhouzhuang was a mystery to them and their only safe haven had become a trap. He peered through the slats to look for the best escape route.

'Hold on!' he called to Amir. 'Something's up.'

Amir returned to the window. Zhen and her grand-mother had stopped in the middle of the old stone bridge, laden with shopping bags. The two black-jacketed men were now purposefully blocking their path. On closer inspection, they didn't look like police or even local security guards. They were more like thugs. One had a flat nose as if he'd fought in too many boxing matches and lost them all. The other sported a thin ribbon of a scar above his left eye.

'*Equilibrium agents?*' whispered Amir, an edge of panic entering his voice.

Connor frowned, unsure. 'Perhaps. But how did they find us so quickly?'

The two men seemed to be questioning Zhen and her grandmother. Whatever they'd asked, Lăolao was shaking her head emphatically. This seemed to annoy Scarface, who reached into one of her shopping bags and stole an apple. He bit into it and spat some at her feet. Lăolao fumed and made a move towards the man, even though he was twice her size. Zhen stepped in to stop her grand-mother. But Lăolao shook her off and began to berate the thug. Scarface blinked in astonishment as a bony finger was wagged before his eyes. Flat Nose, meaty fists planted on hips, laughed at the old woman's attempt to scold his partner-in-crime. Tossing the apple aside, Scarface then grabbed the shopping bags in Lăolao's hands . . . but she refused to let go. A David-and-Goliath tug-of-war began.

'I think they're being *mugged*!' said Amir, incredulous. When Flat Nose entered the fray and seized hold of

Zhen, Connor dashed for the courtyard's front door. But, by the time he'd opened it and run into the lane, he was too late. Lǎolao had let go of her bags . . . but she appeared to have timed this when Scarface was most off-balance. The thug stumbled backwards, shopping in hand, and hit the low wall of the bridge. Then, moving forward with astonishing speed, Lǎolao punched her attacker in the chest. Even from where he was standing, Connor heard the distinct crack of ribs. Eyes bulging, Scarface let out a pained *whoosh* of breath, dropped the bags and tumbled over the side into the canal.

Before Flat Nose could comprehend the extraordinary defeat of his partner, Lǎolao turned on him and took up the crane stance from her tai-chi form. Flat Nose gave the old grandmother a contemptuous snort. Pushing Zhen aside, he advanced on her and swung a boulder-like fist. Clearly having no qualms at hitting an old woman, he struck her full force in the stomach.

But Lǎolao didn't even flinch. It was as if the heavyweight boxer had hit a brick wall. His thick brow creased in dumb disbelief, astounded at the impotence of his punch. Taking advantage of his confusion, Lǎolao drove her own fist into his flabby stomach. By all rights, being punched by an eighty-something-old woman, the sixteen-stone thug should've barely felt a thing. Instead he groaned like a kicked cow, his face went bright red and he crumpled to his knees. Then, like a felled tree, Flat Nose keeled forwards and landed face first on the stone bridge, his already-sorry nose mashed to an even flatter pulp.

Dusting her hands, Lăolao picked up her shopping bags and shuffled home. She passed an open-mouthed Connor with no more than the briefest nod of acknowledgement as she entered the courtyard.

Hurrying after her grandmother, Zhen urgently ushered Connor inside. 'What do you think you're doing out here? Someone might see you!' she said, glancing over her shoulder at the comatose thug on the bridge and the other half-drowning in the canal as a boatman paddled over to help.

'I . . . was coming to rescue you,' murmured Connor, stunned by the miraculous fighting skills of the grand-mother.

'Did we *look* like we needed rescuing?'

'Well . . . err . . . no, but I didn't expect your grand-mother to take out two oversized gorillas single-handedly.'

Zhen shook her head wearily and sighed. 'I did *try* to stop her.' She locked the courtyard door behind them.

'Who were those two men anyway?' asked Amir.

'Local Triad enforcers.' A smirk cut across Zhen's lips. 'They'll think twice about trying to steal Lăolao's shop-ping in future!' Then the smile faded. 'But they *were* asking if we'd seen two foreign kids in the area. Of course, Lăolao said we hadn't and told them to look for someone their own size. That's when the one with the scar swiped an apple. Bad decision on his part!'

Connor was greatly relieved to discover that the two men weren't Equilibrium agents, but the sizeable bounty on their heads was evidently attracting unwanted criminal attention. This would make any getaway to Hong Kong even more risky.

Lăolao seemed unaffected by the confrontation. She was busying herself boiling water and setting a small teapot and a set of cups on the breakfast table. Amir perched on one of the stools, eyeing her with a mix of awe and fear. 'Is she Supergran or something?'

Zhen laughed. 'No! But when she was a little girl the local master refused to teach her kung fu. So she taught herself. Then she went back to the martial arts school and beat the master until he apologized!'

'But *how* does she do it?' Connor asked. 'I've trained in martial arts and never seen anything like *that*. I mean, one of them hit her in the stomach and your grandmother didn't even bat an eyelid. Then she took each of them down with a *single* punch. It's unbelievable!'

Zhen conveyed this to her grandmother. Lăolao appraised Connor a moment, then muttered a few words. Zhen translated: 'She will teach you the techniques of Iron Shirt and Iron Hand.'

Connor couldn't believe his luck. What he'd witnessed was a martial art beyond any other. In the back of his mind the idea kindled that just such skill might give him the edge over Mr Grey. 'When?' he asked eagerly.

Zhen enquired, then turned back to Connor. 'When she's had her tea.'

CHAPTER 29

'Stand like a tree,' Lăolao instructed through her grand-daughter. 'Tall and strong.'

In the centre of the courtyard, Connor grounded his feet, loosened his knees, straightened his back and held his head high. Familiar with *kamae* stances from his martial arts training, the *zhàn zhuāng* pose came naturally to him. He imagined himself being rooted deep into the ground, while the top of his head touched the clouds as if pulled taut by an invisible thread.

Lăolao shuffled round him, studying his posture critically. She tapped his feet with the end of a wooden broom shaft, signalling for him to widen his stance. Then she knocked his knees, for being over-bent. Next she poked his stomach for being too far forward, then his hips for being too far back, and his shoulders for being too rounded. Finally, she lifted his chin a fraction of an inch.

Once satisfied, she instructed via Zhen, 'Cup your hands below your *dāntián.*'

'My *what*?' asked Connor, shooting a mildly alarmed look at his guide.

The corner of Zhen's mouth curled impishly. 'The energy centre just below your belly button.'

'Oh, my *hara*!' said Connor, resting his hands close to his navel. Having a black belt in jujitsu, he only knew the Japanese term for the lower *qi* point.

Following Lăolao's guidance, Connor relaxed his muscles and regulated his breathing. Amir watched from the sidelines, opting to work on the encrypted flash drive instead. An amused grin spread across his face as Connor was made to stand perfectly still, breathing in and out, for several minutes. Losing interest, he returned his attention to the tablet laptop.

'Imagine a ball of fire in your lower belly,' instructed Zhen, translating Lăolao's words. 'Sense it grow with each breath.'

Closing his eyes, Connor concentrated. At first there was nothing. Just a flat cool emptiness. Then a warm tingling sensation, like the heat of a small candle, flickered into life at the pit of his stomach.

'Fuel the fire. Let the light swell into a small sun.'

Channelling each breath to his *dāntián*, Connor felt the energy intensify, the heat spread and the power fill him up like a solar battery. The strange experience would've been unsettling were it not so pleasurable and energizing. The ball of fire now burned hot and bright.

Connor heard Lăolao by his side, speaking.

'She asks, do you feel the *qi* in your stomach?'

Connor gave a nod.

Without warning, Lăolao thwacked him in the gut with

the broom handle. Taken completely by surprise, Connor doubled over with the force of the blow, all the wind knocked out of him. He dropped to his knees, clutching his throbbing stomach, the fire in his belly now for real.

'Looks like you got the short end of the stick there!' said Amir, laughing as he glanced up from his work.

Eyes bulging, Connor wheezed at the old grandmother, 'What was *that* for?'

Lǎolao shook her head in dismay. '*Zài shì yīcì.*'

'Try again,' Zhen translated as she helped Connor to stand.

Rubbing his battered belly, Connor took a moment to get his breath back. 'What did I do wrong?'

'You need to lock in the *qi*,' Lǎolao explained through Zhen. 'Imagine it fusing with your body. Becoming part of you. Otherwise it's like a boat without an anchor. The *qi* will drift and won't protect you. A strike will simply knock the energy aside.'

Taking up his *zhàn zhuāng* stance again, Connor resumed his breathing ritual. Gradually the throb in his stomach abated and the fire returned. He visualized the ball of *qi* hardening, sinking into every fibre of his belly. Lǎolao wound up to hit him again.

This time he was ready. As she wielded the broom handle at him, Connor clenched his stomach muscles. For an old woman she had a surprisingly hefty swing. The blow struck like a battering ram. Once again he collapsed to his knees, pain rocketing through him.

Tutting loudly, Lǎolao waved for him to stand up.

Dragging himself back to his feet, Connor lifted his shirt to examine himself. A long red line cut across his torso like a whip mark.

Zhen winced at Connor's eye-watering bruise. 'Iron Shirt isn't about brute strength. It's about harnessing your internal life force. No tension. Your body needs to be relaxed yet powerful. Like a wave.'

'Like a wave,' repeated Connor, carefully lowering his shirt and preparing for a third attempt.

He adopted the stance. He breathed deeply. He gathered his *qi*. His mind calmed. His muscles relaxed. His body absorbed the energy. He was like a wave . . .

Then the broom handle hit him and he crashed to the floor, winded and beaten again.

Lǎolao stood over him, her wrinkled upper lip curled in disdain at his pathetic performance. She uttered a disgruntled stream of Chinese at him. Zhen smiled down, her grin a little too forced. 'She says you're doing *really* well.'

CHAPTER 30

'The Demon Gate is located *here*,' said Zhen, her grandmother prodding a stubby finger hard as a nail into Connor's chest. Just above his right nipple and between his pectoral muscles, he could already feel a sharp pain from her pressure. After two days of relentless Iron Shirt exercises – where he'd been beaten in the stomach, had heavy bricks piled on top of his chest and lain on sharp rocks to condition his body – Connor had been relieved when Lăolao suggested they move on to Iron Hand techniques. Now he was thinking that he might regret that decision.

'This point should be hit in and towards the spine,' continued Zhen, translating Lăolao's words. 'A strike here disrupts a person's *qi* flow and can cause injury . . . or even death.'

Without warning, Lăolao jabbed hard with her fingers and Connor's chest seemed to implode. A tidal wave of agony crippled him to his very core. As if his life force was swirling down a drain, his body became completely sapped of energy and he dropped to his knees. Unable to stand or defend himself, he could only manage to utter a feeble plea of '*Why?*'

An amused Amir looked on from his usual perch, his tablet and keyboard on his lap, as Zhen knelt down beside Connor in the courtyard. 'Lăolao says, you must experience Demon Gate in order to do Demon Gate.'

'*OK*,' he wheezed with a weak nod, 'that's *enough* experience for one day!'

Zhen beckoned Amir over to help. Lifting him to his feet, the two of them supported Connor as her grandmother thumped him on the back in three specific *qi* points. The reaction was instantaneous. Like a floodgate opening, Connor's energy rushed into him and the debilitating effects of the Demon Gate strike vanished. Aside from a dull throb in his chest at the point where he'd been hit, Connor felt completely fine.

He blinked in astonishment. From his bodyguard training he was acquainted with *kyusho* pressure points – physical vulnerabilities in the human body and nervous system that could be exploited to control or subdue an attacker. But this *qi* style of attack, targeting the energy centres, was a revelation to him. If he could master this particular technique, then he'd surely possess an unbeatable defence against Mr Grey when they next met.

Connor pointed to his chest. 'Is *this* where you hit that thug who took your shopping?'

Lăolao responded with a toothless grin and nodded. 'Combined with Iron Hand, no man can withstand such a strike,' she said via Zhen.

Connor turned eagerly to Amir. 'I *need* to practise this – on you.'

Less than keen at the prospect, Amir began to back away. 'Erm . . . I'm a bit busy with the encryption.'

'Come on – it'll be like Buddyguard training,' coaxed Connor. 'It'll only take ten minutes, promise.'

In fact, it took half that time. Connor's prior skill in martial arts meant his strikes had pinpoint accuracy. After three or so semi-effective attempts, he hit the Demon Gate on the button and Amir dropped like a sack of rice.

'*I think* . . . you've mastered that technique,' gasped Amir as they helped him to his feet and Lǎolao restarted his flow of *qi*.

'A few more goes,' pleaded Connor. 'Just to be sure.'

Gritting his teeth, Amir braced himself as Connor tried again. A second later he was slumped on the floor in an enfeebled heap. After the third successful Demon Gate strike in a row, he rasped, 'I *really* need to get on with hacking that flash drive!'

'Of course,' said Connor, pulling his friend to standing. 'Thanks for your help. I've nailed that technique.'

Amir offered a pained smile. 'No problem,' he replied, rubbing his chest and tottering over to the corner to resume his work. 'But next time you want a punchbag . . . ask someone else!'

But Lǎolao had already set up another punchbag. She'd hung a hessian sack of rice from the top spar of the wooden *muk yan jong* training post, now denuded of coats. She gestured for Connor to hit it.

Connor launched a rear cross, his knuckles striking the sack with a heavy thud. Lǎolao tutted disapprovingly.

'Lǎolao says you're wasting sixty per cent of your potential power,' explained Zhen. 'Iron Hand is not only about making your punch hard; it's about making your fist strong with *qi*.'

Lǎolao shooed Connor aside and lined herself up with the makeshift punchbag.

'By concentrating your *qi* into your fist and energizing your muscles, you can increase the power and efficiency of your punch,' Zhen translated.

Breathing in deeply, her grandmother circled her hands around an imaginary ball as in her tai chi, then clenched her fist and let loose a short, sharp punch. The sack of rice burst apart with the brutal force of her strike, white grains cascading on to the courtyard floor in a shimmering waterfall. Connor stared open-mouthed at the old woman's remarkable feat.

'You're not practising *that* on me!' said Amir from his safe corner in the courtyard.

After Lǎolao had made him sweep up the rice, it was Connor's turn on a fresh sack. He stood before the *muk yan jong*, rubbing his hands together briskly and pulling them apart several times. The twice-daily t'ai chi sessions had helped him control and nourish his *qi*, so he soon generated a flow of inner energy. Then, visualizing a ball of fire between his palms, he closed his right fist around it and imagined locking in the *qi*, before throwing a punch with all his might. His fist pounded the rice and the bag swung like a pendulum.

Connor was chuffed. But Lǎolao wasn't happy. 'Too tense,' she said through Zhen.

He tried again. And again. And again. But still Lǎolao was dissatisfied, and the bag remained stubbornly whole. He kept up the barrage for another twenty minutes before exhaustion and pain overcame him.

'I don't know how you made it look so easy!' gasped Connor, examining his raw and bloody knuckles.

'All things are difficult before they are easy,' said Lǎolao through her granddaughter, before shuffling off to the kitchen and lighting the stove. She scooped out four cups of 'punchbag' rice into a pot and began boiling the water for dinner.

Worn out and aching, Connor slumped down next to Amir. 'Look at my hands!'

'Don't expect sympathy from me,' said his friend. 'My chest is still throbbing!'

Connor sighed. 'Well, I hope you've beaten more out of that flash drive than I did out of the rice sack.'

Amir wearily shook his head. 'It's high-level military-grade encryption. With only this tablet, it's like trying to break into a tank with a can opener!'

'Are you saying you *can't* hack into the drive?'

'It's just the hacker bots available online aren't up to the job ...' Amir's brow creased in concentration. 'But I suppose I could try to write my own decryption program ...' He trailed off, losing himself once again in the code.

Zhen strolled over, carrying a glass bottle of dark-coloured liquid. 'Lǎolao says to rub this into your knuckles.'

'What is it?' asked Connor as he uncorked the bottle, poured some out and applied it gingerly to his grazed skin.

'*Diē dǎ jiǔ*, a traditional Chinese herbal remedy.'

Almost immediately the pain began to subside. 'Wow, that's neat stuff,' remarked Connor.

'Lǎolao's special formula,' replied Zhen with a warm smile. 'It unblocks the meridians and allows the *qi* to flow freely again. You must put it on after every session.'

As he massaged the miracle lotion into his other hand, Connor asked, 'Have you had any luck yet finding us a way to get to Hong Kong?'

'Possibly,' said Zhen. 'My cousin is a truck driver. He sometimes delivers freight there.'

Connor frowned. 'I thought you said your cousin was a girl.'

Zhen glanced away, hiding her embarrassment. 'Er, those were my clothes at the flat. No one else stays there.'

'Oh, of course!' Connor laughed, realizing how obvious it all was now. 'So, when will your cousin know if he's going to Hong Kong?'

'In a day or so, I expect.'

'Well, let's hope it's an easier journey than the one we had getting here!'

CHAPTER 31

'You made a promise to me,' said the Director, peeling an apple with a small silver fruit knife.

Yuan glanced nervously over the gallery's handrail. Spread out below like a monstrous spiderweb was an intricate network of staircases, ramps and floating corridors that formed the hub of the Hive. The interlocking 'air bridges' had once controlled the flow of thousands of cattle as they were herded to the top of the former 1933 slaughterhouse to be butchered. Now scores of workers in white lab coats ascended and descended the grey concrete maze.

'Oh, I've no intention of throwing you over . . .' said the Director, seeing the flash of alarm behind the agent's steel-framed glasses. 'I merely wanted to *remind* you of that promise.'

'I haven't forgotten,' Yuan replied quickly, conscious of the Director's security guard standing at her shoulder. 'My men eliminated the surveillance tutor and captured the colonel.'

The Director cut out a thin slice of apple and popped it in her mouth. 'But still you failed to recover the flash drive *and* allowed Connor and his associate to slip through your fingers.'

The criticism as stinging as a slap to the face, Yuan stood a little more stiffly. 'I've agents scouring the country,' she reassured her boss. 'Eyes are everywhere. Ears are listening. No stone is being left unturned.'

'So, what stone are they hiding under?' pressed the Director, taking a step closer. 'It's been three days already.'

'My agents have reported nothing so far,' admitted Yuan.

'Absolutely *nothing*?'

Yuan squirmed under her boss's fierce gaze. 'Well, a couple of Triad gang members – low-level agents – were beaten up. But that just turned out to be a grandmother who didn't want her shopping stolen!'

The Director raised an eyebrow and pointed the tip of the fruit knife at Yuan. 'Perhaps I should be hiring her instead of you? I needn't stress how vital to Equilibrium's future that drive is. It *cannot* be allowed to leave China.'

Yuan bowed her head. 'I'm aware of its importance. That's why I manipulated the station incident to appear as a terrorist attack. The police and state security are now searching for the fugitives too. With their combined resources, we'll –'

'Ah yes, the station incident. That did draw a great deal of unwanted attention and state involvement. For which I hold *you* solely responsible.' The Director scuffed the sole of her shoe on the ground. 'Do you know why the slaughter-house's floors were made this rough?'

Yuan glanced down at the tiny ridges of concrete beneath her feet and shook her head.

'To prevent the cattle from slipping ... *even in their own blood.*'

Yuan looked up, startled, as the security guard seized her by the roots of her hair and wrenched her head back. The Director leant in and hissed into her ear, '*Equilibrium must remain in the shadows.*'

With one quick slice, the Director drew the fruit knife across Yuan's throat. Blood spurted in an arc over the concrete floor. 'I warned you not to fail me.'

The guard let Yuan's body slump to the ground. As the agent lay dying, Mr Grey strode across one of the air bridges to the gallery, stepping nonchalantly over the rivulets of blood running down the slope.

'Wasn't that a little rash?' questioned Mr Grey, as the Director wiped the blood from her fruit knife and continued to peel the apple.

'Don't question my authority, Mr Grey!'

The assassin observed the guard dragging away the agent's corpse for disposal. 'I only ask because I wonder who's going to lead the operation now?'

'You are,' said the Director, pointing the fruit knife at him.

Mr Grey's nostrils flared and his lips tightened into a thin line. 'I'd best be on my guard then – in case you decide to *terminate* my contract too.'

The assassin locked eyes with the Director. A tense silence fell. Then the Director smiled. 'You're not a man prone to failure, so I don't anticipate having to cull any more of my herd. Now I trust you're coming to tell me you've made progress with the colonel.'

Mr Grey nodded. 'I must admire the man's resilience. It certainly made my work a joy, even if he has made you wait. But they all break eventually.'

'Good. Then talk as we walk.' The Director headed down a flight of stairs and across an air bridge.

'As suspected, Connor has the flash drive,' Mr Grey explained as they marched along a corridor lined with medical labs. 'The contents *are* genuine. Their destination is – or at least was – Hong Kong and ultimately London. The colonel has no idea where Connor and Amir are now. That I'm sure of.'

'What about the local boy?' asked the Director.

Mr Grey snorted. 'Not a contact at all. A mere tour guide. Name of Zhen. No further trace of the boy, although we did find his rickshaw abandoned nearby outside.'

The Director came to an abrupt halt and shot the assassin a look of alarm. 'Outside the Hive?'

Mr Grey nodded. 'CCTV footage shows a boy in a pollution mask approaching the entrance the day before the colonel and his team attempted to flee to Hong Kong.'

'What was he up to?'

'It wasn't the tour guide. It was Connor. I suspect he was trying to contact Charley.'

'*Really?*' The Director's mood lightened. Through a lab observation window, the blonde-haired Buddyguard recruit could be seen struggling with a pair of crutches, a doctor assessing her progress.

'Connor's loyalty to his friends is his weakness,' said the assassin with a disparaging smirk. 'And Charley is his Achilles heel.'

CHAPTER 32

Connor took his frustration out on the *muk yan jong*. He hammered the wooden post with his fists, beating a furious rhythm as he practised his Iron Hand strikes. Over the past couple of days Lǎolao had switched the sack of rice to one of heavy sand, then that morning, gravel, to further condition his hands. She'd continued to test his Iron Shirt technique too and, whether he was getting the hang of it or was now simply numb to the pain, he no longer collapsed every time she whacked him in the gut. Zhen said *that* was progress.

But infuriatingly slow progress was being made with both the flash drive and their escape plan.

They still hadn't heard anything from Zhen's cousin and time was fast running out. As much as he'd built a rapport with the austere Lǎolao – if one could call being beaten daily by a stick a 'rapport' – Connor didn't doubt that her week-long deadline remained in place. They'd be forced to leave their safe haven in less than forty-eight hours. Yet they had nowhere else to go.

The flash drive was their only trump card, their only

hold over Equilibrium. If they could access the information, then they might be able to use it to their advantage – either to threaten Equilibrium or to undermine its efforts to capture them. Sat Buddha-like in the corner of the courtyard, his IT-savvy friend was working all hours to create a decryption program, his brow permanently knitted as he typed in streams of complex coding.

Connor shook the tension from his hands, breathed in and regenerated the *qi* in his fists. The pummelling of the post kept his mind off the constant threat that loomed over them and the impossible task ahead. But he couldn't keep his mind off Charley . . .

Her angelic face haunted his dreams and her gentle reassuring voice interrupted his thoughts. His heart ached at her absence as well as her treachery. He still struggled deep down to believe that she'd turned traitor. Yet Colonel Black had been convinced. The video of her disclosure had been proof, and Mr Grey had confirmed her collusion with the enemy. Her betrayal was irrefutable. But how Connor wished he could still be in her arms – to feel safe, secure and happy as he'd done before his whole world had fallen apart.

Connor resumed his relentless battering of the *muk yan jong*. As he thumped the hard wood, he wondered what had happened to their friends, instructors and the other Buddyguard recruits. Where were they? Was Equilibrium holding them to ransom? Or had they now been killed like Bugsy and Colonel Black? He felt a surge of anger at the idea. Fury fuelling his punches and fanning the flames of his *qi*, Connor let loose a barrage of strikes against the post. The *muk yan jong* rocked under his onslaught . . .

Then Connor stopped, panting heavily, his rage spent. He stared in slack-jawed awe at the post. His knuckles had left *dents* in the wood. In his heightened emotional state, he'd somehow mastered Iron Hand!

But Connor didn't get long to savour his accomplishment. All of a sudden he had the distinct feeling he was being watched. He glanced over his shoulder. Amir's head was buried in his screen. Lǎolao was asleep in her bedroom. And Zhen, he knew, was out shopping.

Then Connor caught a flicker of movement. A young boy's face peered through the slats of the courtyard window. Their eyes met and there was a moment of alarm in both their gazes. The boy bolted before Connor could reach him. At the same time the front door swung open and Zhen came bustling in.

'Good news!' she said, dumping the two shopping bags. 'My cousin has a shift driving haulage to Hong Kong.'

Connor rushed to the shutter. The little window overlooked a narrow dead-end path that was occasionally frequented by old men fishing in the murky canal. But that afternoon no one was there. Then Connor spotted the young boy scurrying across the bridge.

'He says he'll need money to bribe the customs officers and cover his own risk,' said Zhen, oblivious to the fleeing child. She bit her lower lip and looked over at Connor awkwardly. 'Fifty thousand yuan.'

'*What?*' exclaimed Amir, his concentration broken at the startling amount. 'We don't have that sort of money.'

Losing sight of the boy, Connor glanced down at his wrist. 'What about this?' he said, offering Zhen the bracelet the birthday girl Maria had given him in Mexico. In all the frantic and crazy turmoil of the past fortnight, he hadn't taken it off and, until that moment, had forgotten all about it. 'It's solid gold, worth several thousand dollars.'

Zhen inspected the gleaming bracelet. 'That should cover it,' she said, pocketing the piece of jewellery.

'So when do we go?' asked Amir.

'In two days.'

'Two days!' exclaimed Connor, thinking of the little boy who'd spied on them. 'We might not have two days.'

CHAPTER 33

'You need to eat,' said Zhen, urging him to join them for breakfast.

Connor stopped his anxious pacing of the courtyard and sat down. Dour as ever, Lǎolao dumped a large bowl of congee in front of him. He had no appetite; nonetheless he forced a spoonful of the thick rice porridge into his mouth. With the possibility of capture hanging over their heads, this could well be his last full meal for a long while.

'Perhaps the boy didn't tell anyone,' said Amir, half an eye on the decryption program he'd finished late the previous night and was now running on the tablet as he tucked into his own bowl. 'It's been twelve hours and we've seen nothing suspicious. He might not have even made the connection between you and the Shanghai attack.'

Connor desperately wanted to believe that. But the way the boy had fled across the bridge told another story.

'How old was the boy?' asked Zhen, pouring herself a cup of black tea and taking a sip.

Connor shrugged. 'Six, maybe seven.'

'Then, even if he did tell someone, they might not

believe him. Anyway, Zhouzhuang gets lots of tourists. It's not unusual to see a foreign boy around here.'

Connor rubbed the weariness from his eyes. 'I honestly hope you're right. For all our sakes.'

Putting aside her teacup, Zhen offered a reassuring smile. 'You both just need to keep your heads down for another twenty-four hours. We're due to meet my cousin at five tomorrow morning at the highway junction. He'll stop the truck just long enough for you to climb into the back of the trailer. Inside he's loaded an empty crate along with the other containers. You're to hide in there. The trip should take no more than a day. Since you won't be able to come out again until you're in Hong Kong, he's left food and water in the crate.'

Amir cleared his throat. 'What about going to the toilet?'

Zhen grimaced. 'I'm guessing . . . there'll be a bucket for you.'

Wrinkling his nose at the prospect, Amir returned to his decryption program.

'We'll cope,' said Connor, now thinking twice about eating *all* his rice porridge. 'I'll put up with anything to get out of this country alive.'

Zhen lowered her gaze, her attention suddenly absorbed by the tea leaves in her cup. She seemed both sad and troubled. She spoke softly. 'My cousin *can't* guarantee you safe passage. Customs officers may search the truck. If you're discovered, he'll deny everything. You have to understand this plan is very risky.'

'But it's our *only* option,' said Connor, setting down his spoon. 'You're not to worry. We understand the risks. We just appreciate all you've done for us. I don't know how we'd have survived this long without your h–'

'*Zhè shì shéi zuò de?*' Lǎolao interrupted sharply.

Connor looked up, startled, convinced the police were about to break in. But Lǎolao was inspecting the wooden post of her *muk yan jong*, running her gnarled fingers over the indentations in the wood.

'Sorry, that was me,' he replied with a sheepish grin.

When Zhen told her grandmother this, the old woman snatched up the wooden broom handle and gesticulated for Connor to stand.

Connor raised his hands defensively. 'I said . . . I was sorry.'

Zhen laughed. 'She doesn't want to punish you – she wants to test you.'

'What? Iron Shirt . . . *now*?' said Connor. They could be arrested at any moment and the old woman wanted to practise martial arts! 'But I've only just finished my breakfast.'

'Lǎolao says the *qìgōng* porridge will help,' Zhen insisted. 'If you're leaving tomorrow, she wants to know you're ready for anything.'

Lǎolao tapped the ground impatiently. Seeing that the old woman wasn't going to take no for an answer, Connor reluctantly rose from the breakfast table – leaving Amir engrossed in his decryption – and stood in the centre of the courtyard as directed. He breathed deep and harnessed his *qi*, channelling the inner energy to his stomach. Well practised by now, he soon forged a fiery warmth in his belly and readied himself for another pointless beating.

Lăolao wound up to hit him, her narrow eyes glinting fiendishly. At the exact moment that she swung the broom handle at his midriff, Amir cried, 'I've cracked it!'

The wooden handle struck Connor and snapped in half on impact, one end clattering across the courtyard, the other piece still in Lăolao's bony hand.

Connor grimaced. 'Good work, Amir . . . but I think she's cracked my ribs!' However, when he pulled up his shirt, his skin was unmarked – not a bruise or a blemish in sight.

Lăolao applauded, her wrinkled face breaking into a toothless grin. She patted Connor on the shoulder. 'Iron does not bend or break or bleed,' she said carefully in English. 'You strong like iron now.'

Connor could scarcely believe it. Only now was he aware that he hadn't felt a thing or even flinched at the blow. It was as if Lăolao had hit him with a piece of balsa wood, not a one-inch-thick length of hardened oak.

'Connor, you *have* to look at this,' said Amir, urgently waving him over.

Hurrying to his friend's side, Connor saw a long index of folders and files filling the tablet's screen. 'What exactly am I looking at?' he asked.

'This is everything Bugsy hacked from Equilibrium's mainframe,' explained Amir, running his finger down the screen as he scanned the contents of the drive. 'Their organization's structure. Their agents. Their informants. Their finances. Their operations. This is sensational stuff.

A complete record of *all* their activities. No wonder Equilibrium doesn't want this being released.'

Amir opened a folder marked *Operations*.

A seemingly never-ending stream of documents appeared, labelled by name, location and date. Some were chillingly familiar: aircraft hijackings in America . . . shopping mall attacks in Kenya . . . London bombings . . . hostage-takings in France . . . political killings in Russia . . .

Amir gasped. 'Are they responsible for *all* this?'

The list went on and on. Connor's eyes were caught by a file labelled *Antonio Mendez* – a name he recognized. 'Can you open that one?' he asked.

Amir clicked on the file and brought up the document on the screen.

Location: Baghdad, Iraq

Target: US Ambassador Antonio Mendez

Purpose: Destabilization of Middle East. Trigger new US–Iraq war.

Benefit to Equilibrium: Gain control of oil resources. Increase in crude oil price.

Mission detail: Multiple attack on convoy. All vehicles destroyed. Security team neutralized. Target escaped with bodyguard. Bodyguard shot dead. But target reached safe haven and survived.

Result: MISSION FAIL

Connor felt his knees give way. He knew without a doubt that the bodyguard in question was his father. The target,

Ambassador Antonio Mendez, was now the President of the United States. Connor's first Buddyguard mission had been to protect the President's daughter. That's where he'd learnt the truth about his father's death: Justin Reeves had sacrificed himself saving the former ambassador during an ambush in Iraq – as detailed in this very file.

But there was another truth Connor hadn't known until that moment.

Equilibrium had killed his father.

CHAPTER 34

Connor stared watery-eyed through the courtyard's shuttered window at the reflections rippling in the canal. The discovery that Equilibrium was responsible for his father's death had shaken him to his very core. That this mysterious and sinister organization had robbed him of a father and ripped his family and life apart was almost too much to bear.

Sick to the pit of his stomach, Connor could taste the bile in his mouth. Fists clenched, jaw set, he wanted to punch through the wall – and with Lǎolao's Iron Hand training he just might! He was beyond crying. He'd shed his tears of grief for the past eight years. Now only a hard cold anger gripped his heart.

He wouldn't be in hiding from the police and Chinese state security forces . . . if it wasn't for Equilibrium.

He wouldn't be mourning Colonel Black's death, or Bugsy's or Steve's . . . if it wasn't for Equilibrium.

He wouldn't have lost Charley or had his heart broken by her betrayal . . . if it wasn't for Equilibrium.

He wouldn't even have become a Buddyguard . . . if it wasn't for Equilibrium.

And, most importantly, he would still have a father . . . if it wasn't for Equilibrium!

Everything came back to Equilibrium. They were the root cause of all his hardship and sorrow. And, according to the countless files on the flash drive, they were the cause of hundreds of thousands of people's suffering across the world. And to what aim? What reason could they have to wreak such misery and devastation?

Zhen came up to him quietly with a steaming cup. 'Lǎolao says you should drink this.'

'What is it?' asked Connor, the ferocity of his glare making her flinch away.

'Green tea with chamomile,' she replied, her hand trembling slightly as she held out the tea. 'To soothe your nerves and calm your *qi*.'

'I don't want soothing,' snapped Connor.

Zhen turned away, her cheeks smarting red. 'I was only trying to help . . .'

Connor reached out to her. 'Sorry,' he said, realizing he was taking his anger out on the wrong person. 'I've just discovered –' he swallowed hard – 'who killed my father.'

Zhen's hand went to her mouth, her eyes pools of pity. 'Oh, I'm *so* sorry.'

'That's why –' Connor fought his rising tide of grief and fury – 'I need a few moments to myself.'

'Of course,' said Zhen, bowing her head.

He now took the proffered tea and thanked her. Zhen retreated and joined Amir at the breakfast table where he was poring over the files from the decrypted flash drive.

Amir too had tried to comfort him, but had understood that he needed his own space to absorb the bombshell about his father. So, after a heartfelt hug, Amir had focused on the task in hand: studying the files to discover who or what Equilibrium was.

Connor sipped his tea and resumed staring at the water town's reflection in the canal. Equilibrium *had* to be stopped – destroyed, obliterated. Now more than ever, he was determined to get the files out of China and into the hands of the Deputy Director at MI6. Only by doing so could he bring down this evil organization and exact justice for his father's murder.

Whether it was the water's gentle lapping or the herbal power of the tea, Connor's storm of emotions began to ease and he rejoined his friends at the breakfast table. 'What have you found out?' he asked.

'The more I read, the more terrified I become,' Amir replied, a shell-shocked expression on his face. 'Equilibrium appears to be involved in every major terrorist attack, assassination, military coup and civil war for the past twenty or more years. You name it, they've had a hand in it.' He opened up some of the operation files. 'Look familiar?'

Connor swept his eyes over the headers:

Location: Washington DC, United States of America
Target: Alicia Rosa Mendez
Purpose: Undermine American balance of power by kid-
    napping First Daughter.

Location: Indian Ocean
Target: Maddox Sterling
Purpose: Kill media investigation into Equilibrium.

Location: Ruvubu National Park, Burundi
Target: President Bagaza
Purpose: Install puppet leader by military coup and acquire
mining rights to diamond fields.

Location: Moscow, Russia
Target: Russian President
Purpose: Place agent Viktor Malkov in position of power
within Presidential Executive Office. Gain control over
country's vast natural resources.

'These all match *my* assignments!' said Connor, aghast.

Amir nodded. 'You stopped – or seriously hampered –
many of their recent operations. I've found a few others
that coincide with successful Buddyguard assignments
too. This confirms Mr Grey's conversation with you in the
insect market. Buddyguard disrupted Equilibrium's plans
once too often and, when Bugsy began to investigate them,
this triggered their decision to target Buddyguard and stop
any further interference –'

A mobile phone rang, echoing round the courtyard. Its
ringtone unfamiliar, Connor looked to the others. Zhen
shook her head. 'Lǎolao doesn't have a phone, and mine's
in my pocket.'

Hunting around, Amir pinpointed the source of the sound in Connor's Go-bag. 'It's *your* phone, Connor.'

Connor frowned. 'But no one has my number apart from you.'

Dashing over to his bag, he pulled out the phone and immediately recognized the caller's number on the screen. He stared at Amir in shock.

'It's *Charley*!'

'You *can't* answer it,' Amir warned as the phone continued to blare out its jaunty ringtone.

'But I have to,' said Connor, his thumb hovering over the Accept icon. 'It's Charley.'

'She's betrayed us for Equilibrium, remember?'

Connor hesitated. 'I *need* to hear that from her before I truly believe it.'

'No, don't!' pleaded Amir, making a grab for the phone. But Connor held it out of reach. Amir glared at him. 'You answer that, and it'll give away our location.'

Connor glanced at the screen, the flashing number compelling him to respond. 'But you bought these new phones so we couldn't be traced.'

'Any phone can be traced once the SIM card and IMEI number are identified. Besides, it might not even be Charley. You said her number had been disconnected.'

Zhen and Lǎolao looked on with bewildered expressions as the mobile continued to ring in Connor's hand.

'I've *only* phoned Charley on this. Who else could it be?' Despite Amir's warnings, Connor accepted the call.

He knew his heart was ruling his head, but he *had* to speak to Charley, even if it was for the last time. Laying the phone on the breakfast table, he pressed the speaker icon so Amir could hear too.

'Hello? Charley?' he said, hopeful and hesitant.

'I thought your girlfriend's number would get your attention,' replied a cold calculating voice that made Connor's skin crawl.

'Kill the call!' cried Amir, reaching for the phone.

'NOT if you want Colonel Black to live,' said Mr Grey quickly.

'He's *alive*?' gasped Connor, exchanging a stunned look with Amir.

'Well . . . he's still breathing, if that's what you mean.' Connor could almost see the cruel smile slicing across the assassin's anaemic face. 'And, if you want him to continue breathing, I'd strongly advise you to surrender and hand over the flash drive.'

'Never!' said Connor, the word coming out as hard and heavy as a stone. Much as he hated himself for abandoning the colonel in his hour of need, he knew the former SAS soldier would be the first to understand. The flash drive was the only leverage they had over Equilibrium; Colonel Black himself had drilled that fact into him. To give it up now would be to give up everything.

'You're as headstrong as he is,' snorted Mr Grey. 'Perhaps you need some convincing.'

The phone pinged with a picture message. Fearful of seeing Colonel Black beaten, broken and bloody, Connor and

Amir peered reluctantly at the screen. But what they saw gave them a far greater shock. The photo – a green-tinted night-vision shot – showed the grim and claustrophobic interior of a metal shipping container. Packed inside, a cluster of young teenagers and adults huddled together in the almost pitch-darkness. Connor recognized the muscular bulk of Jason, the bleached blond hair of Marc, Richie's round face and Ling's black bob among the frightened captives, a haunted look of despair in all their eyes. Jody, Gunner and the other instructors kept watch over the recruits, but their faces were gaunt and their own eyes sunken with fear and exhaustion.

'Their limited water supply will soon run out,' Mr Grey explained matter-of-factly. 'But personally I'd be more concerned about oxygen levels. Shipping containers are notorious for poor ventilation. They may just ... *suffocate.*'

Connor gripped the table so hard his knuckles went white. Amir slumped down on his stool, their team's predicament hitting him like a punch to the guts. Until that moment they hadn't known what fate had befallen their friends. Now they knew ... *Their friends were in a living hell.*

'Let them out!' he demanded, slamming the table with his fist and causing the phone to jump.

'That's a little difficult,' replied the assassin coolly. 'They're in the middle of the ocean. By the time their cargo ship arrives at Shanghai Port, I don't expect many, if any, to have survived the long journey. Unless someone alerts the captain, of course. But that's *not* going to happen until Equilibrium has the flash drive.'

Connor looked to Amir whose face reflected his own horror at the situation. The stakes had changed. He might have been willing to gamble Colonel Black's life for the drive, but how could he justify sacrificing *everyone* in Buddyguard? Equilibrium had forced them into an impossible dilemma. If they didn't surrender the flash drive, they'd be sentencing their friends to certain death. But if they did hand it over, then Equilibrium would remain in the shadows, free to continue its secret reign of terror.

'Time is of the essence. *Tick tock!*' said Mr Grey. 'Equilibrium expects you to deliver the flash drive in person at their headquarters within twenty-four hours.'

'Err . . . that's a little difficult,' said Connor, echoing the assassin's own words in an effort to regain the upper hand. 'We're already out of the country.'

'Oh, I doubt that very much,' said Mr Grey. 'Your dial tone was local and, according to the network signal trace, you're in . . . Zhouzhuang!'

Amir shot Connor a look of *I told you so*, then buried his head in his hands. Connor cursed his heart's weakness for answering the phone. He *should* have heeded his friend's warning. Now he'd put them both in jeopardy and given Equilibrium back the advantage.

'How convenient for you,' continued the assassin. 'That's not far from Shanghai. I look forward to welcoming you into the Hive. Perhaps on this occasion, Connor, you'll stop by long enough to catch up with your girlfriend. Unless you'd like a word with her now . . .'

There was a muffled sound of the phone exchanging hands.

'Connor! Is that you?' said Charley's voice on the other end of the line, high and panicky.

'Yes,' he replied, his own voice tight with emotion.

'Listen, you *have* to do what Mr Grey says. Otherwise Equilibrium will kill all the recruits – including me!'

'Why would Equilibrium want to kill *you*? You work for them! You betrayed us . . . *didn't you*?'

There was silence on the line. Connor's heart was thumping so loud in his chest that it was all he heard. He'd *had* to ask the question, but now dreaded the answer. Then Charley replied, 'What are you talking about, Connor? Equilibrium kidnapped me. The spinal therapy was just a ruse to get me to China. They *tricked* me.'

'*What!*' exclaimed Connor in horror. Even after everything he'd read in the operation files, he couldn't believe the depths to which Equilibrium had sunk – exploiting a young girl's disability to their own ends. He knew Charley had invested all her hopes and dreams in that one pioneering treatment and he couldn't even begin to imagine the bitter anguish she was now going through. His heart went out to her.

'You know I wouldn't do anything to harm you, Connor,' she insisted. 'I love you.'

These were the words Connor wanted to hear and he felt his throat choke with emotion. 'I love you too, Charley.'

'Then *please* save me,' she implored. 'By the way, are Amir and Zhen with you too?'

'Y-yes,' Connor managed to reply. 'They're right by my side.'

'Good. Now you must –'

The call was suddenly cut off as Amir snatched up the phone. He opened the back, yanked out the battery and prised the SIM card from its slot. Then he snapped it in half, stamped furiously on the phone and threw the broken pieces with all his might over the courtyard wall and into the canal. 'I told you *not* to answer that call!' he shouted, his fists balled up in rage.

'I-I-I had to,' Connor stuttered, never having seen his friend so angry.

'We have to leave, *now*!' ordered Amir, taking charge for once and hurriedly gathering up the flash drive, his tablet and Go-bag. 'Thanks to you, Equilibrium have traced us to our location. But with any luck it'll only be accurate to fifty metres or so. That gives us a narrow corridor to escape *if* we leave now. We'll need to find somewhere else to hide until the truck arrives.' He glanced irritably over at Connor. 'Why are you smiling?'

Connor hadn't realized there was a smile on his lips, but he felt it in his heart. 'Because Charley *didn't* betray us.'

Amir shot him an unexpectedly fierce look. 'Then tell me this – how did she know about Zhen?'

Connor opened his mouth to answer. But nothing came out. He glanced over at their young guide who stood beside her grandmother, watching the frantic packing with increasing alarm. Amir was right. He'd not mentioned Zhen at all during their brief conversation. Charley *couldn't* have known about her.

Amir shook his head in dismay. 'She even got you to reveal we're *all* together. Charley's certainly a class act! Now grab your Go-bag and –'

A knock at the door caused them all to freeze.

Amir's eyes flared in panic. 'They can't have got to us that quickly!'

Connor spun towards the door. 'But would Equilibrium bother to *knock*?'

CHAPTER 36

Zhen ushered Connor and Amir inside the house, while Lǎolao hurriedly swept all evidence of their earlier break-fast into the sink and dumped their bedding into a basket.

The knocking became more insistent.

'Wǒ *láile!*' barked Lǎolao, shuffling across the court-yard at a snail's pace.

Inside the house, Connor and the others hunkered down in the grandmother's bedroom, a threadbare space of lime-green walls and brown lino flooring. Apart from a sagging mattress and rickety bedside table, the only other item of solid furniture was a lopsided wardrobe, its front panels missing and replaced by a striped pink tablecloth. The wardrobe not being a realistic option, there was nowhere for them to hide. So, pressing themselves close to the wall, they peered through the small grimy window overlooking the courtyard.

Lǎolao was still fumbling with the lock, making a show of her frailty. She glanced over her shoulder to ensure they'd had enough time to conceal themselves, then she opened the door a crack. His heart pounding, Connor braced himself for a forced entry by a unit of armed agents. But the door stayed on its hinges. Through the opening, he spied a plump middle-aged man with a salesman's smile. In his pudgy hands he held a string of pyramid-shaped green leaves. He waved them in front of Lăolao's stony face.

Amir looked at Zhen. 'What are those?'

'*Zòngzi*,' she whispered. 'Rice dumplings in bamboo leaves.'

Amir ran a hand through his slick of black hair and let out a sigh of relief. 'Equilibrium doesn't do food deliveries!'

His hammering pulse slowing several beats, Connor rested his head back against the wall. The man was nothing but a street hawker! Lăolao dismissed him with an irritable wave of her bony hand and went to close the door. But the dumpling seller was keen to make a sale. Wedging his foot in the gap, he offered another string of dumplings and lowered his price. When Lăolao shook her head, he produced a couple of bamboo wicker baskets and tried to sell those instead. As the hawker kept up his sales patter, his booted foot still firmly lodged against the door jamb, Connor noticed that the man's watchful eyes kept flicking past Lăolao into the courtyard.

Connor's sixth sense went haywire.

He darted through to the opposite room. In three strides he crossed the drab little lounge, with its rocking chair and antique sideboard, and reached the narrow latticed window that faced out on to the canal. He peeked through the shutter. On first inspection, everything appeared normal: a few boats cruising along the waterway and a handful of people going about their daily business. Then on the far side, down from the bridge, he spotted the round face of the young boy from the previous day. He was tucked into an alley, keenly watching the house. It was at that moment Connor became aware that the streets were rapidly emptying – and that two boats were silently docking alongside the courtyard wall. Partially obscured by the boats' awnings, a squad of armed police in black combat gear crouched shoulder to shoulder, their weapons at the ready.

Connor rushed back into the bedroom. 'The dumpling seller's a distraction! The house is being surrounded.'

Amir's eyes flared wider than a startled owl's. 'Then it's over . . . Equilibrium has us trapped!'

Connor shook his head. 'It's not Equilibrium. It's the police.'

Amir slid down the wall to the floor. 'Great! I hear the police are very hospitable to terrorist suspects.'

'We're not surrendering,' said Connor, pulling his friend to his feet. 'We can't. Not with our friends' lives at stake. We have to find a way out of this.' He looked into the courtyard where Lǎolao was now remonstrating with the salesman, who refused to leave. Their best chance was to take the man on, but who knew how many police officers lay in wait further along the lane.

'Follow me,' said Zhen as she reached behind the wardrobe and pulled out a bamboo ladder bound with twine.

Propping it against the wall, she scampered up, pushed open a hatch in the ceiling and disappeared into the loft's cool darkness. Their Go-bags strapped to their backs, Connor and Amir clambered up after her. The roof space was cluttered with old boxes, cobwebs and birds' nests. Sunlight leaked in through the patchwork of tiles, but the loft itself was a dead end.

'We can't hide up here!' said Amir, coughing from the dust. 'They'll soon find us.'

'That's not the plan,' said Zhen. She prised a tile aside, then another and another until there was a hole large enough to crawl through. 'This way.'

Connor grabbed her arm. 'You can't come with us.'

She stared at him, baffled. 'Why not?'

'At the moment you're innocent. You can claim we forced you to shelter us. But, if you're seen to be helping, the police will arrest you . . . maybe even shoot you!'

Zhen held his gaze. 'Equilibrium know my name. They know where Lăolao lives. Of course I'm scared of being caught by the police. But I'm *more* scared of Equilibrium. If they're as powerful and evil as you say, they *must* be stopped at all costs. You'll never make it out of the country without my help; you still need a guide.'

Connor released his grip on her arm. 'I'm sorry we got you into this.'

Zhen smiled. 'Don't be. I was the one to approach *you* first.' She wriggled through the gap on to the roof.

Amir glanced at Connor. 'She's tough, that's for sure,' he said admiringly, then followed their guide out.

Connor pulled up the ladder and closed the loft hatch before crawling through the hole and kneeling beside the others. Zhouzhuang spread out before them, an undulating sea of dark grey tiles criss-crossed with gleaming ribbons of canals. Below, oblivious to the fugitives on the roof, the armed police unit prepared to launch their assault.

'Will your grandmother be all right?' whispered Connor, glancing anxiously down into the small courtyard to see her beating back the sham dumpling seller with the broken broom handle.

Zhen nodded. 'Lǎolao's afraid of no one. Not even the police.'

Leading the way, she traversed the roof to the adjoining building. Despite the shallow slope, loose tiles made the going treacherous. But the next house after that presented even greater problems – it was separated by an alleyway.

'We'll have to jump across,' said Zhen as she backed up to take a running leap.

'*What?*' hissed Amir, peering over the edge with horror at the ten-metre drop on to the hard stone pavement below.

But Connor was more concerned about the second squad of police hiding further along the alley than any possibility of falling.

Zhen threw herself across the gap and landed cat-like on the opposite roof. She waved for them to follow.

'Here goes nothing!' said Connor. Sprinting towards the edge, he leapt into the air. Beneath him the police officers waited for the green light to commence the raid while, unbeknown to them, their targets were literally above their heads. Connor touched down on the other side, landing as lightly as possible on the balls of his feet. There was still an all-too-loud *scrunch* of tiles and he winced at the noise. Luckily a burst of police radio chatter masked his landing.

Amir now worked himself up for the jump. Sucking in several deep breaths and shaking his limbs out, he took a practice run-up, carefully counting his paces. Then with a final intake of breath he went for it . . . and stopped, teetering on the lip of the roof. His eyes, shiny with panic, flicked between the precipitous drop and his friends.

I can't do it, he mouthed.

Connor and Zhen silently and frantically urged him to try again. Amir backed up as far as he could, then dashed headlong towards the gap. Arms flailing and legs whirling, he soared over the alley and landed on top of Zhen. The two of them hit the roof in a heap of entangled limbs, their heavy collision disturbing a nearby roost of pigeons. Connor, Amir and Zhen all froze as the birds flapped away in a cloud of feathers and cawing. Below in the alley they heard a hushed exchange.

Zhen whispered, 'It's OK. They think it's just the pigeons.'

Connor helped extract his friend from their guide. Amir smiled shyly at Zhen as she dusted herself off. 'Thanks for catching m–'

All of a sudden Amir's foot went from under him as a tile broke loose. Connor grabbed his friend's jacket and yanked him back from the edge, preventing him from plummeting to the ground. But the tile couldn't be saved. It tumbled through the air and smashed on to the stone pavement, fragments flying in all directions.

The unit of police officers all looked up, guns trained on their newfound target.

'Go!' cried Connor, pushing Amir up to the ridge of the roof as a burst of bullets tore into the sky.

There was an angry shout and more gunfire. The three of them fled across the roofs, leaping from building to building. No longer did they care about making a noise or kicking more tiles to the ground. They simply ran for their lives. Below in the network of alleys and lanes, the police relentlessly pursued them, their necks craned for a sighting of their quarry. A detachment of four officers scaled the walls and began to give chase over the rooftops too.

'Canal!' warned Zhen as the roof ahead came to an abrupt end.

'Keep going!' Connor cried, spotting a lower building on the opposite bank.

'Are you crazy?' shouted Amir.

But, driven by fear and the police, Connor, Zhen and Amir leapt from the eaves. Two storeys up, their legs bicycling madly, Connor realized he *was* mad for attempting such a foolhardy jump – they were dropping like stones and didn't look as if they'd make it!

Beneath them a boatman stared up in frog-eyed shock as the three teenagers soared over his head ... to crash-land atop a waterside restaurant. By some miracle they'd cleared the canal but, hitting the tiles hard, Zhen's legs went from under her and she rolled down the slope out of control. Diving for their guide, Connor and Amir caught her trailing arm just before she tumbled over the edge.

'No time for swimming,' said Connor, dragging her back from the brink.

They scrambled up the slope to the next ridge. Behind, the four police officers on the roof reached the drop-off into the canal. Not nearly so desperate or reckless as the, three fugitives, the heart-stopping leap gave the officers pause for thought. They drew their guns but were too late to take aim, the fugitives having vaulted the ridge and slithered down the other side. Then, ordered by their superior to give chase, the four men were forced to take a running jump.

Connor and the others didn't wait around to see if they made it. Scurrying across to the adjoining building, they began to scale the wall to the upper roof. As Connor helped push Amir up, he heard a yell followed by a loud splash. At least one officer had failed to make the distance.

In the streets below, the police squad on the ground had been compelled to take the long way round, going north to the nearest footbridge before they could continue the pursuit.

'What's our plan?' panted Amir, as the three of them fled up and over roof peaks, dodging power lines, skirting gaps and avoiding broken tiles.

'Keep running!' Connor gasped, ducking beneath a telephone wire.

'But where to –'

Their guide came to an abrupt halt. A wide waterway cut them off from the next set of buildings. There was no way they could make *that* leap.

'Back! Back!' she cried. They retraced their steps, returning to a building that connected to a different row of houses. However, by the time they reached the roof's junction, the three policemen who'd cleared the canal had caught up. The lead officer drew his gun and ordered them to stop. As the two other officers cautiously advanced, Connor grabbed Zhen round the throat.

'*What are you doing?*' she exclaimed, her eyes rings of shock.

'What's the word for "hostage"?' Connor demanded in her ear.

'Err . . . *rénzhì*,' she spluttered.

Connor shouted at the police: '*Rénzhì!*'

The officers hesitated, an apparently innocent victim now under threat.

Amir sidled close to his friend. 'Connor, *please* don't make the situation any worse for us!'

'I'm not,' he hissed out of the corner of his mouth. 'I'm giving Zhen an alibi that we kidnapped her.'

One of the policemen edged closer, cutting off their only escape route. Connor shouted '*Rénzhì!*' again and stamped his foot to make his point.

Amir looked wildly around. 'Nowhere to run, nowhere to hide. I think we should surrend–'

In that instant the roof beneath them gave way and the three fugitives dropped through the hole on to a bed below. The metal bedframe collapsed under the impact, the mattress taking the brunt of their fall and saving them from broken limbs. Still beneath the covers, a startled couple stared at them, eyes and mouths open wide like emojis.

'Sorry to drop in on you uninvited,' said Connor. He helped Amir and Zhen to their feet as dust and debris continued to rain down on their heads. 'You all right?'

Zhen nodded, but Amir winced. 'Hurt my knee but I'll be fine.'

Above, the three policemen peered through the hole in the roof. '*STOP!*' commanded the lead officer. But Connor, Amir and Zhen were already running out of the bedroom. They darted down a creaking staircase, through a sparsely furnished living room and out of the front door.

'Which way?' Connor asked their guide.

Zhen glanced up and down the narrow street lined with poky little shops crammed full of plastic gifts and souvenirs. 'Well, not *that* way!' she said, glimpsing the ominous black uniforms of several armed police officers charging up the street.

They raced off in the opposite direction. Connor heard a shout from behind but didn't look back. They sprinted along the road, weaving and barging their way between the shoppers. Yells of complaint and disgruntled glares pursued them. But they didn't care – not with a whole unit of armed police on their tail. Exiting the cobbled street, they came to a canal and turned sharp right. Amir, hobbling on his injured knee, accidentally bumped into a tourist taking a photo of his wife at the waterside. Losing his balance, the man toppled head first into the canal.

'Sorry!' cried Amir as the man flailed in the murky waters. His wife, however, was more furious that her silk dress had been soaked than at the fact her husband had been dunked.

With no time to stop and help, Connor careered along the canal side with the others. People scattered as Zhen yelled for them to move out of the way. But it was the shouts from behind that had greater effect. Connor glanced over his shoulder to see three officers chasing them down. They had their guns drawn but were unable to fire due to the presence of so many tourists. They yelled for everyone to drop to the ground. Then up ahead two other policemen appeared and blocked the path.

'We're trapped!' Zhen gasped, skidding to a stop.

Connor looked desperately around. The two shops on their right offered no escape route, the nearest bridge was a couple of hundred metres beyond the police officers and the only alley was on the opposite side of the canal. The policemen slowed their pace, confident of capture at last.

Then a boat glided by, the little man at the tiller watching the chaotic scene with open-mouthed astonishment.

'Leapfrog!' said Connor to Amir and Zhen as he jumped off the path on to the passing boat. Using it as a mobile stepping stone, he bounded across to the other bank. Amir and Zhen both followed suit, the boatman too stunned to even complain.

Furious their quarry had escaped, a police officer ran up and leapt into the boat after them. But, weighed down by his weapon and tactical equipment, his feet went straight through the flimsy wooden hull. Floundering up to his waist in the murky canal, the officer was subjected to a torrent of abuse from the tiller-man as the boat rapidly began to take on water. Their crossing point now sinking, the remaining officers were forced to run back to the nearest bridge.

Safe on the other bank, Connor, Amir and Zhen darted down the opposite alley. But their frenetic escape was starting to take its toll. Zhen was gasping for breath and Amir was limping badly, his knee worsening with each step he took. Connor felt his own pace flagging too.

'We have to find somewhere to hide,' he panted.

They burst from the alley into a bustling square. Connor looked frantically around. Tacky gift shops, paper lantern stores, sweaty dumpling sellers and countless restaurants ringed the paved square. The old-style curved-roofed wooden buildings, complete with a towering white-and-red pagoda in one corner and a huge stone gateway decorated with carved dragons at the entrance, attracted sightseers to the ancient water town's centre like bees to a honeypot. The place was literally swarming with foreign tourists.

Where better to hide a tree than in a forest, thought Connor.

He grabbed three baseball caps from a gift shop and handed them to his friends. Donning the caps – Zhen scooping her long hair up into a bun – they did their best to blend into the crowd.

'We can't stay in Zhouzhuang,' said Zhen, her eyes darting left and right. 'The police will close the roads and search every house.'

Amir grimaced. 'And I can't run much further.'

A uniformed tour guide was waving a pink flag. 'This way! On to the bus. Quickly now.'

'Then we need transport out of here,' said Connor, steering Amir and Zhen into the heart of a bunch of Western tourists. The group was shepherded across the square, under the stone gateway and over to an awaiting bus. Keeping their heads bowed, Connor, Amir and Zhen climbed aboard with the other tourists. They were not a second too soon. As they took their seats at the back of the coach, armed police officers charged into the square. They hunted through the crowd, making a beeline for any foreign teenager with their parents. Just as the order was given to close the entrances, the tour bus pulled away from the kerb and merged into the town's traffic.

Connor, Amir and Zhen sank into their seats with relief. They kept low and quiet, trying not to draw attention to themselves while they recovered their breath and the tour bus continued to put distance between themselves and the police.

As the coach reached the outskirts of Zhouzhuang and joined the main highway, Amir whispered, 'So what now?'

Connor peered over the windowsill at the passing houses and rice paddies. 'I guess we find out where we're going first.' He leant forward and tapped the immense rounded shoulder of a rosy-cheeked man in the seat in front. 'Where's the bus going next?'

'Haven't you *read* the itinerary?' drawled the red-faced man, a grin stretching from ear to ear. 'Shanghai, of course.'

Connor slumped back against his seat. Amir screwed his eyes tight shut and cursed under his breath.

Zhen, her own face mirroring the two boys' disheartened expressions, sighed. 'Like you English might say, out of the wok and into the fire!'

CHAPTER 38

'Charley's a very *determined* subject,' remarked the weasel-faced doctor as he and the Director studied their young patient through the lab's observation window. 'She'll let absolutely nothing stop her from trying to walk again.'

Crystal-blue eyes fixated on their target, jaw muscles straining, slim biceps bulging and hands clamped to the parallel walking bars, Charley shakily dragged a leg forward in a superhuman effort to take an excruciating first step towards the other side of the room. Her leg moved in fits and starts, her jerks inelegant and awkward; nonetheless she moved *unaided*. With her T-shirt plastered to her body in patches of dark sweat, Charley worked up the willpower to shift her other leg. As she prepared to take the next step, her slender face contorted with focus, fury and frustration. She bit down on her lower lip to the point of drawing blood. Her arms began to tremble uncontrollably. However immense the internal exertion, though, her rear leg seemed to fail her and eventually she collapsed on to the bars, panting and in pain. A couple of technicians rushed to her aid. But after a moment's recovery she shoved them away. Then she lifted herself back on to the bars and began the agonizing process again.

'She's been at this for over an hour.'

'Impressive,' said the Director with a nod. 'But what I want to know is how the neuro-chip is performing.'

The doctor grinned like a rat who'd discovered the way into a locked larder. 'One hundred per cent. The neuro-chip is successfully communicating with the motor cortex and bypassing the spinal injury. The graphene receptors implanted in her lower spinal cord are receiving the wireless signal and triggering nerve and muscle responses.'

The Director subjected him to a sidelong glare. 'Then why *isn't* she walking?'

The doctor stiffened at his boss's scathing tone, then ran a hand over his balding pate, smoothing flat a few loose strands of hair. 'The neuro-chip is only *one* factor in her recovery. The patient needs to retrain her brain to send the correct impulses to her leg muscles. The motor cortex has millions of neurons and only a few thousand are being utilized at this stage. However, with continued practice, greater control will be achievable.'

The Director reconsidered their patient. 'And you're convinced this technology can be utilized to *enhance* a person's natural abilities?'

The doctor nodded. 'Combined with the right steroids, the neuro-chip's signals can be amplified to generate a faster and stronger muscle response. Any modified subject would benefit from extended endurance, greater physical power and increased reaction times.' The doctor turned to the Director, a conniving glint in his narrow eyes. 'You could even *hijack* a subject's body by overriding the wireless signal. Immobilize them, torture them or compel them to do anything you require ... such as assassinate a target.'

A whisper of a smile passed across the Director's face. 'Excellent. Be sure to keep me updated with your progress and let me know when we can have our first trial.'

The doctor gave an ingratiating bow of his balding head and retreated back into the lab. As the Director observed Charley make another punishing attempt at walking, Mr Grey's skull of a face appeared like an apparition in the tinted glass's reflection.

'I can see why Connor admires her so much,' said the assassin. 'She's ... tenacious.'

The Director turned sharply to Mr Grey. 'And *where* is Connor? More importantly, where's the flash drive?'

The assassin stepped into the light, his face no less skull-like close up. 'The police were tipped off before your agents got there. It seems a local boy discovered their whereabouts by chance.'

The Director swore an oath in Chinese, then suddenly exploded into anger. '*Why didn't WE know about the tip-off?*'

Mr Grey took a step back, distancing himself from the Director's erratic behaviour. 'Unfortunately, Agent Yuan is no longer with us,' he explained in a low even tone, 'so the information wasn't passed on.'

The Director scowled at the implied criticism of the agent's execution.

'Don't fret,' continued Mr Grey, holding the Director's red-hot glare. 'Connor and his friends are on their way here.'

This news seemed to pacify the Director. She shrugged off her anger, then asked tersely, 'How can you be so certain?'

Mr Grey glanced into the lab where Charley continued her personal battle, while technicians took neurological read-outs of her labours. 'His weakness for Charley is his undoing, along with his loyalty to Buddyguard – he now knows about his colleagues' limited survival time. I anticipate the drive being in your hands within twenty-four hours.'

The Director drew close to Mr Grey, closer than most people would ever dare. 'Good. Then I'll inform the Board of your *imminent* success. They've been understandably anxious waiting for news.'

The assassin didn't flinch at the Director's threatening tone. 'One last thing.'

The Director raised an eyebrow. 'Yes?'

'Once the drive is recovered, Connor is *mine*. He has a blood debt that needs repaying.'

'We have a choice to make,' said Connor, his voice echoing off the crumbling brick walls of the disused warehouse. Late-afternoon sunlight filtered in through the upper tier of broken and boarded-up windows that shouldered the burden of the warehouse's collapsing roof, while the three of them sat in a tight huddle at one end of the cavernous space.

As soon as the tour bus had arrived at its first destination in Shanghai, they'd disembarked with the other tourists and made a quick getaway. Through a combination of Amir's memory for directions and Zhen's knowledge of the city, they'd managed to navigate their way back to the warehouse that had once been Colonel Black and Bugsy's bunker. Now it was their last remaining refuge in the whole of China.

Connor looked at his two friends. Their faces were washed-out, their eyes ringed with exhaustion. Zhen perched on the old office chair, her knees clasped to her chest, her hair still tied in a bun. Amir wearily propped himself against Bugsy's workbench, the array of electronic equipment untouched since their departure for the train station a week and a lifetime ago. His friend stared off blankly at the far end wall, his body slumped in defeat. Connor himself was bone-tired and almost at his wits' end. They were back where they started, yet in even more peril than before. But with Alpha team and their instructors' lives still in jeopardy, and with the bitter knowledge that Equilibrium was responsible for his father's death, Connor was far from broken.

'We could head back to Zhouzhuang and try to meet up with Zhen's cousin,' he suggested.

Zhen shook her head. She showed them her smartphone, which displayed a news app in Chinese. Connor immediately recognized the photo of the water town with its canals. 'The whole area is swarming with police. They've set up roadblocks. You wouldn't get ten kilometres down the highway before you were captured.'

'Then we look for alternative routes to Hong Kong,' said Connor.

'We've already done that.' Amir sighed heavily. 'Zhen's cousin was our best chance out of here and you blew it!'

'Listen, I'm sorry,' said Connor, feeling the guilt hanging round his neck like a noose. 'I should've listened to you. I was stupid for answering that call, but I *had* to know . . . *had* to speak to Charley.'

Amir nodded, his gaze forlorn and far away. 'I understand. I wanted to know too.' He turned to Connor, his eyes red and rimmed with tears. 'I'm more angry with *her* for trying to deceive us – to our very faces! Like you, I'd clung to the hope that Colonel Black had been wrong, that Charley was still one of us – *our* friend.' He crushed a polystyrene cup that had been left on the workbench and angrily tossed it away. 'She's nothing but a heartless traitor!'

It hurt Connor to hear his friend say such things about Charley. But how could he argue with him? The simple fact was that Charley had betrayed them and now they found themselves in a desperate predicament. 'Well, if we can't get to Hong Kong, what do you suggest?'

'Hand over the flash drive to Equilibrium.'

'*What?*' Connor's jaw fell open. 'We *can't* do that. After everything we've read on that drive, Equilibrium has to be exposed. Destroyed! They're terrorizing the world and no one knows the truth. They murdered my father!'

'I know,' said Amir sadly. 'They also killed Bugsy and Steve. But this might be the only way to save Colonel Black and the rest of our friends. It could just save us too.'

'How? The drive is the one thing that can bring Equilibrium down.'

'I realize that, but I don't see we have any other option. If we can't get the flash drive to Stella Sinclair in London, then we may as well exchange it for the lives of our friends.'

Connor now understood Colonel Black's moral dilemma when he'd insisted that sacrifices might have to be made for the sake of the flash drive and the greater good. They too were now stuck between a rock and a hard place – and all the time the gap between them was closing.

Zhen cleared her throat. 'Once Equilibrium has the drive, won't they simply kill us all to keep their secret safe?'

Connor nodded. 'Zhen's right, Amir. We can't trust them.'

Flicking a stray piece of polystyrene cup off the bench, Amir shrugged in response. 'Then I'm out of ideas.'

The three of them lapsed into silence. Equilibrium had them against the wall. They couldn't escape the country. They couldn't go to the authorities. And they couldn't save their friends *unless* they gave up the drive. Connor held his head in his hands. 'I'm afraid Equilibrium has beaten us.'

'If a battle cannot be won, do not fight it,' agreed Zhen.

Connor looked up. 'What did you say?'

'If a battle cannot be won, do not fight it. The great Chinese general and philosopher Sun Tzu said that –'

'I know who he is. My sensei in jujitsu was always quoting him.' Connor's expression hardened from defeat to determination, a steely glint entering his green-blue eyes. He had the spark of an idea – a dangerous one, a risky one – but an idea nonetheless. 'There is *another* choice.'

Amir and Zhen both stared at him. 'What?' asked Amir.

'We do the one thing Equilibrium least expects: go on the attack.'

Amir recoiled in shock. 'Sorry. Correct me if I'm wrong, but didn't Sun Tzu say if a battle cannot be won, then *do not* fight it?'

Connor nodded and grinned. 'Sun Tzu also said, *If you know the enemy and know yourself, you need not fear the result of a hundred battles.* We know ourselves and what we're capable of. The real question is, *who* or *what* is Equilibrium?'

CHAPTER 40

Without war, there is no peace. Without chaos,
no calm. Without poverty, no riches.

Our role is to keep society in balance.
To ensure no government becomes too strong.
No country too powerful.

Equilibrium is shaping the future. Ensuring we have
a future. A future that we own . . .

'They're a bunch of megalomaniacs!' exclaimed Connor as
they huddled round Amir's tablet and read the document
displayed on the screen.

Amir nodded and continued to study the files. 'Equilibrium is a multinational criminal organization with its
central cell in China. According to this statement, its goal
is to destabilize the world in order to enhance its own global
domination. One method of doing this is to infiltrate governments, then acquire stakes in critical infrastructure and
natural resources.'

'So Equilibrium is ultimately about money and power?' said Zhen.

'Yes,' replied Amir, his eyes racing over the files. 'As far as I can tell, Equilibrium functions like a company with its own Board of Directors, each responsible for a different territory, with China's Director being the chairman of the Board. Think of it like the mythical beast of the Hydra – a many-headed snake that survives even if you cut one of its heads off.'

Connor's brow furrowed. 'Didn't Hercules kill the Hydra?'

Amir nodded. 'He chopped the heads off, then used a firebrand to stop them growing back.'

Connor tapped the flash drive. 'So, this is our Hercules. Somehow we need to expose the Chinese head and stop it *ever* growing back. Then we destroy the others. OK, who's on this Board of Directors?'

Amir buried deeper into the personnel folder, but each file came up virtually blank, only stating a location and contact number. 'As you can see, there's very little, if any, information on them. In fact, it appears they go to great lengths to remain anonymous. I've only a corporate structure to go by for any evidence they actually exist. However, those beneath the Director *are* identified.'

Amir clicked on a link to reveal a greasy black-haired man with a poor complexion and close-set mud-brown eyes magnified behind rimless glasses.

Zhen gasped. 'That's Liu Yan!'

'Who?' asked Connor.

'Chairman of the Politburo Standing Committee. The third most powerful man in the Communist Party.'

'He's not the only one of influence under Equilibrium's employ,' said Amir, opening several more files. 'There's the vice-president of the Xinhua News Agency, the CEO of China Investment Corporation, and even the Minister of National Defence!'

Connor stared aghast at Amir. 'Our enemy's even more powerful than I feared. What information do you have on the Hive itself?'

'As we already know, it's the headquarters of their Chinese operations. But it's also the heart of their cybernetics programme – hence the high-tech medical facilities. Equilibrium's people don't just want to rule the world – it appears they want to rule the future as well.'

Amir pulled up a series of documents with schematics of robotic limbs, microprocessors and human bodies. He ran through them. 'There are projects here for artificial intelligence, voice cloning, biomechanics, genetic modification, human augmentation –'

'Human what?' asked Zhen, struggling to keep up.

Amir leant back in his chair. 'Basically, they're attempting to create super-humans.' He ran his finger down the screen, reeling off the projects. 'Strength enhancement, night-vision capabilities, cerebral uplinks to the internet . . . this is scarily advanced stuff. We're talking real-life cyborgs. Human Terminators!'

Zhen bit her lip anxiously. 'Will *we* have to fight these cyborgs?'

Amir squinted at the screen, then shook his head. 'Most of it seems to be in the developmental stages still. But this is definitely Equilibrium's endgame.'

'They have to be stopped,' declared Connor. 'But, before we attempt to chop the head off this snake, we first need to rescue our friends. If we can locate them and alert the ship's captain, then Equilibrium will no longer have that hold over us.' He looked at Amir. 'Equilibrium must have tracking information on their whereabouts. Having broken the encryption on these files, do you think you can hack into their computer system like Bugsy did?'

Amir whistled through his teeth. 'It'll be risky, but I can give it a go. Bugsy left a pathway link to their mainframe's back door . . . if it's still active, that is.' He went online, his fingers flying over the keyboard. 'First I'll have to set up a Tor router, then bounce our signal through multiple nodes, so our location can't be pinged easily.' After several minutes of furious typing, Amir turned to Connor and Zhen. 'Here goes nothing.'

He executed the link to the mainframe. The screen flashed once, then went blank.

Amir slumped in his seat and sighed. 'Sorry, the link's dead.'

Then a cursor flashed in the top left corner.

'Hang on . . .' He straightened and smiled. 'I think we're in.'

Connor leant over his friend's shoulder as Amir began to tap away on the keyboard. 'This'll be like hunting for a needle in a haystack. It'll take some time –' Suddenly the cursor went haywire and streams of numbers began filling the screen. Amir swore, stabbing at the tablet's power button. The computer refused to power down.

'They're back-tracing all the IP addresses!' cried Amir as he tried to disconnect the flash drive to prevent corruption of the files. But the system was locked down. Amir picked up the tablet and smashed it repeatedly on the edge of the workbench until the computer was little more than fragments of circuit board.

'You're making a habit of that,' said Connor, eyeing the remains of the wrecked device strewn across the bench and floor.

'Old-fashioned kill switch,' said Amir, panting. He looked at Connor, a sheen of sweat on his brow. 'Sorry. Equilibrium blocked the back door and left a trap!'

'Did they locate us?' Connor was already reaching for his Go-bag and preparing to make a swift exit.

'I'd set up the Tor router over a VPN,' explained Amir, as if Connor knew what he was talking about. 'It *shouldn't* have been traceable. I'm pretty confident they didn't reverse-engineer the IPs all the way. Not in the time we were online.'

'Good,' said Connor, settling back down and dropping his Go-bag. 'Now, is there any other way to access their server?'

Amir looked along the workbench, cluttered with piles of electronic gear, a pair of sleek laptops and other high-tech surveillance equipment Bugsy had acquired. 'The only way would be a physical link. Someone would need to enter the Hive and plug a transmitter directly into the mainframe. But we'd have to be *crazy* to attempt that.'

Connor slid one of the laptops, along with a bunch of surveillance gear, over to Amir. 'As Sun Tzu once said, every plan is crazy before the battle, but sane in victory.'

Zhen's brow creased. 'I don't think he ever d–'

Connor kicked her shin under the table and smiled pointedly at her. 'Time to work out a plan.'

'Are you sure you're up to this?' said Connor from the rear seat of the auto-rickshaw that they'd temporarily 'borrowed' from a backstreet dealer. The rickshaw was parked round the corner from the 1933 Building, far enough away not to draw attention but close enough to communicate with the transmitter once it was installed.

Zhen nodded nervously. 'Neither of you can do this job. So I guess it's down to me.'

She wore the familiar black-and-orange jacket of a Sherpa fast-food delivery boy. Her long hair was tucked inside the biker helmet and she carried a black thermabag containing several pots of noodles. Staying out of sight in the rickshaw's rear cab, Connor and Amir had their baseball caps pulled down tight to the eyeline, their faces concealed behind pollution masks.

'*Test-1-2-3*,' whispered Amir into his head mic.

'I hear you,' said Zhen, tapping the side of the helmet on which Amir had inserted a discreet earpiece.

'Good. I'll guide you once you're inside.' Amir studied a blueprint of the Hive on his laptop's screen, detailing the layout of the building, its network of ventilation shafts and the CO_2 fire system that protected the array of computer servers. Then he pulled up a second window, a video feed showing Connor's masked face in close-up and real-time.

'Whoa, look away, Zhen – his face'll crack the screen!' joked Amir.

Connor elbowed his friend in the ribs as Zhen bent her gaze towards Amir instead. 'Good thing your face is covered too, Amir.'

'Well, at least we know the contact-lens camera is operational.' Amir tweaked the focus and colour contrast of the image. 'How does the contact lens feel, Zhen?'

She blinked several times. 'A little uncomfortable but OK.'

Their plan was bold and crazy. Rather than trying to sneak in, the idea was for Zhen to walk straight up to the front entrance in the guise of a delivery boy.

Connor slid the tiny transmitter into the lower seam of her jacket. 'Good luck, Zhen. If the situation gets out of control, just run for it.'

Anxiously clasping the thermabag to her chest, Zhen responded with a hesitant smile, then turned and strode off with her food delivery. The two of them watched her progress on the laptop as she rounded the corner, crossed the street and approached the imposing concrete entrance to the Hive.

Amir put his hand over the mic. 'This is a *stupid* plan,' he hissed to Connor. 'Zhen isn't trained for this.'

'But neither of us look Chinese,' Connor reminded his

friend. '*She* can infiltrate Equilibrium without raising suspicion.'

'Would you be willing to bet your life on that?' Amir pointed to the video feed showing two security guards intercepting Zhen by the front doors.

Connor's heart was in his mouth as their guide was questioned. The conversation was captured by the hidden mic in the metal zipper of her jacket and translated in real-time over the laptop's speakers.

'What's in the bag?' grunted one of the guards.

'Noodle delivery,' replied Zhen.

The guard ordered her to open the bag. Then he searched the contents, opening each pot. 'Smells good,' he said. 'Who's the delivery for?'

'Zhao Wu, Research and Development Department,' replied Zhen, using the name Amir had gleaned from a cybernetics file.

The other guard now patted her down. There was a scrunch as his hand passed over the zipper mic. While the helmet concealed her earpiece, Connor was growing ever more concerned that the transmitter would be discovered. Not able to see where the guard's hands were going, he held his breath in dread anticipation.

The first guard glared at Zhen. 'Are you *winking* at me?'

The video feed flickered as Zhen blinked rapidly, the contact lens clearly causing her irritation. 'Errm . . . no, just a bit of dirt in my eye.'

The other guard completed his body search and stepped away. Satisfied she was clean, he waved her through.

Connor resumed breathing. Fortune had been on their side this once, the transmitter too small to be felt amid the jacket's padding.

Zhen entered through the glass doors and approached the long sleek reception desk. The man behind it observed her with indifference.

'Noodle delivery for Zhao Wu,' she announced.

The man checked his computer, then narrowed his eyes at Zhen. 'Zhao Wu isn't working today.'

'Then . . . I guess you have free noodles!' said Zhen, plonking the pots and several pairs of chopsticks on his desk. 'It's already been paid for.'

The receptionist stuck out his lower lip and inspected the closest pot, giving it a sniff.

'Chicken,' said Zhen helpfully. As the man grabbed a pair of chopsticks and dug in, she asked, 'Can I use your toilet?'

'This *isn't* a public convenience,' said the man snootily, slurping up a long strand of noodle and dismissing her with a wave of his chopsticks.

'But I gave you free noodles,' she protested.

The receptionist ignored her and continued to wolf down his food.

Zhen hesitated, unsure what to do next.

'You *have* to get into that toilet,' Amir whispered to Zhen via the mic. 'It's our only access to the ground-floor server closet.'

Connor and Amir saw Zhen's hands reach up and remove her helmet.

'*Don't* show your face!' cried Connor. But it was too

late. He could picture her long black hair falling down over her shoulders. Now her face was in full view of the CCTV cameras, Equilibrium could identify her.

But her actions had the desired effect. The receptionist's indifferent attitude instantly changed. A cloying smile now graced his greasy lips.

'*Please*,' asked Zhen, her tone taking on a kittenish quality.

'Why, of course,' said the receptionist, only too keen to help the pretty young girl before him. 'Take your time. It's over there.' He jutted his greasy chin in the direction of a white door.

The man's eyes lingered on Zhen as she hurried over to the ladies' washroom, entered and locked the door behind her. There were three cubicles, a basin, a hand dryer and a full-length mirror. But there didn't appear to be any cameras in the room.

'You've got maybe three or four minutes before the receptionist starts getting suspicious,' said Amir. He studied the blueprint of the building on his laptop. 'Can you see the ventilation grille in the top-right corner of the ceiling?'

'Yes,' replied Zhen, hurrying to the far cubicle and clambering on top of the toilet seat. She unclipped the shoulder strap from the thermabag and used the metal fastener to prise open the cover, the grille swinging down on its hinges.

'Now you need to climb up and work your way two rooms across.'

'Good thing Zhen's doing this,' said Connor as their

guide pulled herself up and into the narrow shaft. 'I don't think I'd fit in there.'

They watched the screen go dark as Zhen entered the duct and began to crawl along. A rectangle of muted light appeared ahead as she wormed her way towards the first ventilation grille. In the room below they caught a glimpse of a man hunched over his computer. Zhen carried on, the screen going black again, only the sound of her breathing audible as she shuffled along the shaft.

'One minute gone,' said Connor.

Zhen came to the second grille and peered down. A small room could be seen with a tower of computer servers and switch panels. She forced open the ventilation panel, it swung free and she dropped to the floor.

'Good work,' said Amir. 'Now take the transmitter and plug it into a free socket in the back of a patch panel.'

Through the contact-lens camera, they saw Zhen remove the transmitter from her jacket's seam and approach the back of the server tower. A huge network of cables snaked between the multiple patch panels.

'There aren't any free sockets,' whispered Zhen as her fingers sifted through the cables.

'Then pull out a patch cable and stick the transmitter there,' instructed Amir.

'Which one?'

'Any one.'

'Two minutes,' warned Connor, checking his watch.

Zhen yanked out a cable and replaced it with the

transmitter device. Then she hurried back to the ventilation duct. 'I can't reach the vent!' she muttered in panic.

'Find something to stand on,' suggested Amir. They could only watch as she frantically looked around. Then in one corner she spotted a large bin and positioned it upside down beneath the grille. Stepping on top, she reached up but was still only just too short. Zhen made a jump for the opening, her fingers catching hold of the lip of the shaft. With grunts and strains, she managed to pull herself up.

'Well done,' said Connor as they listened to her panting in the echoing darkness of the ventilation duct. 'But you need to hurry. Three minutes are up.'

'What about the bin?' she asked, glancing down at the floor where it lay tipped over for anyone to see.

'Nothing you can do about that,' said Amir. 'Close the grille and go.'

The video feed jerked and jolted as Zhen wriggled her way back towards the washroom. As she neared its ventilation opening, they could hear banging. The pounding grew more insistent with each passing second.

'Hey! You still in there?' came a shout from the other side of the washroom door.

Zhen slid out of the ventilation duct and landed on the toilet seat. 'Yes!' she called, pushing the grille back into place and flushing the cistern. 'Be out in a minute.'

She dusted down her jacket, shook the dirt from her hair and rinsed her hands of grime. Then, grabbing the thermabag just as the door was remotely unlocked, she emerged from the washroom to be greeted by the scowling face of the receptionist.

'What took you so long?' he demanded.

'Sorry,' she said, clasping her stomach and grimacing. 'Must've been those noodles I had last night.'

The man's expression morphed to one of queasiness as he examined his own pot of noodles.

Zhen left in a hurry, not looking back or at the security guards as she exited the building. By the time she returned to the rickshaw, Amir had already linked up the laptop to the transmitter.

'Great job,' said Amir. 'We're in!'

Connor grinned at Zhen and patted her on the shoulder. 'You'd make a fine spy,' he said.

'I think I'd rather be a bodyguard,' she replied, trying to steady her trembling hands. 'Less dangerous.'

'Not in my experience,' said Connor.

Amir tapped away at the keyboard. 'OK, I've full access to Equilibrium's databases and security systems.'

On the screen he pulled up a matrix of CCTV feeds from within the Hive. White-coated technicians and doctors could be seen scurrying around like lab rats along the warren of concrete corridors and 'air bridges'. Rows of unidentified and identical white doors were kept under constant surveillance, checking people in and out; yet none of the rooms behind those doors appeared to have cameras, their secrets remaining secret. A view of the lobby area revealed the receptionist tucking into another pot of noodles at his desk, greed obviously having overcome his nausea. And, in another frame, a small cell-like room held a silver-haired man who lay shuddering on a cruelly narrow bench.

Connor peered closer. 'That's Colonel Black!'

CHAPTER 42

'Entering the Hive once was crazy, going in *twice* is insane!' exclaimed Amir as Connor kitted himself out with his own contact-lens camera, earpiece and throat mic.

'If we save the colonel *and* locate the others, Equilibrium will hold no power over us. We're back in control,' argued Connor, handing Amir the flash drive for safekeeping. He clambered out of the rickshaw.

Amir grabbed his arm. 'Our plan was to hack into their systems and locate the shipping container our friends are being held in. Nothing more. Beyond that we're jeopardizing the entire operation.'

Connor shook Amir off and rifled through his Go-bag for the iStun phone and XT tactical torch. 'At that time we didn't know where Colonel Black was or what state he was in. This may be our *only* chance to save his life.'

Amir threw up his hands. 'I realize that! But think about what you're doing first. Zhen going in was a risk, but *you* – they're on the hunt for you. How do you plan to get past the guards? As a Western-faced delivery boy? I don't think so.'

'You've access to Equilibrium's security systems, haven't you?' asked Connor, slipping the torch and iStun into his pockets. Amir nodded. 'So we play them at their own game. Deactivate the alarms, then direct me when inside and cover my tracks.'

Amir shook his head in defeat. 'I now see why your previous assignments were all so *eventful*. You're willing to risk everything for one person.'

Connor shrugged. 'I suppose it's the reason why my Principals are still alive.' Then he remembered Eduardo and his face clouded over. 'Well, almost all. Now, can you override the security systems or not?'

Amir sighed heavily. 'Yes. I can disable the CCTV cameras and unlock the doors, but only for a few seconds at a time. Otherwise a security officer is bound to notice.' He pulled up a three-dimensional interactive map of the Hive on-screen, numerous blue dots moving around the various levels. 'The Hive's security tracking system,' he explained. 'It monitors everyone's movements in the building. But I can mask your presence. I can also track you with your thermic smartband and plot your location on to this plan.' He pointed to a room near the top level. 'This is where I think the colonel's being held, judging by CCTV camera reference. I'll guide you there.'

'Thanks,' said Connor, glancing at the wafer-thin electronic band on his wrist. The bio-display showed his heart rate as elevated to ninety-five beats per minute. He was sure that would rise during the coming rescue operation.

'Do you want my jacket and helmet too?' asked Zhen.

Connor shook his head. 'I'm going in the back entrance. No disguises this time. I'll have to rely on evasion, rather than deception.'

'Good luck then,' said Zhen with a tense smile. 'And if the situation gets out of control . . . just run for it.'

Connor let out a laugh. 'Don't worry, I intend to.'

He jogged down a side alley and worked his way round to the back of the 1933 Building. He knew Amir was right. He was gambling everything to rescue the colonel, endangering all of them *and* the flash drive. But he owed it to Colonel Black to do all that he could. Connor recalled a story the colonel had once told him about his father in the SAS – how Justin Reeves had disobeyed a direct order to save the colonel's life, living by the decree: *no man is left behind on the battlefield*. Connor wanted to be his father's son and wasn't going to leave any man behind, especially not the colonel. Having discovered that Equilibrium was responsible for his father's death, he had no intention of letting them kill his surrogate father too.

'Amir, are you reading me?' he asked as he crouched behind a large refuse bin in the rear service yard. The area was unguarded, but monitored from all angles by CCTV.

'*Loud and clear.*'

'I'm by the bins at the rear. Can you cut the cameras and unlock the door?'

'*Done in . . . 3 . . . 2 . . . 1 . . . Go!*'

Connor sprinted from his hiding place and over to the back entrance. The electronic lock beeped green as he approached. He yanked the door open and darted inside

the Hive. He was greeted by a cool waft of air conditioning and the hum of a generator. The room appeared to be
a general storage area and dump zone for rubbish and
recycling before it was transferred to the bins outside.
Sprouting from the ceiling, a CCTV camera was directed
at the rear door.

'*Straight ahead and up the stairs,*' Amir instructed in
his ear. '*Hurry! Remember I can only override the system
for a few seconds at a time.*'

Connor rushed across the room to the opposite door,
waited for the coded digital lock to go green and entered a
deserted corridor. The walls and floor were all grey concrete, broken regularly by white-panelled doorways. He
heard voices echoing from the far end of the corridor.

'*Move!*' urged Amir.

Connor bounded up the staircase ahead of him. He was
almost on to the next landing when Amir warned, '*Stop!
Two hostiles approaching from left.*'

Connor hunkered down in the stairwell, praying they
wouldn't spot him. His smartband was now peaking at a
heart rate of a hundred and sixty beats per minute and he
could hear the blood pounding in his ears. A pair of white-
coated technicians strolled past the staircase, too engrossed
in their discussion to even look his way.

'*All clear,*' whispered Amir. '*Turn left at the landing,
then over the second air bridge on your right.*'

Connor dashed up the last few steps and along to the air
bridge. He glanced up and his breath was taken away by
the sheer complexity of the internal structure of the 1933

Building. The central atrium was a cat's-cradle of concrete walkways and bridges to numerous levels and rooms, spiralling all the way up to a glass ceiling. But the confusion of ramps, bridges and corridors played to Connor's advantage. Like a mouse in a maze, he'd be able to evade the other people walking around the building.

He scampered over the air bridge and up a ramp to the next level.

'*Follow the balcony to the end, then up the spiral staircase,*' instructed Amir.

Connor raced along but as he was about to ascend the staircase Amir hissed, '*Down to the next level, quick!*'

Doing as his friend instructed, Connor heard footsteps on the stairs behind him. He bounded down and kept going, past the ground level towards the basement.

'*No, stop!*'

Connor froze, his ears listening to the ever-approaching footsteps.

'*Wait . . . wait . . .*'

Pressing himself against the wall, Connor fought the overriding urge to run and flee. Against all his instinct he stayed where he was –

'*OK, retrace your steps. They've gone a different direction.*'

Hearing the footsteps fade, Connor breathed a sigh of relief and tore back up to the spiral staircase.

'*Two more levels to go.*'

His heart thudding in his chest, Connor took the steps two at a time. But he was forced to leave the stairwell early as another lab technician descended towards him. Under Amir's direction, Connor shot down a corridor lined with white-panelled doors, a mystery concealed behind each one.

'*Back! Back!*' ordered Amir. '*Hostiles up ahead.*'

Connor spun on his heels and rapidly retreated. He heard Amir swear in his ear at the same time as a door further along the corridor began to swing open.

'*Quick, through the door on your left,*' hissed Amir as voices converged on both sides of Connor, threatening to entrap him.

Connor darted over and wrenched on the handle, diving through the doorway just as two security guards entered the corridor and a technician stepped out.

'No! The *other* left!' cried Amir. But it was too late. Connor had already bolted inside the room and closed the door behind him. And he wasn't alone.

'*Connor?*' said a surprised voice.

CHAPTER 43

Connor slowly turned round, as if his whole world was moving at half speed. The room was painted a stark medical white, the only decoration a Chinese watercolour of far-off misty mountains on one plain wall. A hospital bed, its sheets crisply turned down, protruded into the centre of the room, a doctor's report on a clipboard hanging from the end rail. On the floor lay a yoga mat and a pair of resistance bands. Cluttering up the bedside table was a mobile phone, a bottle of water, a half-used blister pack of painkillers and a well-thumbed paperback book. A second door was partly open, leading to an en-suite shower room from which Connor caught the sharp whiff of disinfectant. And by the window, sunlight glistening off the sheen of her beach-blonde hair, sat Charley in her wheelchair.

'What are *you* doing here?' she cried.

Connor stood in front of her, dumbstruck and motionless.

A smile spread across her face like sunshine. 'Not that I'm unhappy to see you. I mean, I thought I'd spotted you the other day, on the street outside – only I convinced myself my mind was playing tricks on me. But you're actually *here*. Connor, I've missed you so much.'

'*Careful, Connor,*' Amir whispered in his earpiece. '*Don't fall for any more of her tricks!*'

But Charley's heartfelt smile made Connor want to surrender and he battled hard against his natural instinct to believe her every word. He'd seen the video of her betrayal, heard Mr Grey's confirmation that she'd colluded with Equilibrium and been duped once before by her deception on the phone. He *couldn't* allow himself to fall for her wiles again, however sincere she appeared now. Then her smile faded and her expression became strained and unnatural, as if she was trying to burn a hole through the wall with her eyes. Lifting herself up from the chair by her arms, Charley rose unsteadily until she was standing before him, unsupported.

'Well?' she said, spreading her arms. 'Where's my hug?'

Connor didn't know whether to be more shocked that she'd betrayed them or that she was apparently no longer paralysed.

Charley's expectant expression faltered. 'Cat got your tongue? I know . . . it's truly amazing. I can *stand*! The doctors have implanted a neuro-chip into my brain along with graphene receptors into my lower spine. They communicate wirelessly, skipping the injured section of my spinal cord, so allowing me to regain some control over my legs. Look, I'll show you.'

'*That's all part of Equilibrium's cybernetics programme,*'

hissed Amir as Charley's face creased in concentration. *'She must have sold us out in return for this therapy!'*

Connor finally found the words to speak. 'You betrayed us . . . so you could walk again?'

Charley blinked and frowned, swaying as if struck by a thunderbolt. 'Wh-what did you say?'

She attempted a step towards him, but stumbled and fell forward. Connor instinctively rushed to her aid, catching her before she hit the ground. They landed in an awkward embrace on the floor – her soft warm skin against his, the sweet scent of her hair in the air, her mesmerizing sky-blue eyes looking into his. As he held her in his arms, his resistance began to crumble. How could this wonderful girl have betrayed anyone?

'Connor!' barked Amir in his ear. *'Remember she's a manipulator – a traitor. You can't believe her act.'*

'Thanks for catching me,' Charley gasped, a bead of sweat running down her cheek. 'I shouldn't really have attempted that without a walking frame. I just wanted to impress you. I'm not fooling myself. I can't walk, not yet. I need crutches, and then I can only take a few paces at a time. But it's progress. Real progress. There'll be years of physio and rehabilitation ahead – five, maybe more, I'm told. It's going to take a great deal of sacrifice –'

'Sacrifice?' interrupted Connor. 'You sacrificed everyone in Buddyguard!'

Charley stared at him, uncomprehending and shocked. 'Connor . . . what are you talking about? Has something dreadful happened?'

'*Don't* play games with me,' he snapped, extracting himself from her embrace and standing up. 'We spoke only yesterday and you let slip about Zhen. I know you're in league with Equilibrium.'

'*Equilibrium?*' Charley propped herself up on her hands, a hurt and baffled expression on her face. 'I haven't spoken to you in over a week! Not since that party with the fireworks. I thought you were too involved in your Mexican assignment, or else had lost interest in me . . . like Blake did.'

She lowered her gaze. Although Connor had never met Blake, the recruit having left Buddyguard soon after he joined, he knew that Blake had been Charley's boyfriend prior to her accident.

'I wouldn't have blamed you,' Charley went on, her voice now a wounded whisper. 'I realize I've been focused on my treatment and we haven't seen each other for ages. But I don't understand . . .' She looked up again, fearful and confused. 'What's all this talk about betrayal? I haven't done any–'

'*Connor, she's playing you,*' said Amir. '*Keeping you occupied until back-up arrives. There's someone heading for your room. You have to –*'

The door swung open and a doctor strode in. He clocked Charley on the floor, then glared at Connor. 'Who are *you?*'

Connor drew the iStun from his pocket. The doctor rushed towards an alarm button on the wall. But Connor intercepted and jabbed the iStun into the man's side. The doctor jerked, convulsed, then collapsed to the ground. Before he could recover from the debilitating shock, Connor struck him in the neck, momentarily cutting off the blood supply to his brain and knocking the man out cold.

'Why did you do that?' exclaimed Charley, her eyes wide and horrified as he now stripped the doctor of his lab coat and ID card. 'He's my consultant!'

Snatching up the resistance bands, Connor began to bind the man's wrists and feet. He glanced sidelong at Charley. 'Well, if you didn't speak to me the other day, then who did?'

Charley ran both her hands through her hair, pulling at her roots, and shot him a desperate look. 'Honestly, Connor, it wasn't me. My phone's not been working for the past week. Try it yourself if you don't believe me.' She hauled herself back into her chair. Tears stung her eyes. 'I haven't seen you for ages and you burst in here acting all crazy. I've no idea what's going on, why you're here, why you're accusing me of betrayal . . . why you've just knocked my consultant out! Please, *please* explain what's going on.'

Connor finished tying up the doctor, then checked the corridor for more hostiles before closing the door. 'This place – your spinal research centre – is a front for the head-quarters of Equilibrium.'

Charley was stunned into silence.

'Don't pretend you didn't know,' said Connor.

'You mean . . . the criminal organization that was involved with Viktor Malkov?'

Connor nodded. 'Him, and countless other corrupt people around the world. They're responsible for multiple major terrorist attacks. And *you* revealed the location of Buddyguard headquarters to them, along with all our security details. Because of that, people are dead – Steve, Bugsy, and maybe soon the colonel and the rest of our friends – Buddyguard is no more, thanks to you!'

'Steve and Bugsy are . . . *dead*?' Charley's hands gripped the bars of her chair, tightening until her knuckles were white. A shudder ran through her and she fell silent, staring at the floor for a long while.

'Charley, you're not fooling anyone. I've seen the video of you telling Equilibrium everything, even your access codes! Now drop the act.'

Slowly, as if the strain of raising her head was almost too much to bear, she lifted her eyes to meet Connor's. 'I've . . . had bad dreams, nightmares where I thought I said stuff . . . secrets I knew I should never reveal . . . but I thought that was just the side-effects of the drugs the doctors were giving me. They made me hazy and my thoughts sluggish for a while. I couldn't quite tell reality apart. Are you telling me I *did* say those things?'

Connor nodded. *If she's acting*, he thought, *then she's doing a convincing job.*

Tears welled in Charley's eyes. 'No . . . no . . . I can't have . . .' She stared pleadingly at Connor. 'They must have drugged me or something. I didn't mean to . . . I wouldn't ever . . . I could *never* betray Buddyguard . . . or you! You *have* to believe me.'

Connor looked her in the eyes and saw only truth: a shell-shocked realization that her nightmare confessions had been real, a searing grief and pain at the tragic fate of her friends and tutors, and a burning guilt and shame for failing to protect those she cared for. There was no way Charley could fake *that* reaction.

Amir seemed to recognize it too. *'It's entirely plausible that she could've been given a truth drug.'*

Connor recalled the video: in hindsight, her eyes had appeared glassy and unfocused, her manner slightly delirious and odd. 'But what about the phone call?' he whispered into his throat mic. 'That was Charley, wasn't it?'

'Not necessarily,' Amir replied. *'Another of Equilibrium's AI projects is voice cloning. Mr Grey could've used an imprint of her voice to talk to you. To try to manipulate you to hand over the drive.'*

Connor thought about their conversation. When had Charley ever been so self-centred that she only cared about herself? That wasn't like her at all. It *had* to have been Mr Grey on the other end of the line.

'Wh-who are you talking to?' asked Charley, her voice hitching.

'Amir,' he replied.

Charley bowed her head. 'He must hate me too . . .'

'He doesn't hate you,' said Connor, kneeling down beside her and wrapping his arms round her heaving shoulders as she wept. 'Nor do I. We believe you. We know it's not your fault. Equilibrium used you, took advantage of your disability and exploited your vulnerability to –'

'*Connor, more hostiles are headed your way,*' interrupted Amir.

'Charley, grab your things,' ordered Connor. 'We have to get you *and* Colonel Black out of here. Now!'

CHAPTER 44

'You don't need to push me,' said Charley as Connor wheeled her towards the door. 'I can do that myself.'

The urgency of their predicament and her own resilience to tragedy had enabled Charley to regain her composure for their escape, and she was once more her assertive and commanding self. Connor felt reassured by this; it was one of the many aspects he admired about her.

'I know, but I need to look like I'm doing something,' he whispered, his voice muffled behind the surgical mask he now wore. Besides concealing his face, he'd donned the white lab coat and scrub cap that he'd taken from the hog-tied doctor. At a glance he looked like any of the other countless Equilibrium employees wandering the rat-run of the Hive.

'Then walk beside me with the clipboard,' instructed Charley, handing him the medical report from the end of her bed. 'The techs here are used to seeing me get around by myself.'

Having gathered only her essentials, Charley propelled her chair out of the room. Connor closed the door behind them just as two security guards rounded the corner. He tensed, readying himself to fight or flee. The two men approached and Charley greeted them brightly. 'Nǐmén hǎo.'

The guards grunted in response. One of them asked her a question in Chinese. Charley replied fluently, while Connor kept his head bent, as if buried in the medical notes. He felt the guards' watchful eyes upon him, but didn't risk looking up. They'd see the shape of his eyes and immediately know he wasn't Chinese.

Charley continued to talk with the two men. Not understanding a word, Connor started to sweat – were they interrogating her or passing the time of day? And when had she become so competent in Chinese?

Then Charley bid the two men goodbye and glided off. Connor kept pace at her side, playing the role of the preoccupied doctor. His status seemed to preclude any necessity to speak to the guards, for which he was grateful. They turned the corner and left the two security men behind.

'What were they asking you?' hissed Connor.

'Where I was going,' replied Charley. 'I told them to the gymnasium. I'm there most days so it shouldn't raise any suspicions.'

'How come you speak Chinese so well?' asked Connor.

Charley glanced sideways at him. 'I've had a lot of time on my hands in between surgery and physio. That, and the fact I used to speak Chinese with Kerry. You know, my friend who was abducted.'

Connor nodded. She'd once told him all about Kerry,

whose kidnapping was one of the reasons Charley had become a buddyguard in the first place.

Amir's voice came through on his earpiece. '*Up one flight, then third door along the left-hand gallery.*'

'Got it,' replied Connor, relaying the directions to Charley.

'Follow me,' said Charley. Familiar with the complex layout of the Hive, she passed the spiral staircase cornering the vast atrium and headed towards an air bridge that sloped steeply up to the next level. A couple of technicians passed them with no more than a brief acknowledgement.

'Isn't there a lift?' asked Connor under his breath, glancing around for an easier route.

'On the other side, but we don't have time for that,' replied Charley. 'Besides, my chair's powered – remember? And I've been doing a *lot* of physio.'

Connor could tell by the definition in her arm muscles that she'd been training even harder than usual. She took the slope without even having to engage the electric motor. Her wheelchair had been provided by Colonel Black following the tragic end to her last assignment and had been specially designed for close-protection work and hostile environments. Aside from the rechargeable electric motor for an emergency getaway, the chair was equipped with carbon-fibre off-road wheels and run-flat tyres. There was a first-aid trauma kit and three flash-bang smoke grenades stored under the seat. The seat cushion itself, back panel and sides were constructed from Kevlar plates to protect the user against bullets. And, if that wasn't enough, the armrests could be converted into *tonfa* batons for combat situations. The wheelchair was a virtual embodiment of Charley herself – tough, resourceful and a force to be reckoned with.

They reached the next level unchallenged and made their way along to the third doorway. It looked no different from the rows of other nondescript white doors that lined each of the six levels.

'Are you sure this is it?' Connor whispered to Amir.

'Matches the CCTV reference, plus there's a double-layer of security,' replied Amir. *'I've killed the camera, but I'm having trouble overriding the lock. Keep getting forced out . . .'*

'Well, hurry up!' urged Connor. 'Someone's coming.'

He heard Amir's furious typing over his earpiece at the same time as the voices grew louder from the direction of the air bridge. Charley exchanged an anxious glance with him. 'I don't usually come up here,' she said. 'Not sure how I'll explain this . . .'

Connor looked towards the bridge. The top of a woman's head was just visible, along with two other people. She was turning their way –

'Got it!' exclaimed Amir. The coded lock turned green, Connor opened the door and both he and Charley bolted inside. But in their desperation to evade the woman they ran straight into a guard manning a security station within the room.

Startled at their sudden entrance, he rose from his seat and barked a question in Chinese. Rolling closer, Charley replied in what sounded an apologetic tone. The guard clearly wasn't convinced – he went for the radio on his hip. Charley whipped out the right armrest of her chair and smashed the metal bar across his wrist, forcing him to drop the radio. The guard now reached for his gun. Without a pause in her attack, Charley swung her baton into the man's gut. The guard doubled over with a *whoosh* of pained breath. Then she brought the end down hard and fast on to the back of the man's head. There was a skull-splitting *thunk* and the guard dropped in an unconscious heap to the floor.

Connor stared in awe at Charley. 'You've certainly perfected *that* move since you last tried it on Richie!'

Charley reinserted the handle. 'A girl's got to let off steam somehow.'

'*Sorry,*' said Amir's voice in Connor's ear. '*I'd assumed the guard was Colonel Black on the Hive's monitoring system. The colonel must be in the adjoining room. The temperature registers minus four degrees! That's some air conditioning. It must be the reason the signal's disrupted.*'

Through a one-way mirror, Connor and Charley could see a body shuddering on a narrow bench under the glare of a neon strip light. Amir unlocked the inner door to the cell. A blast of sub-zero air hit them. The room was as cold as a meat freezer, chilling them both to the bone as they went inside.

'*Colonel?*' asked Charley, her voice soft and full of concern.

Colonel Black weakly raised his head. His face was a

mess, his nose broken, one eye swollen and several teeth missing. A bandage caked in dried blood was wrapped around the bullet wound in his shoulder. Through his one good eye, he glared at Charley.

'*YOU! YOU TRAITOR!*' he spluttered, lunging for her like a wild dog.

Connor leapt between them. Even though the colonel was enfeebled, he was a heavyset man and Connor had to use all his strength to hold him back. 'NO! Charley's no traitor. They drugged her.'

Colonel Black snarled at him. 'I wouldn't believe *anything* you people say!'

'It's me, Colonel! It's me!' said Connor, removing his surgical mask.

'*Connor?*' he gasped, his one good eye flaring wide. Then all the remaining fight drained out of him and he slumped to his knees.

Connor did his best to hold the colonel up.

'What are you doing *here*, Connor?' spat Colonel Black. 'You swore to me you'd deliver the drive to Stella.'

Taken aback by the colonel's anger, Connor replied, 'We've come to rescue you.'

'I told you sacrifices have to be made,' he growled. 'You disobeyed a direct order!'

'Getting the drive out of the country proved harder than anticipated,' explained Connor. 'Now come on – we haven't much time!'

But Colonel Black didn't move. And Connor couldn't lift him.

'I'm not ... worth rescuing, Connor,' he rasped. 'They've broken me. I don't have the will or strength ...'

'*Get up!*' ordered Connor. 'You're SAS. You're trained to survive. To overcome.'

Connor tried to yank the former soldier to his feet. But the colonel was as heavy and cumbersome as a sack of dirt. There was no life left in him. 'Leave me ... Connor. Get the drive to ...' He trailed off into semi-consciousness.

Charley reached under her seat for her trauma kit. She pulled out an auto-injector and handed it to Connor. 'Give this to him.'

'What is it?' asked Connor.

'Adrenalin. It should boost his system, at least enough to get him out of here.'

Connor jabbed the injector into the colonel's thigh and he came round with a start. His respiratory rate accelerated, clarity returned to his vision and strength seemed to seep into his muscles. The colonel sat up and gave Connor a lop-sided grin. 'You just won't let me die, will you?'

'No man is left behind on the battlefield, right?' said Connor, helping him to his feet.

'You're as stubborn as your father!' The colonel laughed, shaking his head. 'He once saved me; now it's his son!'

'I'll take that as a compliment.'

They staggered out of the bitterly cold cell together, Charley following close behind. The guard was groaning, slowly coming round.

'He'll raise the alarm if we don't deal with him,' warned Colonel Black.

Connor leant the colonel against a wall for support, Charley staying at his side. Then, taking the guard under the arms, Connor dragged the dazed man into the cell. Panting with effort, he dumped him on the chilled floor. Locking the cell door behind him, Connor whispered into his throat mic, 'Anyone in the corridor?'

His earpiece was hit by a burst of static, then Amir's panicked voice came over the airwaves. 'My connection to the Hive's been cut! *Get out of there NOW!*'

Connor heard a pained groan and spun round. Colonel Black was doubled over. Connor watched in disbelief as Charley raised her arm to strike the colonel again.

'NO!' Connor cried, rushing forward to stop her. But he was too late. She knife-handed Colonel Black in the neck and knocked him senseless.

Connor dived at Charley. Suddenly standing, her hand shot out at lightning speed and she caught him by the throat. Stopped dead in his tracks, to Connor her strength was unimaginable, overpowering him and bringing him to his knees.

'*No . . . Charley!*' he spluttered in despair, feeling his windpipe being crushed. Gasping for breath, he clawed at her outstretched arm. But it was no use. Her elbow was locked and her muscles tense as steel. The pressure only increased. As his strength leeched away, Connor stared pleadingly at Charley, unable to fathom her treachery even as tears spilt down her cheeks. Then darkness seeped into his vision and he slipped from consciousness . . .

CHAPTER 45

'The bait worked,' announced Mr Grey, presenting Connor and Colonel Black to the Director. The colonel swayed on his feet, head bowed, the effects of the adrenalin having worn off. Connor himself still felt light-headed, his throat bruised and sore, Charley's fingernails having gouged deep marks into his neck.

The Director sat ramrod-straight and regal behind a metal-framed desk, its feet like talons and its dark polished surface like a shield. Her personal office occupied the entire upper floor of the 1933 Building. The heart of the Hive, the immense chamber was built upon a reinforced glass floor, giving the illusion that the room floated over the plunging central atrium below. Through the tinted glazing at his feet Connor could see white-coated lab technicians scurrying around like worker bees, dutifully carrying out the bidding of their queen. Above his head a large round skylight illuminated the room, spotlighting him and the colonel as they were held at gunpoint by Mr Grey and three armed guards. The roof itself was supported by an intricate lattice of steel beams, criss-crossing the ceiling and reinforcing the unsettling impression of the Director as a black widow spider at the centre of an insidious web.

The Director acknowledged Mr Grey with the faintest of nods, then turned her predatory gaze upon her captives. She directed a viper's smile at Charley. 'Yet again I'm grateful for all your help.'

Connor shot Charley a spiteful look. *How could I have been so wrong about her?* He'd believed Charley with all his heart when she'd said that she hadn't willingly betrayed him or Buddyguard. In that moment he thought he'd seen into her soul, glimpsed her true and pure nature. But her actions had proved her to be a deceiver of the cruellest kind. A traitor without a heart or a soul. Someone, if it were possible, even more evil than Mr Grey.

'I *didn't* help you!' Charley protested, a fierce and desperate expression on her face, her eyes blazing at the Director. 'I *never* helped you!' She turned imploringly to Connor and the colonel. 'You *must* believe me. I had no control over what I was doing. I would never help Equilibrium.'

The Director waved her objection away. 'You may not have *wanted* to help. But you've been crucial to this operation's success. During your surgery you gave up all Buddyguard's secrets. You've helped lure Connor here, even lent your voice to his entrapment. But, most beneficial of all, you've enabled my scientists to perform the first human trial with the neuro-chip. A resounding success, I would say.'

The Director turned to Connor. 'Did Charley explain her miraculous surgery to you?'

Connor glared at the imperious woman. 'It'll allow her to walk,' he said bitterly.

'Oh, it does a lot more than that,' replied the Director with a smirk. 'The neuro-chip in her brain communicates via wireless signals to the graphene receptors in her lower spinal cord. Wireless signals that can be intercepted and overridden.' The Director fished out a small handheld device from her jacket pocket, the size and shape of a smartphone.

'What's that?' Charley asked breathlessly.

'My technicians call it a *neuro-controller*,' replied the Director. 'Not very imaginative, but accurate.' She ran her forefinger across the device's screen. Charley's arm involuntarily shot up in the air and stayed there.

The blood drained from Charley's cheeks. '*What* have you done to me?'

'Given you the chance to walk again,' said the Director. 'So *don't* be ungrateful. Your rehabilitation has to come at a price, though. That price is *control*. And I'm your master.'

She tapped another command into the device and Charley stood up, stiff and sharp. Connor saw the sheer terror in Charley's eyes at being physically manipulated against her will. He now understood that Charley had *never* been a traitor. That her attack on him and the colonel had been engineered by the Director and her technicians. All his despair, sorrow and anger at Charley disappeared in an instant. Instead he was flooded with guilt that he'd doubted her. He realized that the only one to be betrayed in all this was Charley herself – betrayed by her doctors who'd made her a lab rat for Equilibrium's bio-mechanical experiments.

Charley stood looking down at her legs. Legs that were no more hers than when they were paralysed. 'If that's the price for me to walk again, then it isn't a price worth paying!' she spat.

The Director sighed. 'It's a shame you feel that way.' She swiped her finger across the device and Charley collapsed to the floor – just like a marionette whose strings had been cut.

Connor ran to Charley's side and helped her back into her wheelchair. He could feel her body trembling with shock. 'Are you all right?' he asked.

Charley shied away, looking at him as if scared she might harm him again. 'Connor . . . I'm sorry,' she murmured, her voice hitching. 'I tried to stop myself, but I couldn't. I thought I'd killed you . . .'

'No need for tears, Charley,' said the Director. 'You're the cutting edge of technology now, the first in a generation of enhanced humans under Equilibrium's control. You're the future! Unfortunately, your friends here don't have so much of a future.'

Pocketing the neuro-controller, the Director tossed a tiny transmitter on to her desk. 'We found your pathetic little surveillance device. You really should tidy up after yourselves. It was disappointingly sloppy work, especially after such a bold and daring infiltration into our head-quarters. To be honest, I was surprised that you decided to return. Don't get me wrong. It was a valiant attempt to rescue Colonel Black. But would you have risked all if you *really* knew him?'

Connor stiffened. 'What do you mean?' He looked side-ways at the colonel, who was struggling to stay standing.

'Have you never questioned Colonel Black's motives?' asked the Director.

'Why should I?'

The Director drummed a finger on the armrest of her steel chair. 'Well, he's recruiting *young* teenagers like your-self to be bodyguards. To act as shields to the offspring of the rich and famous. That would seem morally question-able to most people.'

'Depends upon your point of view,' Connor shot back. 'Terrorist organizations like yours make us a necessity.'

The Director shrugged. 'But who's to say your life is any less valuable than that of a spoilt rich kid's?'

'They're not always spoilt,' argued Connor. 'Often they're victims of their family's situation, of circumstances beyond their control.'

'That doesn't change the fact you're risking your life for another. That makes you a victim too. Can't you see what the colonel's doing here is *wrong*?'

'No, what we're doing is right!' Connor insisted, becom-ing angry at the Director's line of questioning. 'Protecting the innocent from the likes of *you*. Saving lives.'

The Director tutted and shook her head at his naivety.

She pointed at Colonel Black, who appeared to be on the verge of collapse. 'This man has exploited you. Profited from you. Deceived you. Tricked you!'

Connor took the colonel's arm, doing his best to hold him up. 'The only one into deception here is you,' he replied. 'I wasn't forced to become a buddyguard. I chose to.'

'Did you?' The Director stood up and strode round her metal desk, her steel-tipped heels clicking on the polished glass floor. 'What if I told you that the colonel searches for talented yet *vulnerable* teenagers. Ones without strong family ties. Ones with nothing to lose. Ones with death wishes. Or weaknesses that can be exploited.'

'I wouldn't believe you,' said Connor. 'He selects us on our natural instinct to do good, to protect others.'

The Director gave him a sympathetic yet pitying smile. 'I bet he used your late father to entrap you. Perhaps he even set up a fake incident to convince you of your aptitude for such dangerous work.'

Connor didn't reply. But the silence was answer enough. That was exactly what the colonel had done.

Colonel Black rallied himself and glared at the Director. 'Connor, don't listen to her. She's trying to manipulate you. Turn you against me! She's –'

The guard at his shoulder struck him in the lower back with the butt of his gun and the colonel dropped to his knees, wheezing.

'No, *you're* the manipulator, Colonel Black,' continued the Director, circling the weak and battered colonel. 'Connor, this man gambles with your life for his own profit. The clients who engage Buddyguard pay a small fortune for your services.'

'And we're well rewarded for our work,' Connor defended, thinking of the thousands of pounds that had been spent on medical care for his mother.

'Not nearly enough!' barked the Director. 'In truth, you're nothing but walking targets. *Bulletcatchers* for the sons and daughters of the high and mighty.'

'We're trained for the job!' Connor argued. 'Equipped with the most advanced self-defence gear. We have full support too. The risks are minimized.'

'But not eliminated! When you get injured on an assignment, the colonel awards you with a pat on the back and a gold badge?' The Director bent her gaze towards Charley. 'Is a *badge* really worth such personal sacrifice, Charley? Can that badge ever replace your legs?'

Charley kept her mouth shut, but stinging tears crept into the corners of her eyes.

'Of course not! So why should either of you show loyalty to Colonel Black? Especially when he's hiding darker secrets from you both.'

Connor felt his breath catch in his throat. 'What secrets?'

The Director stopped circling the colonel and approached Charley. 'Have you ever wondered where the recruit Blake disappeared to?'

Charley flinched in her chair at the mention of her former boyfriend's name. Connor's attention was caught too.

'Blake didn't *disappear*. He went home,' said Charley.

The Director gave a pitying shake of her head. 'No, Blake died on a mission. Killed in action.'

Charley's eyes widened in disbelieving shock. Connor swallowed hard, his mouth suddenly dry.

'Of course, you wouldn't know about that, because it would be bad for morale,' continued the Director. 'Recruits *don't* die. You're told they've gone home, been relocated or are on a long assignment. To date three recruits have lost their lives on Buddyguard missions. More than ten have been injured, four seriously and one –' she looked at Charley – 'permanently.'

Both Connor and Charley were stunned into silence. Then Connor asked the colonel, 'Is this true?'

Colonel Black hung his head. 'Yes.'

Connor felt a knot tightening in his stomach. Charley's cheeks flushed with anger.

'But that's not the secret I'm really talking about,' said the Director, a sly smile spreading across her lips as the first seeds of doubt were sown. 'I bet Colonel Black told you that Buddyguard is highly classified. That you couldn't inform anyone in the interests of national security. That his organization is tied to your government's security and intelligence service.'

'Yes, he did,' said Connor. 'So what?'

'Well, your precious colonel isn't exactly being truthful.'

Connor turned to Colonel Black for an explanation, but he refused to meet his eye.

'Correct me if I'm wrong, Colonel,' the Director said. 'Buddyguard was originally sanctioned by the British government's Department for National Security, but the project was shelved. Too great a political gamble if the media got wind of it. However, *you* revived the project on a private-contract basis.'

Connor stared in shock and disbelief at the colonel. 'You mean it's *unauthorized*?'

Colonel Black cleared his throat. 'Officially, at least.'

CHAPTER 46

'*Officially, at least!*' cried Connor, his fists clenched, his eyes burning holes into the back of the colonel's head. Had his whole world been built upon shifting sands? Had Buddyguard been sold to him on a lie? The fate of their fellow recruits buried alongside the truth? If so, then everything he'd believed Colonel Black to be – honest, loyal and honourable – was a sham.

'It was for everyone's protection,' insisted the colonel. 'It kept us under the radar.'

'You *lied* to us,' said Connor, distraught. 'You lied about our recruitment. You lied about the fate of our friends. You lied about Buddyguard being sanctioned by the British government. What else have you lied about?'

Colonel Black looked up at him from where he knelt on the floor, his face a battlefield of injuries, the ragged scar across his throat like a rope round his neck. 'I didn't lie. I was economical with the truth.'

Connor was stunned into silence. He no longer knew what to think.

Her expression taut and pale, Charley appeared to be in

equal shock. 'You told me Blake had returned home,' she said accusingly.

'I'm sorry,' replied Colonel Black. 'I thought it for the best. You were still recovering from your fall at the time.'

Charley looked daggers at the colonel. 'We trusted you with our lives. Our friends *died* and you didn't tell us!'

'In war, soldiers die. That's just the luck of the draw. You didn't need to know the body count. It would've distracted you from your own assignments. Put you at greater risk. But I *never* took any of you for granted. I spared no expense in your training or equipment. I did everything in my power to reduce that risk. My recruits' welfare and safety has and always will be my number one priority.'

'You deceived us,' said Connor. 'You recruited us under false pretences.'

'No, Connor, I saw the *potential* in you. Made you the man your father was.' He looked up at Connor, his flinty eyes rimmed red. 'Yes, I admit that I used his legacy to draw you in. But you can't deny that you wanted to follow in your father's footsteps. That you *wanted* to become a bodyguard.'

'There he goes again, exploiting your grief,' interrupted the Director. She was perched against her desk, arms crossed, watching the scene unfold with malicious delight.

The colonel dragged himself to his feet and lurched forward. 'You cannot let this weasel of a woman twist your minds! She is a master manipulator! She –'

The guard hit him again, this time in the back of the

head. The colonel buckled and slumped to the floor, blood spilling across the polished glass. Mr Grey seemed to observe the spreading pool with pleasure, then glanced sidelong at the guard. 'Careful not to kill the colonel. I haven't finished his dental work yet.'

The guard laughed, but Mr Grey didn't – he was serious. Connor felt sickened and furious. Whatever Colonel Black had or hadn't done, he didn't deserve that brutal treatment at the hands of such sadists.

The Director unfurled her arms and, like a vulture looming over the body of a mortally wounded lion, stood beside the colonel. 'I ask you again, Connor, why be loyal to this man? This charlatan who sacrifices you like lambs to the slaughter, who considers you *expendable* . . .'

She turned to her desk, picked up a super-thin tablet computer and inputted a command. An electronic screen was activated on the wall and Colonel Black appeared: his face ashen, eyes dilated, but all his teeth still present and his nose yet to be broken. He was talking to the camera. 'I use them for human shields . . . They're expendable! So what do I care what you do to them?'

The colonel lay unconscious on the floor, unable to defend himself. Connor knew that he shouldn't believe what he saw and heard, especially after Charley's forced betrayal. Still the words and sentiment stung. Charley exchanged a heartbroken look with him. She was as devastated as he was. She'd previously questioned Colonel Black's integrity. Prior to Connor's assignment in Russia, she'd supposedly overheard the colonel saying: *That's what we train them for. The size of the contract is worth the risk of a buddyguard or two.* Colonel Black had, of course, denied those were his exact words, insisting he'd said it was *never* worth the risk. Still Charley had been deeply concerned at the extreme risks of the operation. And, in hindsight, rightly so. Now, in light of what they knew about the colonel, it seemed her suspicions had been well founded. He was mercenary and dishonest.

Having delivered the final nail in the coffin, the Director settled behind her desk and smiled. 'Now, let's get down to the business at hand. Surrender the flash drive, Connor, and we can put all this sorry mess behind us. You and Charley can walk free.' She looked at Charley in her chair. 'And I mean that *literally*, Charley.'

Connor narrowed his eyes distrustfully at the Director. After everything Equilibrium had done in their attempts to hunt them down and eliminate them, the last thing he'd anticipated was a deal on the table. Not that any agreement was likely to be honoured by the Director. He wasn't that naive. Nonetheless he decided to play her game in the hope of a true opportunity to escape. 'What about our friends?' he asked.

'You mean the ones on the ship?' The Director pursed her lips. 'I'm sure we can come to an arrangement.'

'*Don't* . . . give her . . . the drive,' groaned Colonel Black, slowly coming round. 'You know . . . what's at sta–'

Mr Grey stood on the colonel's hand, grinding the bones with the heel of his shoe. 'Don't interrupt, Colonel.'

Trying to ignore Colonel Black's gasps of pain, Connor made his demands. 'Tell me the ship's location and container number. Once I've had confirmation they're free, I'll give you the drive.'

The Director smiled. 'I'm afraid, Connor, in this negotiation I hold all the cards. Drive first, freedom second.'

Connor clenched his jaw, fighting the impulse to simply leap forward and throttle the woman. 'How can we trust you?'

The Director spread her hands. 'How can you not? Your friends are fast running out of food and water. The longer you take, the shorter their lives will be. Besides, you don't owe Colonel Black anything. So why hold out? Why put your *own* life at risk for something he stole from us?'

Connor looked the Director square in the eye. 'Because Equilibrium killed my father!'

Only the slightest flicker of surprise registered on the Director's face before the mask came down again.

'That's unfortunate, Connor,' she said, her tone briefly sympathetic. 'But I assure you it wasn't personal. So, unless you want to be responsible for the deaths of your friends, I'd advise handing over the drive *right now*. Otherwise I'll be handing you over to Mr Grey. And I can promise that he won't be as considerate as I've been.'

Mr Grey smiled a hyena-like grin at him and Connor felt his chest tighten at the pitiless cruelty in the assassin's ice-grey eyes. He looked to Charley, but the despondent slump of her shoulders told him they were out of options. They had no alternative but to give up the drive.

Then his smartband vibrated gently on his wrist. Connor sneaked a peek at the display, glimpsing the message from Amir:

Green box – Oxygen Masks!

Out of his peripheral vision he spied a green box to his left attached to the wall.

'Well? I'm waiting,' snapped the Director. 'And my patience is fast running out.'

Connor's smartband vibrated again.

Hold your breath.

CHAPTER 47

The fire klaxon was deafening – a screaming siren that brought the whole of the Hive to a halt. The windows and doors of the Director's office automatically sealed shut and a white cloud of gas burst in a hissing roar from piping overhead. The sudden shock of the fire alarm caused everyone in the room to freeze – everyone except Connor.

In the ensuing confusion, Connor – breath held – sprinted for the green box as the huge venting of carbon dioxide filled the room. He yanked the lid open and grabbed a gas mask. Heart pumping and lungs burning, he pulled it over his mouth and triggered the oxygen flow. Then he snatched a second mask and ran back to Charley.

One of the guards had spotted him through the cloud of gas, but was slow to respond. As Connor drew level with him, he summoned up a ball of *qi* energy and drove an open palm into the man's solar plexus. Connor knew the one-inch push was effective, but in this instance the technique entirely floored the guard and he didn't get back up. It was as if the man had no strength left. He simply lay there open-mouthed and gasping like a fish on dry land.

A second guard went to raise his gun, but he fumbled his weapon and dropped it. A moment later he passed out and joined his weapon on the floor. The sudden drop in oxygen levels – the result of a total flooding of the room with carbon dioxide to suppress any fire – caused the final guard to sway, then collapse too.

Battling his way through the roaring fog of depressurized gas, Connor found Charley slumped in her wheelchair. He fitted the mask to her face and turned on the flow of oxygen. Her eyes blinked open and she quickly came round. Connor spun her chair towards the door.

'What about the colonel?' she asked, her voice muffled by the mask.

Colonel Black lay sprawled on the floor in a drying pool of his own blood, his breathing rapid and shallow. Connor couldn't abandon him to Equilibrium and the torturous evils of Mr Grey. So, seizing the comatose colonel under the arms, Connor hauled him towards the door. His mentor's sagging body was backbreakingly heavy and only a super-human effort, aided by the polished glass floor, enabled him to drag the colonel across the room.

The Director, like a ship's captain in a storm, was weakly clinging to her desk, glaring in impotent fury at their escape, too debilitated by lack of oxygen to prevent it. However, she managed to trigger the intruder alarm under her desk before her knees buckled and her whole body caved in. Meanwhile Mr Grey crawled slowly yet determinedly towards the green box on the other side of the room.

Grunting and straining, Connor heaved Colonel Black

the last few metres. As the three of them approached the glazed office door, the lock turned green and Charley shoved it open. Connor pulled the colonel into the corridor and the door swung shut behind them, automatically locking itself and sealing in the suffocating gas.

Panting from his exertions, Connor propped the colonel against the wall, took off his gas mask and placed it over the colonel's mouth.

'What's . . . happening?' groaned Colonel Black, the oxygen reviving him.

'Amir triggered the CO_2 fire system,' explained Connor. 'We have t–'

All of a sudden the glass door exploded and a bullet ricocheted off the wall by Connor's head, plaster spitting out in all directions. In the Director's office, Mr Grey lay sidelong on the floor, still some distance from the green box and its lifesaving masks, but he'd picked up the guard's dropped gun and blasted a hole through the doorway. The rush of air into the room saved the assassin's life. It also began to resuscitate the Director and her guards.

'I can't carry you, Colonel,' grunted Connor, heaving him to standing.

Colonel Black swayed on his feet. 'Give me another adrenalin shot and I'll do the rest.'

Charley reached into her trauma kit and handed him a syringe. He jabbed the needle into his thigh as another bullet ripped into the plasterwork millimetres from them. Mr Grey had by now got to his knees and was taking aim for a third time, trying to steady his hand.

'Follow me!' ordered Charley, propelling her chair along the corridor and down the slope.

Taking one arm over his shoulder, Connor supported the colonel as they limped after her. A pair of guards came rushing towards them, alerted by the intruder alarm. Seeing the three fugitives, they drew their guns. With nowhere to hide, Connor and the others were little more than sitting ducks in a shooting gallery.

But Charley kept going. Accelerating down the corridor, she threw herself and the chair on to its side as they began to open fire. Metal sparking and chair skidding, she smashed into the two guards like a battering ram. The men were bulldozed aside and tossed into the air like victims of a car crash. With a quick flip of her body, Charley righted the chair and rounded the corner at speed.

Connor was stunned at her devastating attack and nimble chair work. Staggering past the battered and broken guards, they found Charley fending off another three men single-handedly. Wielding her armrests like a pair of nunchuks, she seemed to be channelling all her frustration and fury of the past few years into her defence. She swept one guard's feet from under him, struck another guard in the jaw and caught a third straight in the groin. Even Connor felt sorry for her last victim.

'You don't need legs to be lethal!' he remarked as they came up alongside her.

'It's just good to be back in control of my own body,' she replied, clipping her armrests firmly back into place.

The three of them cut across an air bridge and down to

the fourth floor. Racing along the corridor, they barged aside startled technicians trying to evacuate the building and headed for a lower walkway. But, as they turned a corner, a unit of guards blocked their way.

'Get down!' ordered Charley, spinning her chair a hundred and eighty degrees and ducking behind the back of her seat.

The guards let loose a volley of gunfire. Connor and the colonel sheltered in her chair's protection, the Kevlar plates and liquid body-armour panels deflecting and absorbing the deadly bullets, the impacts sounding like heavy hail on a tin roof. They retreated rapidly back round the corner.

'Is there any other way down?' asked Connor, his heart pounding at their narrow escape.

'Not without going the whole way round,' replied Charley. 'But we don't need to.'

Grinning, she reached under her seat and pulled out a flash-bang grenade. 'I've always wanted to use one of these,' she said, tossing the grenade down the corridor.

A deafening explosion and blazing flare ripped through the building. The unfortunate guards were left disorientated and blinded while the nearby technicians were sent into an even greater panic.

Charley, Connor and Colonel Black picked their way through the groaning men and took the walkway down to the next level. Zigzagging back and forth across the network of bridges, the Hive's complex geometry played to their advantage as they evaded the pursuing guards and worked their way towards the ground floor. The rush of people heading for the fire exits only added to the chaos. But, as they went to cross the final air bridge, Mr Grey leapt from a walkway above and landed in front of them.

'I haven't finished with you, Colonel,' Mr Grey called out. 'And I've barely begun with you, Connor.'

Their escape route blocked, Connor and the others fell back behind a pillar before the assassin could raise his gun. Mr Grey slowly advanced as more guards could be heard charging along the corridor behind them.

'We're being surrounded!' hissed Connor.

Charley took out another flash-bang and tossed it up the corridor. They covered their ears and closed their eyes as the grenade exploded. Screams and the confused cries of men echoed through the atrium.

'That won't hold them off for long,' said Charley. 'And I've only one flash-bang left.'

Colonel Black straightened himself and took his arm off Connor. 'Charley, any more adrenalin shots?'

She nodded. 'But you shouldn't take any more. You'll overdose.'

'Just give me it.' He beckoned for the shot.

Charley reluctantly passed him the last syringe.

'I'm sorry that I didn't tell you the whole truth about Buddyguard,' said Colonel Black, ramming the needle into his leg, 'and I may have failed you both in many ways, but I won't fail you now. Connor, I told you that sacrifices may have to be made. Well, this is *my* sacrifice for you.'

With the roar of a lion, he leapt out from behind the pillar and threw himself at Mr Grey. The assassin was quick to react – a shot going off, clipping Colonel Black's arm – but the sheer strength and rage of the colonel took him by surprise. Mr Grey was driven back as he fought off the onslaught of blows. The gun was knocked from his grasp and clattered over the rail. The two men began fighting hand-to-hand.

'GO!' Colonel Black yelled to Connor and Charley.

The two of them sped past the battling men and headed down the slope. Connor glanced back, hoping to see the colonel following them, but he was locked in a life-and-death struggle.

An elite soldier against an assassin, the brawl was brutal and ruthless.

Eye gouges met kidney punches . . .

Knee kicks countered elbow strikes . . .

Headbutts returned strangleholds . . .

Fuelled by adrenalin, the colonel tore into Mr Grey. Then the assassin drew a knife and the fight turned really savage. Colonel Black suffered a bone-deep slash to his forearm as he blocked a cut to his throat before managing to pin Mr Grey against the bridge's handrail. He caught sight of Connor dithering. *'I told you to go. That's an order!'*

In that moment of distraction Mr Grey planted his knife in the colonel's heart.

'NO!' yelled Connor, as he watched the blade sink in and Colonel Black slump to the ground.

The assassin now directed his deadly attention towards Connor and stalked across the air bridge in his direction.

'Come on!' cried Charley, who'd reached ground level and was carving a path through the last line of guards, her adapted armrests flashing with glints of steel and blood as she laid waste to anyone who got in her way. The guards' efforts to stop her were further hampered by the flood of Equilibrium employees evacuating the building.

Against his every instinct to help the colonel, Connor turned and fled. Drawing his extendable baton, he fended off a reception guard. Then at last he and Charley were in the lobby and racing towards the exit.

CHAPTER 48

The glut of people spilling out of the Hive and into the street helped to cover their escape. Charley engaged her wheelchair's electric motor and Connor ran at her side. His breathing was loud in his ears, the whine of the alarm and the guards' angry shouts strangely dull and distant by comparison. It was as if another person, a different body, was fleeing from the Hive, someone else's feet pounding the pavement. He felt disconnected from the world, numb to all his senses.

Colonel Black was dead. His final link to his father had been severed and now he'd been set adrift. The colonel might not have been everything he professed, but he certainly proved to be a courageous man at heart, a loyal soldier and a true bodyguard.

The *zing* of a bullet passing his ear quickly brought Connor back to his senses and he ran even harder. They turned the corner. Amir and Zhen were waiting for them by the auto-rickshaw at the side of the road.

'Where's the colonel?' asked Amir, looking past them.

'Dead,' Connor gasped. 'He sacrificed himself for us.'

For a brief moment it looked like Amir had been knifed through the heart himself. 'So we risked everything for *nothing*.'

'No, we got Charley back,' replied Connor, managing to find a smile amid his sorrow.

'Of course,' said Amir, reaching out and clasping Charley's hand. 'In more ways than one. Sorry I ever doubted you.'

'Sorry I gave you reason to doubt me,' she replied sadly. Her gaze switched from Amir to the Chinese girl in the black-and-orange fast-food jacket. 'Who's this?'

'Zhen, our guide,' explained Amir.

'Then guide us out of here,' said Charley, hearing a shout in the near distance. 'The guards aren't far behind.'

Without needing to be told twice, Zhen leapt into the driver's seat and gunned the engine. The underpowered motor emitted a flatulent *phut-phut-phut* as Amir stepped aside to allow Charley into the back seat.

'Are you serious?' said Charley, eyeing the compact cabin. 'We can't *all* fit in!'

'She's right,' said Connor. 'Besides, this rickshaw will be too slow with four of us aboard. We need another vehicle.'

An Equilibrium guard rounded the corner and immediately called for reinforcements.

'Over there!' said Zhen, pointing to a gleaming black motorcycle with a sidecar. 'Use my rival's ride.'

A Shanghai Insiders tour guide had pulled up on the opposite side of the road and dismounted, giving a potted history of the 1933 Building to a pair of backpackers. With the tour guide's attention on the unique architecture and the apparent fire evacuation, Connor and Charley dashed over to the motorcycle.

Charley swiftly transferred herself into the sidecar. Connor collapsed her chair and hooked it on to the back luggage rack before leaping on the rider's seat. Having ridden mini-motorbikes through Epping Forest as a kid with his father, Connor was familiar with the workings of a bike. He kickstarted the engine, startling the tour guide out of his patter.

'Hey, that's my bike!' the man cried in outrage.

But Connor engaged first gear and hit the throttle before the guide could stop them. The motorbike and sidecar roared away. Zhen and Amir followed close behind as four guards ran into the road to block their escape. Connor kicked up a gear and drove straight at them. A bullet whizzed past his head. Another pinged off the metal nose of the sidecar, forcing Charley to hunker lower in her seat. Holding his nerve, Connor kept his line and the guards scattered a moment before they were mown down.

Chased by the sound of gunfire, Connor accelerated away, gripping the handlebars tight and counter-steering as the bike naturally pulled in the direction of the sidecar. At the end of the street, he bore right, Zhen staying hard on his tail.

'Are you all right, Charley?' asked Connor as they left the Hive behind and crossed a bridge back into central Shanghai.

Nodding, Charley sat up in the sidecar.

'What about the neuro-controller? Any chance the Director could hijack you?'

Charley hesitantly shook her head. 'I think . . . I must be out of range.'

Now they were a good distance down the road, Connor slowed his bike a touch and Zhen's rickshaw came up alongside.

'Where are we going?' Amir cried over the two engines' combined roars.

'Warehouse,' Connor shouted back, weaving his way through the traffic. 'Safest place. Good work on the fire alarm by the way, Amir. You saved our lives!'

Amir grinned. 'Thanks. With all the computer servers in the Hive, I guessed a CO_2 system had been installed. It was separate to Equilibrium's mainframe so I could hack in and control –'

A bullet shattered the back window of the rickshaw and Amir cowered in the footwell, hands covering his head as shards of Perspex rained down on him. In his wing mirror, Connor spotted four motorbikes racing after them through the lines of traffic. He twisted the throttle, and the motorcycle and its sidecar surged forward. Zhen did her best to keep up, the rickshaw's puny engine straining at maximum speed. Only the jam of cars and the nimbleness of her driving allowed her to stay one step ahead of their pursuers.

'We'll never shake them off!' Zhen yelled to Connor as a bullet disintegrated her wing mirror to a stub of metal.

'American Embassy,' Charley shouted back. 'That's close to here, isn't it?'

Zhen nodded, then swerved round a startled pedestrian crossing the road.

'But what about Equilibrium inside agents?' yelled Amir as the rickshaw mounted the pavement and cut through a red light.

Connor followed, horns blasting as he narrowly missed a collision with a taxi. He drew back alongside the rickshaw. 'We have to take the risk,' he replied. 'We can't keep running like this. Zhen, lead the way.'

Zipping in front of a bus, Zhen turned the rickshaw off the main road and headed west from the Bund. Connor swung the motorcycle round, rubber burning as the wheels spun. Behind, the bikers were gaining on them. A volley of rounds peppered the sidecar, most ricocheting off Charley's bulletproof chair, the Kevlar panels once again saving their lives.

'We need to level the playing field,' said Charley, reaching back and taking out her last flash-bang. She tossed the grenade on to the road and into the path of the bikers. A second later the stun grenade detonated with a supernova of a flash and a thunderous bang. Subjected to its full force, the lead biker was dazzled by the blinding explosion and rode straight into the rear of a parked car, cartwheeling over the roof to crash-land in a heap on the pavement.

'One down!' cried Charley. But the three remaining bikers continued their relentless pursuit. The blast had also attracted the attention of the city's police force. Lights flashing and siren wailing, a police car pulled out of a side road and gave chase.

'That's all we need!' said Connor, gritting his teeth as he rode the motorcycle across a junction and through another red light. He caught up with Zhen just as she suddenly split left. But a taxi cut in front of Connor, forcing him to ride straight on. His last glimpse of Amir and Zhen was as their rickshaw ducked down an alleyway, pursued by one of the bikers. Connor had no choice but to keep going, accelerating along the road as the last two bikers and the police car hounded him.

'Where now?' Connor yelled to Charley, lost without their guide.

'I think I recognize where we are . . .' she replied. 'The embassy's down . . . *that* road!'

In his determination to escape their pursuers, Connor almost missed it. He hit the left turn too hard and the motorcycle skidded round the corner. The handlebars were at full lock, but still the bike veered over the white line into the wrong lane. Connor had lost all control over the steering. The sidecar started to lift off the ground, threatening to flip the bike into the path of an oncoming bus.

'*We're going over!*' cried Charley, throwing her body weight into the turn.

Connor leant with her, applying more gas to bring the bike round. At the last second the motorcycle righted itself, its tyres gripped the road and they shot back on to the correct side, clipping the bus and scraping the paintwork.

'That was close!' said Charley, checking her wheelchair had survived the encounter.

Now it was a straight run to the embassy. Connor could see the American flag in the distance, the stars and stripes rippling in the breeze. Throttle at the full, he weaved between the cars.

'We're *going* to make it!' he said, gritting his teeth.

But halfway down Connor spotted the flashing lights of a police roadblock and he was forced to screech to a halt. Further back up the road the two Equilibrium agents made a quick exit before the police car behind braked and blocked any hope of a retreat.

Connor and Charley found themselves trapped. Armed police having them in their sights, they had no option but to surrender.

Connor stared at his reflection in the one-way mirror. He hardly recognized himself. His spikes of brown hair lay flat and matted, his fringe plastered to his forehead. His eyes were no more than dark hollows, their stare slightly wild. His cheeks were sunken, his lips cracked, and his complexion wan and smeared with grime and sweat. He looked, and no doubt smelt, like a runaway who could do with a decent meal and a hot shower.

The police officer who sat opposite him seemed to think the same. He eyed Connor with undisguised disdain, his glare as grim and unsympathetic as the over-starched uniform he wore.

Connor shifted position in the hard metal chair, its feet bolted to the concrete floor. The table was fixed too, its surface scratched and dented. Connor didn't want to think how some of those dents had got there as he leant forward and rested his handcuffed wrists on the table. He hadn't got a word out of the officer in the whole time he'd been cooped up in the dingy interrogation room. He hadn't been given a phone call, the offer of a lawyer or even a glass of water.

Connor had asked repeatedly where Charley was but had been met with stony-walled silence.

He worried for her and prayed that she was being treated with appropriate respect. He himself had not been harmed since their arrest. But he'd been denied everything, including information.

He had no idea if Amir and Zhen had escaped, been arrested, captured or shot dead by Equilibrium agents. Their fate played on his mind, as did his friends in the shipping container. Every minute he was being detained in a holding cell was a minute less that Jason, Ling and the others had to live.

Connor decided to try one last time with the officer. He knew that Equilibrium's tentacles reached far and were buried deep into every stratum of the country's security agencies, but surely not *every* officer in the Shanghai police force could be corrupt or in the pay of Equilibrium. Now that he'd been captured and arrested on terrorism charges, Connor realized he had nothing to lose.

'Please. You *have* to believe me. Equilibrium is holding my friends hostage. The organization is a mass criminal network, extending even up to government level. They *killed* the colonel.' The officer continued to stare impassively at him. 'We were trying to escape before they killed us too. You see, we have information that would expose them and bring the organization down. We're *not* the terrorists. They are! *Don't you understand?*' Connor slammed his fists on the table, the officer's complete lack of interest frustrating him to anger. 'Lives are at stake here! You have to contact –'

A knock at the door interrupted him.

Another grim-faced policeman appeared. He spoke briefly to his associate, then looked at Connor as if he were something scraped off his shoe. 'Translator here now,' he said in English.

'At last!' Connor slumped back in his chair and breathed a sigh of relief. Finally he might be able to get through to someone – explain the situation and give his side of the story.

Then the translator walked in and Connor's hope was crushed like a tin can in a compactor.

'Hello, Connor,' said Mr Grey, the greeting as warm and comforting as a shard of ice.

Connor's eyes widened in horror. 'No, don't leave me with him!' he begged as the police officer vacated his seat and headed for the door. 'He's one of *them*. He works for Equilibrium. He's an *assassin*!'

Mr Grey muttered something in Chinese. The police officer nodded, then left the interrogation room, locking the door behind him. With the click of the latch, Connor felt as if the whole outside world had been shut off from him. The room's temperature seemed to drop several degrees. Now the only reality that existed was him and the devil that masqueraded as a man.

Mr Grey removed his suit jacket and hung it pin-straight

over the back of his chair. Then he sat down opposite Connor, crossed his legs and neatly pulled the cuffs of his shirt into line.

Connor did his best to regain his own composure. With a grin of bravado, he said, 'I see the colonel's left his mark.'

Scowling, Mr Grey touched the cut above his left eye. 'That will heal. Unlike his bleeding heart.'

Fury overruling sense, Connor launched himself at the assassin. Mr Grey didn't even flinch as Connor's shackles cut his attack short, barely reaching halfway across the table. Connor raged like a chained lion.

'Save your energies,' advised the assassin in a somewhat bored tone. 'You're going to need them for what I have planned.'

Realizing the futility of his efforts, Connor fell back into his chair, his chains jangling and his blood coursing hot and angry through his veins.

'The Director is somewhat irritated by your rude departure,' informed Mr Grey, as if Connor had run out of some tedious business meeting. 'So she's handed your *care* over to me.' A fiendish smile now slid across his thin pallid lips.

Connor's stomach twisted into a knot and his throat constricted to the point he found it hard to breathe. 'Are you going to torture me? Like you did the colonel?'

Mr Grey gently shook his head. 'No. Not you.'

At that moment, the door unlocked and the police officer came back in, pushing a wheelchair ahead of him.

'I can do it *myself*!' Charley protested, irritably trying to take control of her chair. 'I said –'

She looked up and saw Connor's horrified face, then the skull-like grin on Mr Grey's, and her objections immediately died away. The police officer ferried her over to the corner of the room, spun her chair to face the table, flipped on the brake, then departed and locked the door once more.

'*No!*' said Connor, looking pleadingly at Mr Grey. 'Not Charley. Leave her out of this.'

'What's going on?' asked Charley, her sky-blue eyes flicking fearfully between Connor and the cold-hearted assassin.

Mr Grey rose from behind the table. 'I'm presuming your associate Amir has the flash drive,' he said, ignoring Connor's impassioned protests. 'The police report doesn't list it in your possession.'

Connor felt a flicker of hope. *Amir and Zhen must have escaped!* But his elation was short-lived.

Like the Grim Reaper identifying his mark, Mr Grey laid an ashen hand on Charley's shoulder. She shuddered under the assassin's touch, then stiffened as he brushed aside her long blonde hair.

'Is this where they inserted the neuro-chip?' asked the assassin, running a skeletal finger along the small scar at the base of her skull. Charley flinched.

'Don't you dare touch her!' warned Connor, straining once more at his chains.

'Oh, I don't intend to,' replied Mr Grey, pulling the Director's neuro-controller out of his pocket. Charley stared in fearful apprehension at the device. 'The doctor reliably informs me that this device has so much more potential than merely the control of a subject. I understand it can inflict pain. Immense pain. Now tell me, Connor, where's Amir hiding?'

Before Connor could answer, Mr Grey pressed his thumb to the neuro-controller's display panel. Charley suddenly went into spasm. Her whole body locked out as if she was suffering an epileptic fit. Her back arched, her arms splayed out, her hands turned to claws and her mouth opened in a silent scream.

'STOP!' cried Connor. 'STOP! You're killing her!'

Mr Grey released his thumb and Charley flopped back into her chair, limp as a rag doll.

'Charley, speak to me! Are you all right?' Connor asked desperately.

Gasping, she appeared lost in a white-out of pain, a sheen of sweat coating her deathly pale face.

'I can only imagine that it must be like molten iron being poured into your spine,' said Mr Grey, his pleasure apparent. 'Or perhaps razors slicing through your nerves?'

He depressed his thumb again and Charley convulsed once more. Her eyes bulged and she seized the armrests of her chair as if she was being electrocuted. Connor yanked on his chains, fighting to free himself. But he was powerless to do anything. He could only sit and stare as she writhed in her chair.

Mr Grey grinned, evidently enjoying the look of torment on Connor's face as much as the agony he was inflicting on his victim.

'*Enough! Enough!*' cried Connor, unable to watch Charley suffer any more. 'You win . . . you can have the drive. Just leave Charley alone.'

The victory his, Mr Grey slipped the controller back into his pocket and Charley collapsed into her chair. 'See? I didn't even have to torture *you*.' The assassin narrowed his eyes at Connor. 'Although I still have that pleasure to come.'

Connor was no longer even listening. Hot tears ran down his cheeks as he sobbed, 'Charley, are you OK?'

But Charley was unresponsive, the excruciating pain having caused her to black out.

Mr Grey coughed impatiently. 'Where's Amir?'

Defeated and distraught, Connor replied, 'In a warehouse. In the –' His smartband vibrated.

Mr Grey grabbed his wrist and read the message:

Call me now.

'Is that from Amir?' he demanded.

Connor weakly nodded, no longer having the strength to resist.

'Then you'd *better* call him,' said Mr Grey, pulling a mobile phone from his pocket.

Taking the phone, Connor dialled the number in the message. It rang only once before it was answered.

'Amir?' asked Connor. He listened to his friend, then, frowning in puzzlement, he passed the phone over to Mr Grey. 'Amir wants to speak to *you*.'

A neon nightscape of dancing lights and towering LED screens, the Shanghai skyline glittered in all its glory. From nearly five hundred metres above the ground, the hexagonal-shaped Sky Walk on the hundredth floor of the Shanghai World Financial Center afforded the most breathtaking views over the endless starlit city. To Connor, the skyscrapers of Pudong – that had looked like steel giants from the river level of the Bund – now appeared like a flashing forest of toy Christmas trees.

He stood close beside Charley upon the vertigo-inducing glass floor of the Sky Walk, only a few inches of glazing separating them from the abyss beneath their feet. Charley had recovered from her torture, but was still somewhat subdued, the invasive control over her body having unsettled her to the core. Connor held her hand, but there was no strength to her grip.

The Director and Mr Grey waited with them, flanked on either side by a requisite pair of guards, guns concealed and blank innocuous expressions on their faces so as not to draw any undue attention. Whatever strings had been pulled and pockets lined, Connor and Charley were no longer in police custody. They were the property of Equilibrium.

In his phone call Amir had demanded an exchange. The flash drive for Connor and Charley – eight o'clock sharp at the top of the Shanghai World Financial Center. Connor could now see why his friend had chosen that specific location. The Sky Walk was busy with tourists gazing at the views and taking photos of themselves, revelling in the optical illusion that they were floating in mid-air above the gleaming city. It was a very public place with obvious CCTV cameras and conspicuous security guards. If the Director tried anything here, she risked exposing herself and Equilibrium.

'Your friend best not be playing any games with us,' snapped the Director, glancing impatiently at her watch. 'Otherwise you two will be taking the *express* elevator down.'

Connor guessed that she didn't mean the lift behind them. Three floors beneath their feet was the lower observation level of the building's world-famous trapezoid structure, the reason the skyscraper was called the 'bottle opener' of Shanghai. Then beyond that was a vertiginous drop to the street, precisely four hundred and seventy-four metres below. It would be a swift and permanent exit.

Yet Connor hoped that Amir *wouldn't* turn up. That he wouldn't attempt something so foolish as to trade their lives for the flash drive. The Director was not a person to be trusted or bargained with. He understood *why* his friend was trying to save them, but the contents of the drive were too important to be given away in a hostage exchange – an exchange that risked Amir being captured too.

But dead on eight o'clock Amir appeared at the other end of the Sky Walk. Separated by over fifty metres of glass walkway and a throng of tourists, their eyes briefly met, a look of apprehension shared between them before Amir smiled in an effort at reassurance. His friend was alone and apparently unarmed. He put a phone to his ear, and a moment later Mr Grey's mobile rang. The assassin answered, switching it to speakerphone.

'Send Connor and Charley to me,' demanded Amir, sounding impressively in command.

The Director cupped a hand to her ear. 'Sorry, didn't quite catch that. It's too noisy in here. Let me sort that out.'

She clapped her hands twice, sharp and loud, cutting through the noise and chatter. The tourists all stopped what they were doing. Then in a disturbingly quiet and orderly fashion they filed out of the exit doors at each end and down the stairs. In a matter of seconds the Sky Walk had cleared of people.

As if he was dropping in an elevator, Connor felt a plummeting sensation in the pit of his stomach. Just as he'd feared, Amir had played straight into the Director's hands. The Director laughed at the shocked look on Amir's face, her laughter echoing off the glass walls of the transparent and now-empty Sky Walk.

'I bet you thought this was a secure place to make your

exchange,' said the Director. 'But Equilibrium *owns* this building.'

Lowering his phone, Amir replied, 'It changes nothing. Release Connor and Charley, guarantee our safe passage out of the country, then I'll hand over the flash drive.'

With her hands planted on her hips, the Director glared scornfully down the walkway at Amir. 'You're in *no* position to make such demands.'

Amir stood his ground. 'If you don't, I'll release the files online.'

Connor was proud of his friend. He could tell Amir was nervous but he hadn't allowed his nerves to enter his voice.

'Go ahead then,' said the Director with an indifferent shrug. 'Release the files. Equilibrium controls the Chinese internet. Any mention of Equilibrium will be automatically blocked and deleted. *Nothing* will get past the government's Great Firewall.'

'That may be true,' replied Amir. 'But I've created a program to dump the files *en masse* via ghost servers and phantom VPN tunnels. All Equilibrium's nasty secrets will be leaked on to the web. At the same time a multiple denial-of-service attack will overload the firewall's defences. Something sensitive is bound to get out. It *always* does.' He held up his smartphone, his thumb hovering over the screen. 'All I need to do is give my associate the command.'

The Director let out a derisive snort. 'You'd first have to break the mutating encryption key and there's no way a little runt like y–'

'I already have,' Amir replied.

The Director stiffened. 'Prove it,' she spat.

'OK,' said Amir blithely. 'Liu Yan, Chairman of the Politburo Standing Committee, is one of Equilibrium's agents. So too is Zong Li, the vice-president of the Xinhua News Agency; Chen Feng, the CEO of China Investment Corporation; and even the Minister of National Defence, Ren–'

With each name mentioned, the Director's temper grew until she stamped her foot furiously on the glass floor. '*Enough!*' she shrieked. 'I'll *kill* every last one of my IT security team! They told me the encryption was *unbreakable*! I'll have every bone in their puny little bodies broken for this –'

'Before you do that,' interrupted Amir, holding his phone threateningly in the air, 'let Connor and Charley go.'

The Director clenched her fists and glowered at Amir. 'Here, have your *precious* friends!' She shoved Connor in the back.

Connor exchanged a doubtful look with Charley. *Had Amir really outsmarted the head of Equilibrium?*

'You heard the Director,' said Mr Grey, kicking off the brake on Charley's chair. 'You're free to go.'

Slowly Connor made his way down the Sky Walk, Charley at his side, her wheels squeaking over the polished glass floor. The financial district of Pudong twinkled far below them, the rear lights of taxis flowing like blood cells along the veins of the city. At any moment Connor expected a bullet in his back, the Director merely toying with Amir, distracting him with their release so that one of the guards could shoot him before he initiated the command to release the files.

Charley wheeled her chair along, her jaw set and her eyes fixed on Amir. Their friend gave them both a nervous smile as they drew ever nearer. Connor wanted to run, but didn't dare give the guards cause to open fire or the Director the satisfaction that he was panicking. Surely she wasn't simply letting them go free. But, with every step further along the Sky Walk, Connor's expectation and hopes grew.

They were over the halfway mark when the Director called out, 'That's far enough.' But Connor and Charley kept going, too eager to escape. 'I said, *that's* far enough!'

This time Charley was forced to an abrupt halt, her arms locking out against her will. Connor stopped too, glancing back to see the Director with the neuro-controller in her grasp. A flicker of fear passed across Charley's face at being hijacked once again.

The Director, having made her point that she was still ultimately in control, released Charley, then demanded, 'Now the drive.'

Connor felt dangerously exposed in the middle of the Sky Walk. He and Charley were in no-man's-land. Amir may have negotiated their release, but they were far from free yet.

Amir wet his lips nervously, a bead of sweat running off his brow. 'I'll give you the drive once you tell us where the hostages are being held.'

The Director narrowed her eyes. 'That wasn't part of the deal.'

Amir waved his smartphone, his thumb primed over the screen like a grenade pin. 'Do you really want the Chinese government knowing Liu Yan actually works for you?'

The Director sneered. 'He's not the only government stooge in our pay.'

'Fine,' Amir replied. 'But are you sure you want Russia knowing that you tried to take control of their country by installing a puppet leader?'

'And we would have succeeded if it wasn't for Connor's interference.' The Director glared at Connor.

'Or that you stole over fifty million dollars' worth of

diamonds straight from under President Rawasa's nose in Burundi?' continued Amir.

'It was a *hundred* million,' she corrected. 'And what do I care about a tinpot leader from a third-world country?'

'How about a first-world country then?' said Amir, his thumb still hovering over the button. 'I'm sure the American President would love to know that you were the one responsible for attempting to kidnap his daughter. I hear the United States' Navy SEAL team are experts in kill-or-capture operations.'

'This is getting *tedious*,' snapped the Director.

'Then tell us the location of the hostages,' said Amir.

The Director scowled at him. 'You drive a hard bargain, young man.' She nodded at Mr Grey.

Through gritted teeth the assassin said, 'They're on the MV *Halcyon*. Shipping container CSQU8463725.'

'Now where's the drive?' demanded the Director, growing ever more impatient.

Connor shook his head vehemently at Amir. '*We need to get out of here first!*' he hissed.

Amir gave an apologetic shrug. 'A deal's a deal. Besides, there's no other way to do this.' He spoke into his throat mic. 'Zhen, send up the drive.'

A tense sixty seconds ticked by as everyone waited for the flash drive to arrive. Connor's eyes darted around, assessing their escape routes. As soon as the Director had the drive, he realized they'd be executed on the spot. There were the exits through which the phoney tourists had departed. But Connor didn't fancy racing down over two thousand, seven hundred steps to reach street level and, as able as Charley was with her chair, a hundred flights of stairs was too much of a challenge even for her to negotiate. The only realistic option was the lift. All of a sudden Amir's choice of location seemed even more foolhardy. *What had his friend been thinking?*

The Director tapped her foot impatiently. Mr Grey stood stone still, his very lack of motion more threatening than any movement, like a cobra primed to strike. Then the lift behind them pinged and its doors slid open to reveal a tiny flash drive in the middle of the floor. The Director clicked her fingers, ordering one of the guards to retrieve it.

'How do I know this is the *real* drive?' she asked, inspecting the device in her hand.

'Check it for yourself,' suggested Amir.

Connor began wheeling Charley down the Sky Walk towards Amir. But now the neuro-controller was no longer hijacking her system she soon took over and they both raced for the exit.

'Let's go,' Connor urged Amir, pressing the call button for their own lift.

Handing Mr Grey the neuro-controller, the Director pulled her tablet from her jacket pocket and wirelessly connected to the drive. A login window appeared. 'Not so fast!' she said. 'A password's required. What is it?'

'*Hercules*,' replied Amir.

The Director typed the word and a list of folders immediately popped up on her screen. A satisfied grin spread across her face as she inspected a few random files. 'Well, this appears to be genuine,' she said, somewhat surprised. 'You're clearly a man of your word, Amir. Unfortunately, I'm not. Guards, seize them!'

'But we made a deal!' Amir protested as her two guards strode down the Sky Walk towards them. Connor stabbed at the call button, willing the lift to appear as a third guard entered via the fire exit. The lift doors opened a moment later – only for them to be greeted by another Equilibrium agent.

As each and every escape route was blocked by a guard, the Director laughed. 'Did you really think that a mere child like you could threaten and bring down Equilibrium? An organization that controls governments throughout the world?'

'Yes,' replied Amir, oddly unfazed by their predicament. 'Because I assumed that you wanted to keep Equilibrium a secret.' He pointed out of a window in the Sky Walk where a drone hovered in the night, its lens focused on the Director. 'Wave to the camera!'

The Director's eyes flared with rage.

'Oh, and just in case you're wondering,' continued Amir, 'this whole encounter is being beamed live to everyone on the Bund. So I'd advise against doing anything rash in full view of several thousand witnesses.' He indicated the towering LED screen on one of Pudong's skyscrapers. A twenty-storey-high image of the Director's livid face appeared. Beneath the picture ran a real-time translation of their conversation. 'So I'd let us go if I were you.'

The Director rounded on Amir. 'You still don't get it, do you?' she snarled. 'I own the police! I own Shanghai! I OWN CHINA! I can do whatever I please. I can get away with *murder* if I want.'

She stormed into the lift behind her. As the doors closed, she gave Mr Grey and her guards one final command. 'Shoot the drone. Then shoot them!'

CHAPTER 52

'It was a good plan, Amir,' said Connor as the three of them were surrounded by Mr Grey and the four guards. He offered his friend a conciliatory smile. 'Just a shame it didn't work.'

'The drone was supposed to be our insurance policy,' Amir replied with a deflated look.

'Well, for what it's worth, I thought your bluff was pretty impressive,' said Charley, reversing her chair until she was back to back with Connor and Amir. As the guards closed in on them, she took Connor's hand and squeezed it tight. 'If we're to die, Connor,' she whispered, 'at least we're together.'

Connor clasped her hand even tighter. 'And always will be.'

'Ahhh, young love,' said Mr Grey in a sickly-sweet tone. His upper lip curled in disdain. 'Only leads to heart-break.' In one swift and sudden action the assassin drew his gun.

'No!' cried Connor, but was too late to stop him pulling the trigger. The gunshot echoed through the Sky Walk, loud as thunder. On instinct Connor threw himself across Charley. But Mr Grey hadn't been aiming at her. The bullet pierced a side window instead and obliterated the drone. Its rotors shattered, the drone spiralled out of control and dropped from the sky like a dead bird.

'I don't like an audience,' said Mr Grey as the wind whistled through the hole in the window, cracks fanning out like a spider's web in the glass. He eyed Connor sprawled across Charley. 'How valiant of you to want to protect your sweetheart. Unfortunately, no human shield will save her . . . or Amir . . . or *you*.'

The assassin planted the cold hard tip of the barrel against Connor's forehead, forcing him to stand. Connor glared at the ashen-faced assassin – the killer who'd murdered Colonel Black, tortured Charley and been the bane of his existence ever since he'd joined Buddyguard. Mr Grey had haunted his missions, at first at the fringes, then circling ever closer like some flesh-eating vulture. Looking into his glacial eyes, Connor could see no trace of humanity. Only darkness. There would be no point in pleading or appealing to this man's better nature. For he had none. He was the devil incarnate.

Mr Grey barked an order in Chinese at the guards. Two of them now drew their handguns and fixed their sights on Charley and Amir.

'I had wanted to extract my pound of flesh from you, Connor,' said Mr Grey. 'Repay you for shooting me in Russia. But you've become somewhat tiresome. So a simple execution will suffice.'

'Go to hell!' spat Connor.

Mr Grey smiled. 'I expect I will.' He glanced round at the heady view, the city lights glimmering below like jewels in a mine. 'At least dying this high up, *you're* part way to heaven.' He cocked his gun. 'Any last requests?'

'Yes!' Amir begged, clasping his hands together in supplication. 'Allow us a final prayer.'

Mr Grey rolled his eyes, then sighed. 'If you must.'

Amir turned to face Connor and Charley. They formed a tight circle, a final bond of friendship, amid the ring of Equilibrium guards. 'Bow your heads and close your eyes,' said Amir softly.

Connor did as his friend asked, putting his hands together in prayer. He hadn't taken Amir to be the religious type, but in these last moments of life he could understand anyone wanting spiritual comfort.

'Almighty Lord, hear our prayers . . .' began Amir, then added in a whisper that was barely a breath. '*Cover your ears!*'

Connor and Charley had but a second to do so before the doors to the nearest lift pinged open and a black tube rolled out on to the Sky Walk. The guards were given no time to react, the stun grenade detonating only a few metres from them. The flash was like a blinding supernova in the night, visible even from the Bund over one and a half kilometres away. The ear-splitting bang reverberated through the enclosed corridor of the Sky Walk, amplifying its effects so that even Connor's covered ears rang. This was followed by a blast wave that almost knocked everyone off their feet, and Connor was left momentarily stunned as if he'd been punched in the face.

The guards reeled from the unexpected attack, staggering around like drunks, their senses blown. Charley was the first to recover and react. She yanked her chair's armrests free and smashed the gun out of the nearest guard's grip. Hooking his ankle, she then swept him off balance and struck him in the chest as he fell. The guard hit the floor, cracking his skull on the glass and knocking himself out cold.

Next Amir thrust his iStun into the side of the other armed guard. Already disorientated and dazed, the man convulsed, dropped his weapon and slumped to the ground.

Charley and Amir then turned to the other two guards. Blinking like moles in the light, their sight blurred, the men drew extendable batons to fend off the advancing teenage bodyguards. They swiped wildly, Amir ducking then thrusting with his iStun while Charley blocked the attacks, her metal armrests clanging with each deflection.

Of all the Equilibrium agents, Mr Grey appeared least affected by the stun grenade. With reactions as quick as a snake's, he'd shielded his eyes and after a few seconds shrugged off the disabling effects of the blast. Discovering the guards in disarray and in retreat, he raised his gun to shoot Amir in the back.

But Connor leapt on him, grabbing his arm and wrestling for control of the weapon. Surprise working to his advantage, Connor managed to force the gun down. But

Mr Grey's finger was still on the trigger and the gun kicked, letting off a shot. The bullet barely missed Connor's right thigh before drilling a hole through the glazed pane at his feet. Fractures spidered out like veins in the glass.

Mr Grey glared at Connor. 'I hate wasting bullets!'

As the two of them battled over the weapon, Connor heard his combat instructor's voice in his head, urging him from the grave to *Seize, Strike* and *Subdue!* Connor tried to summon up his *qi* to punch the assassin, but it took all his strength and concentration just to keep hold of the weapon. He managed to get in a couple of elbow strikes. But Mr Grey was like hardened steel, every strike failing to leave even a dent in him. Despite Connor's furious determination, the assassin's gun hand slowly yet steadily rose up again. This time the barrel's sights fixed on Charley as she fought off her guard.

Mr Grey leered at Connor. 'Do you want to pull the trigger? Or shall I?'

Connor roared in rage and redoubled his efforts to overcome the assassin. However, Mr Grey, skilled in weapon retention, defeated any attempts to rip the gun from his grasp. Connor made a last-ditch attempt, wrenching hard on his arm –

There was a deafening *bang* as the weapon went off. The round struck Charley dead centre in the back. Connor watched in horror as she bucked from the impact. The guard took advantage of her pain and hit her across the shoulder with his baton. Charley cried out and almost dropped her *tonfa*-armrest. But she hadn't been mortally wounded by the bullet, her wheelchair's Kevlar panel having protected her from the round. But she was weakened by the two blows and was now in retreat from the guard.

'Looks like we need a head shot,' said Mr Grey as he realigned the weapon's sights.

Connor knew it was only a matter of time before the man hit his mark. Risking everything, he let go of the gun. Even Mr Grey was taken aback at this tactic. And in that split-second moment of distraction Connor drove his fingertips like a dagger into the assassin's chest, targeting the exact point between the pectoral muscles that Lǎolao had shown him.

The Demon Gate.

It couldn't be a more appropriately named *qi* point for the assassin. The sudden and debilitating shock of the strike sent Mr Grey lurching backwards. All strength draining from him, the gun grew super-heavy in his hands and he sank to his knees.

'*What . . . have . . . you . . . done to me?*' he gasped, his eyes bulging.

Connor grinned. 'Oh, it's just a little trick I learnt from an old grandmother. Effective, isn't –'

But Connor didn't get to finish his sentence. The glass pane beneath his feet suddenly disintegrated and he dropped like a stone through the Sky Walk.

CHAPTER 53

The wind whistled, chill and sharp, its gusts pulling at Connor like claws. He swung precariously over the abyss, clinging on for dear life as shards of glass spun and sparkled into the city's night. The glazing, weakened by the bullet, had given way under his weight. On pure instinct alone his hands had reached out and caught the lip of the frame, preventing him from plunging to certain death. Now he hung, small and fragile as a fruit bat, from the underbelly of the Sky Walk.

'*CHARLEY!*' he screamed at the top of his lungs.

Mid-fight she glanced his way, but didn't see him at first. Then she looked down and stared in horror at his terrifying predicament. Seizing upon her distraction, the guard swung his baton at her head. At the last second Charley ducked, but she still caught a glancing blow. Then, with the fury of an avenging angel, she laid into the guard, her *tonfa*-style armrests becoming a blur of steel.

But all the while Connor felt his grip slipping . . .

He looked to Amir, but his friend was in serious trouble himself. The other guard had him pinned against the wall, throttling him with his baton. Amir gasped and spluttered, his eyeballs bulging and his fingers clawing at the man's face.

Mr Grey, kneeling close by, watched the chaotic scene with blithe amusement. '*I* would help you, Connor, but I'm a little incapacitated at the moment.'

Connor thought the only help the assassin would give him would be to help him on his way. So, muscles straining and pulse pounding, Connor tried to pull himself back into the Sky Walk. The glass gave him little purchase and the sweat on his fingertips only added an unwanted slickness to his grip. He cried out in horror as he lost hold with one hand and dangled by a single arm in the darkness. Like a leaf waiting for a final gust to blow it off the branch, Connor clung on.

The ache in his muscles grew unbearable and his grip weakened with every passing second. He knew in his heart that he was going to fall, that he would plummet to certain death – either on to the observation deck below or all one hundred floors straight down to the concrete paving of the street . . .

Then he heard a dull *thunk* and a guard's bruised face appeared in a nearby pane, his features squished against the glass. A second later Charley skidded to a halt by the hole, locked out her brakes and reached down with the end of her armrest.

'*Grab hold!*' she cried.

Connor seized the metal tube with his free hand and began to pull himself up. Charley, teeth gritted and muscles straining like the cords of a rope, took all of Connor's bodyweight. Slowly but surely, Connor worked his way back into the Sky Walk. But, as soon as he laid an arm on the floor, Charley kicked him in the face!

Connor reeled and almost dropped back through the floor. Charley then stamped on his hand. Connor gasped in pain and shock.

'NO!' she cried, her eyes wide with panic as Connor struggled to keep a grip. 'It's not me!'

Glancing sideways, Connor spotted Mr Grey with the neuro-controller in his hand. A cruel smile cut across his lips. 'Oh dear, Connor, your saviour has just become your executioner!'

The assassin pressed the controller's display panel and Charley's leg began to rise.

'You will *not* control me!' yelled Charley fiercely. Her face contorted into a knot of furious concentration as her foot went to stamp on Connor's hand again.

Connor clung desperately to the edge, powerless to stop her. He saw Charley trembling in her chair as she battled against the impulse to kick him to his death.

'*You will NOT control me!*' she screamed, and, with a super-human effort of willpower, she forced her leg back on to her chair.

Mr Grey stabbed at the controller, but Charley's limbs refused to obey its command. Somehow Charley had overridden the neuro-controller's signals.

'Well, if I can't control you, I'll just have to torture you,' he snarled, pressing another button on the screen.

All at once Charley began to convulse. Her knuckles went white as she fought against the crippling pain to keep a grip on the handle of the armrest.

'*I . . . can't . . . hold . . . any . . . longer . . .*' she gasped with a look of despair at Connor.

'It's all right,' said Connor as her body jerked violently and she was forced to let go.

No longer supported, Connor plummeted back through the hole. Grabbing for anything he could, his fingers clasped around a carbon-fibre spoke of Charley's wheelchair. With the last of his strength he began to pull himself up again. But his weight was dragging the wheelchair towards the edge, its rubber tyres squeaking across the glass floor.

'Now that's a real catch-22,' said Mr Grey with a cruel laugh. 'Save yourself . . . or Charley?'

The chair slid another fraction of a centimetre closer to the edge.

'I wouldn't judge you for saving your own skin, Con–' Suddenly Mr Grey went into spasm. The assassin let go of the neuro-controller and collapsed to the floor. Behind him stood Amir, bruised and bloody, iStun in hand.

'*AMIR!*' shouted Connor as the wheelchair shifted to the very lip of the hole.

His friend dived for him, grabbing his wrist and pulling him to safety. Then he dragged Charley's wheelchair away from the edge. Connor lay panting at Charley's feet, unable to quite believe his near-death experience was finally over. 'Are you OK, Charley?'

Charley nodded. Her face grey and washed-out, she looked utterly drained, as if the plug had been pulled on her. 'Sorry . . . for kicking you,' she murmured.

Dragging himself to his feet, he kissed her on the cheek. 'Forget about it. It wasn't you. I'm just amazed you managed to override the commands.'

'It was like having a fight with myself,' Charley explained weakly. 'Two voices battling in my head.'

'Well, let's get rid of that other voice,' said Amir. Picking up the neuro-controller from the floor, he prised open the back and, after cursory examination, tore out the electronics. 'That's the end of *that*,' he declared, tossing the remnants down the hole.

The three of them watched the pieces twirl away into the night.

'So what did you do to *him*?' asked Connor, nodding at the final guard flopped against a window, his mouth open and drooling.

Amir raised an enigmatic eyebrow. 'While you were hanging around, Connor, we were dealing with the bad guys!'

They both laughed, but Connor's laughter was cut short when he saw Mr Grey looming over his friend. 'Behind you!' he cried.

Spinning round, Amir drew his iStun and jabbed the metal prongs into the assassin's side again. But Mr Grey didn't even flinch.

'Run out of charge?' asked the assassin, glancing at the red light blinking on its display. With brutal efficiency, he knife-handed Amir in the neck, striking his carotid artery and instantly blacking him out. Amir slumped to the ground.

With Amir out cold and Charley weakened to the point of infirmity, only Connor and Mr Grey were left standing.

'Whatever you did to me, Connor, it appears your friend's stun-phone has *recharged* me!' The assassin bent down and reclaimed his gun. But, rather than taking aim, he holstered the weapon, strolled over to a comatose guard and picked up a baton instead. 'I've decided I'm not going to shoot you after all, Connor . . . I'm going to *beat* you to death.'

The assassin advanced on him, tapping the stick in his open palm.

'So much for a simple execution!' said Connor, looking for something to defend himself with. He spotted Charley's other armrest lying on the floor. He darted for it –

But Mr Grey lashed out. Connor dived to one side and made a desperate grab for the armrest. Almost at once the baton came back, smashing down on to the floor and catching his outstretched hand. A rocket of pain shooting up his arm, Connor was forced to roll away. He'd barely got to his feet when Mr Grey brought the weapon round towards his head. Connor ducked and the baton struck the window behind him with such force that it smashed the pane, glass showering down.

'You can't dodge me forever!' said Mr Grey.

The assassin drove Connor back with a series of brutal

swipes until he was trapped against the windows on the opposite side of the Sky Walk. Connor realized the assassin was right and braced himself for the inevitable blow. Mr Grey feigned an attack to the left before swinging in hard to the midriff.

Connor took the impact full force – a bone-sickening *crack* reverberating through the Sky Walk. But it wasn't Connor's ribs that had snapped. It was the baton! Mr Grey stared at the broken stick in his hand, then at Connor, who still stood before him, unbowed and unbeaten.

A flicker of incomprehension passed across his ice-grey eyes.

Connor simply smiled. Just as Lăolao had taught him, he'd locked in his *qi*, fusing his life force with his body and turning himself into a human shield . . . *Iron Shirt*.

Before Mr Grey could overcome his astonishment, Connor concentrated all that *qi* into his fist and punched the assassin in the solar plexus with the devastating power of Iron Hand. A sharp *crack* of ribs now did echo through the Sky Walk. The assassin exhaled in open-mouthed shock, his eyes wide in both pain and disbelief that a mere boy had the skill and speed to defeat him in combat. Unable to recover his breath, he staggered, then stumbled over the body of a guard and fell . . .

'Watch out!' cried Connor, instinctively trying to save the man as he tumbled through the hole in the floor. But it was too late. The assassin dropped three storeys straight down to crash into the skylights of the lower observation deck where he sprawled lifeless on the cracked glass.

CHAPTER 54

'Is it over?' asked a timid voice from the end of the Sky Walk.

Connor turned to see Zhen peeking nervously through the lift's open doors. He nodded. It certainly *was* over. The Sky Walk was littered with broken glass, weapons and comatose bodies. Chill night air and the sounds of far-off traffic leaked in through the hole in the floor. And Mr Grey, the ruthless and cold-blooded assassin, was finally dead. Connor slid to the floor, his legs no longer able to support his weight. A combination of relief, injuries and exhaustion had rendered him weak and battle-worn. He had no fight left in him.

'My ears are still ringing,' said Zhen, putting a finger in her ear and waggling it.

'Don't worry – that'll fade,' said Charley, her strength having recovered enough to wheel herself over to Connor. 'Are you OK?' she asked.

Connor gave her a thumbs up. Charley smiled and everything seemed to be all right with the world again. He glanced over at Zhen. 'You certainly saved us with that flash-bang!'

'That was Amir's back-up *back-up* plan!' explained their guide, working her way through the debris of bodies to check on their friend. 'He told me to hide in the basement. If I heard the trigger phrase "final prayer" over the comms, I was to send up the stun grenade.' Kneeling down, she brushed the hair out of his eyes.

Amir groaned, slowly coming round. 'Am I . . . *dead*?' he murmured.

'No, of course not,' said Zhen, resting his head gently in her lap.

Amir smiled dreamily. 'Then why am I seeing an angel?'

'Forget the chat-up lines, Amir – we have to go!' said Connor as the guards began to come round too. Struggling to his feet with Charley's help, he headed for the lift. In the streets below, a column of flashing blue-and-red lights could be seen making a beeline for the Shanghai World Financial Center. The distant sound of sirens grew steadily louder.

'Come on,' Connor urged as one of the guards feebly reached for his gun.

Charley purposefully ran over the guard's outstretched hand with her wheelchair as she passed. 'Oops, mind your fingers!' she said.

Supported by Zhen, Amir followed Connor and Charley into the lift. In less than a minute the elevator took them down all one hundred floors to the ground floor. Since no one was expecting them to appear, there were no guards waiting for them. And, with the tourist entrance closed under the Director's command, the lobby was empty so they were able to reach the nearest fire exit unchallenged. Outside, the four fugitives rushed across the road and down a side street, mere seconds before the police convoy screeched to a halt in the front of the building.

The embassy official scratched at his beard, peering at the four slightly dishevelled teenagers over the top of his glasses. When the nightwatchman at the front gate had radioed that an odd bunch of kids were seeking sanctuary, the man hadn't been wrong. Sitting before him in the air-conditioned interview room of the US Consulate were a young blonde girl in a wheelchair, one of its armrests missing, a skinny Asian boy with bruises to his face and blood on his shirt, a Chinese girl in a black-and-orange Sherpa delivery jacket, and a tall muscular lad with a shock of brown hair and a distinct military bearing.

The official leant forward in his chair and rested his elbows on the desk. 'So, you want consular protection?'

All four of them nodded.

'Who exactly are you wanting protection from?' asked the official. 'The local police?'

'No, not the police,' replied Connor, although he knew this was a half-truth since the police and national security forces were after them too.

The official tapped his pen on top of his notepad. 'Then from whom?'

Connor exchanged a hesitant look with Charley and Amir. They *had* to take a risk. They had no other option but to put their faith and fate in the hands of this man. 'Equilibrium.'

The official frowned. 'Who?'

'It's a multinational criminal organization with its central cell in China,' explained Amir.

'Oh, right,' said the official, making a note on his paper pad. 'And why are they after you?'

'We know about their organization,' replied Connor. 'Know of its existence, what they've done and who's involved in it. They've infiltrated numerous governments, stolen billions of dollars and are responsible for terrorist attacks worldwide.'

'*Really?*' said the official, taking off his glasses and giving them a polish.

Amir nodded earnestly. 'They just tried to kill us at the top of the Shanghai World Financial Center!'

The official put his glasses back on and gave them a hard stare. 'I heard about that PR stunt for a new TV crime show being beamed out live over the Bund. I suppose you kids thought it would be funny to play along and waste my time.'

He began to put away his pen and notepad.

'It wasn't a TV show. It was *real*,' insisted Connor. 'The police arrived just as we escaped.'

'Did they?' The official began to examine the three passports and one Chinese identity card laid out on the desk before him. He came to Connor's and shot him a probing look. 'You have a *US* passport? But you sound British.'

'I am,' replied Connor. 'The President personally gave me that passport.'

The official snorted. '*Our* President?'

'Yes,' said Connor earnestly. He leant forward, hands clasped and expression sincere. 'Listen, there's some urgency. Equilibrium is holding our friends hostage in a shipping container out at sea. The cargo ship's name is the MV *Halcyon*, and this is the container number.' He pushed a scrap of paper across the desk towards the official. 'They don't have long to live.'

Eyeing the piece of paper dubiously, the official nonetheless made a note of the name and serial number, then stood. 'This all sounds very serious. I need to speak to my superior. I won't be long.' Gathering up the passports and identity card, he left the room. They heard the door lock behind him.

'Do you think he believed us?' asked Amir hesitantly.

'We can only hope,' replied Connor. 'If he checks out our story of the World Financial Center with the police, he might.'

Charley turned to him. 'You don't think he's connected to Equilibrium, do you?'

Connor shrugged. 'Well, he didn't react when I said the name.'

'But would he?' asked Zhen. 'If he's an undercover agent for them?'

Connor sighed. 'Good point.'

Amir frowned deeply. 'I can't recall how badly the American consulate in Shanghai had been compromised. I'd barely managed to skim the surface of what was on that drive.'

'Even if he isn't with Equilibrium,' said Connor, 'he'll

soon discover we're terrorist suspects wanted by the Chinese government. Then he'll probably hand us straight over to the authorities . . . aka Equilibrium!'

'He can't!' cried Charley. 'The American Embassy *has* to provide assistance.'

'*You* may be an American citizen, but I'm not,' reminded Amir. He glanced at their guide, who sat anxiously between them, her eyes darting like a sparrow's as she followed their conversation. 'And neither is Zhen.'

The four of them waited in silence, the clock on the wall ticking loudly with each passing minute. The air-conditioning unit in the room strained with a monotonous *whirr, whirr, whirr.*

'He's been gone a long time,' said Amir, shifting uncomfortably in his chair.

'Maybe that's a good sign,' replied Charley. 'Maybe he's tracking down the ship or –'

Suddenly the door burst open and two men in dark suits strode in, their expressions grim and their heavyset physiques defying anyone to challenge them.

'Come with us,' ordered the lead man. Bald-headed and with a hammer jaw, he wouldn't have looked out of place in a cage-fight. Only his shirt and tie lent him a veneer of respectability.

'Who are you?' Connor demanded. 'Where's the other guy?'

'Move!' snapped the cage-fighter, pulling Connor roughly from his chair.

They were escorted out of the room, along a corridor and into a lift. Descending two levels, they entered an underground car park and were bundled into the back of a blacked-out minivan. The rear doors were slammed shut and a moment later the vehicle roared away.

'What the hell's happening?' exclaimed Amir as the vehicle cornered and he was thrown against the compartment's side. Zhen clung to him nervously.

'I guess Equilibrium *has* infiltrated the US Embassy,' Connor replied grimly, clinging on to Charley's wheelchair.

Charley tried the rear door's handle. 'Locked!' She cursed.

With the windows blacked out and the rear compartment blocked off from the driver's cab, there was nothing any of them could do. They huddled in the gloom of the muted overhead light as the minivan tore through Shanghai city. Connor felt a growing sense of panic. Once caught, there seemed to be no escaping Equilibrium's web.

After about thirty minutes, the minivan came to a sudden halt and the rear doors were flung open. Cage-fighter and his companion beckoned them out. A roar of jet engines assaulted Connor's ears as he stepped on to an airport runway.

'Apologies for the rushed departure,' said the cage-fighter as his companion helped Amir and Zhen lower Charley and her chair to the tarmac. 'We didn't have much time to extract you. The Chinese government had started to ask tricky questions and Equilibrium's people were closing in.'

He handed Connor back his American passport, saluted, then gestured to the awaiting private jet.

'President Mendez sends his regards. So too does his daughter. Have a safe flight home.'

Connor's jaw dropped. He stared a moment at the US secret agent. His second passport *had* come in handy after all. As he was hustled aboard the jet along with Amir and Charley, Connor glanced back at Zhen, who was still on the tarmac. He raised a hesitant hand in farewell.

'Don't worry about Zhen,' called the US agent. 'We'll take care of her.'

'That's one hell of a story,' said Stella Sinclair. The Deputy Director of MI6 laced her long black fingers together and subjected Connor to a piercing look. 'Do you have any proof?'

Connor sat between Amir and Charley in the top-floor office of the SIS building. Through the floor-to-ceiling bulletproof windows the majestic vista of the Thames could be seen winding past, the familiar London skyline offering a reassuring yet awe-inspiring backdrop to their meeting. The office itself was slick and modern, much like the Deputy Director herself, who wore a tailored charcoal-black jacket with a mauve silk shirt, her hair cut short and her choice of jewellery – a single silver chain and a slim stainless-steel fitness tracker – as minimal and effective as her manner.

Connor shook his head. 'We had to trade the flash drive for our lives.'

'That's understandable ... yet regrettable,' acknowledged Stella. 'Without proof, though, this remains nothing but a story.'

Connor's shoulders slumped. They might have escaped China with their lives, but ultimately Equilibrium had won. The organization would remain in the shadows, unseen and unstoppable. And the three of them would remain targets for assassination. 'You don't believe us then?'

'I didn't say that. Colonel Black's word goes a long way with me.' The Deputy Director gazed out of the window at the clouded sky, appearing to focus on something far off in the distance. Connor sensed there'd been more to their relationship than merely professional respect. 'News of his death greatly saddens me. He was a fine soldier and a good man.'

Connor felt a sharp pang in his own heart, a twist of regret and loss – regret that the colonel hadn't been the honest and principled man that Connor had believed him to be, and the loss of a friend and mentor, a man of true courage and conviction. But Colonel Black's sacrifice had saved them when he'd exchanged his life for theirs. And in that single act of true selflessness he'd redeemed himself in Connor's eyes. He'd been the ultimate bodyguard.

'We lost a number of good friends to Equilibrium,' explained Charley. 'Surely there's something that can be done?'

Stella leant back in her chair. 'Your testimonies will certainly help our agents. You see, MI6 have been aware of –'

A knock at the door interrupted the Deputy Director. She looked up as a young man in a crisp pinstripe suit entered the room. 'What is it, Henry?'

*

Ling sat slumped in the darkness, her back against the rough metal of the shipping container, her head resting wearily on Jason's shoulder. There were a few whispered conversations going on, but most of the captives remained numbly silent. After being confined for so long, they were all too weak to do much more than exist. Their rations of food and water had run out the day before. The temperature was stifling and ever rising. The air was stale, suffocating, and stank of urine and excrement from the buckets festering in the far corner. Their past efforts at escape had turned to mere survival. There'd been no communication with the outside world and a fear had been steadily growing among the captives that they would be entombed inside the shipping container forever.

Then the stomp of boots broke Ling's malaise. 'Did you hear that?' she croaked.

Jason nodded. Barked commands followed the heavy footsteps and they both sat up, sharp and alert. Jody and the other instructors came to their senses quickly too. They ushered the recruits away from the doors, cautious and fearful as to what was coming next.

A bone-like *crack* was heard, then the metal *clunk* of the padlock dropping to the deck.

Hunkered in the darkness like cornered animals, Ling and Jason prepared for the worst. The container's doors swung open and the silhouette of a US Marine officer appeared before them.

'Seagull One to Control,' growled the officer into his head mic. 'Hostages located and secured.'

A flood of tearful relief swept through the recruits as more marines entered the container and hurried to the captives' aid. Unsteady on her feet, Ling emerged with Jason, blinking in the bright sunlight . . .

'They're really free?' asked Connor, exchanging a look of astonishment with Charley and Amir.

Stella nodded. 'A US Navy vessel intercepted the cargo ship an hour ago. I've been informed all the hostages survived the ordeal, just some cases of severe dehydration and mild trauma. They'll be flown home in the next few days.'

Connor felt a huge weight lift from his shoulders, an immense relief rolling through him like a cool breeze. Although they'd managed to obtain the name of the ship and the container's number, he'd feared that Mr Grey had lied to them. Evidently he hadn't anticipated the three of them escaping and so had told the truth. Equilibrium might have won, but their victory was no longer total.

'As I was saying,' continued Stella once the three of them had calmed down, 'MI6 have been aware of Equilibrium for quite some time. But the organization has been like a ghost to us. We haven't been able to gather any concrete evidence as to their operations or personnel. There have only been rumours and hearsay.' She shook her head in frustration. 'What I'd give to obtain some solid proof of their activities!'

'What time is it?' interrupted Amir.

Stella frowned, then glanced at her tracker. 'Coming up to midday. Why?'

Amir looked up at the ceiling, appearing to do some calculations in his head. 'That should be long enough for it to be embedded. Can I access your computer terminal?'

'This isn't an–internet cafe!' said the Deputy Director firmly. 'But you can use that laptop over there. It has guest access.'

Amir went over to the conference table and booted up the computer. Connor and the others joined him as he tapped away at the keyboard. A login window popped up on the screen and the edge of a smile crept into the corner of Amir's lips.

'The password is *Gabriel*,' said Amir, stepping aside for Stella. 'Would you like to do the honours?'

The Deputy Director typed in the password and a drive opened up, listing thousands upon thousands of folders. 'What am I looking at?' she asked.

Amir folded his arms and puffed out his chest. 'All Equilibrium's databases,' he replied.

The Deputy Director did a double-take, then began to sift through the files. 'But you said you had *no* proof.'

'Well, we do now,' said Amir smugly.

Connor stared at Amir. 'But how? We surrendered the drive and they disconnected our transmitter.'

Amir grinned like a Cheshire cat. 'Trojan horse!'

'Explain,' said Charley, as stunned as Connor by their friend's miraculous accomplishment.

Amir cleared his throat. 'Well, I realized we'd never get that flash drive out of the country, not with our lives at least. So I thought I'd return the drive in exchange for you

347

two . . . along with a little extra "e-gift". When the Director connected her tablet to the flash drive at the World Financial Center, a building I *knew* she owned, her actions immediately compromised their security systems. As soon as she entered the new password I had created, a drive-by download was triggered and a Trojan horse installed.'

'What sort of Trojan horse?' asked Stella.

Amir grinned even wider. 'A special program I'd personally coded to create a back door into their mainframe. By installing it on her very own tablet, I knew the malware would be buried deep and be spread wide. No one would suspect her device to be the culprit.'

'So, you mean . . . you had this planned, all along?' asked Connor.

Amir nodded. 'I have to admit, though, it didn't go as *smoothly* as I'd hoped.'

'Why didn't you tell us?' said Charley.

Amir shrugged. 'I didn't know if it would work.'

Connor clapped his friend on the back, then hugged him. 'Well, it did! Amir, you're a genius!'

'You're more than a genius, young man,' said the Deputy Director, calling her assistant into the room. 'You may well have just brought down the biggest criminal network in the world.'

'Don't give him a bigger head than he's got already!' Charley laughed. 'We'll never get him out of MI6.'

Stella appraised Amir with a shrewd look. 'After this technical display, we might not let him.'

She issued some quiet orders to Henry and within

minutes her office was an intense buzz of activity as a select unit of analysts and agents pored over Equilibrium's files. Once the hubbub had died down, the Deputy Director delegated specific tasks and the agents split off to back-up the files, initiate in-depth analysis and develop plans of action to curtail Equilibrium's operations and bring the perpetrators to justice.

Connor, Amir and Charley were left alone with the Deputy Director. She gestured for them to join her at her desk. 'So what are your plans now?' she asked, settling back into her chair.

'Honestly, I don't think any of us have really thought that far,' Connor replied.

Stella Sinclair pursed her lips and regarded them intently. 'All three of you have shown great courage, impressive initiative and true loyalty to one another. To survive what you've just been through takes real talent and skill. You're a credit to Colonel Black's memory and his training.'

She glanced past them, checking that her door was closed. Then in a quieter, more confidential tone, she continued, 'I was, of course, aware of Buddyguard, having been one of the initial supporters of the concept. I considered it a great shame that the project wasn't officially endorsed. Colonel Black was bold and ambitious to pursue the idea. And, of course, he proved the concept was not only viable but supremely effective. There are many in government and this organization who secretly approved of his venture. That's why he was given such free rein. Sadly, without a captain to steer the ship, I foresee that Buddy-guard will have to be shut down for good.'

Connor looked at the others, their downcast and anxious expressions mirroring his own feelings of loss and confusion as to what the future might now hold.

'However, I do have a proposal for you,' said the Deputy Director, leaning forward on to her desk and drawing them in closer. 'MI6 run an off-the-record project called Guardian. It involves intelligence gathering as well as close protection. I'm afraid I can't expand any more on the role at this stage. But, with your training and experience, you'd make ideal candidates. So, how would you like to work for *me* instead?'

CHAPTER 56

'A fire? That's terrible,' said his mum, after Connor and Charley had arrived unexpectedly at his family's poky terraced house in East London. Propped up by pillows, she lay in the metal-framed bed, thin and fragile as a bird with a broken wing. Connor had been shocked by how frail and pallid his mother looked, the multiple sclerosis that she battled evidently having the upper hand that day. Her face was etched with pain and a slight yet constant tremor gripped her wasted body. But as ever his mum's concerns were for other people rather than her own sufferings. 'Was anyone hurt?'

Connor nodded. He felt Charley squeeze his hand for support. 'The headmaster and two of the teachers died.'

His mum gasped in shock. 'Any pupils?'

'A few were injured,' Connor admitted. 'They're recovering now, but the school's been closed. Permanently.'

His mum reached out and took his other hand, her trembling grasp weak but full of love. 'Oh, I am sorry, darling. I know how much you enjoyed it there. What a terrible thing to happen.'

'Thank the Lord you two are safe, that's all I can say,' remarked his gran, shuffling into the room with a glass of water and a plastic pot of pills on a tray. She gave both him and Charley a grave but tender look, not for one minute fooled by their story of an accidental fire closing the school. Putting down the tray on a bedside table, she tapped out a couple of capsules into the palm of her wrinkled hand and passed them to Connor's mum. 'Sally says to take two of these. They'll help you sleep. She's off home now Connor's here, but will be back in the morning.'

Seeing the state his mum was in, Connor was glad Sally had been around to take care of her, as well as his gran. And Sally would continue to do so for the foreseeable future. For Colonel Black had been true to his word when he'd said that his recruits' welfare and safety were his number one priority. A comprehensive insurance policy had been taken out in the event of Buddyguard's demise, ensuring that every recruit was financially secure and any contractual arrangements honoured until the recruit reached adulthood. Connor felt a further pang of grief in his heart at the loss of the colonel. He might have been gruff and stern of manner, but he wasn't the mercenary exploiter that the Director had tried to paint him. Colonel Black had been a father figure, a mentor and, ultimately, a hero.

'I suppose we need to think about a new school for you,' said his mum, swallowing the capsules with a swig of water.

'An alternative arrangement has been offered,' Connor replied. His gran stiffened, her small pinched eyes drilling a question into him from behind her glasses. 'But . . . I'm not sure if it's right for me.'

His gran's bony shoulders relaxed and her expression softened somewhat, although her mouth remained tight and thin. Connor anticipated that she'd be interrogating him later. But he wasn't sure how much, if anything, he could tell his gran about the Guardian organization or his future intentions. Following Stella Sinclair's confidential proposal, he'd initially declined her offer. He was long overdue a break and had no wish to dive headlong into another covert operation, especially when he had no idea what the Guardian role might entail. Yet he could already feel a familiar pull, a yearning for the 'combat high' that only came from being in the field. It was an irresistible draw that his father had experienced and often succumbed to, and that Connor craved too. But, for the moment, he was simply happy to be back home and to be with Charley.

For Charley had also declined the Deputy Director's offer. She wanted to focus on her rehabilitation. She had a dream, a goal in mind. Equilibrium, for all its devious intentions, had implanted into her a remarkable piece of cutting-edge technology. So, rather than be controlled by it, she planned to master it. And Connor wanted to support her every step of the way.

Amir, on the other hand, had eagerly accepted the proposal to join the Guardian team. Stella had enticed him with the promise of a specialist IT role, and the prospect of becoming an intelligence agent was too much of a temptation for his computer-loving friend. His decision had led to his swift enrolment in the programme, the Deputy Director's PA leading him away for further briefing. Their parting had been bitter-sweet, Connor happy that Amir had found his true purpose but knowing that he'd miss his friend. They promised to stay in touch.

Notwithstanding their own decisions, as both he and Charley left her office, the MI6 Deputy Director had told them in no uncertain terms that her door was *always* open should they change their minds.

'Luckily, the school holidays are coming up,' said his mum, stifling a yawn. 'We've time to sort things out. I'm just glad you're home, safe and sound, and not involved in any of this . . .' She patted the newspaper on her lap. 'I don't know what the world's coming to.'

On the newspaper's front page ran a headline story about the terrorist attacks in China, referring to a recent incident at the famous Shanghai World Financial Center that had proved a significant lead on the perpetrators of the railway station shooting. Alongside this feature was another article about people-smuggling, and the disturbing evidence that children were being abducted and transported within shipping containers.

'It's certainly a dangerous world out there,' agreed Connor, sharing a rueful look with Charley.

His mum yawned again, the pain etched in her face easing away like the sands in an hourglass.

'Your mum needs her rest now,' said his gran, ushering them out of the bedroom.

They made their way downstairs, Charley using his mother's stairlift. Entering the front living room, Connor's eye was caught by a photo on the mantelpiece. He took it down and settled into the comforting recesses of the sofa.

The picture was of his father. Smiling and handsome, dark brown hair clipped short, the green-blue eyes that he'd passed on to his son blazed with a sharp intensity. Connor recalled that this particular photo had been taken the month before his father had left on his fateful mission to Iraq. Bitter tears sprang at the corners of Connor's eyes. His father's death had gouged a huge hole in his heart, a gaping void that no other person could fill. But when he'd discovered how his father had *really* died, how he'd sacrificed himself to protect the American ambassador, a man who went on to become President of the United States, his heart had swelled with pride. The hole was still no smaller, but there was an understanding that his father's death had counted for something, had somehow been of real service.

Yet there was always an unquenched fury deep within him at the injustice that his father's killers had got away. It was partly what had driven him to excel at kickboxing, had compelled him to become a bodyguard, then had carried him through all the trials and ordeals of his assignments – a determination and crusade to protect others from the same fate.

Connor realized that the burning hole in his heart would never fully go away, but it was now more manageable. He'd uncovered those ultimately responsible for his father's death. He'd been instrumental in bringing his father's killers to justice. And over the coming months he'd be able to savour their destruction as Equilibrium's empire was torn down piece by piece. It was only a matter of time before the Director herself was captured and punished for her crimes.

Then his father's soul could finally rest. And so could he.

'Your dad would be proud of you,' said Charley, coming up alongside the sofa and putting an arm round his shoulders.

Connor smiled sadly at her. 'I just wish he was around to meet you. He'd have really liked you.'

There was a knock at the front door.

'I'll get it,' called his gran from the kitchen. She shuffled past through the hallway.

'Well, if it's any consolation,' said Charley, 'we'd never have met if you hadn't had a reason to join Buddyguard. So maybe he's the one who brought us together.'

His gran came into the living room. 'Connor, there's someone from your old school to see you.'

Connor looked up expectantly from his father's photo. Then all the blood drained from his face. Charley gripped the armrests of her chair in shock.

'Hope I'm not disturbing you two lovebirds,' said Mr Grey, limping into the room.

'I'll get us some tea and biscuits,' announced his gran, departing the lounge after she'd shown Mr Grey to an armchair.

The assassin put aside his walking cane and stiffly seated himself. Connor and Charley hadn't dared to move.

'You don't seem pleased to see me,' said Mr Grey, pulling at a loose thread in the chair's armrest.

'*How* . . .' began Connor, his chest so tight he struggled to breathe. 'I saw you fall. You were *dead*.'

'Not quite!' replied Mr Grey acidly. 'You wouldn't make a very good assassin, Connor – that's twice you've tried to kill me and failed. The glass roof broke my fall. I don't pretend it didn't hurt. I've a number of fractures, on top of the broken ribs you gave me – *Charley*, hands in your lap, where I can see them.'

He drew a Ruger SR9c semi-automatic pistol from inside his jacket and aimed it at Charley's chest. She immediately retracted her hands from where they'd been reaching beneath her chair. The assassin then took a silencer from his jacket pocket and began to slowly screw it on to the gun's barrel.

'Don't want to disturb the neighbours, do we?'

'This is between you and me, Mr Grey,' said Connor, glancing towards the door where he could hear his gran tinkling with cups and saucers and boiling the water. 'Leave Charley and my family out of this.'

Mr Grey snorted. 'Connor, this is now beyond personal. Which means *anyone* associated with you is a target, especially family and loved ones.' He coughed into the back of his hand, wincing in pain, speckles of blood appearing on his lips. Connor went to make a move, but the gun was on him in a heartbeat. '*Sit down!*' the man ordered. 'As I told you at the insect market in Shanghai, the snake always gets the mouse –'

'Tea anyone?'

Mr Grey discreetly hid the gun in his lap as Connor's gran entered with a tray loaded with biscuits, china cups and a steaming teapot. She poured out a cup for Mr Grey. 'Milk? Sugar?' she asked.

'Black, two spoonfuls.'

Connor's heart pounded as his gran heaped in the sugar, gave the tea a good stir and passed Mr Grey his drink.

'Thank you,' said the assassin with a tiger's grin.

Connor desperately tried to catch his gran's eye, to silently warn her, as she poured her own cup. But she seemed oblivious to his palpable alarm. 'Help yourself to biscuits, you two,' she said before settling into the armchair opposite Mr Grey.

A long moment of uncomfortable silence ensued. Mr Grey eyed the three of them with cool calculation. Connor could see the barrel of the gun poking out between his leg and the side of the armchair, its sights targeted on Charley as she sat frozen in her seat. Then his gran broke into a smile and toasted their guest.

'Chin-chin!' she said, raising her cup to her lips.

Mr Grey returned the gesture and sipped his tea.

'So, you're one of Connor's teachers?' asked his gran.

'You could say I've taught him a lesson or two.'

'What's your speciality subject?'

'History,' replied the assassin, adding with a devious smile, 'I'm very interested in *dead* people.'

Mr Grey took a long draught of his tea, his eyes not leaving Connor. The assassin seemed to be enjoying drawing out Connor's torment at their perilous situation. Connor thought about tackling the assassin while he was off-guard and drinking his tea. But the sofa was soft and low and difficult to get up from. Connor couldn't be certain that he'd cross the living room fast enough to prevent Mr Grey shooting Charley first.

'What period of history in particular?' his gran asked. 'I've always been fascinated by the Victorian age, such a time of invention and social change. Queen Victoria herself was a truly remarkable woman. Did you know that she was an accomplished linguist?'

'Yes, I did,' grunted Mr Grey.

'How silly of me, a man of your intelligence,' said his gran. 'I understand that she spoke fluent English and

German, and studied French, Italian and Latin too. Am I right in saying that later on in life she even learnt the Indian language of Hindustani? I find that incredible . . .'

His gran droned on and on, the assassin nodding curtly at appropriate moments. Then, growing bored with the conversation, he drained his cup and set it aside, almost missing the saucer.

'More tea?' asked Connor's gran brightly.

'No,' said Mr Grey, his head drooping forward. 'It was a little . . . strong for my liking.'

'How about a biscuit then?' She picked up the plate and thrust it towards him.

Mr Grey waved it away. 'No . . . slank you . . .' he slurred, his eyes narrowing. 'I've come . . . to exterminate a mouse . . .'

'Oh, I can assure you, we don't have mice in *my* house.'

'But we get the occasional *rat*, don't we, Gran?' said Connor, frantically trying to hint at the danger they were all in. He tensed, Charley's eyes widening in alarm as Mr Grey fumbled for his gun.

But the weapon slipped from the assassin's grasp and fell on to the carpet at his feet. Connor's gran didn't seem at all surprised at the sight of a loaded weapon in her house. Mr Grey groggily reached for it, slumping sideways in his chair . . . before passing out entirely.

'Phew!' said his gran, putting down the plate of biscuits. 'I was starting to get worried there. I'd given him enough of your mother's sleeping tablets in that tea to knock out a horse!'

Connor and Charley both stared at her in astonishment.

'You *knew* he was an assassin?' asked Connor breathlessly.

Rolling her eyes at him, his gran rose from her chair and picked up the gun. 'I always knew you'd bring your *homework* back with you one day!' she replied. 'Now, Charley, be a good girl and call the police before he wakes up.'

CHAPTER 58

The waves rolled in, glassy, even and glistening in the California sunshine. They peeled in perfect lines from the tip of the San Clemente pier all the way to the golden sands of the shoreline, transforming from a pure aqua green to a foaming white froth. A surfer at the edge of line-up paddled hard and caught a clean break . . . he rode the wave in, but lost his balance halfway and was axed by the lip of the wave. Drilled under the water, the unfortunate surfer was barrel-rolled until he bobbed to the surface, spitting and gasping.

'Aren't they a little big?' said Connor, eyeing the waves dubiously.

'For you maybe,' Charley shot back as she made the final checks to her adapted surfboard.

'What if you get into trouble?'

'That's what you're here for. You're my bodyguard, aren't you?' She teased him with a wink.

Connor pulled on his rash shirt. He didn't know what *he* was so nervous about. Although he'd never surfed before, it was Charley who was taking the biggest risk.

After only two months of intense therapy, she'd decided to visit her home beach in San Clemente in an attempt to conquer her first wave. Thanks to the physio sessions and her growing proficiency with the neuro-chip, she was gaining more control over the lower half of her body. She couldn't walk yet. She might never walk. But she was determined to surf.

'Are you coming or not?' asked Charley.

Connor's phone buzzed with a text. 'Hang on a sec.' He picked up his mobile from his towel and read the message.

Shanghai surprise! Like my bike?

A photo downloaded of Zhen sitting astride a gleaming Chang Jiang 750cc motorbike with sidecar, her company logo *Shanghai Surprise* emblazoned on the side. She was grinning and giving the camera a big thumbs up. Evidently the US government agent hadn't lied when he said that Zhen would be taken care of.

Smiling, Connor texted back an emoji of a thumbs up, along with a reply:

Must remember to post that review on TripAdvisor!

Ever since Amir had provided unrestricted access to Equilibrium's servers, MI6 in combination with other intelligence agencies around the world had systematically infiltrated the clandestine criminal organization and arrested those involved. One of the first and most significant to fall was the Director herself, then the Chinese cell was swiftly rounded up and put behind bars. When Connor heard the news, a peace settled in his heart. His duty to his father was done.

It also meant that Zhen was once again safe in her own country – and she was clearly doing a roaring trade as a tour guide. In fact, the world as a whole was a safer place thanks to the sacrifices made by a few unknown and unnoticed individuals. While Buddyguard's role in Equilibrium's downfall would remain unacknowledged, Connor was under no illusion. Bodyguards would always be needed and would always make a difference. But, for the time being, the world could carry on without the need for *his* services.

He turned back to Charley. 'Hey, look at this. It's from Zhen!'

But her wheelchair was empty. Connor's eyes followed the groove in the sand to where Charley had entered the water. She was *supposed* to have waited for him.

But Charley, independent and determined as ever, was already halfway out, paddling her adapted surfboard into the wash. She duck-dived, nosing the tip of her board beneath an approaching wave, and carried on paddling, the action as natural as breathing for her. Connor scrambled to get his gear together. He was attaching his leash to his ankle when he heard a scream. He looked up in panic, his eyes scanning the ocean for Charley, praying that she wasn't already drowning.

But it had been a scream of delight as Charley caught

her first wave. Lying down on her board, she leant into the ocean surge, staying just ahead of the peeling tube of water. Like a pro, she rode the wave all the way in to shore, skimming over the foam to Connor. The smile on her face was wider than the ocean and brighter than the sun in the sky.

'I'm actually *surfing*!' she yelled, splashing the water around her. '*Surfing!*'

Before Connor had a chance to respond, she'd pivoted her board and was paddling back out. Connor watched her go with a swell of pride. He knew how much this moment meant to her. Despite the constant barriers life had put in her way, she'd never given up hope. She'd battled every obstacle to achieve her dream. He truly admired her for that.

Charley had told him her life story, and there was a piece of advice she'd once been given that had helped carry her through her darkest times. It had stuck in Connor's head too. *We cannot change the cards we are dealt, just how we play the hand.*

Well, whatever cards he'd had in the past, Connor had certainly been dealt an ace with Charley. Spurred on by her daredevil antics, Connor picked up his own surfboard and dived headfirst into the waves after her.

FUGITIVE
ACKNOWLEDGEMENTS

Connor has completed his final mission. I too have completed my assignment with this last book in the series . . . *or is it*? A door has been left open for further adventures, but it will be down to you, my readers, to make this happen. Fans of the Young Samurai series have relentlessly promoted those books to their friends and are soon to be rewarded with a *ninth* book! So, young bodyguards, are you up to the challenge?

In the meantime, I must thank all those who have supported me through the creation of this bulletproof series:

Charlie Viney, my agent, friend and mentor, we still have a long way to travel.

Tig Wallace, my editorial assassin, your sharp mind and pinpoint attention to detail are two of your greatest weapons.

Wendy Shakespeare, the one Puffin I can *always* rely on.

My bulletproof team at Puffin – Helen Gray, Rebecca Booth, Lucie Sharpe and everyone else who has a hand in making the series a success.

All the librarians and teachers who promote my books and tirelessly work to enhance children's lives with the pleasure of reading.

A special mention must go to Shanghai Insiders (www. shanghaiinsiders.com) and my guide Luca who took me off the beaten track and introduced me to the underbelly of Shanghai and some great locations for this book. Riding a sidecar through the Shanghai streets is an experience of a lifetime!

And, most important of all, my two shining lights – Zach and Leo. You are my inspiration and my happiness. I promise to protect and care for you with my life.

Stay safe.
Chris

Any fans can keep in touch with me and the progress of the Bodyguard series on my Facebook page, or via the website at *www.bodyguard-books.co.uk*

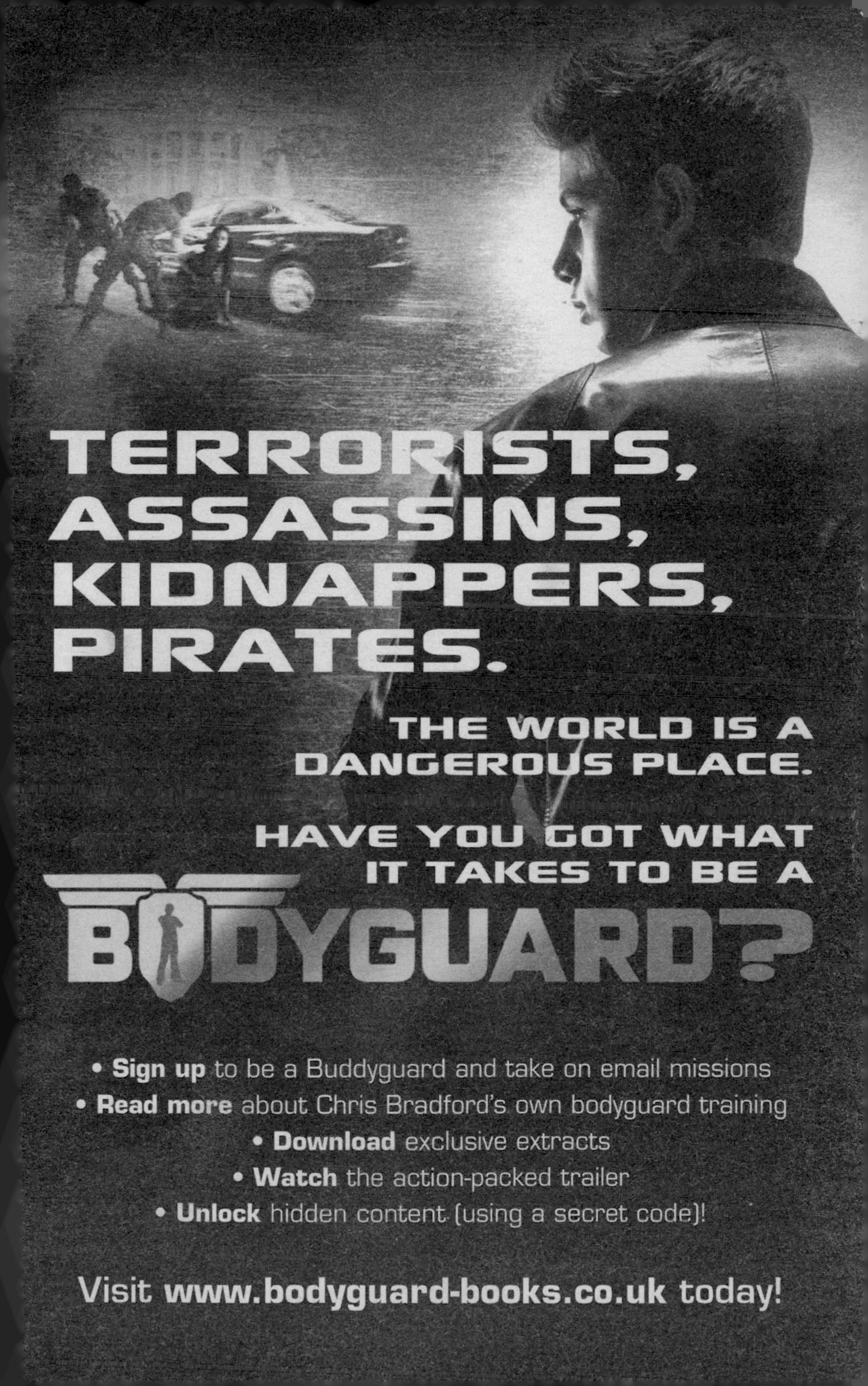
TERRORISTS,
ASSASSINS,
KIDNAPPERS,
PIRATES.
THE WORLD IS A DANGEROUS PLACE.
HAVE YOU GOT WHAT IT TAKES TO BE A
BODYGUARD?
• Sign up to be a Buddyguard and take on email missions
• Read more about Chris Bradford's own bodyguard training
• Download exclusive extracts
• Watch the action-packed trailer
• Unlock hidden content (using a secret code)!
Visit www.bodyguard-books.co.uk today!

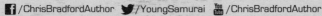

THE RETURN OF THE WARRIOR

COMING SOON

CHRIS BRADFORD

THE SOUL PROPHECY

'DEATH IS ONLY THE BEGINNING'

COMING NEXT FROM

CHRIS BRADFORD